SCARLET ASHES

MIANKE FOURIE

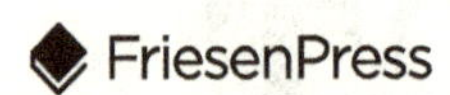

One Printers Way
Altona, MB R0G 0B0
Canada

www.friesenpress.com

First Edition — 2025

ISBN
978-1-03-832008-7 (Hardcover)
978-1-03-832007-0 (Paperback)
978-1-03-832009-4 (eBook)

1. FICTION, ROMANCE, FANTASY

Distributed to the trade by The Ingram Book Company

To my dad for telling me all those **horror** stories.

Elot 24'

PROLOGUE

DOMINICA

2003

"Are you sure this is the right place?" I ask Austen as we near an abandoned factory building in the industrial area of our city. Austen creeps toward the building, and I reluctantly follow him. The location is disturbingly quiet for a few seconds before whispering flutters around me, and I whip my head around. I look around quickly, but there is no sign of movement. No sign of life. I'm starting to hear things, and upsetting thoughts are beginning to plague my mind. *What if we get caught? What if we get surrounded?* Panic threatens to pull my chest apart since we aren't supposed to be here.

"Yes," he whispers. Austen looks up at the building and points to a broken window on the second floor. "Aha, there's our point of entry."

I look up at where he's pointing and groan softly. "And I guess you want us to climb this unstable stack of boxes to get there?"

Austen turns to me, and a wide, excited grin spreads on his lips. "You bet your ass we are."

I close my eyes, sighing. "Fine, let's do this."

Austen got a lead on a vampire clan hiding in this building, and he wanted us to check it out on our own and do recon before giving the information to the heads of our organization. It's idiotic, but we must show the Association that we can work independently.

A chill runs down my spine the moment we enter the second floor. "Let's split up. You take the west, and I'll take the east. We'll meet back here if anything happens," I tell him after looking around the space. It's dark and damp here, and there are too many variables and spaces where vampires can hide and ambush us.

"Yeah, yeah." He rolls his eyes.

"Austen, I'm serious. Please don't be stupid, and *don't* do something we both will regret. Please."

He gives me that crooked smile, which almost always means he will cause trouble for both of us before he turns and moves in the direction that I pointed out earlier.

I huff a frustrated sigh through my nose as I pull the stake from my boot and the bowie knife I got as a graduation gift from the sheath hooked into my belt. Turning the knife in my hand, I admire its feel and look again: it has a dark and light wood handle with a Damascus steel blade. It's not only a beautiful blade but deadly as well. What makes the blade deadly is the fact that it's laced with silver. The edge is dipped in a kind of silver that never dulls the sharpness, but yet it deposits some into the vampire to weaken it. I'm not sure how they came up with that idea, but it's ingenious. All I need to know is that my blades work perfectly.

Our mentor, Sam, gave each of us a blade that matched our personalities on the day we became full-fledged hunters in the Vampire Hunters Association (VHA). A hunter's sole purpose is to rid the world of the vampire infestation. We are trained to kill them. A hunter is made when they make an oath to the VHA. It's an old magic that we know little about. All I knew was that I had to make my family proud. I finished first in my class and am incredibly proud to say that.

There are only a handful of female vampire hunters, as most did not make the cut, which makes my achievement even more impressive. The boys, on the other hand, aren't pleased about it.

Some of them think I don't belong here, but I proved all of them wrong during training. I'm not as strong as them, but I'm cunning and know how to take them down without using brute force. Now, I must prove them all wrong in the field.

Focus, Dom. I scold myself when I realize how far I've walked into the building without noticing. I clear my mind of all distractions and walk down the hallway I find myself in. Every step I take makes me cringe. My footsteps aren't as quiet as I want, with all the debris lying on the ground. The paint is peeling from the walls. Papers and a sticky substance I can't place cover the floor. It's not blood. I can tell that much. I shudder to think what it might be. Returning my attention to what's in front of me, I spot a door down the hall. I sigh, knowing I have to check it out. I look behind me once more. There's nothing there, and I don't hear any other sound that indicates Austen may be in trouble. I take another deep breath before moving down the hall toward the door, trying to tiptoe around most of the debris.

When I reach the door, I notice the window in it, so I hunch over slightly, taking calculated and slow steps, trying to make as little noise as possible. I take a minute to listen for movement.

The door is cracked open, but no sound comes from the other side. Come to think of it, there is no sound, period. The silence that fills the hall is deafening—no crickets chirping, no bats squeaking from the ceiling. Not even the wind is blowing outside. These are all sounds you would expect to hear in an abandoned building. Even if none of those sounds were present, some other echoing sound would exist. But there's nothing.

Goose bumps cover my skin, and my nerve endings are shot. Everything in me is screaming to get the hell out of here.

Steeling my nerves, I slowly push open the door with my foot and brace for anything that might jump out at me. My heart slams against my rib cage so hard—almost like it's trying to break through and run away.

The room is dark except for a few strands of moonlight slipping in. I frown as I look around, noticing the windows are painted black. The one who did it must have been in a hurry as they missed a few spots.

I carefully step into the open space, keeping my ears trained on noise from anywhere in the room or beyond. I didn't think it possible, but the silence in this room is soul-crushing—even worse than when I stepped into the building.

Suddenly, the air changes. Charges somehow. The hairs on the back of my neck rise, and I spin to find the cause of the disturbing feeling.

Shit! It's a trap, and we fell for it. *I* fell for it.

A dark figure blocks my path out of the room. The figure's essence screams pure hatred and evil incarnate.

He steps into the room toward me. I don't hesitate to move as I mimic his pace and step away.

Dammit, how can I be so stupid?

"Calm your nerves, Dom, slow your heart rate, and assess your surroundings. Look for advantages that you can use to slay the beast or, at the very least, to escape and get back up."

My mentor's words ring in my head as the figure steps closer still.

I step back once more and feel my back hit the window. Shit, I broke one of the most important rules of my trade: never get backed into a corner.

It will be an advantage for me tonight, as it triggers my fight-to-survive mode.

The vampire takes one more step closer to me. The little moonlight that enters the dark room falls on the lower part of his face, but his hatred filled emerald eyes glow through the darkness. His nostrils flare, and he gives me a feral grin. His fangs gleam.

I still and swallow visibly. Fear has no business here tonight, so I let my breathing calm as I regulate my heartbeat like we were taught. "Tsk, tsk. Didn't your clan leader tell you never to trap a hunter?" I tease, hoping the vampire will not catch the panic in my voice.

The frown on his face is all the distraction I need. I lunge, the stake already in my hand and ready to strike.

He is fast, moving to the side, and dodges my assault, but not fast enough as I bury the knife I had concealed in my other hand in the side of his chest when I turn to the side.

The scream leaving the vampire's mouth is haunting, to say the least.

He stumbles into the light more, and anger-filled horror covers his face as the silver burns him. There is only a second for my mind to spring to work, and I use his stunned demeanor to my advantage.

Ramming him with my shoulder, I drive him backward until his back hits the wall with a loud thud.

The vampire hisses at the impact, my knife still buried in his side, and swipes his clawlike hand at me. I rip the blade from his side and dodge two blows, but I'm too slow for the third, and he connects with my shoulder—dragging those sharp things down, sending curses flying from my mouth.

I stumble back, my knife slipping from my grip, and look down quickly. I assess the damage and see that it's not too deep. The pain, though, becomes like a buzz in the back of my mind. I don't feel it as the adrenaline pumps through my veins at an alarming rate.

I'm *so* in over my head, and panic threatens to consume me, but I will it away.

The bastard is strong, and I need to think on my feet. I jump back from him when he swipes at me again. Looking around quickly, I notice that we've traded places, and I'm practically at the door. I need to get out of here—now. I turn swiftly and dart from the room down the hall toward where Austen and I last saw each other.

I don't make it far before bony fingers fist into my hair and pull me backward, sending me flying into the opposite wall.

As I hit the solid concrete wall, the air gets knocked from my lungs, and I see stars. I fall to my knees, gasping for air. I press my hand to my chest in the hopes of helping it draw in a breath, but it doesn't work.

Heavy steps thunder toward me, and I manage to clear my mind just enough to grip my stake for a quick strike, but my hand is empty.

Looking up just in time to see a boot coming toward my face, I dodge the blow and roll to the side as it stomps down with a loud thud where my head would have been.

"You piece of shit, hunter. You are going to die here tonight," he snarls as I scurry to my feet when air caresses my lungs.

"Hmm, here I'm thinking the same thing. The only difference is I will be leaving here, and you will blend in nicely with the rest of the dust on the floor, don't you think?"

His pale face turns hues of red I never thought I would see on a vampire, and he charges me.

Stupid asshole … I smile, not moving, and the moment he is within striking distance, I bring my steel-toed boot up, kicking him in the groin.

Without hesitation, he drops to the ground—another brutal scream leaving his mouth—grabbing his throbbing balls. I swear, if it's possible, he's going to have to massage them down from his throat.

Looking around quickly for something I can use as a weapon, I spot some broken glass on the floor next to the shattered window of the door we had just come out of.

I bend down to pick up a jagged piece of glass but miss it when he grabs my ankle, pulling my feet out from under me.

I fall forward, bracing myself on my hands and knees. The impact almost sends the air rushing from me again. I kick back like a horse trying to get rid of its rider when the panic threatens to claw its way out again.

The next moment, my heel connects with something hard, and I hear bone cracking, knowing I connected with his face somewhere.

The vampire roars, his hands flying up as I roll to the side, catching a glimpse of his face and the blood streaming from his nose.

I stumble to my feet, run down the hall, then skid to a stop when I see more broken pieces of glass lying on the floor.

It won't be fatal, but it will slow the vampire down long enough for me to escape.

My heart pounds so hard it's difficult to concentrate, and the ringing in my ears isn't helping either.

I grab the broken shard and twist around just as the vampire tackles me to the ground.

My grip on the glass tightens when I go down. The glass cuts into my skin, sending a wave of pain down my arm. I don't let it register, either. It's the nearest thing I have to a lifeline, and I don't plan to lose it like I did the stake.

When my gaze falls on him, his eyes flash, and he hisses as the scent of my blood hits his nose. The vampire scrambles on top of me, his eyes crazy. He pushes me onto my back, pinning my hands to my chest, and drops his head down. The snarling coming from him sounds animallike, sending terrors through my body. He pushes my head forcefully to the side and sinks his fangs into my neck.

The moment I feel the sharp sting, my adrenaline kicks in again. I buck my hips, but he sits steady. I buck again, twice this time, and manage to throw him off balance and regret the decision at once when his fangs tear from my neck.

Shit, shit, shit!

Forcing my knees up, I throw him off me this time, and I scamper to my feet. The blood from the gaping wounds in my neck runs down and stains my clothes just as he lunges for me again. *Sam is going to kill us,* I think to myself as my looming death lingers in front of me.

I quickly make the decision not to run since it will send my heart into overdrive, and the blood loss will only make me lose consciousness.

Bracing myself for the attack, I wait for the moment he grabs me, and I plunge the jagged piece of glass into his heart.

He wails and shoves me away, the force sending me bouncing on my ass when I hit the floor again. I cry out as the pain shoots up my spine, and my legs lose feeling momentarily.

The vampire's wailing bellows through the empty building just to be answered with hissing from the top floor.

Feeling returns to my legs, and I force my aching body up. Now is my only chance to get away. I don't stick around to find out if the vampire is dead or not.

Who am I kidding? He won't be, but I hope I never cross paths with him again. I push my legs faster as I run for the opening Austen and I came through.

Reaching our meeting point, Austen appears out of the dark, his face as pale as the whitest sheet. I knew this was a mistake, but like always, I let him talk me into this kind of shit.

"Shit, Dom! Are you okay?" Austen reaches for me, and his eyes go impossibly wide when his gaze falls on my neck. I quickly cover the wounds with my hand when I remember the vampire's fangs tearing from it.

The fear running through me drives me to get out, and I just shake my head at Austen. We don't have time to discuss this now.

"Let's go. I'm fine. We need to get out of here!" I snarl through my teeth as I apply pressure to my neck.

"But your neck—did it turn you?"

"No, Austen, now let's go."

Austen grabs my hand, and we run for our lives as we hear footsteps thunder our way.

CHAPTER ONE

DOMINICA

2023

"This day can't get any better, can it?" I mumble, mindlessly driving through town. I spot a bar just off the side of the road and decide on a whim that maybe alcohol will be my only remedy for the image seared into my retinas.

It's not one of the classiest bars in town, but I don't care. Alcohol is alcohol. The flickering sign has multiple missing lights, and the name is only legible since it's the middle of the day. I sigh. Not having the strength to search for another place selling alcohol, I bite the inside of my cheek and get out of my car.

I stroll into the Sorbet bar, wrinkling my nose when the stench of stuffiness hits it. The bar is practically empty except for a few guys sitting in the corner in one of the booths—way at the back.

It's eerily quiet except for the whispering from the men in the corner. The expected boom from the music is missing.

Rolling my shoulders, I try to rid myself of the tension still building in them, contemplating if I should just skip the alcohol remedy and head home, but that's the last place I want to be.

The scenario gives off horror movie vibes as an unwanted chill crawls up my spine, but I shake it off.

Thinking it best to refrain from interacting with people today, especially intoxicated men, I sit on one of the bar stools at the bar, which is the nearest to the door and the furthest from said men.

The men in the booth quiet down when my stool scrapes on the floor, sending the sound echoing through the bar. I catch them eyeing me.

Rolling my eyes, I don't entertain their chatter and keep my gaze trained in front of me. I hope they get the hint of the *stay-away* look I'm trying to give off. It usually works, but I struggle to keep up that facade today.

Their interest peaks when I take my leather jacket off and hear one say that they've got company. I clasp my hands in front of me, closing my eyes momentarily as I breathe in deeply, hoping they stay where they are.

I'm in no mood for flirting, drunk bastards today.

I lean over the bar counter and look for the bartender, who still hasn't shown up. I groan irritably and rub my hands over my face when I don't see anyone.

After a while, I tap my fist on the counter and look around again. This time, I glimpse one guy staring at me as he talks, and he nudges his head in my direction. The same chill from earlier runs down my spine again.

"Can I get you anything?"

I startle when the bartender speaks right in front of me. I hadn't heard him walk over to me, and the fact that I'm so bloody distracted doesn't help much, either.

It's pissing me off, to be honest, since I'm not supposed to be distracted easily. It takes a lot to throw me off my game, but clearly, that's not the case today.

The bartender clears his throat when I still don't answer him, and I snarl inwardly. *There I go again, being distracted AF.*

"Um." I clear my throat. "Yeah, just a Coke, please."

He nods, and as he leaves to get my drink, I call for him to bring me a shot of tequila. I'm here for the alcohol, after all.

He smiles, nodding again before disappearing into the back. It doesn't take long for the bartender to bring my Coke, and he places it in front of me before he turns to pour me a shot of tequila. He frowns as he places it in front of me.

Ignoring the look that he gives me, I grab the shot and throw it down my throat, relishing the burning trail it leaves as it gets to my stomach. The burn does wonders for my peace of mind.

I close my eyes, take a deep breath, and let it out slowly as I place the shot glass down and pick up the glass of Coke. I take a slow sip and notice him still staring at me.

"Yes?" I place the glass back down on the bar.

The bartender clears his throat again as he takes the shot glass from the counter.

"Why's a pretty little thing like you sitting alone in a bar on the bad side of town at this time of day?" I look around, seeing all the guys in the booth looking this way again.

"Not much." I am trying my best not to sound rude. "Sorry, but I'm having a very shitty day and don't really feel like talking, so if you don't mind."

"Hey, just doing my job." He shrugs and moves to the other side of the bar again. I huff a breath through my nose, lowering my head and thinking of how my boss made me leave his office. That image alone makes my stomach churn.

"Dominica, so nice to see you again." Brian's secretary greets me as I walk toward his office. "Brian is unfortunately very busy and doesn't want to be disturbed."

"Hi, Agnes. Don't give me that shit. He's the one who summoned me," I bluntly state as I stroll past her desk.

"Dom, I wouldn't go in there," she warns as she rises behind her desk to stop me. I glare at her, which makes her halt her pursuit. What is going on with these people today?

First Tony, with his hands he can't keep to himself—well, he will now, and now Agnes.

"Dom," she yells after me as I push through the office doors.

I stop dead in my tracks as the scene before me knocks the air from my lungs.

On the oversized chestnut oak desk lies Jessica, her legs spread so wide I swear her hips will pop from their sockets any second. She's completely naked and moaning like there is no tomorrow.

Brian is on his knees in front of her, nose-deep as he ravishes her. His grip on her thighs is so tight there's no doubt in my mind that it'll leave bruises.

They don't show any inkling that they know I'm watching them, but I can assure you they sure as hell heard me walk in.

After a few seconds, Jessica screams as she reaches her climax, her eyes falling on me the moment that happens. She smiles wickedly and grinds herself on Brian's face until she's fully satisfied.

"You have to be kidding me," I snarl under my breath. Brian's gaze falls on me when he looks up and dares to roam it over my body before pinning me with a lust-filled stare. The anger building in my chest flares, and I narrow my eyes as I cross my arms.

The previously mentioned whore grins up at me like a cat who's gotten the cream. Well, in a manner of speaking, she certainly did.

I feel the red blush creep up my chest and face as I stare at them.

Why the hell am I *blushing?*

That's one thing about myself: I absolutely loathe the fact that I blush beet red for the simplest things.

Clearing my throat, I tap my foot irritably. I try to rid myself of the images now seared into my memory forever. "You wanted to see me?" I grit my teeth.

Brian smiles as he gets up from the floor. He, like Jessica, is completely naked and still very much turned on.

I don't know exactly what's running through his mind, but by the look in his eyes, I can only imagine, and believe me, it's not going to happen. Threesomes have always been one of Brian's favorite pastimes.

"You know what? Screw this. Next time, call me rather than summoning me to your damn office for this shit show."

I turn on my heel and storm out of the office before he or the slut draped over his desk can say anything.

What did he think he was going to establish with this display? Brian has been trying very hard to get into my pants since the first day I started at the VHA. Obviously, he always fails. And he will always fail.

"Dom, I tried to warn you," Agnes says, pity covering her whole face.

"Next time, try harder, won't you? Or just tell me he's fucking someone in the middle of a business day," I bite out as I walk past her desk.

I don't stick around to listen to the flimsy excuse she's trying to give me. I need to get some fresh air.

I rub my temples. Why the hell is this upsetting me so much? Why he sees the need to show me he can get any woman he wants is beyond me. Don't get me wrong—when I started at the VHA, I had a massive crush on the guy, with his muscular body, square-cut jawline with the neatly trimmed beard, and well-dressed attire, but then he showed his true, bombastic colors, and I refuse to be a notch on someone's post. Thank you very much.

I sigh, lowering my head into my hands as the memory loops in my mind again. I wish I could scrub it out.

A stool scraping next to me rips me out of my thoughts. I don't move, recognizing the clothing of the man next to me as one of the guys from across the bar when he enters my peripheral.

"Hi there, sweetheart. Need some company?" the asshole says as he sits down. I consider someone an asshole if they invade my space, especially in a situation like this. But most of all, it's a part of my job to read people and their intentions, and this guy's intentions are screaming vile things.

Ignoring him, I raise my head and take another sip from my Coke, staring straight ahead. I don't want to have a conversation with him. His entire vibe gives me goose bumps and makes the hairs on the back of my neck stand on end.

Why do these kinds of men always feel the need to approach me? I don't get it. Do I have a damn flashing sign on my forehead or something?

"Come on, darling, don't be like that," he coos and leans sideways, his head propped up by his hand on the bar counter.

He tries to sound sweet and flirty, but it makes my stomach turn. The guy reeks of smoke and bourbon mixed with sweat and other nasty smells I can't pinpoint. It makes me want to hurl.

"What gives you any idea I want to talk to strangers?" I snap as I glare sideways at him. "Aren't you a spicy little thing? Come on, darlin', we're just lookin' for some fun." I almost jump out of my seat when asshole number two speaks from behind me, his breath hot on my neck. He really is too close for comfort.

My back goes rigid, and I ball my fist on the counter next to my glass. My other hand slowly moves to my thigh, where my ring daggers are strapped, and my hand folds over the handle.

They fit my hands perfectly, like they were molded to fit there. It's my weapon of choice. I got them when I lost my bowie knife in that factory twenty years ago. I'm still bummed about it.

I didn't come here for a fight, but if these assholes don't leave me be, I will give them one. Why does trouble seem to follow me?

I turn to asshole number one—who dares to sit down next to me—and I give him a stiff smile.

He beams at me, showing his pearly whites, which, in all honesty, he will lose in a few seconds if he doesn't take his friend and mind their own business.

He probably thinks I will give in to them when I'm scanning my surroundings.

I can't find their other friend when I look around the room again. Weren't there three of them?

My shoulders tense. Great, they probably have me surrounded. My suspicion is confirmed when an overly warm, sweaty hand grabs my shoulder from the other side. I grit my teeth. My entire body stiffens from the touch.

Being touched is still something I can't swallow, especially by men who think they have the right to do so. I have romantic partners, but that's on my terms, and I must mentally prepare myself every time. It has been like that since my time at the Academy—overeager potential male hunters who think they are allowed to touch what doesn't belong to them. Being cornered in the girls' washroom is still something that haunts me, but that's a story for another day. If it weren't for Austen who came to help me, I probably would be less tolerant.

"Sir, I kindly request that you remove your hand from me," I state flatly, looking down at the hand on my shoulder before slowly looking up at him.

"Or what, baby girl?" He laughs mockingly, his teeth stained yellow from taking abuse from all the smoking.

"Or you are going to lose it," I snap.

He tightens his grip, clearly not happy with my statement. I close my eyes, forcing myself not to react on my instincts, now practically screaming at me to react. This ass *really* doesn't know who he's messing with. "Sir, I will not ask you again."

"Oh, really, darlin'? What gives you the right to talk to a man like this?" he growls in my ear, gripping my shoulder harder.

One moment, I'm sitting, trying to get a hold of my temper, and the next, I fall. The bastard with his hand on me pulls me backward, and an involuntary yelp leaves my mouth.

I grab my glass of Coke and throw it in asshole number one's face—who is still sitting next to me with that shit-eating grin—as I let myself fall.

He screams angrily and jumps up from his seat when the cold drink hits his face just as I topple over. I've now pulled the ring dagger free from the sheath on my thigh.

I swing my legs back with the momentum of my fall, kicking asshole number two in the chest, sending him flying backward into some tables.

At the same instant, my legs make contact with the douchebag's chest, and his friend lunges for me as I make a perfect somersault, landing on my feet in a crouching position.

I kick off from the ground, moving toward him fast, and he curses violently when I force him to stop in his tracks. My dagger digging into his throat.

"You bitch!"

"As I recall, I did warn you all to leave me alone and especially not to touch me, but that seems to slip your mind," I tell him, my face inches from his.

"Hey, you are the one stepping into a bar dressed like that in the middle of the day. Women only dress like that for this kind of attention." He chokes out the last part of his sentence as I increase the pressure of my dagger on his trachea.

I look down at myself. Frowning up at the asshole, I tilt my head in confusion. What the hell is he talking about?

I'm wearing tight-fitting black denim and a black tank top—normally with my black leather jacket, but it's on the floor with my chair now.

My go-to color: it's easier to hide certain stains.

The tank top is cut low, exposing some of my breasts, but not low enough for them to get an idea like this.

But then again, these kinds of men will see any piece of clothing as an invitation to do whatever they want to some unsuspecting girl.

The mistake these assholes make is assuming that *I* am one of those unsuspecting girls.

"You see, and therein lies my problem," I sneer as I step closer to him, pressing my dagger just hard enough to draw blood. "It doesn't matter how a woman dresses; you have no right to claim her just because of that."

Asshole number two stumbles to his feet, glaring at me as he rubs his chest before taking a menacing step toward me.

"Ah-ah, I wouldn't do that if I were you," I say, catching the movement and forcing my dagger deeper into his friend's throat, making him choke.

"Hey, lady, come on. Just leave, okay, or I'm calling the cops," the bartender says, his eyes wide as he watches me.

I snort at his pathetic comment. These assholes disturb *my* peace, and he wants to call the cops on *me* for protecting myself.

This world has indeed become a place I loathe. I meet more and more men who feel threatened by an Alpha female. They prefer you to be meek and not in control of your own decisions. It's disturbing.

In my world, it doesn't quite work that way. If you are weak and can't fight, you will definitely die.

Granted, it's a problem of everyday life, but it seems worse somehow. I *know* there is worse shit out there. I deal with it daily or, to be more precise, nightly.

My job is to deal with the lowest life-forms, the creatures of the night, and now I have to deal with their human counterparts.

"Fine," I snarl.

I pull my dagger from asshole number three's throat, wipe the blood on the blade on his shirt, and sheath it back in its place as I step back.

Eyeing the other two, I pick my jacket up from the floor. Taking my wallet from my jacket pocket, I pull out a couple of dollars and toss it on the bar before I walk out.

Asshole number three spits on the floor where I stood, rubbing at his throat, his eyes screaming murder.

"Watch your back, princess," he sneers at me.

"I always do, asshole." I laugh dryly and let the door slam behind me before any of them can say another word.

I take a minute to settle my temper. I let my head fall back, closing my eyes and soaking up the sunlight before sunset. This day is just getting better and better, isn't it? Hopefully, tonight will be fruitful, and I can relieve all the tension. I pull on my jacket and stroll to my car.

"I hate Halloween," I grit out, avoiding a punch to the face. I dodge a second punch to the stomach by jumping back and landing a solid kick to its chest.

"It's a dumb and useless holiday. If people only knew what it stands for, they would not dress so ridiculously and be out at night when it's the most dangerous and mock the undead. People will never believe what crawls around their homes at night, and when they do see something, they chuck it off as paranormal or some other kind of shit."

"I'm about to kill you, and you're having a useless conversation with yourself," the vampire growls as he rubs his chest and rises from the ground.

"I'm getting bored, so I have to do something to make it entertaining," I say, placing my hands on my hips before continuing, "and you thinking that you will kill me is a little funny. Well done."

The vampire snarls, evanesces, and appears at my back. I roll my eyes and forcefully bring my elbow back to collide with his face. He stumbles. I quickly turn and kick him in the chest again.

"Case in point." I laugh darkly, drive my stake through the vampire's heart, and watch his form being reduced to ash.

Rising from the ground, I dust the asshole from my clothes, coughing as I step out of the filth that's left behind from my kill.

The tension is already seeping from my muscles. There is nothing like slaying the soulless beasts of the night to calm my nerves and make me feel productive. Especially after the day I've had.

I clench my jaw as the images plague my mind again. It's getting ridiculous. I really need to let it go.

Scanning my surroundings, I spot Austen and Silvia, each staking a vampire as two more approach them.

They rise simultaneously and stand back-to-back when the bloodsuckers launch their attack. It doesn't take long for them to finish off the vampires, and they high-five when the dust settles.

I chuckle, shaking my head. Luckily, I'm not the only one who enjoys this job. Silvia smiles brightly and laughs when Austen says something I can't make out. They do make a good team.

"Austen, I'm going to check the western part of the corn maze," I call as I walk toward the maze.

"Dom, please be careful." Austen pauses and frowns. "Where is your backup?" he yells as he ducks from a punch flying by his face.

Another vampire has emerged from the shadows without anyone noticing. Luckily, our instincts are a force to be reckoned with.

I laugh dryly, rolling my eyes again. I turn as Austen lands another blow to the bloodsucker's jaw, and I walk away, not even answering him.

What kind of question is that?

Every vampire hunter usually has a partner. For our safety, of course. I am the only one who doesn't have one, and I sure as hell don't need one.

Brian, our commander in chief, and I have fought about this subject many times, but I always get my way.

I don't want to be responsible for someone else's life, and they know it. I'd rather it be just me, and then I won't get distracted.

Annoyance flares in my veins. It isn't my first rodeo, dammit. I pull my face at the cliché venue we find ourselves in. Why do these bloodsuckers like school grounds so much? For Pete's sake, I couldn't wait to get away from school when I graduated, and the eternally undead tend to drift back to it.

I round a corner and sigh. The maze is eerily quiet. It won't be for much longer, though. The school's Mayhem and Murder-themed Halloween night drew in many people this year. As did it draw in the wrong crowd. The entire focus is on the maze in the middle of the schoolyard. It's easy pickings for vampires since the humans don't suspect danger. They come for the occasional scare, but few realize there could be something much worse out there.

The human traffic flow has died down as we near the 3 a.m. mark. My heavy boots echo in the empty schoolyard as I approach the maze, and the sound bounces off the school building's walls, making it sound eerie and ghostlike. I revel in quiet moments like these, but this one is short-lived when a faint chuckle fills my ears, and I stop dead.

Here we go.

I flick the ends of my assassin's coat back and pull my ring daggers from the sheaths tied around my thighs before the fabric falls into place, swinging them around my fingers before gripping them tight. I can't help but briefly close my eyes. The feel of them in my hands awakens utter contentment in my soul.

I stroll toward the maze, catching my appearance in one of the school windows as I pass it. A giggle slips from my lips as I twirl my finger in my hair.

My look isn't exactly original, but hey, can you blame me? I grew up watching movies like *Blade* and *Underworld,* and I just love the look of the main characters since my world is kind of wrapped up in the same shit as those movies. The only difference is that I'm *not* a vampire. *I* am the thing they fear.

Dominica Salvatore. The name that sends any vampire running except for one. *Damn Xavier Valin.* My archenemy.

He's the only vampire that slips through my fingers each time our paths cross. Ever since that night in the abandoned warehouse when he almost killed me. There's this *dance*—if we can even call it that—between us, and frankly, it's disturbing. He loves messing with me. There is another element that drives me insane, but I refuse to utter it out loud. I struggle to deal with it as is. But that's something for later.

I've made quite a name for myself. I'm ruthless and have absolutely no mercy. I use my looks to draw them in and then strike like death itself.

Within the first year of joining the Vampire Hunters Association, the supernatural started trembling at the mention of my name.

I prefer it if they run at the sight of me. It makes for a more exhilarating hunt if you ask me.

The chuckle from earlier echoes through the night again, this time a little louder and more menacing. "What's with the Chucky cackle, dude? Really? Just come and get the poor helpless girl walking alone at night," I call into the night air as the laughter rings out again.

My appearance can be misleading if you don't pay close attention. My features are almost angelic if you will, which draws them in even more. They are the polar opposite of how I carry myself, though. Having the face of an angel adds to the whole "save me" theme. Growing up, I despised it, but I saw the advantages when I became a hunter. You bet your ass I was riding that train then. Stupid bloodsuckers can't resist it.

Some say the blood tastes sweeter.

No vampire has ever gotten close enough to sink a fang into my flesh—not since Xavier—and I prefer it that way.

Anger fills my being again at the thought of his mouth on me. I can't believe I was so stupid once. I vowed that it would never happen again, and I've been able to keep that vow.

Before any of them ever get a chance to come near my neck with those disgusting fangs, they either end up with my daggers digging into *their* necks or a stake in the heart.

My hand drifts up absentmindedly. I trace the scar at the base of my neck—knowing its exact outline. It drives my purpose more.

I think that is one of the main reasons I hate him more than the average vampire. He scarred me for life, and he caused a lot of unwanted problems for me that night.

I shake my head, ridding myself of the memories of the night I met Xavier.

A shiver runs down my spine at the thought of that night and how stupid Austen and I were. We were lacking street smarts. Luckily, my skills have become much more honed as the years have followed.

Training and determination taught me that not all hunters have it easy. My talents come naturally since my bloodline is ancient—which isn't common knowledge; not even the VHA knows—and adding my lineage with my innocent beauty makes for one lethal weapon. With nearly flawless alabaster skin, raven black hair, piercing blue eyes, and a tiny build, I'm truly poison in a small five-five package. So, let's just say it doesn't take much effort for me to do what I do. It takes even less time to lure the beasts out.

Straining my ears, I listen for any sound coming from the bloodsucker when rustling comes from the maze up ahead.

Guess the asshole decided he wanted to play hide-and-seek tonight—*game on, asshole.*

I turn away from the building and enter the western part of the maze, following the deranged laughter, my daggers ready to strike like a pissed-off king cobra.

Turning a corner that veers left into the maze, I hear more rustling ahead just past the scarecrow, and I approach cautiously.

Look, don't get me wrong; I don't fear these assholes, but I'm still not stupid, and I damn as hell am not trigger-happy. I don't run into scenarios guns blazing, so to speak.

The rustling becomes louder as I get nearer. It's the only sound in the chilly night air before a scream pierces it. I whip my head in that direction. The maze winds to the right and ends abruptly. The only way to go is either left or right.

Shit. Which way?

Whimpering comes from the right, which sends my cautious mode into killing mode hyperdrive.

Panic envelops me, and I run toward the sound just to find three vampires pinning down a woman not much younger than me. Then again, hunters age differently than normal humans. Our aging slows drastically, so we might look twenty-five but are more like thirty-five.

Anger fills my chest, but I force it down. Nothing good ever comes from acting in anger. I quickly assess the situation. One vampire drinks from her neck, the other from her breast, and of course, they go for the femoral artery, as the third has his head and fangs buried near her private area, as he drinks from her thigh.

The poor woman didn't stand a chance, not until now. "You better let her go, boys, or we are going to have a problem here," I say softly, my voice dripping with forced innocence.

All three vampires' heads snap in my direction, hissing as they hold the woman tighter. One snaps his jaw as he assesses me with a hateful glare.

I keep my hands behind my back, concealing the daggers from view. I sway from side to side. "Oh, come on, guys. I also want some fun. Don't be so selfish."

The vampire at the girl's throat gives me a feral smile. He releases her and saunters toward me. His head swivels like a snake, inhaling the air and pinning me with a hungry stare. His fangs gleam in the little light provided by the overhead lights. "Hmm, pretty girl. Don't you smell delicious?"

"Really? I didn't notice. What do I smell like?" I ask, batting my lashes. "Like forbidden fruit," he says and sniffs the surrounding air again. His mouth is literally watering.

I smirk and tilt my head to expose my neck to him. His eyes turn dark as he watches my every move. "Such a willing little succulent, aren't you? So naive," he purrs as he lowers his head to my neck.

His lips touch my throat, and I chuckle. He draws back, confusion on his face. "Something funny? You clearly don't know the danger you are in, do you?"

Is that amusement in his eyes? "No. Nothing funny. You're correct about the danger, but *I'm* not the one in danger." I pout and drop my hands to my side, exposing the daggers.

He frowns and looks down. His eyes round, and with a hiss, he steps back quickly. I'm well-known for my weapons, so if a vampire doesn't recognize my scent, they sure as hell do my daggers. "Ah, so you know these?" I ask amusingly, bringing the daggers up to eye level.

His gaze jumps from my hands to my eyes, slowly retreating from me. The thrill and amusement at this very moment will never get old. That look on his face, the look they get when they realize who I am, is like a rush.

He brings his hands up in front of him in surrender, still backing up toward his friends.

The vampire swallows visibly when I step closer, moving with him.

"Leave the girl," he hisses when he nears his friends. They don't listen, and the panic I know he feels shows on his face when he kicks the one at the girl's thigh. "Dammit, I said leave the girl." The other two growl in frustration and look up at him, confused.

I swing my daggers around my fingers, catching their attention, and they pinpoint the cause of the fear and panic in their friend's voice.

I will never get used to the exhilarating feeling of a vampire fearing me. I worked hard for my reputation, and none of these assholes will ever get the chance to destroy that.

They tried, but they have yet to triumph. I have scars all over my body that tell tales of the ones that, indeed, were more of a fight than others.

"What the hell?" The vampire at the woman's breast hisses. He lets her go, grabs the collar of his friend's shirt, and drags him up from the ground.

Their sudden release makes the poor woman fall to the ground, and she cries out in pain, which in turn makes my eyes flash in anger, but I keep my composure.

"Oh, come on, boys. Don't tell me you are afraid of little old me?" I pout, still swinging the daggers around my fingers, catching them occasionally.

Their eyes jump between the daggers as I walk closer to them.

"Listen, hunter, we don't want any trouble," one of them says, his voice trembling.

I'm not sure which one said that. I don't see faces anymore. I only see fangs and the exact spot where I drive my stake through. The daggers are fun to use, and the silver on the blade's edge helps weaken the target, but a stake to the heart is more effective.

Every vampire hunter needs to have a stake and some other weapon made from silver in their arsenal. I chose the daggers since they are great for getting up close and personal, and besides, they look epic and make me feel badass.

There's something feminine about ring daggers, yet the danger looming with them makes the draw irresistible.

"Could have fooled me," I laugh as I strike.

Within a minute or two, all three vampires are crumpled at my feet, cut up and whining in pain. They must be newly made because an older vampire's strength is something else. It's more of a challenge, if you will. Their strength, resilience, and fighting skill can bring down the most experienced hunter if we're not careful.

I grab the front of the vampire's shirt, the one who approached me, and yank him toward me. "Where is the rest of your coven?"

"Fuck you," he grinds out.

"You wish," I laugh darkly, and my voice drops to a venomous whisper. "I will not ask you again."

He hisses and bares his fangs just before I pull the stake from the back of my skirt and drive it through his heart. The dust that was the vampire doesn't get a chance to settle before I move to the second one. I grab him by the front of his shirt and ask the same question. He glares at me, defiance screaming from his eyes and every pore. I smile wickedly and push the stake into his chest—slowly, oh so slowly—stopping just before piercing his heart, and he screams. His breathing becomes labored as the wood scrapes against his heart. "They aren't here," he huffs.

"Bullshit," I snarl. "Where. Are. They?"

"They don't know we are here. We took it upon ourselves to come for a hunt." He sounds almost desperate.

"Oh really?" I raise my brow, unimpressed.

"Yes, now let me go," he pleads.

"Oh, pretty boy. You are sorely mistaken. I never said you would leave this place alive. With the wind, yes." I snicker as his face turns white, even though they are naturally pale.

To an outsider, my actions might seem cruel. Why do I mock them and make it torturous? The answer is simple. It's pure nature for a vampire to torment their prey, scaring them to the point their heart gives out, and then, just before it does, they pounce.

So, I am just returning the favor. And besides, why do I need to have mercy when they don't possess the thought process to give any?

I push the stake into his chest further, watching as his eyes freeze in horror just before he, too, is reduced to ash.

The last vampire scurries backward and gets up, running into the maze. I guess he hasn't mastered evanescing yet. I curse under my breath and dust vampire number two from my skirt. Huffing a frustrated sigh, I roll my shoulders and run after him.

It's the part I love the most about hunting. There is something poetic about the typically hunted now doing the hunting. The thrill, coupled with pure adrenaline, is intoxicating. But for some reason, I can't seem to feel the exhilaration. All I feel is irritation and a boatload of anger.

"You can run, but you cannot hide," I call as I run after him.

CHAPTER TWO

XAVIER

I am so damn bored. Ugh, bloody newlings. Why the hell am I entertaining these assholes by coming here? Babysitting duty sucks ass.

What the hell is taking so long? Tapping my fingers on my folded arms, I look at my watch again as I lean against the exit part of the maze wall.

I watched as two beautiful and luscious girls walked into the maze, giggling like schoolgirls—which they weren't—looking for the thrill of being frightened. They did not know that they would get that in abundance.

I sent the three newlings in after them: boom, easy as pie. It's been over an hour, and none of them are back yet.

It's not that difficult to hunt down prey. I mean, really, do I need to bite the girls for them as well?

A frustrating growl rumbles in my chest, and I roll my eyes and push myself off the wall. I should probably look for them, or there will be hell to pay from their sire.

It's because of this exact reason I refuse to join a damn coven. I can't do this for the rest of eternity. And besides, I like being by myself. No orders that need to be followed or a chain of command. Just me, myself, and I.

The thought makes me smile. The sooner I get out of here, the sooner I can return to my everyday life. That life entails traveling to wherever I want to and dabbling in the smuggling of precious artifacts. In the past, my role as enforcer for the newlings' sire was all I had time for. Now I only get called to rid our Society of the most bothersome of enemies.

Right, back to the present, to the newlings. I can't help the snarl that slips out next. This shit-ass situation is starting to get on my last nerve. I straighten my spine and pull at my jacket before I stroll into the maze, shoving my hands in my pockets.

After about five minutes of easy navigating through the maze, I stop dead when a familiar voice reaches my ears. *You have to be kidding me.*

I shove my hand through my hair, knowing exactly why the newlings aren't back yet.

Stupid-ass hunters.

Irritation flares through me. I don't have the patience for this tonight. No, it's not just any hunter—why would it ever be so easy? The most dangerous one in an exceptionally long time. I drag my hand over my face. Where are the days when you can go out for a nice hot meal, and no one tries to kill you?

My kind isn't like they used to be either, so I can't complain. They have too many *feelings,* and their damn shitty opinions count more than the fact that they are bloodsucking vampires. This is yet another point why I don't belong to a coven.

The only reason I'm here is because my remarkably close friend—and sire to these newlings—asked me to take them out hunting.

I wasn't thrilled, but he didn't have the manpower to set someone aside, and besides, I can handle my own when encountering hunters.

Not to toot my own horn, but I'm rather good at hunting and not drawing attention, until I met Dominica Salvatore.

That woman drives me bloody insane. She always ends up where I am and seems to know my every move, no matter how hard I try to avoid her.

If I didn't know better, I'd swear she's stalking me.

Well, maybe the other way around. I love taunting her. I even have a nickname for her, and every time our paths cross and I want to piss her off, I just drop the name.

Laughing, I make my way to the commotion filling the air now. Turning a corner in the maze, Riley, one of the newlings, comes running straight into me, making him fall on his ass. I stare down at him and raise my brow mockingly. "Really? Are we running from a *hunter?*"

"Xavier, it's not any hunter. It's her. It's the *Reaper.*" Riley's eyes are as big as saucers, and his breathing is ragged as he stumbles to his feet. He's trembling, and his body is bloodstained.

I look him over and notice the cuts are slowly healing. Clearly, Little Deadly is in the mood to play with her kill tonight. The cuts she left on him aren't life-threatening but will still hurt like a bitch and slow him down.

Those damn ring daggers of hers are worse than a bloody stake. She's done quite some damage to me whenever my focus is off.

Reaper. The name leaves a bitter taste in my mouth. Really original, but I do get why they associate her with the Grim Reaper. She's just as deadly as the mythical floating ghost.

On the other hand, my name for her has nothing to do with that. She's a bloody deadly sin, *mine,* to be precise.

My body reacts to her in ways not reserved for your enemy. Every time I see her, it's like I come alive, and try as I might, my damn dick has a mind of its own.

I hate her so much more just because of that, not to mention the fact that she killed quite a few of my friends—close friends, to be exact—ones that were more than four hundred years old. But the genuine hatred comes from the first day I met her. She almost killed me, and then she came back with the Association, and they bombed the whole building. I narrowly escaped with my life.

It's with those killings she made her name, not that she got off unharmed, but still, she's the one who walked away from the fight. It took me a month to recover.

The bombs the VHA uses are laced with silver particles, so even if you survive the initial blast, the particles enter your blood, heart, and everything. Your body absorbs it like it's nothing, weakening you and acting like a damper on your healing ability.

I'm so lost in my thoughts that I don't see the dagger flying in my direction. I look up into Little Deadly's face only when it's lodged in my shoulder and the pain registers.

I grunt and pull the dagger from my shoulder. I can't keep the wince off my face as the metal burns my flesh—damn *silver.*

"Thanks for that," I growl, tossing the dagger to the side.

"Always a pleasure, Xavier," she says, hatred lacing every syllable.

Little Deadly curtsies and my attention snags on her outfit. I raise my brows as my gaze drags up and down her body. *That wasn't a good idea.*

She wears an assassin's coat, big enough to fit me, but it's not what catches my attention. It's what she wears underneath the coat. On her feet, she's wearing combat boots going up to her mid-calf. I trail my eyes up, and the fishnet stockings make me want to laugh aloud. *Where did she even find those?*

Her skirt has pleats that flare out so much that if there is a slight breeze tonight, it will not cover anything. Not that it's covering much as is. I force my gaze up, and they snag on the tight-fitting black tank top, which accentuates her breasts.

Cursing, I snap my gaze up to her face so quickly that one of my vertebrae cracks. My anger rises. The image of myself latching onto one of her nipples and grazing my fangs across it just before

I suck it into my mouth slithers into my mind. The thought alone makes my mouth water.

I clench my jaw so tightly my teeth crack as a smile runs across her mouth.

"Are you checking me out?" Little Deadly flicks her coat away from her side to place her hand on her hip, her brow raised.

Shit, I need to recover from this, or she will never let me live this down, especially now that Riley is here to witness our interaction.

Strangely, I want to rip his eyes from their sockets. I don't want anyone to witness our little banter. It's private and only for my pleasure—and torture. "Wouldn't you like that?"

"No, not really. It disgusts me to know that you are trying to undress me with your damn eyes," Little Deadly retorts and makes a gagging sound as she picks at her nails with the remaining dagger.

My temper flares at her insult, and I bite my tongue, tasting blood. This little vixen is asking for a spanking. "Well, we sure are lowering our standards, aren't we?"

She tilts her head, and the frown on her face makes her angelic features more alluring.

I motion to the newling hiding behind me, and the recognition on her face makes me want to slap her smug smile from it.

"Oh, poor baby, feeling a little protective of your kitten there?" she mocks. A growl rumbles through my chest, and she raises her brows at me again.

"Growling like a little puppy dog isn't helping your case much, X, but hey, whatever rocks your boat. Can we just get on with this fight so I can get rid of some tension?"

I frown and realize her smile is off as well as her usual banter. A crazy thought worms its way to the front of my brain, and it disgusts me.

The thought of ripping out the throat of whoever upset her—the one that's caused her to act and feel this way needs to hope they never cross my path, or they will surely regret it. But I can't decide if it's the thought that disgusts me or the actual feeling associated with it.

CHAPTER THREE

DOMINICA

Of course, I run into none other than Xavier. Why am I even surprised? Since we met in that abandoned building—how long ago, I can't even remember—we never seem to be rid of each other.

I can only explain the feeling as debris pulled toward a class five tornado.

It must be a cruel game, but I have learned to accept that no matter how hard I try to avoid Xavier, he is wherever I find myself.

An outsider is probably thinking, if it bothers me so much, why haven't I just killed him?

Well, the answer is simple … I don't know.

This job has become so monotonous that I may be looking for something thrilling again. I'm stupid and playing with fire, but I can't help it.

I catch Xavier assessing my wardrobe, and I can't help the hot feeling building down below when his eyes rest on my breasts. Still, he snaps his head up so quickly that he looks like a boy getting caught doing the nasty.

Dammit, what is this asshole doing to me? I hate him with every ounce of my being, yet my body screams for him.

I shake my head to rid myself of the new images in my mind, cursing inwardly that I just can't escape this shit. It has to be because of what I saw earlier. If not, I seriously need to get my head checked.

"So? Are we fighting or what?" I ask, forcing a mocking smile but feeling more irritated currently than at the start of the chase.

"Nah, *Little Deadly,* not tonight. It seems like you make trouble wherever you go, and now, I have some explaining to do. I think it's torturous enough to let you steam out your demons rather than me getting staked." Xavier smirks, shoving his hands in his pockets.

His demeanor is pissing me off with every syllable leaving his mouth, and my anger rises to a boiling point, but the moment the stupid nickname he has for me registers, I see red.

I despise being called that. I know Reaper is one of the names the vampire community has given me, but being called *Little Deadly* pisses me off more than anything else.

He started calling me that after the second time he narrowly escaped my stake, and he gets the same damn reaction out of me every time.

And naturally, I feel the blush coming up from my chest and settling in my cheeks.

Xavier's smile only stretches wider as he sees the rage building behind my eyes. His gaze doesn't leave mine as he grabs the other vampire behind his neck and says, "Come on, asshole, before we both join your friends because of your stupidity."

"Don't you dare!" I warn him, sensing his next move. Xavier laughs maliciously and evanesces before my eyes.

I scream in frustration, stomping my foot like a child. Not the best behavior from someone like me, but it just came out.

How dare he leave without a proper fight? Especially tonight when I need it most. That is yet another of the many reasons I hate that bastard. He brings out weird behaviors like this. No vampire has ever made me throw a damn tantrum. *What the actual hell?*

I ball my fists and scream out again and again. My throat is raw, but at least it makes me feel somewhat better, like I can rein in this anger until I can find a proper way to release it. I sigh heavily, pinching the bridge of my nose.

I regain my composure and look around, listening for anything coming my way since I wasn't quiet. When nothing happens, I decide that maybe I should call it a night and just go home. The thought of a hot shower and a tub of ice cream sounds like the best remedy.

I stride to where Xavier tossed my ring dagger, pick it up, and wipe it clean on my skirt. The prick almost threw it away, and these are my favorite ones. The amount of blood on it makes me smile. At least I hurt the bastard, and the wound will cause him discomfort for a while.

"*Dom!*" Austen calls as he and his partner, Silvia, run around the corner. I rise from the ground, turning to find him hunched over, his hands resting on his knees as he tries to catch his breath. He gives me his famous scowl.

"What the hell?" he snaps at me.

"What do you mean?"

"I heard you scream, and here you are, looking bored and unbothered."

"Just letting off some frustration. Damn vampires got away," I huff.

Austen narrows his eyes on me and folds his arms over his chest when he stands upright. I raise my brow at him. He knows better than to challenge me.

"Fine, I won't come running next time you scream."

I let out a sarcastic burst of laughter. "Yeah, right, you'll always come running. You want to know how I know that?"

"Hmph, enlighten me?"

"You can't resist the urge to tell people that you saved the one hunter who thought she could work alone, and you had to come to my rescue," I say, folding my arms.

With a burst of laughter, Austen says, "Yeah, right! Keep telling yourself that."

"No need, my friend." Austen's laughter is infectious. "Come on, let's get out of here. I need to get home. I am so over this day."

CHAPTER FOUR

XAVIER

"I am going to get my ass handed to me. Do you realize that?" I ask Riley as we walk into Alex's compound.

"It can't be that bad, can it?" He looks at me and then at his arms, where the cuts were just a few moments ago.

I huff air out through my nose and roll my now-healed shoulder. The sting of the damn dagger still lingers, and I shake my head at the newling. So much to learn. I do not have the time or the patience to deal with a newly made vampire. It's like training a damn puppy. "You have *no* idea."

"What's the worst that can happen? He won't kill me, will he?" I tap him on the shoulder reassuringly and force a smile as we approach the door of Alex's office.

Riley stares at me, and I don't know what to say. I will obviously do my best to ensure he doesn't lose the new life he has just been granted, but I can't promise anything.

The doors open, and we enter, Riley trailing behind me, dragging his feet. I look over my shoulder at the kid; he catches my eyes and hurries to catch up.

If there is one thing I can teach him, a vampire does not lag. We don't drag our feet or shy away from danger. It just ruins the illusion of what we are, and besides, it's just rude.

Alex sits behind his desk with a scowl, his knuckles white from gripping the device in his hand too tightly. Curses falling from his mouth.

"Sire—" Riley starts to say and almost runs up to the desk. Alex only lifts one finger, cutting Riley off before he can talk further. Riley stops, shuts his mouth, lowers his head, and waits for Alex to address him. I shake my head at the new vamp.

Idiot …

I stroll to the desk and slap the newling behind the head as I walk past him, sitting opposite my friend. I thank my lucky stars for not having to deal with this much longer.

"What the hell happened?" Alex snarls, looking up at me.

"Hunters happened. One specific one," I tell him nonchalantly as I lean my head back against the chair. Alex likes having dramatic furniture. The chair I have my butt placed in can pass as a poor man's throne, with the high back and carved ruins. Alex has a bigger build than me. In fact, he is the total opposite. He has shoulder-length brown hair and a full beard; where I am much slimmer built with black short hair that I wear slicked back and no facial hair. I don't care for it much.

Alex lifts his brow and pulls his tongue over his teeth, contemplating my words before tossing his phone on the table. "*That* hunter is really getting on my last nerve. She's a thorn in the side of the entire Vampire Society, and she needs to be taken care of. Sooner rather than later."

I hum low in my throat, agreeing with Alex, but the thought of never having one of our iconic fights leaves a bitter taste in my mouth. I shake my head at the absurdity of the thought plaguing my mind and say, "That's easier said than done. The last hunter that posed a semblance of a threat took an entire army to take down.

The threat the Reaper poses falls in a whole different category." I tap my finger on my lower lip before adding, "Now, we will need to be more discreet about how we handle this, with technology and all." Humans are still mostly unaware of our existence. Granted we keep a low profile but then you get instances where haze-clouded vampires can't keep to the shadows. That's when it gets interesting. Damage control can go either way depending on when the hunters show up.

"Tell me about it," Alex growls and nudges his head to the phone.

I frown, take the phone from the table, and look at the YouTube video repeatedly playing. You have to be kidding me. I tap on the play button and look at the imagery unfolding in the video.

It's of the three newlings feeding on one of the girls in the maze, and the video goes dark just as Dominica comes running around the corner. I can hear the person who took the video's breathing pick up. I assume they must be hiding.

The imagery might be lost, but the audio is clear as night. I can hear the whole exchange between hunter and vampire. *Dammit.*

"If that whole video's imagery were shown, we would have a whole lot more shit to deal with than we have to at this stage," he says, rubbing his temples.

"What do you suppose we do to erase this?" I ask, placing the phone down on the desk. I glance over my shoulder at the now ghost-white newling.

"Nothing now. We can trust that the VHA will take care of that problem since they don't like losing control of the public knowing too much of our existence." Alex sighs.

"Guess there is something we can be thankful for about the Association." Alex lets out a huff and leans his head back on the chair. He takes a deep breath, and after a long pause, he lets it out slowly and looks at Riley. "Go get yourself cleaned up, please. We will talk about being discreet later. I don't have the strength to deal with this now."

I frown again, noticing the slight snarl on Alex's lips. Looks like there is more brewing under this whole facade than he's letting on. I wait patiently until the door shuts behind Riley, then turn back to Alex. "Okay, my friend, spill it. What happened?"

Alex sighs and rubs the back of his neck. "What makes you think there is something else?"

I shake my head, roll my eyes dramatically, and feign being hurt. "Really? Like I haven't known the inner workings of your mind for the better part of two centuries. I can't believe you insult me so."

Alex laughs tiredly, and he gets up from his seat. He walks to the window and looks out at the compound.

It must be something big because I had only seen him react like this when Dominica and her squad blew up the previous compound building. That night, we lost quite a few newlings and elders.

Something similar might have happened. Alex confirms my suspicions when he turns to me with a grim expression. "Okay, now I am officially worried. What the hell is going on?"

"The VHA blew up another compound across town … there were no survivors. Sofie was there, Xavier. My sister … " Alex's voice breaks, but he composes himself and continues, "she was there for a meeting with the clan leaders, and I haven't heard anything from her. I fear the worst."

I'm struggling to absorb the news. Shit, I didn't even know Sofie was back in town. Alex and Sofie are the only ones left from the Velgara family. They are incredibly close and have been around since the late 1500s. The only thing that would keep Alex from going off the rails is reassurance, which I'll give him. "Sofie is resilient, my friend. She would have gotten out beforehand. She escaped death too many times to be killed by something so trivial," I tell him, but I can see how much this is getting to him.

"I don't know, Xavier. This time feels different. This is exactly why you must stay with us. I need you by my side. The VHA has eliminated most of the other clans, and I fear we'll be next if we don't resolve this soon." I know he means getting rid of Little Deadly and reclaiming control of our territory, and I'll do what I've always done for my Society and take out the threat.

My insides grind at the thought of never leaving. I know Alex needs me, but I can't. Clan life is not for me. I've lived in the compound for a while, but the hive mentality was unbearable. "Alex, my friend, you know I will always come when you call and be by your side, but I can't stay here. The coven life was never for me, and you know how I get with crowded spaces."

Alex looks resolved. He knows I don't do well in covens, so he never pushes me to join one. I understand why he's asking me this, but it doesn't sit well with me. I sigh. Maybe I should've killed Dominica that first time we faced off in the warehouse. The stupid girl is proving to be one hell of a nuisance, and I curse myself for keeping her alive.

My inner war still rages on. I don't even understand why this is happening, though. I've never once hesitated to kill a hunter in my entire existence. In fact, it's one of the things I am known for. Killing vampire hunters is sort of my specialty.

I decided that if they wanted to disrupt all our lives and hunt us for sport, I would make it my mission to hunt them out of existence. I'm the sole reason a specific, well-known family of hunters only exists in history books. After a while, it became tedious, and so I only went after the most renowned, resourceful, and powerful ones like Dominica.

It's been quite some time since I came across a female vampire hunter as strong as her. I think that's why I haven't killed her yet. I'm afraid it will take ages for another like her to come around and challenge me the way she does. Besides, it's too much fun to toy with her, making her life more difficult than snuffing it out.

You don't live as long as I have and manage to not get bored with your surroundings. You search for something that will just make you feel alive, wanted, and challenged. Nothing seems like a threat anymore, which becomes a problem for an old vampire like me. Feeling like nothing can touch you or come after you, and success makes you cocky and full of shit, and that's usually when your ass gets handed to you on a silver platter.

Well, maybe I should just get on with it, especially now that they are bombing the compounds of so many of my kind. The look on Alex's face drives that nail home, and I can *feel* his worry for his sister.

"Don't worry, okay? I will stay until this is sorted out and our kind and your sister are safe again," I tell him, trying to keep the snarl from my voice.

"Thank you, Xavier. It means the world to me, my friend. Now if I can just know my sister is alive and well, I can relax, and we can strategize about a way to take out that bitch of a Reaper and her whole Association."

CHAPTER FIVE

DOMINICA

"Dom, I would greatly appreciate your attention to this meeting," Brian all but growls at me.

I raise my brow and lean back in my chair as he berates me for my performance last night and the fact that two vampires escaped me.

We are all seated around a conference table at the Vampire Hunters Association's head office's main room, making the humiliation worse because he doesn't hold back.

After I got home last night, I took a long soak in a hot bath and was getting ready for bed when I got a rather rude text from the boss man over here to be at this particular meeting.

I usually skip these as they are tedious and a waste of time, but hey, I must come when summoned, so here I am listening to the shit he's spewing.

On the other hand, my attention isn't on the current topic, which clearly does not sit well with our first in command. Before Brian thought it reasonable to elaborate on my mistakes, as he likes to call them, they spoke about another building that was blown up where they thought more vampires were hiding.

Look, I am all for killing these assholes, but bombing an entire building is reckless. There could be civilians, and the fact that they think of them as collateral damage does not sit well with me.

I do not agree with some aspects of the VHA, but I tolerate them because I want to do this world a favor by eliminating the vermin and protecting the innocent. Of course, keeping my mouth shut is an entirely different topic.

“Listen, I still took out twice as many vampires last night as any of the others, and you still feel the need to tell me that I didn’t do well. Is this really about my performance out in the field, or is it that I walked in on you and the daily slut?”

Brian, who is busy looking through the next few topics and waiting for me to explain myself, obviously did not expect my answer. He looks up from his papers, and the look in his eyes can only be described as murderous. It would send a lesser hunter running for the hills.

Everyone knows Brian and his sex drive, so why he feels the need to glare at me now is beyond me. Did he think I was going to keep my mouth shut after what he did to me? Well, I guess he forgot that I am the vindictive type.

“Dominica, you are pushing your boundaries a little too far this morning, and I am not going to stand for that,” he says every word painstakingly slow, his nostrils flaring.

I roll my eyes and cross my arms in front of my chest. “You are the one to talk.”

“Dom, drop it,” Brian warns.

Austen turns to me with a frown, and I just shrug. Fine, whatever, this is useless anyway. I don’t have the strength to deal with this now or ever.

“What is the next mission?” I ask Brian as if nothing had just happened. He stares at me for a few more seconds and looks at everyone sitting at the table before he clears his throat and moves on to the next mission.

I feel every person in the room's eyes burning through me. The disapproving glares from the older hunters cause me a little more discomfort than I'm willing to show. This isn't the first time they've stared at me; it certainly will not be the last.

"What the hell was that?" Austen whispers to me when Brian talks to Silvia about what he expects of them tonight.

"Nothing ... aren't you supposed to listen to what he tells Silvia? That is expected of you, too. You know that, right?"

Austen gives me that *I don't care* grin and shrugs. "You know I don't listen in these meetings, and I do as I please out there. It's a live-or-die situation, and nothing these suits say counts out there."

"True, but you need to take responsibility for what you do out there."

"Yeah, yeah, Miss Smarty Pants. Now, don't think for one second that I'm distracted from the little situation between you and Brian. You will have to tell me sooner or later, and I would prefer it be sooner because you know I hate being in the dark."

I snort, which gets me a glare from Brian and scowls from the older hunters at the table. I just raise my brow and stare each one of them down. I really don't give a rat's ass if they approve of me. I've shown my worth a hundred times over so all of them can kiss my ass.

Austen softly clears his throat and wiggles his eyebrows at me, and I suppress the urge to smack him upside the head. "I'll tell you later. Now leave me alone."

He smiles broadly and turns to Silvia to learn what their assignment is. Stupid idiot always has a knack for making me smile, especially when I don't want to.

"Dom," Brian says, pulling my attention back to him. "Surveillance tonight." I sit upright quickly, throwing my hands in the air. "You are kidding, right?"

"No," he says, not even looking at me.

"This is bullshit, Brian, and you know that."

Brian looks up from his agenda again, this time looking pleased with himself. Realization hits. The bastard is trying to get back at me for undermining him in front of his peers. His professionalism sucks, and he acts like a child seventy-five percent of the time.

I know *my* professionalism is something to be desired right now, but I'm so over this.

He smiles triumphantly. "Now, we both know you are one of the best in surveillance, Dom, and we need you at the docks tonight."

"Flattery is getting you jack-shit, and you *know* I'm your best hunter. You are deliberately taking me out of the field because I wasn't keen on your threesome idea with Jessica," I spit as I rise from my chair.

"Dom, I'm warning you—"

"Or what, Brian? Are you going to fire me?"

"No, but I can suspend you or keep you on desk duty if you don't stop with this shit right now."

I slam my palms on the table just before pushing my chair back, causing it to topple over. Then I storm out of the office before I say or do something I will regret.

The day goes by too slowly, and eventually, I find myself at the docks setting up cameras and audio equipment. I hate doing surveillance. It's boring as hell, and what am I supposed to do with myself the entire night?

I'm vibrating for a fight or just something to let off some steam, but now I have to sit here and be a *good little hunter.* Ugh, sometimes I want to kick my ass for not keeping my mouth shut. These last couple of days aren't something I want to do over.

I walk to my station, a small room in an abandoned part of one of the office buildings overlooking the docks. All the monitors come together, and I take my seat in front of them.

I sigh, thinking of my situation again and that everything feels beyond my control. There isn't much I can do about that now. I turn on the screen in front of me.

I take my phone out of my pocket and review the assignment details again. The mission is as follows: I am supposed to get intel on where the rest of the covens in this shitty city are after the bombing of that other warehouse. Getting audio is preferred, but video with audio … ooh, now *that* will be epic. Usually, getting those two things in missions like these is rare since the vampires pick up on the humming of the cameras. But I've managed to once or twice.

Brian's been raging about this reliable source who feeds him information but can't give him all the details as they would be compromised if they do. I don't know how I feel about that faceless source. I'm *not* impressed that I have to sit here on the whim of a ghost. It's very suspicious if you ask me, but I was shot down the one time I brought up my concern. How I've kept my mouth shut about that is beyond me.

He only mentioned the docks and said that some of the leaders of the remaining covens are meeting here tonight. This source is starting to piss me off. His info always lacks vital parts. I tend to be the one who gets the assignments created by this person's intel, and it's starting to get on my last nerve. It's like Brian deliberately sends me on wild goose chases or missions that flop. I shake my head, pushing the thought out of it. *Don't get paranoid, Dom.*

I finish setting up the system and pull my massive coffee jug from my bag. At least I have enough coffee to get me through this horrible, time-consuming night.

Switching on another set of monitors, I connect the different feeds and pour myself a cup.

I sit back in my chair with the steaming brew and look at each screen, ensuring the feed is clear, catching all the angles I need to see, and taking a sip. A satisfied hum leaves my lips.

"Well, well, aren't we cozy?"

I jump, pulling my dagger from its sheath at my thigh, spilling coffee down my hoodie as I spin at the sound of the voice.

"Dammit, Austen," I yell when I recognize my friend and feel the coffee burning my skin as it soaks through the material.

Austen bursts out laughing, wheezing when he sees my face. I grab some tissues and start wiping at the spot on my top, mumbling under my breath about shoving the thermos up his ass. His joke doesn't impress me, and now I am covered in coffee.

"I am *so* happy you can find humor in my discomfort." Irritation laces my voice as I try to wipe the hot liquid from my top again.

"Not your discomfort, Dom, but the look on your face—it's priceless." He laughs and slaps me on the shoulder.

I shoot him a glare. "What the hell are you doing here, anyway?" The snarl in my voice is unmistakable as I throw the tissue in the bin, seeing that the coffee stain has only spread.

"I wanted to come and tell you the news. I thought it best you hear it from me personally," Austen says sheepishly, rubbing the back of his neck.

I cock my head, frowning as I pull the hoodie off. My gaze falls on Austen's, which is on my chest, and the tight-fitting tank top clinging to my curves, and he swallows before clearing his throat.

I shake my head and roll my eyes. It's not the first time I've caught him staring at my boobs. That's not what irritates me. It's the fact that he has seen me wear this top a thousand times, and his eyes snag every time. It makes me feel dirty, which grinds my gears more than anything else. "Hello, eyes are up here," I scoff.

Austen coughs and smiles slowly as he drags his eyes to mine. "Uh, so Brian called me into his office after the meeting and—"

"Hopefully, he was fully clothed," I mutter.

Austen frowns before cocking his brow. "You care to elaborate?"

"No, not really."

"Are you sure? You're hanging on to something making you act all *girly-like*, and it freaks me out." He makes a move with his hands that looks a lot like jazz hands at the word "girly-like," and I have to keep from smacking him.

"You're being stupid. What is it you wanted to tell me?"

"Okay, here goes. So, Brian calls me to his office, and he—" Austen's sentence gets cut off again, but this time by a loud explosion coming from the docks behind one of the containers out of my camera perimeter. I spin and look out of the office window to where the cloud of smoke billows into the air. Six figures run from the site where the bomb exploded.

"Shit!" Austen and I yell simultaneously, running from my vantage point. "What the hell was that?" Austen yells over the roaring of the flames and falling debris as we near the site.

"Looks like vampire activity if you ask me!"

"How did they know you were here?"

"The hell if I know, but I smell a damn rat," I snarl as we come to a stop a few feet from the inferno spreading among the dried pieces of driftwood and empty containers.

"You don't think we got rotten intel?" Austen says with his hand in front of his face to protect his eyes from the heat of the flames.

"That's exactly what I think. Someone is lying—"

My sentence gets cut short when Austen shoves me so hard I almost fall on my ass. I have a sound mind to hand him his ass when Austen jumps out of the way just in time as a car comes barreling through the burning pile of stacked pallets and the spot I stood mere seconds ago.

"Austen!" I jump up, running to where he gets up quickly. "Shit, are you okay?"

"Yeah, you?"

The car, which nearly flattened us, skids to a stop and turns around to face us again.

"Yeah, I'm fine." I take an attack stance and wait for the car to come at us once more.

Austen looks from me to the car and then back again, bewilderment on his face. "Dom, you're insane. Are you seriously considering jumping a speeding car?"

I look at Austen quickly, frowning and shaking my head at him before returning my focus to the vehicle. I can't believe he just asked me such a stupid question. "The assholes in that car just tried to run us over, and you expect me to what, turn around and run away? You bloody well know me better than that."

At that moment, the car's engine revs to life. I pull my ring daggers from the sheaths strapped to my thighs and time the exact moment I am going to jump so I can land on the car. The black-tinted windows make it extremely hard to see inside. It can only be vampires, as no human can see through that dark tint.

When it spins around, I spot a sunroof on the black sedan. It will be a perfect entry point. The car speeds toward us again, and just before it hits us, I jump into the air and land on the sedan's hood. I grab to get a hold on the hood and scramble to get my footing. The moment I do, I make my way to the roof, but the car swerves, and my foot slips.

"Shit!" I hold on for dear life as my right foot dangles from the car. The car swerves again, this time to the other side, and my body is thrown to the left. The good thing is both my legs are on the vehicle now, and I quickly find my footing again.

The car swerves violently again, and I stab my dagger into the sunroof, causing it to shatter on impact. Grabbing onto the opening, I pull myself up just as a vampire pushes through the opening. The next thing I know, the car stops abruptly, and I'm thrown off the roof. I roll to a stop, stumbling to my feet quickly.

The car doors swing open, and six vampires exit. Their faces are full of menace, and the driver smiles viciously.

I look around for my backup, who has somehow now disappeared. *What the hell, Austen?* I don't have time to think about where my friend can be as they evanesce and reappear, surrounding me.

I take a deep breath to calm my nerves. The driver standing before me now is much taller and more muscular than the others. I cringe inwardly.

This one isn't going to go down quickly. It's not my first time fighting a big guy, so I just have to make some extra-calculated moves and ensure my surroundings are clear when I take him down.

Where the hell are you, Austen? I am officially worried. The vampires close in. I notice every movement from the corner of my eye but don't react to it.

This particular situation feels so familiar. It reminds me of the time Xavier had me surrounded when I tracked them down to a casino in the Nevada desert. The week before, there was an attempt on Brian's life.

"Hiding, are we?" Xavier calls a few feet from where we took cover. I'm catching my breath behind a large boulder—clearly not *large enough for him to see me. We've been fighting for over three hours, and now the remaining hunters and I are surrounded.*

"Don't be so full of yourself, X. I'm just catching my breath. I'll be right there to hand your ass to you," I grit out, pressing down on the wound in my side. My voice drips with sarcasm as I finish tying a piece of torn shirt around my bleeding arm. "I thought the undead are supposed to be so patient, but it looks like that quality skipped you."

"Oh, you are asking for it. You know what? Take your time. Killing you will solidify my status in the vampire world and *yours, so please, take all the time you need, Little Deadly," he chuckles darkly.*

I clench my jaw, balling my fists. Does this bloodsucker really think he's going to be able to take me out? Ha, think again, asshole. *I dare a peek around the boulder I deem my hideout—a relatively poor one. My eyes widen. The number of vampires collected around Xavier is too many for us. It will be nothing less than a slaughter. "Shit," I mutter.*

Closing my eyes, I fight the defeat in my body as my mind races to think of a plan. I look to where Maya is tending to two other hunters who are severely wounded and then to Steff as he vigorously explains a contingency plan to get us out of this situation. We won't be able to get away without some sort of distraction. "Dammit." I roll my eyes, knowing that the only distraction worth mentioning—is me.

I can't think of anything besides getting my injured team out of here.

"Steff," I call under my breath.

Steff looks at me, and I beckon him to move to me. He will not like my idea, but he just needs to get over it and do it.

"What's the matter, Dom?"

"Listen, we need to create a distraction. It's the only way we can get a fighting chance. I am going to draw the vampires away from you, and you get the rest of the team to safety—"

"No! Are you insane? You're going to get yourself killed, and I can't have that on my conscience," he interrupts me.

I close my eyes in frustration and pinch the bridge of my nose to keep from snapping at him.

"Steff, please, we don't have time to argue. They will not hold back any longer, so just do what you are supposed to—"

"Tick, tock, Little Deadly," Xavier calls mockingly.

I grit my teeth and press my lips into a thin line. That damn name! *The bastard is listening in on my conversation, and like a true sadist, he plays on the hope that lingers just to snuff it out.*

"Move, Steff," I hiss before moving out from behind the boulder.

Looking back quickly, I make sure Steff isn't standing there like an idiot, and I huff a sigh of relief when I see them move away from my position.

I turn my attention back to Xavier when I hear him snicker and glare at him. This idiot likes to bring out the worst in me. "Here I am, asshole. Come and get me," I drag out and open my arms wide, taking a bow, my eyes never leaving his.

"Ha, so eager to die today, I see."

"Let's see if you can actually touch me today because, let's be honest, you are totally lacking … " I trail off, gesturing my hand up and down his body with a disapproving look.

Xavier growls, baring his fangs, and the rest of the vampires do the same.

"Touchy, aren't we?" I laugh dryly.

Xavier tilts his head like something possessed, and that creepy feral smile forms on his face. Without warning, he evanesces out of sight and appears right before me. I startle. Cursing loudly, I punch him quickly … Twice. Once in the gut, making him hunch over and bringing him to my level, and then in the jaw, sending his head flying sideways. I back away quickly, leaving enough space between us.

He growls, moving quickly, and grabs me by the throat, lifting me into the air without effort.

He laughs aloud as I struggle to draw air into my lungs and claw at his wrist. The not-quite-human sound chills me to the bone. "Any last words, Little Deadly?"

The fight has taken more out of me than I care to admit, but that bloody nickname makes my blood boil. I swear that name will bring me back from the brink of death. That's how much I despise him calling me that.

I huff out a weak-ass growl, making Xavier laugh again, this time throwing his head back as he does—golden opportunity if you ask me. Taking my chance, I bring my legs up and kick him as hard as I can in the chest, which sends me flying backward but, better yet, gets his death grip off my throat.

"Are we bothering you, hunter?" I'm pulled from my memory. Shit, what the hell is going on with me that I am so distracted lately?

"Nah, just bored out of my mind." I try my best to sound bored. He growls at my mockery and nods his head toward me. The vampires surrounding me step closer at his command, baring their fangs. "Come on, guys, I don't have all night," I say impatiently.

I swing my daggers around my fingers. The moment my daggers sing, the vampires' faces pull in disgust. I smirk, catching the daggers in the palms of my hands, blades pointing down. I grip them tightly and stab backward, hitting flesh as the first vampire attacks. He's not as quiet as he thinks he is, sneaky bastard and a damn coward if you ask me.

The vampires to my left and right charge while my daggers dig into the first vampire's chest. I yank them out, and he screams in agony.

I turn to the left quickly and throw one of the blades toward the vampire, watching the blade sink deep into his abdomen. Then my fist collides into the right side of the vampire's jaw, making him stumble backward.

Ripping my stake from my boot, I stab the vampire on my right in his heart and see him turn into dust. I linger too long on my last kill, and when I turn—too slowly—toward my next attacker, radiating pain pulses through my head. I have just enough time to see a massive fist swing for my head when the big-ass driver connects with my cheek, hitting his target.

The punch disorients me, and the next one he lands sends me flying backward with the force of it. I hit the ground with a sickening thud, and my ears ring from the impact. My remaining blade still clutched tightly.

I shake my head, trying to get my bearings back in order, just as the big guy grabs me by my flimsy tank top and lifts me effortlessly into the air, ripping it and exposing some of my lacy sports bra underneath.

When I open my eyes, I look directly into his, and the evil radiating from them is unmeasurable. He sucks in a breath, and his eyes roam over me, making me feel violated.

I spit in his face, and he hisses and bares his fangs. Anger flashes behind those dead eyes. *Dammit, my head still feels like mush, but I need to focus, or I am going to be dinner tonight.*

Think, Dom, think. I sink my teeth into the big guy's hand, and he bellows. *These assholes aren't the only ones who can bite.*

He yanks me closer, and when he does, I sink my blade into his throat, causing blood to spray in my face and down my exposed chest. His bellow cuts off, and the anger in his eyes is replaced by surprise and uncertainty.

It's now or never. I grab hold of his wrists, which are still clutching my tattered top, plant my feet on his chest, and push back with all my strength. I pull myself from his hold, ripping the tank top entirely from my body. I fall backward, my now-bare back hits the ground unnecessarily hard, and I cry out in pain. At that moment, I grip my stake with both hands and hold it, sharp point up, against my chest, bracing for impact. I'm sure of two things at this very moment: my body is going to hate me for the abuse it's taking, and this guy is going to be dust in three, two, one …

The big guy hits me like a wrecking ball to a building, and like in some dramatic play, he inhales deeply before he poofs into dust around me. My heart pounds in my chest, and my vision threatens to "exit the building" as black spots appear in the corners of my eyes.

The dust particles settle around me, and I cough as I inhale the stupid asshole. I get up a little disoriented, shaking my head. There is a throbbing pain in my head from the hit I took, but I will deal with that later, not to mention the burning coming from my scraped-up back.

There are still two more vampires to deal with, and on cue, they curse, seeing what's left of their friends.

"Come on then." My voice sounds slurred. The hit must've been harder than I initially thought. My focus is shot as the throbbing becomes more prominent.

"Looks like the big guy made our job a little easier." The cowardly vampire laughs. "Yeah, I agree," the second one concurs before addressing me. "Not looking so good there, Reaper. I guess the stories doing the rounds in our circles are greatly exaggerated."

"I disagree with you on one thing, though." Sir Coward laughs as his eyes roam my semi-naked figure. "She *does* look good, and it makes my mouth water." The two vampires look at each other and smile darkly, licking their tongues over their fangs and dragging them over their lips.

I take a deep breath, squeezing my eyes shut for a quick second. Their incessant, irritating voices aren't helping this headache at all, and the stiffness in my back only adds to the drained feeling. "Are you done?" I ask, pressing my fingers into my temples.

They look at each other again and then snort before stepping to me. Ugh, can we just get this over with? I need a damn Advil and maybe a shot of tequila, but that's debatable. But before any of that, I need to find my friend. If he's not hurt, I am *so* going to kick his ass.

I hold up a finger, and they stop, frowning. I turn to the dust pile, bend down, grab my stake from the ground, and kick through the dust until I hear metal clanging.

I pick up my dagger from the ground before glancing at the bloodsucker who attacked me from behind. He has my other dagger in his hand. I see red. I don't like it when anyone touches my weapons, let alone a vampire. I will not tolerate the enemy attempting to cut me with my own blade.

"If you give me back what belongs to me, I might consider letting you go. What happens after tonight is not guaranteed, though," I drag on, trying to add more boredom to my voice.

Not that I'm *not* bored, but my head is starting to give me trouble, and my vision is becoming blurry. I think I have a concussion, but now is not the time to analyze my injuries. I need to focus on the asshole in front of me.

"You truly are full of yourself, Reaper, aren't you?"

I shrug, regretting the motion immediately. "What I am is over this fight. Either you give me my dagger, or I take it from you, and believe me, the latter will be really bad for you."

He looks tauntingly at me, lifts the dagger into the air, and points the blade in my direction, smirking.

Sir Coward opens his mouth to mock me again, but before the words leave his mouth, I flick my wrist, and the dagger in *my* hand flies through the cool night air and pierces his throat.

His eyes almost bulge from their sockets. His friend looks from him to me with a mixture of horror and anger.

"You're next, right?" I stroll closer to them, rolling my neck on my shoulders—the second vampire still rooted in his spot. The one with the dagger in his throat falls to his knees, grabbing it. Just as I approach him, he pulls it out, tossing both at my feet.

He looks up at me expectantly, and I tilt my head, frowning, before looking at his friend as I stop before them.

"There are your damn blades; now let us go as you said," the second vampire says cautiously.

I huff a laugh and pick up my daggers from the ground, wiping them somewhat clean on my pant leg before placing them back in the sheath on my thigh.

"Okay, so I need some information before we do anything else."

"What information? We don't know anything," vampire number two says, and his friend nods tightly.

I roll my eyes. "Come on, dude? Do you expect me to believe you just happened to run into me tonight? That you just *happened* to carry explosives with you and then just *happened* to see me and my friend and then thought it would be cool to run me over?" I sigh, their inferior poker faces are giving them away. They don't speak. Their jaws set. "Really? Nothing?"

"Listen, lady, I don't know what you want me to say."

"I need to know who sent you, and since you are the only one able to say anything now, seeing that your friend here doesn't have vocal cords for another few hours, I expect answers." The annoyance I'm trying to keep at bay is poking out its ugly head.

His eyes dart between me and the car behind me. He wrings his hands, and the image almost makes me want to laugh. I have never seen a nervous vampire before.

He looks frantically from his friend to me and takes one step back. I clear my throat and reach for my daggers, which makes him stop in his tracks.

"I'm not asking you again. You are getting on my last nerve," I say, tapping my fingers on the dagger's handle.

"Okay, fine, we got an anonymous tip that hunters were setting up shop in one of our regions." His voice trembles with every word.

"And?"

"And nothing, we were given an order to take out the hunters."

"Don't act stupid, asshole, who gave you the tip?" I say, narrowing my eyes. "I don't know, I told you—"

"You told me nothing," I cut him off. "Everything you just said is vague as hell, and you want me to believe that is all you know." My voice rises slightly as my anger builds again. I'm not getting any information from the bottom-feeders of this chain of command, so I might as well stop asking.

"I swear, Reaper, I don't know anything else."

Twirling the stake in my hand, I look down at it and then lift my gaze slightly before I drive the stake into vampire number two's heart.

The vampire with the hole in his throat gurgles in surprise and falls back on his ass and tries to scurry away from me as his friend turns into dust. "Aww, where is that mocking smile now?" The vampire snarls pathetically, and I raise my brow as I cross my arms in front of my chest.

"So, since you're as useless as your friend over there," I point to where his friend just stood, "I think it's time to put you out of your misery."

The pathetic asshole shakes his head, his eyes as big as saucers. He coughs and tries to speak, but only blood spills from his mouth. His body is struggling to heal since the silver in the blade stints their healing.

I frown at the fear in his eyes. "What's with the fear? I mean, I thought you guys no longer have these emotions?"

He looks around frantically, his eyes falling on something behind me. I look behind me, but he grunts and turns into dust before I have time to register.

I whirl around, pulling my dagger from its place on my thigh. My eyes dart from one shadowy spot to another until a person appears from behind a container. I squint my eyes and make out the frame of Austen, and when light hits his face, a smile dances across it. Maybe I'm imagining things, but Austen's smile looks wicked and unsettling. As soon as he steps into the light of the overhead spotlights, there is no trace of the former smile.

I frown. Are the lights playing tricks on my eyes, or maybe I'm just seeing shit. Austen's gaze falls on me, and it sends a chill down my spine, but it's gone so quickly that I once again feel like I am imagining things. I shake my head lightly and start walking to my car.

My head is killing me, and my back is protesting with every move I make. I'm going to throw up if I don't sit down for a few minutes.

"Shit, Dom, are you okay?" Austen asks frantically when he reaches me, his eyes snagging on my shirtless body.

"Where the hell were you?" My voice sounds a lot more accusing than I intend it to be. I stop and turn to him when he doesn't answer me. Does he really need to think about his answer?

"I had some trouble of my own back there."

I inhale deeply and close my eyes to keep from vomiting before crossing my arms over my chest. *It's a lame-ass excuse.* "What trouble exactly?"

"Well, the vampires you fought weren't the only ones. The moment you jumped the car, the others came from somewhere over there." He looks behind him for too long and then points to some random place.

I narrow my eyes and open my mouth to tell him to stop bullshitting, but the throbbing in my head is now screwing with my thought process, and my vision becomes spotty.

I squeeze my eyes shut and drop my head in my hand, pressing on my temples. "You know what? We can continue this conversation later. I need to get a damn Advil and lie down for a few hours—"

"Dom, look at me," Austen interrupts, stepping closer and touching my face. The worry in his voice is so at odds with the look I swear I saw just after he stepped out from behind the container.

"Dammit, Austen, what the hell are you doing? I'm tired, and my head is killing me. I need to get home before I pass out behind my steering wheel." I can't help but feel annoyance toward him.

"There is absolutely *no* way you are driving anywhere. You have a concussion, and your back isn't looking so great," he says as he grips my shoulders and turns me, so my back is to him before turning me to face him again. The action is too fast for my concussed brain to handle, and I heave before hurling the contents from my stomach on the ground. Austen jumps back and curses loudly. "Shit! I have to get you to a hospital."

I drag the back of my hand over my mouth, wiping away the bile. Throwing up only made the throbbing worse. "I don't want to go to a hospital; you know I despise them, and the food sucks."

"Dominica Salvatore, we are *not* going to argue about this. Get in my damn car and let me get you checked out."

I sigh heavily. I hate hospitals; it's like being locked up in a prison, and I don't want all those people around me. "Fine," is all I manage to get out as the blinding headache worsens.

"That was easy." Austen frowns but walks to his car with me following suit. "I really thought I was going to have to throw you over my shoulder and force you there."

"Austen, please. Not now."

Austen laughs and opens the car door for me. I scowl at him but don't protest as I get in. I'll deal with his lack of presence later. All I need now is my bed and something to get rid of the throbbing that feels like someone keeps banging on my head and back.

The hospital visit was as expected. I have one hell of a concussion, and my back is scraped and cut up badly, but it will heal fine. *I just have to keep still. Pfft, I doubt I will manage that very well.* The doctor wanted to admit me, but being true to myself, I gave him and the staff, including Austen, enough grief that the doctor agreed to let me go home under supervision.

I was happy to agree, but we both knew that I, and no one else, would fill the supervision part. I don't want anyone in my apartment to look after me, and I don't need anyone to fuss over me.

Austen, on the other hand, doesn't agree with me or the doctor who sent me home—hence my current situation.

Austen is driving me home from the emergency room and losing his shit. He hasn't stopped spouting bullshit about how I'm not supposed to be alone and the fact that someone needs to be there to make sure that I do not fall asleep.

"Can you please just stop screaming? I don't need a damn babysitter, Austen. Dammit, you are supposed to know me best. When have I ever needed someone to look after me?"

Austen's face turns red from anger, and it might as well be heading toward purple from lack of oxygen at my last statement. "First of all, I am not screaming. Second, I am getting really tired of your so-called independence." Austen grits through his tightened jaw, his knuckles turning white from gripping the steering wheel too hard. "When will you accept that it is okay to depend on someone other than yourself?"

Leaning my head back on the headrest, I close my eyes as he rants. The shirt they gave me is scratchy. Austen won't shut up; I am astounded that he can rant for so long without stopping to pull air into his lungs for longer than a second. It isn't helping my head much, and the uneven road has no mercy on my back against the car seat. Each bump feels like someone is dragging a cheese grater down my back.

I am so tired, and keeping my eyes open is challenging. I don't have the energy to argue with him.

Austen has known me for the better part of my life, and we always seem to have this "discussion" when I get injured. I mean, really? Does he forget what we do for a living? We are bound to get injured. It's a given.

"Dom!" Austen shakes me and screams my name, startling me awake. *What the hell?*

"I thought you weren't screaming?" I croak, my voice sounding groggy.

"You aren't supposed to fall asleep for the next four hours, and you want me to believe and trust that you will look after yourself without help?"

"I'm fine. Stop babying me, man. It's just a quick nap," I tell him, trying to sound unbothered. But let's be honest: if I cannot stay awake while he is going off like this, what will happen when everything is nice and quiet?

"Dammit, Dom!" Austen's voice rises again.

"Austen, if I agree that you can look after me for four hours, will you please stop screaming? My damn head is going to explode with the overload of your incessant nagging." I pinch the bridge of my nose, squeezing my eyes shut. This is really getting the better of me, and I will do anything to get him to shut up.

Austen huffs his reply but stays quiet. The car is silent for the first time since we left the hospital, and it's music to my ears. I know he won't agree with the four-hour thing, but I don't really care. I will deal with that problem when I get to it.

Luckily, we arrive at my apartment shortly after, and before long, I'm sitting on my couch with a warm cup of tea.

Austen isn't taking any chances with me falling asleep, as he keeps on trying to feed me various kinds of fruits and continuously tries to offer me something to drink, although he just gave me the damn tea.

"Dude, please just calm down and sit still for a few minutes," I huff. "You are driving me insane."

"I'll sit and enjoy a cup of coffee if you promise not to fall asleep."

"I promise. Now please just sit your ass down," I say, rolling my eyes. *It's going to be the longest night of my life.*

CHAPTER SIX

XAVIER

When we get to the docks, I can hardly contain my anger. Alex asked me and some of his most trusted guards to come and see what was taking so long with the team he sent out nearly five hours ago. It's quiet, except for the massive inferno in front of us. There are signs of a fight, but I can sense it's been over for a while now. I get out of the car and stroll toward the black sedan with the rest of the guard on my heel. I round the vehicle's rear, and I'm stopped in my tracks.

The six piles of ash just beyond the unmarked car are enough to make any vampire's blood boil. *What the hell went wrong here?*

The wind shifts, and a hint of a familiar scent wafts through the air as I make my way from one ash pile to another. I can't control the growl climbing up my throat. I crouch and run my hand through one of the piles of ash.

"What the hell happened here?" Hector, the head of the unit I'm with, asks from behind me. "Who could take out Steven? He was the strongest warrior I know, apart from our king and you."

Silence falls, and I have to gather every ounce of my self-control not to react. "Dominica." Her name falls from my mouth like rotten blood. That woman is cruisin' for a bruisin'. Alex won't be happy with what happened here tonight.

Looking around for clues, I spot a camera on one of the overhead cranes and another on one of the nearest office buildings.

I rise from the ground and walk to the one on the office building. I rip it off and examine it closely. These aren't ours. They look too familiar to deny that the VHA isn't behind this.

"Wait here," I tell the guards, following the familiar scent leading me to Little Deadly's surveillance equipment. *This is odd. Why would she leave everything here?*

An unnerving feeling settles in my stomach that doesn't make sense. *Worry. It can't be.* Am I really worried about that vixen?

No! I hope she got what came to her. As Alex said, she's been a thorn in our sides since the day she became a hunter, and the sooner she's taken out, the sooner we can rebuild our Society.

I sit behind the monitors and access the recorded footage. Within minutes, I'm watching Dominica and her stupid friend. *What's his name? Aubrey? No, Ashton? Whatever.* They are running to where our guys must've planted the explosives, which just went off.

She jumps the car and is surrounded by Steven and the other vampires. Steven is one of our elite vampires and has seen a lot of action throughout his life, especially when he was turned about four hundred years ago. Alex only sends him when a situation is beyond the guard's control.

A fist clenches my heart as Little Deadly faces off with Steven. Again, I'm not sure if the worry is for her. The fight between her and Steven at first looks like he caused quite an amount of damage when his fist connected with her cheek. The unsettling feeling grows in my gut when he rips her top and exposes her breasts. I swallow visibly when I spot the lace bra, and my blood boils when he drags his eyes over her semi-naked body. But before the anger can settle, the fight on screen quickly becomes worse.

A snarl escapes my lips the moment Dominica drives her stake through his heart, and I slam my fist on the desk.

Steven wasn't a tiny vampire, and the power behind that guy wouldn't soon be replaced. How could she take out someone as seasoned as that man? I mean, it didn't take her long to snuff out his life.

I rest my elbows on the table and briefly cover my face with my hands. I cannot understand how she can outwit even the most experienced vampire, but I am watching her do just that. I don't know why it catches me off guard. I drag my hand roughly through my hair, looking at the screen again.

Dominica must have taken a few hits to the head as she stood and stumbled before shaking her head and getting her weapons from the ground. The stiffness in her back is apparent, and her movements are crisp. The wince on her face confirms my thoughts.

My anger gets the better of me, and I sweep my hand across the desk, shattering the monitors and equipment to the floor. The overwhelming feeling of avenging my fallen brethren is something I can't keep contained. Especially not after seeing Alex so distraught when he found out Sofie didn't survive the bombing of the warehouse the other night. I was stunned when he told me. I didn't have the words to express my sorrow for Sofie and my friend.

He assures me Dominica planted the bombs herself, and she is the one who killed anyone who survived the blast.

If I only took that bitch out the day I met her, none of this would have happened. How could I have been so stupid? Have I become so bored with my basic vampire nature that I abandoned everything I was supposed to do?

A growl leaves my throat as I stomp my foot down on one of the remaining screens displaying the last of the fight. I can't watch it anymore.

The feelings that start in my chest soon fester into a hatred I thought impossible, but here I am. I didn't want to be a part of this stupid war anymore, and now I am smack-dab in the middle of it again.

I walk out of the building to the waiting men. The somber look on all their faces makes me want to rip something to shreds. The fallen men were friends, brothers, sons, if you will. I only shake my head when one of them steps forward.

They look from one to the other before each of them bares their fangs in unison, an act of vengeance and respect for the fallen.

There is no stopping what's coming. That bitch hunter has an Empire State Building–sized target on her back, and her life is going to get a lot more difficult now than it ever was. I sincerely hope she is ready for it because I sure as hell am.

I will stand by my reputation and take her out of this world. Playtime is over, and fangs will slice so much deeper now.

I walk to the car as the building I just came out of catches fire, and before long, all evidence of what happened here tonight goes up in flames.

"Are you telling me she killed Steven?" Alex snarls.

"Yes, and the rest of the crew you sent."

Alex curls his hands into fists, trying to keep them from trembling. These last few days weren't the greatest, but we must stay focused.

"What is your plan, my friend? What do you need me to do?" I ask as I walk over to Alex, who stands at the fireplace, gripping the mantel so hard the wood cracks and splinters, and gently place my hand on his shoulder.

"I want her dead, Xavier. Put as many men out there as we need, but I want her dead and gone before the next full moon," Alex demands, slamming his fist into the wall.

"I know. I'm on it. We need to think of a way to lure her out, but we also need to think of a way to end the VHA once and for all."

"You're right, but all I can think about is how Sofie must have suffered at her hands. The only thing I see is red, and all I want is revenge," he says, sighing heavily.

"I feel the same, my friend. Sofie was like a sister to me just as much as she was yours. We will get vengeance, I promise."

"So you are rejoining our war, my friend?" The hope in his voice is hard to miss, and I can't let him go through this alone.

Alex may be the king of all vampires and have the strongest coven in the territory, but he still needs to be kept grounded and needs advice since he tends to blur lines when he's not thinking clearly.

"Yes, I will stay and help you; you have my word," I promise. Alex's eyes widen in surprise.

A vampire's word is sacred. It's not something you give or take lightly. You are bound by it, literally, and when broken, the consequences can be something you'd rather wish to avoid. It sucks the life out of you when that person betrays you by taking advantage of it. Let's just say the only way out is by killing the one you gave your word to.

I've only given it once in my life, and it bit me in the ass. Alex knows this, so the utterly surprised look on his face makes complete sense.

"Xavier … " he trails off before grabbing me and giving me a bear hug. "You have no idea what this means to me."

"Well, you know exactly what it means to me, so do not make me regret giving it to you."

Alex pulls away and nods, his eyes serious and brooding. He steps away and sits behind his desk again. I take my seat across from him and wait for him to speak. The atmosphere is heavy, and the surrounding problems make it much heavier.

"I'll make sure that the staff readies a room for you, and then you can send for your belongings," Alex says as he picks up the phone to call goodness knows who.

I only nod and let him handle this. It may give him back some feeling of control. We need him focused. I can't run this place, and I'm not going to if, for some reason, Alex is out of commission.

Many years ago, I was chosen to be the king of this coven, but I refused. I didn't want to be in charge of their lives, and all that pressure wasn't something I needed at the time. Again, the hive mentality is something I struggle with. They wanted a ruthless leader at the time, but I was consumed with wiping out a certain family of hunters: the Van Helsings. Ugh, thinking of them awakens the burning hatred again. They were a menace, and it became an obsession to kill them out of existence. I couldn't focus on ruling, so I suggested Alex.

Now, almost 160 years later, Alex has done very well in his position, which suits him. Sofie would want me here, and I know she would kick my ass if I left her brother to deal with this alone.

While I wait for Alex to finish on the phone, I get up and stroll around his office, taking it in for the first time since I came here. It has mostly stayed the same, but the paintings of him and Sofie stand out more than they did in the past.

She was truly beautiful. Her deep sapphire eyes and icy-white hair complemented her pale skin perfectly. I've never seen a painting depict the very essence of a person as the one I'm looking at. Sofie's cold stare was exactly as it was in real life. Alex once thought Sofie and I would marry and start our own journey, but we were never more than friends. She might have had some feelings for me, but she never acted on them or told me otherwise.

"It's done, my friend. Your room is ready, and I asked Reggie, my assistant, to go by your place and get the necessities. If there is something specific you want, you can just let him know."

"Thank you, Alex."

"Now, shall we go for a drink? I am starving, and I haven't had anything since before the tragic news of my dear sister," Alex says somberly as he motions to the door before leading the way out of his office.

"That's very generous of you. Do you have any blood bags, or are all your meals straight from the source?"

Alex turns mid-stride and frowns at me before tilting his head in confusion. "You mean to tell me you don't drink from the vein anymore?"

"No, I do … but I prefer not to. The groupies one gathers are rather distasteful, and I prefer to have my food without being groped."

Alex chortles, shakes his head, and begins to walk again. "No need to worry about that here, my friend. I assure you that the food is professional. You can have your fill in peace." I laugh with Alex and nod my thanks to him.

I mentioned earlier that I am known for hunting, but sometimes my alluring features don't work in my favor, or at least they don't always say what I want them to. Being attractive has its downsides.

I'd rather my prey be afraid than willing, which means I can have what I need, and when I'm done, they don't want to ask a thousand questions afterward.

Alex clears his throat, and I'm back to the present—frowning at my train of thought, I step past him into the room.

The "dining room," as it's called—I know, cliché, right?—is delicately decorated with old furniture and trimmings. The old Victorian-style couches are placed strategically around the room. On each couch sits a beautiful human woman or man, whichever one you prefer, dressed provocatively. The women are dressed in tight black corsets with loose black lace skirts, and the men only in black dress pants, their necks wholly exposed. Each wears a black mask with intricate decorative patterns that conceal their faces. They must still be young by the smell of their blood, maybe in their early twenties. The mixture of scents drives my hunger into overdrive, and I swallow hard, my mouth watering.

"Take your pick." Alex motions again. I scan the room, and, at the back, hidden just beyond the light, sits an alluring dark-haired girl waiting. Her head is down, eyes cast to the floor. Her hands are in her lap, and her back is as straight as an arrow.

I meticulously walk to the back of the room and sit down next to her, making her jump a little. I can't help but notice the tremble in her body. "Is this your first time?" I keep my voice low and quiet to not frighten her, but she must be on edge because it makes her jump again. Vampires have the unnatural ability to sit almost statue-like, which only makes us seem more dangerous and unnerving. I need her to understand that even if I am dangerous, I am not barbaric.

I patiently wait for her to relax, even if it's only a little. When her breathing calms, I clear my throat and repeat my question. She stiffens again.

Turning to me with a bow of her head, she says, "How may I be of service tonight?" A low rumble sounds from my throat, and her eyes snap up to meet mine. She still trembles, and I lift my brow questioningly.

"Yes … sir," she hesitates, and I wonder if the staff told her not to speak to us. My suspicion is confirmed when I see one of the guards, who is stationed around the room, step closer menacingly, and a sob slips past her lips before she can catch it.

"Look at me," I tell her calmly. She hesitates, but her gaze falls on mine again after a few minutes, and I smile at her. Okay, maybe I shouldn't have because that usually gives them the sense that you are more than just a feeder, and they would seek you out. But this poor girl will die from fright even before I touch her, and I am not going to leave her to the mercy of some brute who cannot control himself. The moment our eyes meet, I will her to calm down, and she does.

Let's be honest: the magic that comes with the eye lock and the smile helps a lot. It places the prey in a trance if you desire it. "They will not harm you."

She swallows visibly, and her eyes dart from one guard to another. "It's not me I am worried about, sir. Not so much … It's my sister," she whispers.

"What do you mean?"

"My sister is with the master of the house, and they told me if I don't behave, he will kill her."

"Are you talking about Alex?" She nods, looks past me, and her eyes widen. The fear behind them grows as she stares behind me. I turn and find Alex watching us. This is precisely the kind of shit I want to avoid. We have bigger fish to fry.

I sigh, following a snarl, and get up from my seat. I need clarity here. As I make my way to Alex, he smiles at me, but his gaze still has the girl pinned.

"We need to talk." Alex nods toward the chair opposite him. "I thought we got rid of some barbaric old ways, my friend. What's with the godfather threats?" I say when I sit.

Alex chuckles. "Some people need persuading, and there is no better way than threatening their families."

Shaking my head, I roll my eyes and look over my shoulder at the girl. She doesn't look our way, but I can smell the fear radiating from her.

I prefer them to be frightened, but the preference is that they fear me and not something else. It makes the blood taste bitter, and I don't care for it.

"Don't you like our selection tonight?" Alex tries to change the subject, but I raise my brows unimpressed.

"What do you want me to say, Xavier?"

"Our kind is no longer a secret, and there are so many people willing to be food that you have a much wider selection than you did a few centuries ago. Why feel the need to capture those who can cause more harm?"

Alex rests his elbows on the armrests of his chair and brings his fingertips together, narrowing his eyes at me. "Don't be so dramatic, my friend. I know we have a wider pool, but I like the occasional family drama. It brings some life into these old walls, and playing on their fear is something I've always enjoyed. You know that." Alex's bored demeanor makes me want to punch him in the face.

Look, I don't mind the mind games. I also like to play with my food occasionally, but we are supposed to be evolving. It only keeps us in a primeval kind of mindset, and it stops our kind from seeing the bigger picture. It might seem trivial, but it is a small stepping stone, if you ask me.

"You are making it difficult," I tell him before returning to the girl.

Alex's chuckle rings through the room, but I ignore it. Instead, I focus on my meal. I will deal with this when I have time.

"I'm sorry, but I need to feed. Just ensure you keep *your* side clean, and neither you nor your sister will be harmed … much." I bob my shoulder. "He likes playing with his food, so just do as you're told, and maybe you will go home." Moving fast, I push my hand into the back of the girl's hair, and with the other planted on her waist, I push her down on the couch.

The girl sucks in a breath, and her eyes fall on mine once again, the fear now shifting to me and not her surroundings. I inhale her scent deeply. That's much better. I can't have this girl seek me out. I lower my head to her neck, and as soon as she starts to tremble, I sink my teeth into her. Her blood is rich, and the tang of fear laced with it makes my adrenaline soar. I drink deeper, and she grabs onto my arm, digging her nails into the fabric of my leather jacket.

I hum low and deep in my chest as her warmth fills me, and all I can think about is how a certain hunter's blood will taste the day

I kill her. I will drink her dry as a punishment for what she has done to my kind.

I had only tasted her blood once, and it was like nothing I had ever tasted before. It felt like euphoria, and the craving for it afterward was like coming down from a stint on some kind of drug.

It took me years to get that taste from my mouth and out of my system. One of the reasons I prefer blood bags is that the taste of blood straight from the vein has never really tasted the same after I tasted *her* blood. Blood bags aren't any better, but at least there isn't a face going with them, and no one is trying to have a vampire boyfriend like in that movie.

The moment I feel the girl go limp in my arms, I force myself away from her. Her breathing is shallow and quick. She isn't at death's door yet, but her condition will put her out of commission for a while. At least I can save her for a few days, if not anything else.

"Keep your nose clean, and you will be fine." I turn on my heel and stride out of the dining room.

CHAPTER SEVEN

DOMINICA

"Will you please stop buzzing around me?"

"*I am not buzzing.* I'm just making sure you're okay," Austen says, throwing his hands in the air.

It's been two days since the fight at the docks, and Austen doesn't want to leave. He slept in the guest room and was up and making breakfast before I even woke up, which is weird because he never gets up that early.

I, on the other hand, *am* starting to get twitchy. I appreciate what he's doing and that he looks after me, but I'm not used to having someone in my apartment, not this long anyway.

Sure, Austen has been to my place often, but not like this. We watch occasional movies and have poker nights frequently, but this is pushing the boundaries.

"I've told you ten thousand times that I am fine now and that you can go home. I appreciate everything, but come on, man, I have taken many more serious hits than this one."

Austen frowns at me from behind the kitchen counter as he places the bacon onto our plates. "Shut up and sit down. You are making it weird," he tells me, ignoring my statement.

I huff in frustration and take a seat opposite him. He pushes the plate to me and turns to get the two cups of coffee he made before plating the food.

I must admit, he knows how to make one hell of a breakfast, and the coffee isn't half bad. Digging into my food, he takes the chair beside me and brings it to where he prepares the food to sit down. He watches me for a few seconds while I stuff my face, and when I look up at him, there's a weird grin on his face.

"What—" I say with my mouth still stuffed with bacon and pancakes.

"Nothing," he laughs.

I chew the hobble of food and swallow it with some coffee before asking the same question again, and it just gets me the same stupid answer.

I hate it when Austen does that. He clearly wants to say something, but he knows how much it bugs me to pull information out of him, so he does it on purpose.

"I am going to throw something at you if you don't spill it," I warn him, narrowing my eyes.

He shakes his head and takes a big bite of his food. I grab the nearest towel and throw it into his face. He chokes as he swallows, and I only laugh when he scowls at me.

"Damn you, Dom," he laughs. "Can't a man eat in peace?"

"Not if that man deliberately withholds information from me, no," I tell him as I cross my arms.

Austen coughs a few times, and his face turns serious for a moment. "Okay, so I tried telling you this the other day when you were setting up surveillance … "

He trails off as he watches me. I can't recall him telling me anything, but then again, that explosion could distract the most focused person. "Go on."

He clears his throat. "So, after the meeting the other day, Brian called me into his office … Shit, I don't know how to say this."

Irritation builds in my chest, and I snap at him. "Just spit it out, dammit." Austen shifts in his seat. "Don't be mad, okay? I didn't ask for this, but I feel like I do deserve a shot, so please just keep that in mind—"

"For Pete's sake, Austen, just tell me!"

Austen raises his hands and continues, "Brian, put me in charge of the next mission." The words tumble out of his mouth, almost like he wants them out before he stops himself from telling me again.

I expected as much, but I didn't expect it would be so difficult for Austen to tell me. I mean, I know I can get testy if Brian places a moron in charge of dangerous missions, but I am happy for my friend. Obviously, the jealousy monster rears its head, but I force the stupid emotion down and focus on being happy for Austen.

I am so lost in my thoughts that I don't notice Austen watching me in anticipation. He clears his throat. It takes me a few seconds to look at him, and when I do, I see the worry in his eyes. "It's okay, Austen. I am happy for you," I tell him with a smile.

"Are you sure?" he asks hesitantly.

"Yeah, I mean, it's about time. I just don't like the way it's being done, though. I don't want you to resent me later when this game Brian plays backfires."

Austen frowns, and I sigh. I don't want to take this away from him, but I know my friend, and I know he will not take it well if Brian decides midway through the mission that he is tired of punishing me and then shifts gears and takes the mission from Austen.

"What do you mean by that?"

"Never mind, I *am* happy for you. Let's go out and celebrate." I smile again, but I know it will give me away.

I get up from my chair and walk to my room, my appetite nonexistent now.

"Dom, don't change the subject," he calls after me as I leave the kitchen.

"I'm not. I am trying to show you that I am happy about this; hence, I am going to get ready." I turn to him quickly to gesture at my pajamas before turning my back on him again.

The stool scrapes on the floor, and he hurries after me. "Then why would you say something like that if you didn't mean anything by it?" He sounds irritated.

I stop at my bedroom doorway and turn to face him again. "Brian is being an asshole. Not for giving you a mission but for how he treats me. That's what I meant, so can we please move on to another subject?" I counter, feeling exasperated.

Austen narrows his eyes and watches me for a moment before turning and going into the living room.

I sigh dramatically, me and my big mouth. Why can't I just say *wow, that's great,* and that's the end of it. No, my big mouth blabbers everything my brain is trying to figure out.

Groaning, I follow him into the living room and sit next to him on the couch. The disappointment on his face breaks my heart as he sits looking defeated, hands in his lap, head hanging.

"I'm sorry, Austen. I didn't mean to sound so negative. I am genuinely happy that they see you are capable of running this mission, and I will be proud and honored to work with you on this," I say softly and place my hand on his knee.

Austen inhales deeply, looks at my hand, and then at me, his eyes shifting from sadness to something I haven't seen before.

He takes my hand and moves closer to me. My spine tingles from the discomfort now creeping down my back.

"Are you sure it won't bother you that I am in charge? I know you wanted this mission, and I don't want hard feelings between us," he says, his voice low.

I swallow visibly as he looks deep into my eyes and inches closer to me.

I clear my throat, feeling like a huge lump is stuck in it. "I am sure, and you know that I don't mind working with you. You know how to plan and do your work properly … "

I trail off when Austen is mere inches from me. He leans in and kisses me softly. I am so caught off guard that my brain lags for a couple of seconds before it finally registers. My back goes rigid, and I push him away, getting to my feet. I pace the floor like an idiot as Austen sits on the couch with a satisfied smile covering his face now.

There is silence between us for almost ten minutes as I try to compute what the hell just happened. *How did this happen? Where is this coming from? Am I missing something?*

"Are you going to say something?" Austen asks, leaning with his arm on the backrest of the couch. The teasing look in his eyes sparks anger in mine.

"Why did you do that?" I snarl.

"Because I've wanted to do that for a long time, and I thought the moment was right. Dom, I like you, and it's been killing me that you don't see it. I have tried to show you so many times, but now that you know I am worthy of you, I think we can take a chance on us."

My breath is knocked from my lungs as I listen to his confession. How did I not see this coming? I have a knack for picking up these kinds of feelings from the opposite sex, but this one has flown straight over my head. I don't know how to feel or what to say.

Anger. Disbelief. *Anger.* I want to scream at the amount of rage pumping through me. *Yeah, that's the feeling I'm going with.*

I've stopped pacing and only now realize it. Biting my tongue so as not to yell at my friend, I just stare at him. Austen rubs his hands on his pants a few times and gets up from the couch, moving to me. He takes me into his arms and lowers his head to kiss me again.

"Austen, what the actual hell!" I yell, pushing him away more aggressively this time. "Where the hell is this coming from?"

Austen stumbles back and frowns. "I told you I have liked you for quite a while, and I never felt worthy of mentioning it to you, but now that the VHA has acknowledged my success, I feel that I stand a chance to be with you."

"*You feel?* What the hell are you talking about?" I exclaim, feeling extremely annoyed now.

"Yes, can't you see we would make the ultimate power couple? We can take our world by storm, and there will be no one as strong as us. No one will love and care for you like I do," Austen coos and tries to caress my cheek, but I gently push him away again.

"Austen, you know I love you," his smile spreads wider, "as a friend. You will always be my best friend and my go-to person, but I don't see us being together."

I thought he knew this, that he knew me, but with the look on his face, that wasn't the case. I thought our friendship was important to him, but this will ruin it. Look, I'm not blind. Austen is an extremely handsome guy, with his sand-blond hair and honey-colored eyes. He's about five-eight and built like a brick wall, which is very alluring, but I just don't see him like that.

He crosses his arms over his chest. Silence falls once more, and this time, it's deafening. I genuinely hope that he'll see reason and that we can go back to our friendship without this bullshit. But I know I'm kidding myself; nothing will ever be like it was.

"Austen, please talk to me. You know I'm right."

Austen is quiet for a while longer, and when he eventually looks at me, there is an odd expression in his eyes, but before I have a chance to really comprehend it, he closes them and turns away from me.

"I think I'd better go," he almost whispers.

"No, please don't. Let's just discuss this," I plead as he walks to my front door and takes his jacket from the closet.

"There was enough said, don't you think?" he retorts.

I hurt his feelings, and that wasn't my intention. I have just never looked at him in the same way, and the thought of "us" has never crossed my mind.

"No, please. We need to discuss this," I all but beg again, grabbing onto his arm to make him look at me.

Austen rips his arm from my grasp more aggressively than is needed and storms out of my apartment, slamming the door behind him.

A heavy sigh leaves my chest. I know my friendship with Austen is beyond repair and will never be the same again. But I have to try because my concussed brain can't fathom not being able to talk to him the way I used to.

I don't care how awkward it will be initially; I just have to try to fix this.

I sigh again, dragging my hands through my hair, and walk to the bathroom to take a long, hot shower to relieve the tension in my back and shoulders.

I pull off my shirt and turn to see my injured back in the mirror. Some of the scrapes and cuts have bandages on them, and I pull them off to see the full extent of my injuries.

Lucky for me, hunters have the ability to heal, but slower than vampires. We do heal faster than normal humans, though, and the stronger and higher you are in the ranks of the VHA, the more that ability develops. The stronger the magic becomes. Hunters start out as normal humans, but the day you make the oath to the VHA, the magic is bound to your life force. Your abilities enhance and hone you into the perfect weapon to fight the evil that is vampires.

For example, my back looks like I was dragged around about a week ago, not two nights ago, which greatly helps.

Well, I need something to get rid of this ugly day, and I decide to face the shower head on as if it were one of my enemies.

Hissing at the sting of the tape pulling from my skin, my chest sags as I take in the full view of my once not-so-bad back. It looks like I am trying to collect as many scars as possible, although I am not.

I would not trade some of my scars, as they represent my growing ranks in the VHA. The one so prominent on my neck, though, I would trade for almost anything.

Trailing my finger over the jagged marks of where Xavier's fangs ripped from my flesh the night we faced off for the first time, I am taken back to the aftermath of that night.

Sam was not happy with either Austen or me, to say the least. We were scolded beyond redemption, and when Sam saw the extent of my injuries, it looked like the vein that was already popping in his head would explode.

I was rushed to the VHA hospital, and they did extensive tests on me to make sure I wasn't turned, no matter how many times I assured them that I did not consume any of the vampire's blood and that he did not drain me as I am still my charming self. That's the only way a vampire can turn a human. They have to drain you completely, and then you need to feed from them to complete the transition.

All that got me was several snaps of "be quiet" and "not now, Dominica" accompanied by Grand Canyon–sized scowls.

I was under close watch for seventy-two hours and was kept in isolation the entire time. That is really unpleasant, and I would not want to go through that again.

I feel as helpless tonight as I did that night. So stupid and inexperienced. I close my eyes and sigh, hitting the mirror out of frustration. *How could I have let this happen?* I mean, really, all I had to do was pay attention, but that seems to be at a loss these last couple of months.

I hit the mirror again and again until it shatters around my fist. When I open my eyes, eventually, the feeling hasn't subsided, and it makes me scream out until my throat is raw.

Why the hell does it feel like everything is turning into shit? My whole life feels like a very badly plotted movie. Okay, I may be a bit dramatic. It's not my entire life, but the last few months, absolutely.

I discard the rest of my clothing and turn on the shower. This is going to hurt like a bitch, but I need to get rid of these absurd feelings that I have let my friend down, building in my chest that I don't have any control over.

I watch the water fall and let the whole bathroom fill up with steam. I inhale deeply as the hot air fills my lungs. I let out my breath slowly and step into the warm water. Turning, I gnash my teeth as the water hits my back. It's painful but feels good at the same time.

Tomorrow, I will have to go and speak with Brian to make sure that this mission he gave Austen is legitimate and that he needs to assure me that this isn't one of his revenge plots. I won't be able to give Austen my heart the way he wants me to, but I sure as hell can make sure that his pride doesn't get another hit from Brian.

I turn to face the water as the sting in my back dissipates and scrub a hand over my face, feeling much more determined than a few minutes ago. Maybe this way, I can show my friend that I do care for him, even if it isn't the way he likes. Maybe one day he can accept it.

Yes, that's it. I will make sure this mission of his goes down without a hitch, which will solidify his rank in the VHA and hopefully bring back some form of friendship between us.

The calm and tension-reducing shower only lasted about thirty minutes. My phone has been going off nonstop, driving me insane. Brian is blowing up my phone and bombarding me with seven thousand questions in that time frame, and I am going to lose it if he does not back off. Hence, I am dressed and out the door of my apartment all in the span of thirty minutes. I don't make it to the end of the hallway before my phone rings again, and I answer it with a huff. "Dammit, Dom, how come you always need to make it so difficult to get a hold of you?" Brian's irritated voice booms through the speaker, and I need to hold it at least an arm's length from my ear.

"Are you done screaming? My head still hurts, and I don't need your screaming in my ear at this particular moment," I force out as politely as I can.

I don't want to give Brian any reason to screw this up, so I need to be on my best behavior.

Brian snorts on the other end of the line before continuing, "Don't get smart with me. Where the hell have you been the last two days?"

I frown. *What the hell does he mean? Where have I been? Didn't he get the bloody memo?* This is going to be harder than I thought.

"I'm struggling to discern if you are being serious with this line of questioning or if you are just screwing with me," I tell him, stopping mid-stride.

Sometimes this organization lacks common sense more and more since Sam was in charge. Brian is Sam's nephew and does not have the leadership skills his uncle had. Apart from being a handsome, bombastic, self-centered prick, he struggles to get the same loyalty and work ethic from the hunters as Sam did.

With Sam, leadership came as easy as breathing, but with Brian, it sometimes looks like he's choking more than anything else.

Screwing the next "hottie"—his words, not mine—that comes to work for him is higher up on his list of duties than the actual work that needs to be done. Don't even get me started on the not-so-reliable information he gives out. Case in point, my surveillance operation from the other night.

I've had my suspicions about him dealing with some shady characters, but it's not like I can walk in and demand an investigation of our chief in command.

"Dominica?!" Brian yells into the phone again. I roll my eyes. "Sorry, concussion," I lie as I play on my injury. Well, I'm not entirely lying; my head still hurts, and my attention span isn't quite up to par yet.

"Where the hell were—"

"Didn't Austen fill you in on what happened?" I interrupt him and can practically feel him fuming on the other side.

"He did, but he was vague on details and what happened," he says, his voice clipped. I don't even know what he is trying to convey, but this conversation is tedious and wasting my time.

"Brian, I will be at the office soon. I'll give you a play-by-play. How does that sound?" I force the politeness again, and it's actually painful.

There is silence on the line for what feels like an eternity, but after a while, I hear Brian inhale deeply and let out a growl. "Fine, I'll see you in a bit."

"Oh, and Brian?"

"What?"

"Please be sure to have your party favor wait until we are done before you enjoy yourself too much, as I don't need that visual again."

The line goes deadly quiet once again, and all the answer I get is a string of curses, then the line goes dead. I smile to myself, feeling somewhat pleased with my little jab. I know it will bite me in the ass later, but I don't care.

Placing my phone in my pocket, I make my way out of my apartment building and to my car, which Austen had arranged to be dropped off at my residence after the other night.

Let's just get this meeting over with so I can fix the shit between my friend and me before it becomes irreparable.

CHAPTER EIGHT

XAVIER

A growl leaves my chest, deep and low. I am so over this strategizing bullshit. No one is listening anymore, and it's turned into a pissing contest.

Let me catch you up. After our somewhat *entertaining* meal, I stalked to my room to unpack, and Alex followed suit. He wanted to get started on our plan to take out Dominica and the rest of the VHA as soon as possible, with the main focus on the Reaper, of course.

I didn't want to discuss plans or strategize now; I want some time to myself. I am usually calm and collected and have a clear mind, but that's after I have time to process my day and the things that bring out my darker side.

Since I've agreed to stay with Alex at his compound, I struggle to find my inner peace and collect my thoughts as he's almost like a shadow. He needs a plan *now*, or he is going to lose his mind, but little does Alex know that I am not far from losing mine, and that will not be pretty.

Hence our current situation. I lost my temper *and* my manners with it about three hours ago. I had to force myself to step away, or I would rip off the heads of the vampire council members.

They aren't particularly happy that I am second in command. They feel that since I abandoned my duties so long ago, I do not have a say in the council decisions, nor am I an adviser to the king or how matters will be handled.

I tried explaining my side to them, but they kept interrupting me, and now I am struggling to rein in my temper. I called all of them pompous bastards—I know, not quite original—and said they need to wake up to what the hell is going on around them.

Alex flipped his desk just minutes after I had my outburst, and that's where we stand now, most of the council members looking at Alex as if he had lost his mind and others scowling my way for being a bad influence on the vampire king.

"That's enough," Alex snarls.

"But, sire, don't you see that this traitor and outsider is just here to create doubt and make sure you are distracted—"

Alex inhales deeply, and the vibration from the growl coming from his chest reverberates through the entire room, making the council member shut his mouth, his teeth clacking on impact.

"Xavier has never once shown us that he can't be trusted. I know him, and I have known him for longer than some of you who serve on this council. I will not hear another ill word spoken against him."

"But, sir," another council member pipes up but is silenced just as fast when Alex's glare falls on him.

I must admit that glare is damn scary. If there was a way for Alex to have heat vision, he would use that glare to scorch people to ash.

"Not. Another. Word," Alex grits out.

A tension-filled silence falls in the room. I clear my throat, and Alex's gaze falls on me, but he nods at me when I raise my brows.

"I think I've had enough for one night. If you don't mind, Your Majesty, I am going to retire to my room." I address Alex formally in front of the council now, trying to avoid another set of glaring eyes and scoffs.

Alex sighs and closes his eyes before he raises his hand to pinch the bridge of his nose. "I suppose we aren't going to get anything done tonight. You are free to go."

I nod and give him a slight bow, a hint of mocking in my eyes. Alex's lips twitch as he tries to keep from smiling, and I leave the room.

I stroll down the absurdly long hallway. My mind is racing. There is so much wrong in our world, and I know it won't be fixed in just a matter of days, but we need to start somewhere.

If it was up to me, I would get rid of that damn council and all the vampires that have the same mindset as them. The council and many other vampires feel that we are the superior species and we should overthrow the humans and just take what we want. They are like parasites feeding off the power around them, spreading faster than I'd like to admit.

One moment, I'm plotting the demise of the council, and the next, the sound of a yelp draws me back. Without thinking, I grab the person when I see them fall. I didn't even register bumping into someone. Realizing it's a human woman, I wait until she finds her feet before letting go. She moves out of my reach quickly while apologizing profusely.

I frown, noticing the girl's features. Well, would you look at that? It's the same girl I had for lunch. *Great! Just bloody great.*

Her eyes widen when she recognizes me, her hand shoots to her neck, and her cheeks flash bright red.

"I-I'm so sorry I didn't see you, sir. Please—"

I hold up my hand when she starts to stutter another apology. She goes quiet at once, watching me intently. My eyes roam over her body and fall on her hand, which she now lowers slowly to her side.

"I'm happy to see that you are up and not looking so pale," I mock as I look her up and down.

"I … um … I was hoping to see you again," she says quietly, and I narrow my eyes.

"Really, and why is that?"

"Well … " she starts to say as she throws her weight from one hip to the other. "I was hoping you could help me get my sister away from the king and help us escape … " She trails off and looks behind her when she hears some voices coming from the hallway. I've heard them coming for a while, obviously, but they belong to some of the servants that work for Alex, and she isn't talking loud enough for them to hear, so why interrupt the poor, nervous girl?

I stay quiet, and she watches me nervously as the servants near us. I lean against the wall with my shoulder and fold one leg over the other, shoving one hand in my pocket and inspecting my thumbnail on the other. The servants pause. "Is the blood source bothering you, sir?" one of them pipes up and shoots the girl a dirty look.

"Do I look bothered in any way?" I snarl at the servant, making her tremble.

"I'm so sorry, sir. Please forgive my forwardness, I—"

I run my tongue over my right fang, pulling my lip up threateningly. "You are dismissed." The two servants look from me to the girl and then back at me before bowing and scurrying off. I train my sight back to the girl, and she squirms under my glare, rubs her thighs together, and clasps her hands in front of her. That blush runs up to her cheeks again.

I must admit it's turning me on, and that does not happen often with human girls. I push off the wall and shove my other hand in my pocket. I need to keep them to myself, with the thought of pushing her up against the wall and taking her here and now plaguing my mind.

I stroll to her slowly. Her throat bobs. "Are you sure that is why you are seeking me out?" I ask her as I come to a stop mere inches from her.

Her eyes dart from mine to my mouth, then jump back to my eyes again. Her breathing hitches, and that blush on her cheeks only gets deeper. "I … I … " she trails off again, letting her gaze fall to the floor.

The girl looks so damn delicious in her vulnerable state. I can't resist the urge, so I hook my finger under her chin, bringing her face up. She keeps her eyes down even though I've lifted her head. A deep rumble from my chest makes her look at me instantly, and I cock my head, expecting an answer.

"No, sir. I was hoping I could give you something to thank you for saving me from the brutality of some of the feeders," she sighs after a few minutes.

Why is this girl intriguing me so much? I mean, there were a lot of experienced blood sources tonight, but she pulled me to her like a moth to a flame.

She pushes her hair behind her ear and places her hands together in front of her again. She looks up at me through her lashes, and I can smell the arousal on her.

I am treading dangerous waters now, and I know that, but I have little control over my senses. Maybe it's because I have denied myself for so long and because the girl is the first fresh blood source I've tapped into since I bit Little Deadly. Maybe this is why I can't focus clearly: perhaps I'm blood-drunk and didn't have my fill.

I dip my head to her neck, which startles her. I pause until I can hear her heartbeat calm slightly. I drag my nose down from under her chin to the hollow of her neck, inhaling the delicious scent, which makes her gasp.

Pulling back from her quickly, I drop her face as I step away from her. What the hell am I doing, indulging in this? I know where this will lead and can't let that happen. *I do not need a damn groupie.*

"Did my scent offend you, sir?" she asks as she approaches me. I clear my throat, and my eyes flash. I can't understand why this girl has this effect on me.

"What's your name?" I ask her, but it comes out as a growl. The breath catches in her throat, and she closes the gap between us, placing her hands on my chest. This bloody girl makes me swallow hard, and I can't seem to step away from her.

"Tasha." She smiles.

"Well, Tasha, do you know you are playing with fire now?" I warn, but honestly, I don't know if the warning is for her or myself. She looks at me with those innocent doe eyes and nods her head slowly. I can feel myself getting hard, which means she does as well. Maybe just for tonight, I can let go of my rules and rid myself of the tension that's been building in my neck and shoulders since I can't even remember when.

I snake my hand behind her back and pull her flush against my chest. She rewards me with a little squeak, and I crash my lips onto hers. The kiss is rushed and dominating, but I don't let up. She doesn't protest as she gives in to me and opens her mouth, giving me access. Our tongues battle it out, and a groan leaves my throat when she rubs herself against me.

I break the kiss and look behind me when I hear Alex's voice coming from his office. If he finds me here with this human girl, he will want in on the fun, and I am in no mood to share, *ever.*

I growl as I pull away from her, picking her up, and throwing her over my shoulder. She squeals, and I rush to my room, slamming the door behind me and letting Tasha down from my shoulder. I only let go when I see she's stable on her feet again. "Are you all right?" I ask her, deliberately keeping my distance from her.

"Yes, thank you. Why did we come here?" Tasha looks around my room and frowns. Apart from the stacked bookshelf and the desk with some of my prized possessions, there isn't much in this room.

Tasha walks to the bookshelf with my diaries and some first-edition novels. She whistles low when she takes *Pride and Prejudice* from the shelf. "Wow, this is quite a collection you have here." She places the book back, looks at the titles of the others she recognizes, and strokes the spines of each book she touches.

I pace the room, keeping my distance and watching her intently. My fangs ache, and I can feel my self-control slipping. "I heard Alex and the council coming our way, and I thought it was good not to let him see you, or he would demand to be part of it … … " I trail off, not knowing exactly how to describe the situation.

She tilts her head and looks at me like she's also struggling to understand what we're doing. She wants help with her sister, and now we are in my room, which isn't the best place to be in my current mood. I would say we are entirely off topic.

"Listen, Tasha, I think you better go. I am not myself tonight, and the self-control you saw isn't quite present at this point." I turn my back to her. She is looking more and more appetizing. My focus should be on the problems with the hunters rather than creating more for myself. I walk to my desk and grasp the chair hard enough that my knuckles turn white. If this girl doesn't leave now, I am going to lose it.

There is silence in the room, and I can still smell the aroma of her arousal. It's coating the air, and my mouth waters. The lock on the door clicks, and I tense up, feeling the hold on my control slipping to the point where my hands are shaking, the wood of the chair cracking under my grip.

The sound of clothes being removed fills the space. "Tasha," I warn with a low rumble. The moment her corset hits the floor, I have her pinned against the wall, a snarl on my face, baring my fangs, my breathing heavy. Tasha's eyes are round with shock and fear, but she doesn't move to push me away. This damn girl is playing with fire and making me lose my damn mind.

"What the hell are you thinking?" I snarl at her, my eyes going dark, our noses touching. She takes a shaky breath and drags her tongue over my bottom lip, catching me off guard. Fuck this, I can't take anymore. I kiss her feverishly, and she moans into my mouth, making my cock twitch. I lower my hands to her ass, which is still covered by a thin layer of lace. Grabbing hold underneath her ass and lifting her so she can fold her legs around my waist. She breaks the kiss, gasping for air, and I roam my eyes over her breasts, her nipples pebbled. I take one into my mouth, and she throws her head back with a moan as I drag my fang across it before sucking on it again.

Tasha grasps my arms as I suck and flick her nipple with my tongue a couple of times before doing the same to the other. I pull away, her pants sending lust-filled chills through my body. My fangs ache to taste her, and as if she can see it in my eyes, she nods and pushes her breasts out more.

"Lock your ankles behind my back, and don't let go," I tell her as I move my right hand to the middle of her back. She does as she's told.

It will be unpleasant for her for the first few seconds, but then she'll enjoy it just as much as I am.

My lips twitch in anticipation, and I sink my fangs into her left breast a second later. Tasha gasps and squeezes her legs around my waist, her grip tightening on my forearms. I give her a few seconds to adjust to the pain before pulling a gulp full of blood into my mouth. The blood is sweet and spiced with adrenaline, making it much sweeter. I drink a little before letting go. I don't want to spoil the fun by taking too much.

I hum low and deep in my chest as I lick the remainder of the blood from her breast. Tasha's breathing comes in short huffs as she adjusts yet again to the loss of blood.

"How are you feeling?" I ask her.

"That was painfully blissful," she says, smiling at me. "If it makes any sense." I chuckle and, without warning, rip her skirt and lace panties from her waist. Tasha yelps, and within seconds, she's completely naked. She is beautiful, and her body would surely bring any mortal man to his knees, but at that very moment, Little Deadly's face flashes in front of my eyes, and my back goes rigid.

What was that? I inhale sharply as I close my eyes, shaking my head, trying to rid myself of her image. I open my eyes to find Tasha looking at me worriedly. "I'm fine," I growl, taking her mouth with mine again.

Turning us, I walk to the bed and drop her onto it. I kick off my shoes and unbutton my shirt, taking it off slowly. Tasha watches me with hungry eyes, dragging down my torso and falling on the bulge in my trousers.

She swallows and bites her bottom lip as I start to undo my pants, and they drop to the floor. When I look into Tasha's eyes and see the blush creeping up her cheeks again, Little Deadly makes another appearance in my head, and no matter what I do, I can't rid myself of her. I only see her face now, and that disturbs the shit out of me.

I grab Tasha's hips and flip her onto her stomach, pulling her up on her knees. I shake my head again, trying to rid myself of Little Deadly's face.

Dropping my boxers, I align myself with her core, feeling just how wet she is. Tasha squirms, and I slap her ass. "Please, sir. I can't take anymore."

I pull back slowly and, without warning, drive into her. She gasps and fists the sheets into her hands.

With every thrust, I only hear Dominica's moans in my head. I can't seem to shake it. I flip her over and fist a handful of her hair at the back of her head, twisting her head to the side, exposing her neck.

I start to move again. Our breathing becomes heavy with pleasure, and just before she reaches her climax, I sink my teeth into her neck, driving her over the edge. The blood tastes the best at this exact moment. A vampire can actually get drunk off it if they don't know how to handle it.

I groan from the pleasure of the blood running down my throat, and my own climax peaks.

We stay like this for a few seconds while she catches her breath. When I hear her breathing and heartbeat calm down, I pull out of her and lick the blood from her neck.

Getting up from the bed, I pull my boxers up and get dressed. Tasha covers her face and groans, "What have I done?" She scurries off the bed, grabs her corset from the floor, and then turns around to look for her skirt. Sighing, I look at the tattered material on the floor—*shit.*

Why do I always need to tear the damn clothes off the women? It looks like it doesn't matter how much time passes between sex; I will not get rid of that habit, and it leaves me in this mess each time.

My head whips to the door, and I intently listen as the voices approaching it become louder.

Shit!

I walk to my closet and grab a shirt from it, tossing it to Tasha. "Put this on, and hurry, we have company." Tasha's eyes widen and she fumbles with the shirt before pulling it on and standing awkwardly in the middle of the room.

I roll my eyes and walk to the door when Alex finally knocks. Dammit! I am in no mood to explain this to him or anyone else, but it seems I don't have a choice.

Opening the door, Alex pushes past me into the room, still talking on his phone. He stops as he spots Tasha and turns to give me a wicked grin, never missing a beat as he speaks.

I sigh as I lean against the open door. Tasha looks from Alex to me, and the moment Alex approaches her, she trembles and steps back.

"Listen, I have to call you back … Yes, I know this is important, but I have shit to deal with now, so I will call you back in a few minutes," Alex tells the person on the other end of the phone somewhat irritably, and without waiting for them to answer, he ends the call.

"Well, well. Aren't we having fun?" Alex laughs as he turns to look at me again. "I thought you would never take a human girl again. It seems like this one has caught your attention properly. Isn't this the one you had for lunch?"

"Don't be a dick," I huff, annoyed now.

Alex laughs aloud and turns back to Tasha, stalking forward. Tasha whimpers and moves back again. Her eyes fall on mine, pleading for me to do something. Shit, I am going to regret this. "Why are you here, Alex?" I ask quickly, trying to pull his attention away from Tasha.

Alex pauses and looks at me over his shoulder. I'm unsure if he's contemplating answering me or wants to continue stalking the prey in the room. Luckily, he settles on answering me.

"Tasha, you are dismissed. Please make sure to take enough fluids," I tell her before Alex can change his mind. She frowns, and when I let out a low warning growl, she quickly nods and rushes out of the room.

"You're no fun, do you know that?" Alex huffs and falls into the wingback chair in the corner of my room.

"So," I urge as I shut the door behind me. "You were saying?"

"*So,* we have a lead on the Reaper, and I need you to assemble a team. Surveillance only, for now. We need to get enough information on the VHA and the Reaper before we strike," he says, his face turning serious.

"I'm listening."

"Okay, so I let one of the guards leak some information about a 'coven' in the city," he smiles wickedly as he continues, "this 'coven' has some of the deadliest vampires of our kind and is planning to attack the upcoming Light Festival that the city is hosting."

Walking over to my desk, I turn and lean against it, crossing my arms in front of my chest. "What exactly are you trying to accomplish with this? You are going to get more of our kind killed, and we cannot afford that—"

Alex raises his brow, looking unimpressed by my interruption. I inhale deeply and, after a few seconds, let my breath out through my nose in a huff. "My apologies, please continue."

"The main purpose of this is to examine their inner workings and find weaknesses. Obviously, there isn't going to be a coven, and there will not be an attack on the people that night, but if everything goes well, we can take out a few hunters in the process."

"So, you are leaking false information to draw them out, and then what?" I ask, seeing the massive gaps in this plan.

"Always the bloody pessimist," Alex growls as he rests his elbows on the arms of the chair and entwines his fingers.

"Alex, don't piss me off. I haven't quite settled my temper, nor did I have a chance to fully clear my head. Now, you want to poke a sleeping beast. This is why I am here, remember? I am here to make sure there are no plot holes, and you get the support you need," I force out, trying to be as calm as possible.

"Xavier, stop doubting me and my leading capabilities, for Pete's sake. I appreciate what you are doing, but I am still king, and I am only sharing this out of courtesy and because I regard you as a close friend."

A growl vibrates from my chest before I can stop it, and I cut it off the moment it happens. I am in no mood for this shit, and I tell Alex as much.

"My *friend,* this is getting us nowhere. Fighting among ourselves does not help anyone. We shouldn't lose sight of the real enemy. I understand that this is frustrating and that you need vengeance for Sofie, but we can't run into this without addressing every possible problem. You know I am right."

Alex watches me with his eyes narrowed while I speak. His jaw ticks, but he doesn't interrupt me. He knows I speak the truth, but it's difficult for him. He isn't the kind of leader who can sit and wait for something to happen. He needs to be the one who makes it happen and fast.

Alex inhales deeply, slowly, and blows his breath out as he rises from the chair and moves to the door.

He opens the door and steps out, but before he leaves, he turns and looks at me. "You are right, my friend. I apologize for my behavior. We are going ahead with this plan, though, and I need you to turn these stones, as you call them, and do it quickly. I want results within the next week."

With that, he turns and slams the door behind him. I let out a string of curses, knowing full well that he could still hear me. I'm not sure what bullshit the council planted in his head about me when I left, but if he is behaving like this, it can't be good.

I slam my fist on my desk and grunt in frustration. That fuck session did nothing for my resolve. To be honest, it only added to it. Seeing that damn vixen while being with another woman isn't ideal.

What the hell is up with that? I mean, the hate that boils in my heart whenever I think of her is like nothing I've ever felt toward anyone else, so how does it make sense that I see her face in that intimate moment?

I rub my temples. My life has become quite complicated the last few days, and I don't really care for it. I miss my carefree days and not worrying about anything or anyone other than myself. The faster we get this operation up and running, the faster I can live my life in peace. That means I will finally rid this world of Little Deadly, and that is for the best.

An uncomfortable feeling takes root in my chest at that thought. Clearly, the idea of Little Deadly not being part of this world anymore doesn't sit well with my heart. It's confusing as hell.

CHAPTER NINE

DOMINICA

"Hi, Agnes," I greet Brian's secretary when she looks up at me.

Agnes has a somber look on her face, and she only nods my way and looks back at her computer screen. *What the hell is her problem?* I mean, really, the last time I saw her, I was the one being humiliated, and you don't see me looking like that. "Is Brian in his office?"

"Yes, he's waiting for you. You can go in."

"Are you sure he isn't with someone?"

"Dominica, do not make the situation worse. I beg you," Agnes sighs. I roll my eyes and turn to open Brian's office door. I pause, thinking it best to knock ... Just in case. Brian can be pretty spiteful if he wants to be.

"Enter," Brian calls, and I walk into his office and sit in front of his desk.

"Since when do you knock?" Brian asks, feigning surprise. "Since you leave nasty-ass surprises when you summon me," I counter, and the mocking look on his face turns dark.

I hold my hands up in front of me, and he leans back in his chair, crossing his arms in front of his chest. I blow my breath out and rest my elbows on the chair's arms.

"Okay, truce. I promise not to bring up your little 'lunch date' again if you promise me one thing."

Brian stares at me, looking unimpressed. I am in no mood for a fight, so I close my eyes and try my absolute best to keep calm. I remind myself why I am doing this and that I cannot fail because if I do, I can lose my friend.

"You know I don't make promises unless I get something out of it, and I've heard nothing of value yet," Brian states.

"Other than the fact that I will let go of you screwing in your office in the middle of a business day?"

Brian only shrugs, not saying anything else. He knows how much this irritates me and is trying to get a rise out of me. Screw him, I will not fall for this trick of his.

"Fine, I will tell you what I want, and then you can tell me what you want in return. How does that sound?" I say slowly.

The smile that forms on Brian's face looks inhuman, but he nods and waits for me to continue. I haven't said anything and a feeling of danger and dread settles in my stomach. I am about to make a deal with the devil, but my friendship is at stake. "Okay, so here it is. Austen tells me you made him the lead in the next mission—"

Brian laughs, shaking his head, and says, "Thought you might be upset about that."

"Brian, please shut the hell up and let me finish! You are making it extremely difficult to stay civil with you, and I would appreciate it if you could control your urge to act like a damn fool," I snap, the words leaving my mouth before I can stop them.

Dammit!

How do you know when Brian is about to lose his shit? You just watch his face as he turns shades of red and purple before going off like a bloody bomb. I quickly try to recover from my outburst when I see Brian's face turning red. "I apologize for my outburst. Please just let me finish."

My apology must have surprised Brian as his mouth pops into an O-shape, but he stays quiet. I take this opportunity to continue and hope for the best.

"I'm not upset that you assigned Austen to this mission. I'm happy you finally trust him enough to let him run it. What I want from you is to stay true to your word. Please, don't get his hopes up just to crush them so you can get back at me—"

I raise my brow as Brian starts to defend his actions, and he stays quiet, which is very unlike him, but nonetheless, I continue quickly before he has a chance to change his mind.

"He needs this, and I will do anything so he can have this time to shine," I finish my pathetic pleading, and the silence that follows is deafening.

Brian watches me for a few more seconds before tilting his head. "Well, well, this was something I thought I would never see. The all-powerful Dominica pleading for someone else to take the lead in an important mission," Brian snickers.

"Don't be a dick," I snap again. It's humiliating enough to ask him for this; he doesn't need to rub salt in the wound.

"Is that it, though?" Brian asks, this time more seriously. "Yup, that's it." I shrug and lean back in my chair.

"So, if I keep Austen as the lead on this mission, you will do anything for me in return?" I don't like where this is going. The way he phrases the question makes it sound like I am going to regret the deal.

"Within reason … Yes," I say cautiously, eyeing Brian.

"Hmm … Sounds manageable." He smiles, and I already regret my decision. "Austen can stay as the lead on this mission."

"Thank you, and what do you want from me?"

"That, my dear, is to be determined."

Oh crap. I don't like how he is saying that and how he looks at me. I swallow the lump in my throat. I can't think about the consequences of what I just did. I can save my friendship, which is all that matters now. I will deal with this when the time comes.

I nod and make to stand, but Brian holds his hand up, and I pause in my seat. I sigh and sit back in my chair when he gestures for me to wait. "Yes?"

"You haven't told me what happened with your surveillance operation from the other night."

I tell Brian every single detail of the other night's events, but while I do, I keep a close eye on his reactions. As expected, they are forced and not quite how you would expect your head of office to react.

When I frown at him, he quickly makes up an excuse for why he is reacting the way he is. His explanations do not make any sense, and when I tell him that I suspect his little bird feeding him the information is corrupt, he loses it. "Are you accusing me of something, Dom?"

"No, I am merely stating my suspicions. That is my job, after all." Brian huffs but still fumes, and before he dismisses me, he fills me in on the mission he gave Austen. He doesn't ask if I am all right, and he dismisses the whole thing as a write-off, which I'm fine with. However, the way he tries to get rid of me after I tell him what happened is not sitting right with me.

When I leave Brian's office, I don't feel like I have accomplished anything. In fact, I feel more unsure of what happened on the failed surveillance mission than before, and I'm not sure he will keep his word.

I need to get to the bottom of this. I don't like being in the dark; it feels like a big secret is hanging over my head, and I am the only one who is oblivious.

I walk out of the office building and make my way to my car. I have to find Austen and see if he needs any help with the mission, which is happening tonight.

Calling Austen seems to prove fruitless. I have been driving around town to all his usual hangouts, but I can't find him, and he will not answer his phone. So, I am left with one last option, which I swore I would never ever resort to.

I have to call Silvia.

I roll my eyes and shake my head. *Great!* And guess what? The stupid girl will relish in the fact that I need her to get to my best friend.

I don't have anything in particular against Silvia per se, but I hate that she always tries to best me in everything. Emphasis on *tries.*

Silvia has tried her best to be assigned as my partner since the day she started at the VHA. She has told me multiple times that she has admired me from a young age, which is stupid since she is five years younger than me.

When she failed in that, she tried to turn *into* me. I always tried to be friendly and polite. I tried my best not to hurt her feelings whenever I declined to have her as a partner, but I drew the line when she came into the office one day dressed like me—to a tee.

She didn't take that very well. I still cringe at the way I handled it, but I'd had enough at that point. Let's just say she left the office in tears, and everyone was staring at me like I had stolen the damn crown jewels.

After that day, she never really tried talking to me, and it suited me, to be honest. What caught me off guard was when Austen told me he felt bad for her and asked her to partner with him. I wasn't happy, but I thought that maybe that way we could become somewhat friends, and then this tension could be resolved.

Well, nope. That was not the case: Silvia not-so-subtly tried to rub it in my face that Austen was becoming very close with her. It was clear that she was still trying her best to be me and to replace me everywhere.

I just had enough and told her to get her own damn life and that she would never be anything to Austen other than a work partner. She obviously didn't like that.

Sighing, I roll my eyes. Here I am now, needing to call the bitch to find Austen, and oh boy, will she milk it. I take another deep breath before hitting the call button when I find her name under my contacts. The phone starts to ring, and for some stupid reason, I feel anxious.

Austen really screwed up with his dumb-ass love confession. The phone rings three times before she picks up.

"Well, isn't this a surprise?" Silvia's voice comes through the phone. I can practically see the smirk on her face.

"Silvia," I greet, trying to not sound condescending.

"And to what do I owe the pleasure?" She laughs sarcastically.

"I'm looking for Austen. Is he with you?"

Silvia is quiet for a few seconds before she bursts out laughing. "Isn't this wonderful? The almighty Salvatore asking me for assistance—"

"Silvia, please, I don't have time for your games," I force through my clenched jaw. Biting the inside of my cheek, I wait for her answer.

"Yeah, he's here at my house, but we are very busy. He clearly chose not to do this mission with you. He prefers me, so you can just sit back and relax."

Cursing inwardly, I pinch the bridge of my nose. "Thank you for the useless piece of news. Tell Austen I need to speak to him. I'll be there in a few minutes."

Silvia starts to protest, but I hang up. I'm in no mood to listen to her shitty voice complaining about shit she knows nothing about. I throw my phone on the seat beside me and start my car.

I *will* talk with him, and he *will* listen to what I have to say. I need to make him see my side; hopefully, he will understand.

CHAPTER TEN

DOMINICA

I pull up in front of Silvia's place and park my car. I sit, watching the house as I try to get my thoughts in order. I only hope Austen will listen and let me aid him on this mission. He can't deny that I'm an asset and that he needs my skills. He's always felt that way, so hopefully, that much hasn't changed.

Taking another deep breath, I get out of my car and walk up to the front door. Before I can knock, Silvia pulls open the door and glares at me.

"Where's Austen?" I ask rather impatiently. My no-bullshit tone is likely not helping, but I'm in no mood to argue and play her silly little games.

"Didn't I tell you we are busy, and you aren't wanted?"

I let out my breath in a huff and push past her into her house. I really can't have a bitch fight with this girl. Not now, anyway. She wants to be a part of our circle so badly that she doesn't even know what it entails. "Silvia, I won't ask you again. Where the hell is Austen?"

"What do you want, Dom?" I hear from the left of me.

I look in the direction of the voice, spotting Austen with a couple of hunters we could never stomach. I narrow my eyes at my friend but leave my commentary to myself. The situation is fragile as is, and I don't want to cause a fight by questioning him in front of "his team."

"I need to talk to you." I force my tone to sound as calm as possible. "I can't, I have a mission to get to, and I really don't feel like being rejected again." Austen averts his gaze, sounding somewhat defensive. "So please, can this wait?"

"Austen, just hear me out?" This is humiliating at best, and I hate pleading with anyone, but I will do it to save my friendship.

Austen glances my way again and watches me for a few seconds before he looks at Silvia, who is shaking her head furiously, and then looks back at me.

He sighs and then gives me a curt nod. Silvia clearly doesn't know the word "discreet," gaping at Austen before snapping her mouth shut. I bite the inside of my cheek to keep from saying something that will make the situation worse.

"Thank you. Can we talk in private?" I sigh, feeling a little relief washing over me. Maybe there is more hope than I thought.

Austen gives me another nod and walks past me. I turn and follow him out of the house. We walk around the house and to a shed hidden at the back of the property. I frown but don't say anything as he holds open the door for me to enter.

Once inside, I look around and clench my jaw at the contents on the shelves surrounding the walls. The chill that runs down my spine is unnerving, but I school my face into one of indifference.

The shed is old, and it looks like it could collapse at any moment now. I turn, taking a better look at my surroundings. This is a makeshift office of some sort. In the middle of the space stands a desk with a laptop on top, and covering the walls are weapons of all types—grenades, semiautomatics, fully automatics, and a whole lot more.

Where did Silvia get these? Some weapons are military-grade and can only be acquired through the VHA. They may only be used when going on specific assignments. When said assignment is complete, we must return them and log them back into the system.

I bite my tongue as the reality of the situation becomes clear. Austen is testing me by bringing me into this shed with stolen VHA weaponry and equipment. He wants to test my loyalty, but this is going a little too far.

I clear my throat and return my attention to him. Austen stands in the middle of the room now, his feet shoulder-width apart and his arms crossed over his chest, watching me. I will not fall into the trap he and Silvia are trying to set for me.

"I'm here to help you on the mission," I say simply, folding my arms to hide my balled-up fists.

"And why would I need your help?"

I frown at my friend. What the hell happened to the Austen I knew? This really can't be because I don't feel the same way he does. I know he is upset, but this side of him is new. He's never treated me like this before.

"Really? You know I'm an asset to your team, and I want to help you succeed."

"I don't need your help, Dom. I have Silvia, and we will do this on our own." I throw my hands up in the air. "What the hell is going on with you? Since when do you refuse help from me? We swore we would always be there for one another, and now you are acting like a dick."

Austen chuckles darkly, shaking his head, and then narrows his gaze on me. "Since I told you how I felt about you, and you didn't even consider giving this a chance," he says, gesturing between us.

A pang of guilt runs through me, and I huff out a sigh. I don't know what to say anymore. Everything I want to say isn't anything Austen would like to hear. At least not now.

I understand he's upset, but shit, the way he's acting is childish at best. I can't help that I don't see anything more between us other than being friends, and I'm trying my best to save said friendship. "Don't you think you're acting a bit like a twelve-year-old?" The words slip out before I can stop them, and I close my eyes in frustration. I rub my hand over my face, already regretting my words.

"Ha! Nice one. I don't know what you want from me—"

"I want to help you, that's all. I am trying to show you that I am here for you, even if it's not how you want. I will always have your back, no matter what you think of me," I say softly. This vulnerability is exhausting and not something I often let myself feel.

Austen huffs out a sigh, and after what feels like hours, he nods his head slowly. "Fine, you can help, but remember that this is *my* mission, which means I am the lead on everything, and Silvia is my second in command."

I roll my eyes but nod my agreement, not saying what I actually want to. I am just happy he's willing to let me help.

An awkward silence falls between Austen and me. After a while, he gestures to the shed door, and I move out of the way so he can pass me. "Lead the way, boss." Austen snorts, but a small smile forms on his lips.

That's right, you can't be mad at me forever. I knew I could get through to him. Feeling like we're getting back on the right track, I follow Austen out of the shed and into the house again. When we enter, I can clearly see the discord on Silvia's face. A triumphant smile spreads on my lips, and I raise my brows at Silvia, almost challenging her to say something that I know she's too pussy to do in front of Austen. *Suck-up.*

Austen takes his place at the head of the table, and Silvia almost falls over her own feet as she tries to get to Austen. I stand aside and let her pass me without even trying to intervene. She will be her own downfall.

I take up a space opposite Austen, and he fills me in on what they have discussed so far. The rest of the team glances at each other every few minutes, but I ignore it for now. That unnerving feeling still lingers in my chest.

"Now that you are caught up, we can continue this meeting. We have nine hours until takeoff, and we can't waste another second," Austen says, his eyes falling briefly on me before he looks back at the maps in front of him.

I curse inwardly, *dick.* He is milking this, and I bite my tongue, or I will honestly say something I shouldn't.

"The plans are as follows," Silvia pipes up. "We got intelligence from a private source that there is going to be an attack on the Light Festival and that the strongest vampires have clans set up and are already nested here," Silvia says as she points to isolated parts of the dock area.

I frown when I take a closer look. That's not possible. I've been to that part of the docks, and there is no way that a clan the size Silvia is describing is nested there. Something seems off the more she tells us about the source and the intel he gave them. My senses run in overdrive as the discomfort takes root in my chest. This does not seem legitimate. How is Austen even taking this into account?

When I look up at Austen to ask what he is thinking, I find him watching me. There's a challenging glint in his eyes and something else. It reminds me of the other night he disappeared when we were attacked at the same docks he wants to attack tonight.

Austen tilts his head, challenging me to say something, challenging me to tell him he is making a mistake, but I don't.

I just nod, and the smile on his face is foreign, so out of character. Why does it feel like I'm still in the dark? It's almost like they are deliberately keeping information from me. I can't put my finger on it. My suspicion is confirmed when a sly smile appears on Silvia's lips, and she crosses her arms in front of her chest, her gaze locked with mine.

"So, like Silvia said, the intel we received seems accurate, and this is our only window of opportunity. We don't know exactly when they will attack, but we can't take any chances. The city needs to be protected, which means we need to eliminate the vermin *before* they can carry out their plan. What *we* need to do is make sure we plan and execute everything to a tee," Austen continues where Silvia left off.

After about three hours, we all became quite familiar with the plan, and I have to admit that the plan wasn't half bad, my paranoid feelings aside.

My instincts are screaming at me, and they are never wrong, but tonight, I will try to ignore them for Austen's sake. It's stupid, but maybe this time they're wrong.

Austen seems so confident. I can't bear the guilt of ruining this for him. I'll just be on my best guard and make sure everything runs as smoothly as possible.

So basically, I'm babysitting.

Another three hours later, we head out to our destination. The nagging feeling that something is wrong just about drives me insane, but I push it aside again and focus on the mission ahead.

CHAPTER ELEVEN

XAVIER

"This is a surveillance mission at best," I tell the assembled team before me. "I don't want any rogues on my team. You only attack hunters when they attack you. We need to stay out of sight as much as possible. The main reason for this surveillance is to collect the VHA's patterns of how they work and see where we can find any weaknesses."

The assembled vampires look wary, but they nod in agreement. This is going to be a long night.

After Alex leaves my room, I try to get some sleep, if nothing else. That, of course, turns out to be a waste of time. I try writing in my journal, but it too proves futile. Not even the workout I put myself through does anything to rid my mind of all this pent-up energy and aggression. Not to mention the unsettling feeling building in the back of my mind.

This feels wrong on so many levels, but the king has spoken. Alex came to me a couple of days later, and when I presented him with all the plot holes in the plan the council had decided on, he dismissed everything I had put before him.

It's frustrating as hell. I know Alex sees what I see, but his absolute need to do something overwhelms his common sense.

So here we are: it's the Light Festival, and the council's plan is underway.

"The source," as the VHA knows him, brought back some intel of his own. I still can't understand how the VHA hasn't figured out that the information they get from "the source"—which is a vampire, by the way—is botched.

I shake my head and huff out a laugh. *Stupid bloody humans.* Granted, hunters aren't like normal human beings. They live much longer than the average human, but they are still humans nonetheless. They can still die from wounds, sickness, and so on, but it takes some effort as they heal faster than the average human as well. Not as fast as we do, but it doesn't take as long, depending on the injury they sustain.

Some hunters are mortally wounded and don't make it. If they have the willpower, others will survive, but it will take some time.

With that in mind, I tell my team that we don't wound, but we kill when the opportunity arises.

Let's get back to the point here. The vampire who leaks false information informed me that the mission is run by Little Deadly's best friend.

What's his name again? I can't seem to remember. Yet again, I don't have any interest in remembering his name. He's just one more meal to consume.

Snickering at my little joke, I notice the second in command watching me. He has been questioning my every move. Granted, he had been in command for a few years until I came along, so I expect him to be unhappy about being demoted. "Yes, Damion?"

Damion frowns and narrows his eyes at me but doesn't answer right away. I simply place my hands behind my back and cock my head at him.

"Why the hell are we doing this? I know you say it's to gather intel, but it seems fruitless," he snaps.

"This is a direct order from your king. I am here to make sure it happens just like he said and to give him what he needs. If you have any second thoughts, you are more than welcome to sit this one out and discuss it with the king himself," I say mockingly.

Damion's eyes widen slightly, but he pulls himself together and stands taller. "That won't be necessary," he mumbles.

"Hmm, thought so. Since I have your attention, gather the team and get loaded up. We leave in ten minutes."

As I turn to get my coat, Alex enters the operations room. The determined and driven look in his eyes is unmistakable. "Ready to head out?"

"Just about. Is there something else you need before we leave?" I ask curtly. I am still unhappy about this plan and how I was ordered to do it. I am not a part of this clan, and I am only here because of Sofie and Alex, and I gave my word to Alex. It seems that this also came back to bite me in the ass.

"Don't seem so unhappy, my friend—" Alex starts to say but cuts off his sentence when I glare at him.

"Do *not* tell me to *not* be unhappy about this. I gave you my word, and now it seems like you are taking advantage of it," I all but snarl at my friend.

I am trying to control my temper, and now the remaining vampires are staring. I don't want to disrespect their king in front of them, so I close my eyes and take a deep breath. After slowly releasing it, I open my eyes and look at Alex, resentment, and disappointment rising in my chest. "I'll keep you up to date with the happenings of the evening." Turning on my heel, I move to leave the room. I stop at the door and look over my shoulder at my friend. "I hope this is worth sacrificing our friendship and trust?"

"Xavier, this has nothing to do with our friendship but everything to do with getting rid of the enemy. I haven't betrayed your trust, nor have I taken advantage of your word," Alex states irritably.

I huff out a laugh. "By ordering me around like I am your servant, dismissing valuable information I give you, and by not listening and still going ahead with this ridiculous plan is doing all of the above shit you just denied," I bite out.

Alex's eyes flash with anger, and I sigh, cursing under my breath. I can't believe I let my emotions get the better of me.

"I'll keep you updated," I snap and walk to the waiting car.

We're early when we get to the docks where the VHA wants to set up a perimeter. We are near the burned-down building where I found Little Deadly's surveillance equipment. I order my team to the opposite side of the docks, where an outlook tower looks over the bay area and the docks.

The Light Festival is held at the pier. The best way to stay undetected is to ensure that we always have a bird's-eye view of the enemy.

I tell my team to stay low for now. We don't want to reveal our position so early in the night, and it's crucial that the VHA does not see us coming.

"Okay, seems like we can take a few seconds and go over some details—"

"We don't need to go over anything, Xavier. This isn't the first time we've done this, so you don't have to treat me and my team like a bunch of moronic newlings," Damion snarls.

I clasp my hands behind my back and wait for him to stop ranting. We can't afford to have divisions in our ranks. That has never played out well, and I will not be held accountable for this shithead's hot-tempered behavior.

"Are you done?" I ask him, sounding extremely bored. "The sooner you learn your place in this ranking, the better off all of us will be. You're a hothead who is going to get *your team* killed. So, for the sake of your coven and king, do as you are told."

Damion, who clearly does not like being put in his place, snarls at me, baring his fangs. He straightens his spine and squares his shoulders as he steps forward.

I snort as I raise my brows, not moving from my stance. What this little Bo Peep does not know is that I have almost two hundred years on him, and I can easily hand his ass to him without breaking a sweat. That's if I still could break a sweat.

"Do not insult me in front of my men!"

"I will insult you in front of your king, you arrogant prick." I grit my teeth, my temper rising. "You will fall in line with my orders, and you will do it without a fuss." I step toward Damion, my anger vibrating in my veins. My eyes flash, and I'm digging my nails into Damion's throat before I know it.

He gasps and hisses at me while he claws at my hand and wrist. I tilt my head slowly, menacingly. "Don't fuck with me, little boy."

Damion's eyes turn round with fear as I increase the pressure around his trachea. I need to control myself, or I am going to rip his throat out.

"Sir, he will fall in line. I give you my word," one of the soldiers says, his voice panicked. I snap my head his way. A relatively young vampire looks back at me. Does he not know what the consequences will be? I fight to rein in a semblance of my temper. "Who is this to you?" I ask the young vampire as I shake Damion a little.

Damion's eyes are still filled with fear, but he snarls at me again, "Leave him alone." I slowly turn my gaze back to Damion and then to the young vampire again. The resemblance between the two men is uncanny.

"He's my sire and my great-grandfather, sir," the young vampire says hesitantly.

I nod in acknowledgment to the young vampire and turn my attention back to Damion. Narrowing my eyes, I watch him for a few seconds.

"You know the consequences for a vampire if they do not keep their word in a case like this, right?"

"Yes," Damion forces out as he gives me a curt nod.

"*You* will be responsible for the actions of your sire," I say slowly, turning my attention back to the young one. "If he steps out of line again, you will pay with your life. Is that clear?"

The young vampire's eyes widen in fear, but he lowers his head in resolve after looking at his sire pleadingly. Of course, I won't kill the poor kid if his asshole sire steps out of line, but I need to scare some sense into him and teach him what it means to give out your word so easily.

"Very well," I say after a while, dropping Damion from my grip. "Looks like we are all sorted out."

I look around the group, challenging each of them to try anything. When they bow their heads slightly, I smile, satisfied. "Back to business then—"

My orders get cut off again when the rest of the group and I pick up on faint chatter coming from the direction of the burned building.

I place my index finger in front of my mouth. They nod in agreement, and we listen as the sound of the voices becomes louder and louder as they near the tower.

"Okay, guys, we have enough time to set up our equipment and establish a decent perimeter. The festival isn't starting for a few more hours, so we can set up and head out into the crowd if needed. For now, though, I need everyone here and vigilant." That friend of Little Deadly speaks up. His voice sounds like metal scraping against metal in my head.

"Austen, if I may?" Little Deadly says, but the way she addresses him sounds off. I catch her scent before hearing her speak, and my mind and body are at war once more.

"No, Dom. You said you are here to support *me,* and I am in charge. You can leave if you can't accept that," Austen snarls. I frown at the little prick. Suddenly, the overwhelming urge to rip out his vocal cords consumes me. I grip the side of the window to ground myself before doing something stupid and close my eyes when I feel them darken. *She's the bloody enemy,* I remind myself. *Dammit!*

I gather my composure before opening my eyes and looking out the window again. Little Deadly raises her brow and then places her hands out in front of her in defeat. "Fine, just as you want."

The anger is clear as day in her eyes, but she manages to keep it out of her tone. I do admire someone who can master that skill. I, of course, have never been able to do that, and I've been around for a while.

The friend smiles and orders the rest of the VHA to set up camp. The asshole keeps going over his plans with his team as he walks around doing nothing. What kind of leader is that? I shake my head. Self-centered assholes, the lot of them.

We absorb as much information about how and what they plan to do once they spot us. They are planning to capture one of us to interrogate. Nothing new there. We definitely won't make it easy for them.

Listening to the humans is undoubtedly taking its toll on my team. Some of them start to fidget and become agitated, and others have a permanent snarl on their faces. They are fixing for a fight the more they hear what the hunters plan to do once they encounter us. Their eyes scream vengeance, but they need to keep all of this under control until the right moment.

Strangely, though, through all the chit-chat, I don't once hear Dominica indulge in conversation with the rest of the hunters. She keeps to herself as she sharpens her ring daggers, her eyes wandering over to each hunter. The frown that develops between her eyes has one starting on mine.

Why would she look so upset with her fellow hunters? It doesn't make sense. There's a reason why the vampires know her as the Reaper. She is relentless and merciless and strikes quickly. She doesn't back down from any challenge.

I force myself to drag my eyes from her to her friend. He's standing to the side with that blonde partner of his. Every once in a while, the partner looks over her shoulder at Little Deadly and then talks feverishly with the friend.

I focus my hearing on the pair and find myself confused again. First, it doesn't happen often, and second, it sounds like the friend is unhappy with Little Deadly. The blonde girl, Silvia, looks over her shoulder again, and when she turns back to Austen, she scowls when I hear her talk again. "Austen, why the hell did you bring her with us? We can do this without her. Why would you let her hurt you again? I am your girl. I will have your back no matter what." She smiles, reaching over and running her fingers down Austen's arm.

Austen stares at Little Deadly, not even registering Silvia's touch. This brings another unsatisfying look to the girl's face, and she actually bares her teeth as she hisses, "Austen! Forget about her and focus on what you need to do tonight."

Austen turns his attention back to Silvia and frowns at her. "You're right. I can't lose sight of what we're working toward. I just feel like maybe if we tell Dom what we plan, she will be willing to participate and share the victory—"

"No! Do not tell her anything. You know as well as I do she will not be willing to break the rules, not even for you." Silvia snarls again, but she catches her tone and softens it. "You don't need her, Austen. You can do this and prove to everyone at the VHA that you are the better hunter."

I am intrigued by what these two are discussing, but my attention is pulled to the rest of the VHA group on the ground when one of them yells and points our way. *How did they see us up here?*

I don't have time to figure out the gist of the situation before there's a sound of an RPG being loaded and fired in our direction.

Just before the missile hits our location, we scatter in different directions. The blast is powerful enough to knock me off my feet, even though I run faster than a speeding bullet.

Yeah, I know Superman won't be happy with me using his lines, but I can't think of a better way to describe it.

The flash is blinding, and the moment the force of the blast hits, I'm pushed forward. I manage to push some of the vampires running with me out of the way before I hit the ground. I shake my head, trying to rid myself of the flash of pain in my head. *Great, this is going to be a hindrance.*

My hearing comes back in a rush, and the sounds rushing in make me jump to my feet. My head still spins from the fact that they knew where we were hiding, and now we are in a full-on fight with the hunters.

"Xavier! What the hell happened?!" Damion yells, ducking as a bullet whizzes past his head.

Damion launches his body at the hunter who tried to kill him mere seconds ago and tackles him to the ground. Biting down onto the hunter's throat, I hear bone crack and flesh tear before he rips the hunter's throat out with his teeth.

The bastard is vicious; I'll give him that. Damion rises from the ground, blood dripping from his chin, and he spits the remnants of the hunter to the ground. A vicious smile on his face. I walk over to Damion as he turns and wipes his mouth on the back of his hand. "I have no idea what the hell just happened. I can't understand how they saw us or even knew we were there … " I trail off, narrowing my eyes at Damion. "Did you have something to do with this?"

"What! No, I would never let my men be harmed just to get rid of a disturbance like you." There's genuine shock on his face, which means we still have a rat among us. *That rat will wish he never was turned when I get my hands on him.*

I give Damion a sharp nod. "Very well. Make sure the team is intact, and you go for the kill. I want no survivors."

That vicious smile from earlier creeps back on Damion's face, and he turns on his heel, running into the fight. He slices the back of a hunter on his way through. The human screams out in pain, and I can't help but smile too.

I turn to go in another direction when a fist hits me across the face, making me stumble. I shake my head, rub my jaw, and look in the direction of the punch. To my surprise, the pretty blonde girl stands before me, and she swings again.

I dodge the blow as I laugh at her, making sure the sound leaving my throat sounds menacing and dark. Her eyes flash in anger, and she pulls out her stake.

Silvia storms toward me, stake at the ready. When she reaches me again, she brings the stake down, but I slap it away and jump out of her way again.

"Tsk, tsk, hunter. Now, that wasn't very nice of you, was it?" I laugh, watching Silvia turn red with anger.

Silvia snarls as she pulls out a gun from the back of her waistband and points it at me. I narrow my eyes at the stupid girl before crossing my arms in front of my chest.

"Ahh, getting lazy now. I guess I should expect this from the newer generation of hunters. Your pathetic race is so predictable. You have forgotten the rules of engagement and your trade," I snarl at Silvia, baring my fangs in disgust.

"What do you know about rules of engagement and rules in general? Your kind destroys as they go, and you want to be mad that I brought a gun to a fang fight." Silvia laughs sardonically before pulling the trigger.

The bullet grazes my shoulder, and I barely register the pain. I lunge at the blonde huntress, my fangs bared.

Silvia squeals when I reach her, and I wrap my hand around her throat. She pushes the gun against my chest and pulls the trigger again. I brace for impact as I squeeze the air from her throat.

Click. Click.

I look down at the weapon against my chest. The gun jams and a feral smile stretches across my lips. Silvia fumbles with the gun before dropping it to the ground. She gasps for air as I lift her off the ground. Her feet kick in my direction as she claws at my hand around her throat. Her breath becomes ragged as I slowly increase the pressure, feeling the life leave her body.

This is going to be over quickly, but before the life leaves her eyes, she rears up and weakly kicks me in my chest as she gets a final burst of adrenaline. I pull her to my face and cock my head, bearing my fangs as I snarl at the girl. I will make sure my face is the last thing she will see. Staring into her eyes, I feel her go limp, her eyes roll back in her head, and her lips turn blue. Silvia's hands fall to her sides lifelessly.

I smirk before tossing her to the ground and turning to the rest of my team.

A horrendous scream fills the air, and I turn back to see that stupid friend of Little Deadly run toward his fallen partner, screaming her name over and over again. Good riddance to one more threatening hunter.

As I search for Little Deadly in the horde of the fight, my sense of satisfaction dwindles, and my smile fades.

I realize that the threat was more to Little Deadly than to me, and I am angered by the fact that I didn't kill the stupid girl for my kind but seemingly for that vixen.

Snarling, I take off running into the fight. I will not be made a fool.

CHAPTER TWELVE

DOMINICA

What the hell are Austen and Silvia discussing that makes her look at me every few minutes? I'm starting to lose my cool, and I'm about to get up and confront them when the cracking sound of an RPG being fired hits my ears. One moment, I'm feeling pissed, watching my best friend talking shit about me with his partner, and the next, all hell breaks loose.

I whip my gaze to the hunter with the weapon in his hand just before the loud boom of the missile hitting its target almost deafens me. I barely have time to react when the blast's shockwave hits us. I'm thrown backward. My ears ring, and my vision blurs momentarily before the sound of vampires hissing and fighting filters through.

I stumble to my feet, looking around frantically. I catch a glimpse of Austen as he helps Silvia up, and within seconds, they run into the fight as the vampires attack with no mercy.

Anger fills me, and I retrieve my daggers from the ground where they had fallen and run into the fray of the fight.

The fighters on both sides are relentless, killing without thinking twice.

I dodge blows and slashes as I make my way through. My heart beats a million miles per second, and I can't seem to slow it down. There are screaming and bone-crushing sounds from all around, and I stop to center myself. I can deal with chaos, but I don't feel like myself. With everything happening with Austen and the VHA, I don't know who has my back anymore. The bravado isn't present as much when you're alone. *Alone.* I hate that word and the feeling even more, but I've never felt it more than I do now.

Another scream wrenches me into the now, and I scan the fight only to spot a brute of a vampire with a vindictive smile on his bloody face. He stalks nearer to an unsuspecting hunter distracted by three vampires attacking her.

"Hey, asshole!" I call out and run in his direction, palming my daggers and tightening my grip. The handles cut into my hands, grounding me even more.

He snarls, pulling his lip up to bare his fangs as I near him. He's tall with broad shoulders and bulky muscles, built like a mountain. I quickly scan his body to assess the most accessible striking points that will bring him down to my level.

My attack points stand out like Christmas lights, and I connect with the first. I slide to the ground from my running position, going for the home run, and aim for the brute's Achilles tendon, slicing it as soon as I reach his heel.

The big guy roars out in pain as he drops to one knee. He looks at me over his shoulder, and I can see his face more clearly now. He has scars all over his face, and the emptiness in his eyes looks like black holes in space. It makes me shiver.

I get to my feet quickly and slice my blade across his back, making him arch backward with another bellowing scream. I don't hesitate, moving to his front and grabbing him behind the neck, pulling his head down, and bringing my knee up to his face.

When I hear bone cracking, I grab my stake from my boot and bring it down onto his back. But just before I drive the stake through my enemy's heart, a hand wraps around my wrist, halts my strike midair, and the other slams into my chest, sending me backward.

I stumble before righting myself. Furious, I look for the attacker only to look into those deep green eyes that haunt my dreams during the night and my thoughts during the day.

Xavier's taunting smile pulls at his lips as he steps between me and the brute. "Get out of here now," he tells the beast of a vampire, who, in turn, snarls his disdain but does as he's told.

"What the hell, X!"

Xavier laughs deviously and turns his head just as a devastating scream pierces the night. I whip my head in the direction of the soul-disturbing sound, and I almost drop to the ground in disbelief when I see Austen kneeling next to Silvia's lifeless body.

It feels like someone has punched me in the stomach as the air leaves my lungs. My eyes meet Xavier's again, and the satisfied smile on his face lets me know there is no mystery about who killed Silvia.

There is no coming back from this, and there is no chance I can play this cat-and-mouse game with Xavier anymore. He has to die, and he has to die *now.*

I find my second burst of energy and take off running toward Xavier. I swing once, twice, three times, but he dodges every blow effortlessly.

With every hit I try to land on Xavier, Austen's sobs ring in my ears, but I can't hit my target. I am too emotional, and it will be my downfall if I don't get a hold of myself. I didn't even like Silvia, but the finality of her death hits me more than I'd like to admit.

Xavier snickers and slaps me in the face. That bastard! I swing again, this time making contact with Xavier's rib cage. His breath escapes through his throat in a huff, and he doubles over. I pull back to swing again, but Austen comes barreling through the fight and tackles Xavier to the ground, pushing me out of the way.

I get to my feet quickly. Austen gets on top of Xavier and starts swinging his fists, connecting with Xavier's face with each blow. Xavier, in turn, lies on the ground laughing, taking every blow with ease. I'm frozen to the spot. My mind struggles to wrap around what I'm watching.

Xavier takes every hit. Something's wrong with this picture, and then my eye catches Xavier's hand rising slowly as his nails turn into claws. My eyes widen, and I run to where Austen still throws his weight into every punch, his fists bloody.

"*Austen!*" I try grabbing his arm, but he pulls out of my grip, using the momentum to land a punch to Xavier's rib cage.

"You bastard!" Austen screams violently, landing two more punches to Xavier's ribs. "She was my partner and my friend!"

In all this chaos, Xavier says nothing as he prepares to strike. I can't wait anymore; if I don't act now, I will lose Austen, too.

I wrap my arm around Austen's throat and lock him in a choke hold, pulling him off Xavier. My actions are going to bite me in the ass at the end of this, and Austen might never forgive me, but I have to save him.

Austen struggles in my hold, cursing at me. I tighten my grip, not wanting him to hurl himself at Xavier again.

"Get the hell out of here now!" I yell at Xavier, who is slowly getting to his feet; his face is already healed. He narrows his eyes and tilts his head, wiping the blood from his nose, watching me.

"I'll deal with you later," I grit out, still struggling to keep Austen from getting out of my hold.

Xavier doesn't take his piercing gaze off me but lets out a high-pitched whistle. The sound travels quickly through the night, and within seconds, the vampires evanesce. Xavier is the only one left. He doesn't move, his eyes still pinning me to the spot as Austen screams, clawing at my arm.

The sound of yelling hunters breaks his stare, and he looks behind him, then back at Austen, still cursing, then once again to me and evanesces, but not before giving me a knowing smile.

I'm so screwed.

When I know it's safe, I let go of Austen, stepping away from him, my hands in the air, and prepare myself for the onslaught of curses and maybe a fight coming my way.

Austen whirls around, glaring at me as he rubs his throat. The statement, "If looks could kill," can't be more accurate at this very moment.

"What the hell were you thinking, Dom?!" Austen screams at me, his voice delirious. "I was saving you from getting eaten by a deranged vampire," I state flatly, crossing my arms in front of my chest.

Austen pulls his lips into a flat line. Still glaring at me, he rubs his throat again before turning to the other hunters who are trying to revive Silvia with CPR.

"I'm sorry if you feel like I wasn't, but you didn't see the rest of the vampires close in on us, and I couldn't risk it—"

" 'Risk it'?" Austen asks, his voice low and full of hatred. " '*Risk it*'?" Austen lets out a laugh, but it sounds more like a sob before turning and wailing at me.

"You couldn't risk *what* exactly?" Austen's nostrils flare as he narrows his eyes. "The fact that I decided to place all my faith in someone other than you?!" He steps into my space. "I took a leap and told you how I felt, and you dismissed me like a damn stray dog, and now you want to tell me you couldn't *risk* it!"

"Austen, I—"

"Screw you, Dom. I just lost my partner, and you still think everything needs to revolve around you," Austen snaps before he walks away from me to where the team has gathered around Silvia's body.

I'm left with my mouth hanging open. Did he really just accuse me of being self-centered?

It's so far from the truth. Yeah, I didn't like Silvia, but I would never try to take away the fact that she faced that piece of shit alone.

Although Silvia was self-absorbed and annoying as hell, she was still brave and one hell of a hunter.

How can Austen even think I would care for my own feelings at a time like this? I mean, really? I have never been the kind of person who puts myself first, and now the one who is supposed to know that acts like he doesn't even know me.

Sighing, I lower my head and rub my temples. How am I going to explain this? No one is going to believe that what I did was purely to save my friend and not the vampire, especially not Austen.

Austen kneels next to Silvia, and he slowly takes her hand, tenderly even, as a heart-wrenching sob leaves his throat.

I can kill every last vampire on this planet with how I feel. I hate seeing my friend like this. I hate that he has to deal with losing a partner and someone so close.

I let out my breath slowly and make my way over to them. The rest of the group watches me closely, some frown while others look angry. *They can judge me however they like. I did what I had to.*

I reach out and place my hand on my friend's shoulder, trying to comfort Austen and let him feel that I will always be there, but he jumps to his feet and shoves me away. I stumble backward. "What the hell was that for?"

"Leave, Dom! I don't want you here. This is *your* fault," Austen seethes as he steps closer to me, pointing at Silvia. "*LEAVE!*"

CHAPTER THIRTEEN

DOMINICA

"Where the hell were you?!" Brian yells at me. "Since when do we protect the enemy, Dominica?"

I'm finding myself in Brian's office, which is packed with all the VHA hotshots. They aren't happy, and for some reason, they blame me for this mission's failure.

"I was right there, waiting for instructions, when some idiot fired off the biggest weapon he could get his hands on," I respond irritably. I look around the room again, searching for Austen. "Where is Austen? Why isn't he here being debriefed?"

Remember when I said you can see exactly when Brian will blow a gasket? Well, that's happening in three, two, one …

"AUSTEN IS IN THE MORGUE, MOURNING THE LOSS OF HIS PARTNER, WHO YOU CONVENIENTLY FORGOT ABOUT SO YOU COULD LEAVE YOUR TEAM—TO DO WHAT?"

What the hell is this idiot spewing? I didn't leave my team. I was ordered to leave.

"Where did you get your information, *boss*?" I am so bloody angry that tears sting my eyes. I force the last word through my clenched jaw.

"Oh, we debriefed the team already; since you weren't on the scene, we thought it best to do it here." Brian motions with his hand to the office and the members present. "This also counts as a hearing for going AWOL on your team when they needed you most. And don't get me started on the fact that you protected a damn bloodsucker." Brian fumes as his face turns purple.

Agnes rushes into the office, pushes a glass of water into Brian's hand, and makes him take one of his pills that help with high blood pressure.

I can't believe my damn ears. Who would tell these assholes I abandoned the team? I have never in my entire career left a man behind. I almost died numerous times, I might add, because of that, and now I'm being accused of being a deserter.

That's utter bullshit.

Brian swallows his pill and sits down in his chair, breathing heavily. My head is spinning. This must be some kind of joke.

"I don't understand. I have never deserted any of my teammates in my entire career, and you are going to sit there and accuse me of exactly that? Did we change timelines somehow?" I rake my hands through my hair.

Brian glares at me, but one of his superiors speaks up. "We have multiple witnesses telling the exact same story. Are *you* telling us that all of them are lying?"

"Well, if the damn shoe fits," I snap, glaring at the man on Brian's left. His suit is immaculate. He is among the few higher-ups who have never set foot in the field but feel entitled to judge me.

"Okay, let me ask you this then," Brian spits as he folds his hands on his stomach. "Did you or did you not choke the lead of the mission to get him off the vampire he was about to kill?"

My mouth falls open, and Brian's eyes light up. They twisted the truth to fit their lies, and anyone who knows me knows I'm not going to lie. I clench my jaw and ball my fists, deciding to keep quiet.

A dangerous smile stretches on Brian's face as I'm sure he sees the acknowledgment on mine. "Answer the question, Dominica."

"I did," I say simply. It's not going to matter why I did it. Every single person in this room had already decided my fate and had turned against me at the drop of a hat long before I even sat down.

Brian nods, looking satisfied. "You are being suspended until further notice and awaiting trial for the death of Silvia Horn. We will contact you with the details. Hand in your weapons."

"What?" My head spins again. "Suspended? Awaiting trial? For following orders?"

"You heard me," Brian says again. "Now, hand in your weapons, and don't make this more difficult on yourself."

My back goes rigid as two of the members of the VHA, whom they deem as enforcers, if you will, approach me to strip me of my weapons and to strip me of my dignity.

"Don't touch me," I snarl my warning, and both men stop dead in their tracks. It's good to know they still fear me. I take my stake from my boot and place it on the desk. Turning, I make my way to the door, but the two assholes block my way.

"The daggers, too, Dominica," Brian says nonchalantly.

"There is a snowball's chance in hell that I am giving you my ring daggers, Brian. These are private property, and you will have to take them off my dead body if you want them." I reach for the handles of *my* weapons—just in case.

"Are you threatening me, Miss Salvatore?" Brian rises from his desk slowly. Every eye in the room watches us intently. The tension can be cut with a butter knife. Brian was never able to beat me in any fight. He only challenges me to exert dominance in front of his peers, which he could never do with me.

"No, *Mr. Dickhead,* just a friendly warning," I state flatly before turning to the door again and walking up to the men blocking it. "Are you going to move on your own, or am *I* going to move you?"

I raise my brow, my hands still firmly wrapped around the handles of my daggers.

The two men blocking the door look at one another. To their credit, they abruptly move out of the way. I open the door and before I leave, say over my shoulder, "Gentlemen, I can't say it was a pleasure, but I *can* tell you all to go screw yourselves."

With that, I slam the door behind me and make my way out of the office and down to the parking lot. My heart is racing, and my world is spinning. I get in, slamming the door with so much force, I'm astounded that the window didn't crack. Tears stream down my face, and I scream, hitting the steering wheel over and over again.

I know better than to ignore my damn instincts, but I did it anyway, and now look where I find myself.

I've ignored my instinct only once before, and it ended badly for myself and the rest of my team. Tears keep running down my cheeks as I think of the last time I promised myself I would *never* ignore my instincts again.

"Dom! What the hell are we going to do now?" Jason yells over the noise of gunfire. Jason and I are the only ones left from an eight-man team. We were sent to the caves just outside the city, which are believed to have tunnels leading under the city's architecture. They—being the VHA—believe that's how the vampires can access the city without being seen.

Our mission was to infiltrate the cave system and kill as many of the vampires living there as possible. It sounded simple enough, and I was keen on going as soon as we could. But as the deadline for our departure neared, my gut screamed at me. I had a bad feeling the whole week, but I decided I was only nervous to go on the mission since it was the first one I would lead.

I've worked my ass off to be able to be seen as one of the best hunters in the business, and I wasn't going to let some scared feelings stand in my way.

"I don't know. Just give me a minute to think, will you?" I yell back at him as he dodges the bullets coming his way.

"We don't have time to think, Dom, so please get your ass into gear—" Jason grunts and slumps to the ground. "Shit," he groans.

"What the hell happened?"

Jason clutches his side, but the blood pools and runs past his fingers too quickly. Dammit!

"We got another one!" the vampires cheer.

We are in deep shit, and I can't seem to think my way out of this.

Replacing Jason's hands with my own on his wound, I apply pressure on his side, making him scream out in pain. "Breathe through the pain, okay? I'm going to get us out of here, I promise," I tell him quickly, but he looks warily at me.

We both know his wound is going to slow us down immensely, but I don't care. I am not going to lose another one of my team members. I can't, I just can't.

Think, Dom, think. *My brain is muddled by fear and uncertainty, and I draw a blank. The cave entrance is in the opposite direction, and we need a miracle to get past the horde of vampires that block our path. We can't go deeper into the caves since it's like a catacomb down here, so our only way out is the direction we came from. Shit, shit,* shit.

Jason's breathing becomes shallow, and his head drops. I push down on the wound a little harder, and he grunts but lifts his head. I'm not entirely sure if the sound that left my mouth was a relieved sigh or a sob.

"Dammit, Jason, stay awake." I look down at the pool of blood, and my heart sinks. We don't have any more time. We need to move. "I'm not going to lose you, too. Come on, get your ass up," I say as I duck my head underneath his arm and pull him up from the ground.

Jason isn't a small guy, and it's proving difficult to keep him up and walking without some of his help. I manage, though, and I move him out of the line of fire.

The moment we set foot in the caves, we were in over our heads. "Ill-equipped" was the understatement of the century. The horde we were dealing with went rogue. They raided an illegal weapons dealer's warehouse, deciding to fight the hunters with firepower instead of following the standard combat rules.

Just as I place Jason back down, a loud explosion blasts through the cave, and I cover his body with mine. Debris and rocks fly everywhere. The smoke cloud from the grenade is thick and suffocating. I cough violently as I try to cover my face with my shirt and try to do the same for Jason. His breathing is labored, and we need to move. Now.

I tap Jason's cheek. "Hey, stay awake. Come on, we're moving." I stay low for a few seconds more, straining my ears for any sounds coming from the direction of the cave entrance. It's eerily quiet, which means it's now or never.

I duck under Jason's arm again, and he groans in protest. "None of that. We need to move, and I need your help," I say, adjusting his weight. "This is our only shot at getting out of here alive. So please, just a little bit more, and you can rest when we get you to a hospital," I plead as I adjust Jason again so I can take more of his weight on me.

"I can't, Dom. Leave me; I'm done. Save yourself, please," Jason groans in agony, but I only clutch him harder as we start to move, and at first, I'm dragging his weight with me. "Don't give me that bullshit, Jason. Man up and push through," I command, and to my astonishment, he shifts some of his weight so he can move with me.

"Little Deadly! *Are you still breathing in there? Come on out to play!" My blood chills when Xavier's taunting voice rings through the cave and echoes off the concave walls.*

No. No. No!

Jason frowns as he looks down at me. I place my finger on my lips as we maneuver through the bodies and debris.

"Aww, come now! We never finished our fight in the desert. I know you are here; I can smell you. I will always smell you, especially after

I tasted you! How could I not? The taste of your blood lingers far longer than any other," Xavier calls out, almost singing. His voice grows dark at the last part of his speech, and I can practically hear his mouth watering.

My heart slams against my ribs like a bird trying to free itself from its cage. I swallow nervously and look at Jason.

He scowls at me, and I shake my head. I don't have time to explain, and no one knows what happened the first night I encountered this specific vampire. I tried my best to always cover the scar, and after a while, everyone thought I got it from one of my many battles.

The VHA hid the file and reports of that night very well, and I never really wanted anyone to know that a vampire got the chance to taste my blood and said vampire is still walking on this earth.

We move agonizingly slowly through the cave, using the lingering dust as cover. Just as we're about to lose hope of ever seeing the outside world, some light shines in, and I can see the cave entrance up ahead.

"Come on, almost there," I whisper as low as I can so Jason can still hear me, but another pair of ears hear me, too.

"There you are!" *Xavier's voice booms from a few feet behind us. "Come on, Little Deadly. Since when do you run from a fight?" Xavier laughs maliciously.*

The panic I forced down the entire time starts to rise in my chest. I don't have the strength or the time to fight Xavier.

If I don't get Jason out of this cave, he is going to die, and I know I won't be able to take on a strong vampire now. Shit. I am so screwed.

I force us to a stop, shifting my grip on Jason. I need a free hand. I pull the dagger from the sheath around my thigh and step backward, hiding us in the shadows of the cave wall.

"What are—" Jason starts, but I shoot him a glare, and he shuts his mouth.

I try to slow my racing heart with my breathing to not give away our position, but it's difficult since Jason can't control his labored breathing.

Dammit, I need to move fast and can't hesitate.

I can hear Xavier coming closer, taking his sweet time to instill more fear in us. It's working. My traitorous heart gallops like a prized stallion. I'm tired and injured; honestly, my control could use some … well, control.

Xavier laughs sardonically before saying, "Fee fi fo fum, I smell the blood of a huntress being dumb."

I roll my eyes and clench my jaw as I keep the retort forming on my tongue suppressed. Ugh, why do I indulge this asshole? *I should have killed him the first time I laid eyes on him.* And I actually need to follow through on that statement instead of just saying it every time, *I berate myself.*

The dust clears somewhat. Xavier is mere feet from us, and I brace myself as he sniffs the air. His head twists creepily to the side, and he slowly turns in my direction. Xavier's eyes darken as that evil smile spreads, fully showing his fangs.

Everything happens so fast. One second, I'm staring into those dark eyes across the cave, and the next, they are in my face, and Xavier wraps his hand around my throat.

I gasp, but he tightens his grip, restricting my throat, and I struggle to breathe. I fight against his hold and wrap my hand around his wrist, but I don't relinquish my grip on my dagger.

Xavier hisses, baring his teeth as he pulls my face to his. "Stupid bitch," he spits in my face. "Did you really think you could hide from me? With the blood your friend is losing, it's not difficult to smell you from across the city." He looks past me and reaches down, grabbing Jason's throat as well and lifting us into the air.

We're in so much shit. *My mind spins, and I fight to gather my thoughts like I struggle to pull air into my screaming lungs.*

"F-f," I try to force out.

Xavier's gaze falls on mine, and he turns his head, his ear to my mouth, mocking me as I try to stutter my words. "Speak up, Little Deadly."

Black spots appear in my vision, and I can't hear Jason's breathing anymore. My other hand still clutches my dagger like the lifeline it is.

I try to speak again, and Xavier turns his ear to me again, and at that moment, I drive my dagger into his neck. He roars as the silver-laced dagger slices through his flesh.

Xavier's grip on us loosens, and I pull the dagger from his neck and stab into his rib cage under his arm. He screams again and drops us completely, staggering back.

Jason falls to the ground with a thud. My heart sinks to my stomach. Shaking my head to clear my vision, I scramble toward Jason. He's not moving. I feel his neck for a pulse, and to my absolute horror, there is none.

"Shit." I slam my fist on the ground. Tears sting my eyes. My entire world crashes down around me, and I start to hyperventilate. How could I let this happen to my teammates? I was supposed to lead and protect them but failed them miserably. The tears threaten to spill past my lids, and my breathing becomes ragged.

The sound of Xavier snarling behind me pulls me out of my spiral. I look behind me as he staggers to his feet. His eyes are murderous. I force my entire being to get up and run. I hate leaving my men behind, but I can do nothing for them now. At least they are already dead and can't be tortured by the vampires or worse—be turned.

I slam my fist on the steering wheel again as everything spins out of control. I can't handle this. How did I let this happen? One moment, I'm at the top of my game and one of the best hunters in the world, and the next, the rug is pulled from under me.

I lost my best friend and my career in a matter of days. Gripping my steering wheel, I lower my head. What am I supposed to do now? I have no one to go to.

The only person I had left in my life who was like family was Austen. Who hates me now. The pressure on my chest is something I struggle with. I have to believe that Austen will forgive me for what happened and that we can move past this. If not, I don't know what the hell I am going to do.

The flashback is giving me a migraine with the added stress of the night's happenings. I told myself I wasn't going to think of that night ever again, but it looks like this night's shit is going into that same vault. If I can just keep it closed this time, I can rebuild my life and handle the shit show like a professional.

I sigh heavily. Well, there's no use in staying here any longer. I might just as well head home and wait for the VHA to call me so we can get it over with. It's my word against the whole team, so I don't see any hope of returning to the organization anytime soon, but I will end this chapter of my life with dignity.

I start my car and pull out of the VHA parking lot. As I drive by the front door, I see Austen staring at me. The look of betrayal on his face makes my heart break into a million pieces.

CHAPTER FOURTEEN

XAVIER

"I need to know what happened out there. *Now.*"

Am I imagining things here? Did Dominica really pull her friend off me? I'm sitting in Alex's office as Damion and the rest of the team are being debriefed. My attention is obviously not at the meeting, and it seems to go unnoticed for the first half.

"Xavier!" I look up at Alex's annoyed face. "Where the hell is your brain?" I shake my head slightly. "Sorry? What?" It's quiet, quieter than I remember, and I notice the room is empty except for Alex and me. I frown. Did I really zone out so much that I missed the entire meeting?

"What the hell happened tonight?" Alex asks expectantly, though his voice is still laced with some irritation.

"We got there as planned, but something went wrong," I say more to myself than to Alex as I stare at nothing in particular, trying to make sense of the last few hours. "Or we have a rat in our midst. I don't know, but I will definitely find out. We were well hidden, but the hunters knew exactly where we were. It doesn't make sense. Apart from you, the only people who knew about the exact details of our plan were the team."

Everything feels off. This whole event smells like a setup, and I can't understand the motive behind it.

I look into Alex's eyes, and for a split second, just mere milliseconds, I swear I see guilt. No, wait. I *am* imagining things now. It's screwing with my sanity.

"Are you sure you aren't overreacting, my friend? Maybe they just saw you since Damion told me he was insubordinate. It sounds like he changed his mind about you after you saved him from the Reaper," Alex says, looking impressed. His look darkens as he continues, "What I can't fathom is why the hell you let *her* go when you had the opportunity to kill her and be rid of her."

My mind is racing, and I struggle to keep up with Alex's words. I shake my head again, trying to focus. I need to get out of this compound. I need to clear my head and gather my thoughts.

"Uh." I close my eyes, rubbing them in frustration with the heels of my palms. "I couldn't. Before I could strike, her stupid friend came out of nowhere and took over the fight. I let him get a few shots in before driving my claws into his side to pierce his heart, but that bitch-ass Reaper pulled him off me," I say, opening my eyes. Confusion, my one and only emotion.

Alex is quiet for a moment as he listens. He rises from behind his desk and walks around it. I look up at him when he sits down on the edge of his desk, and the look on his face is weird. I can sense a wave of betrayal coming from Alex, but again, it doesn't make sense.

"This is difficult to say, Xavier, so please just listen," Alex says cautiously.

I scowl. Is he really chastising me? I am the one who got his people out of there alive and made sure there was one less hunter to worry about.

"I can already see that you aren't going to take this very well," Alex says reservedly.

"Take what well?"

"I've had a few complaints over the years, and rumors are making rounds, too, and it's picked up more in the last few months. The council and the rest of the vampire community are concerned," Alex says carefully.

Narrowing my eyes, I lean back in my chair, resting my elbows on the armrest and folding my hands on my stomach.

I don't speak, not wanting to give him more reason to doubt my resolve. After a few seconds of silence, I raise my brow, urging him to continue.

Alex clears his throat. "Some of the vampires have noticed that you faced off quite a few times with that bitch Reaper and not once tried to kill her. I'm just wondering if there is truth behind it, and *if* there is, why you didn't get rid of her?"

I huff out a sarcastic laugh. So, my suspicions are confirmed. There is someone or quite a few *someones* here that want to turn the king against me and remove me from the equation. Why else would anyone bring up something so trivial like this to their king? "What exactly do you want from me, Alex?"

"I talked with Riley while you were out, and he told me what happened on Halloween. It just seems odd that you two exchange banter, and then you don't even try to kill her after she killed two of my newlings. I get the part about taunting the enemy, but not following through baffles my mind."

"I still don't know what you want from me. Are you doubting my capabilities?" Alex takes a deep breath and lets it out slowly. "I'm starting to wonder if I can trust you, Xavier. It seems to me that the council has a point—"

"Oh really? Care to enlighten me on that point?" I interrupt as I get to my feet, the anger rising in me dangerously close to exploding.

Alex rises as well, and there, in his eyes, is the betrayal again. He clenches his jaw and turns toward the window, not saying a word.

"Spit it out, Alex," I grit out.

"They think you are the traitor, and I am beginning to wonder if there is truth there. Are you plotting against me? Are you really after my crown?" Alex spits as he turns to face me again, glaring.

A snarl pulls at my mouth as his words settle. Balling my fists, I turn my back on Alex, trying not to lose all semblance of control.

"I think that these so-called council members are poisoning your mind and turning you against the one being who has stood and fought by your side." My lip curls as my hostility grows. "I gave you that crown, remember?"

"You did, but what's keeping you from taking it now?" Alex growls. The trust between me and my centuries-old friend wanes with every question.

"I gave you my *word* that I would help you avenge Sofie and get your kingdom back to its former glory, and now you are insulting me by asking me these stupid questions," I force through my clenched jaw.

Alex looks me up and down, unconvinced at my words, making the fury burn even brighter in my chest. I can't believe my ears.

"You refuse to answer me about the Reaper and why you haven't killed her yet. You dodge the question, and that is alarming to me. When did you decide to go against your own kind?"

He really believes what they are saying about me. I can't defend the fact that I had multiple chances to take out Little Deadly or why I didn't tonight, and believe me, if I told anyone of my kind what I was doing and how I was feeling about this, they would consider me mad. *I* am starting to believe that I might be going crazy.

I've never in my entire existence heard of a vampire mocking a hunter just to get a rise out of it and *not* kill them just so the excitement and exhilaration of that rise could last a little longer.

How am I supposed to explain that to my friend, who is so easily swayed by the people trying to take the crown from him? I should have left the moment the shit hit the fan, but no, I had to be loyal and throw my word around like it was nothing. Now, I'm bound by it and can't leave until it's completed. *Dammit,* when am I going to learn that you can't trust anyone?

Exhaustion from the night hits me like a truck would a small car. I can't remember the last time I felt so weak from being tired. I look at Alex again, and the resolve mixed with bitterness in his eyes makes the tiredness feel so much worse.

"I can't do this now. I need to clear my head and decide what to do with what you said. I am considering stepping down as your adviser and confidant." I huff a sigh. "It seems that the centuries' worth of trust and friendship between us wasn't as strong as I thought it was," I tell Alex as I shake my head slowly, feeling the hurt of my friend's betrayal crash over me.

"Don't be unreasonable, Xavier. I am merely trying to find the underlying cause of some rumors and complaints. Maybe I lent my ears to the council, which wasn't such a good idea, but I need you by my side." Alex now tries to downplay the accusations.

"I'll talk to you when everything has calmed down a bit. I think we have said enough for tonight," I say tiredly.

I turn on my heel as Alex tries to apologize, but I don't listen as I walk out of his office, closing the door behind me. I need to get out of this hellhole. I've said it a few times, but the pull to get away from here is overwhelming.

I don't know where I'm going, but it won't be anywhere near here, I think to myself before evanescing.

CHAPTER FIFTEEN

DOMINICA

I haven't stopped crying, and the feeling is foreign to me. I don't cry, not since I became a hunter, anyway. It's useless and only leads to a migraine, but here I am, bawling my eyes out.

I still can't for the life of me understand what went wrong—or, let's say, when everything went wrong. I lost my only real friend since childhood, and now my career is in shambles.

When I got home from the VHA after they so maliciously threw me under the bus, it felt like my whole world was crashing down around me, and I had no one to talk to. So here I am, crying out all the pent-up feelings I pushed down for so long. My head throbs and it's never going to stop.

Austen lost his partner, and what did I do? I took away his chance to avenge Silvia. What the hell was I thinking?

Honestly, I could chastise myself as much as I wanted to, but I know I did the right thing. Austen was distracted and overrun by his emotions. If I hadn't stepped in when I had, he, too, would be dead now. I grab my phone from the coffee table and unlock it. Maybe if I just explain it like that to Austen, he will see reason.

I hastily open my messages, finding a text from Austen—sent about an hour ago. I sit upright and roughly wipe my tears from my face. *Why didn't I hear the message come through?*

My chest is tight as I stare at the unopened message, and for some stupid reason, I feel nervous about opening it.

What if he writes me off completely?

Panic rises in my chest as the thought threatens to manifest. *Stop it, Dom.* I close my eyes and take a few calming breaths. Dwelling on thoughts like that will only make the situation worse. I sigh as I click on the message.

AUSTEN: Dom, I'm sorry for yelling at you.

I need my friend. Will you please meet me in the schoolyard?

My heart is ten times lighter when I finish reading. I read it twice more just to make sure I'm not imagining Austen's words. I don't waste one more second to answer. I will do anything to be there for him and to show him that even though I don't romantically feel the same, he can still count on me otherwise.

I'll see you in thirty minutes.

I get up from the couch, wiping at my tear-stained face again. Shit, he can't see that I've been crying. I run to the bathroom and open the tap at the basin, letting the water run to a lukewarm temperature. I fill my hands and splash it over my face, hoping it will do the trick. I look at myself in the mirror, and I cringe a little. Well, it will have to do.

I'm still in the clothes from the mission, and they still have Silvia's blood on them, so I also go to get changed. When I pulled Austen from Xavier, the blood on his clothes got onto mine, and I didn't even notice until I got home. I don't want to remind Austen of what he lost tonight.

Grabbing my keys from the cupboard at the front door, I all but run out of my apartment.

I am the first at the schoolyard, so I sit at one of the picnic tables the kids use to eat lunch. The night air is chilly, but it's refreshing. It's quiet out tonight, sparking the all-too-familiar uncomfortable feeling that something is amiss. I'm so used to fighting and vampires snarling at me when I find myself here that the silence is unnerving.

"Dom," Austen calls from behind me. I look over my shoulder; a pang of sadness runs through me at the distraught look on his face.

"Hi," I greet softly as I get off the bench and stroll to Austen. "I'm so happy you want to talk. I've been racking my brain to find the right words, but I come up empty every time."

"Yeah, well, there isn't much you can say, is there? Silvia was murdered, and you stopped me from killing the bastard who did it," Austen says bitterly and shoves his hands in his pockets.

I tilt my head, frowning at his harsh tone, and it's like the wind is knocked out of me. "I did that to protect you. I couldn't just let Xavier kill you."

Austen's eyes widen when I let slip Xavier's name. He balls his fists at his sides as he watches me. I instantly regret naming the one vampire who haunts me every damn day.

"What did you say?" Austen sneers, visibly swallowing. "Since when do we know the enemy by name?" Austen's demeanor changes as he walks closer to me, almost menacingly. I frown as I look at him. His eyes are dark; try as he might, I can see storms brewing behind them. I put my hands up in front of me in surrender, stepping back as he advances.

Austen steps closer, and then I notice he's still fully dressed in his battle gear, his hair disheveled, and his face dirty from the blowback of the explosion. There are clear tracks where tears ran down his face from crying, and honestly, he looks a little crazy.

"I-I don't. I just heard it when one of the others said it tonight." Figuring that telling the truth now will only make matters worse, I decide to lie. One thing I swore I would never do, but here I am.

"Don't lie to me, Dom. I know you better than anyone else on this earth. You have always tried to best me in everything I do. And when I opened my heart to you, you didn't even try to consider it. You only have eyes for a certain kind, yeah? You can't seem to live without all the attention being on you, and when it's not, you make sure you get it back," Austen spits.

Austen's face is covered in an emotion that makes no sense. I frown as I walk closer to him, unsure if I heard him correctly. *What is he talking about? He's all over the place.* "What did you say?"

"You heard me, Dom. You are an attention whore!"

"Excuse me? How dare you?"

Austen laughs dryly as he pulls his sword from its sheath on his back. He starts pacing as I stand rooted to the spot.

"Where is this coming from?" My head is spinning. The look on his face starts to register as hate and loathing. Still, my mind struggles to process that emotion—especially toward me.

We have been friends for so long; I don't even remember a time when he wasn't part of my life.

Shit, we have literally taken bullets for one another. He's my confidant and the one I never would have thought could look at me like he is now.

"Really? Are you really that stupid? I am so tired of being in your shadow all the time. I fell for you like a lovesick *idiot,* and you discarded me like I was nothing. And then add the fact that I am out here every night doing more than what's expected of me." He stops pacing and glares at me. "All I hear is praise for *you,* and now I lost a partner, and it's all your fault."

The hatred in his eyes makes me reel. I stumble backward from the impact of the hate, and the action makes him laugh bitterly.

"I don't understand. That's not true, Austen, and you know it," I say, but my voice is barely a whisper as my brain still cannot comprehend his words.

"You need to stop insulting me, Dominica. Are you saying I'm delusional or something?" he yells now, raising his sword and pointing it at me.

Finally, my anger awakens as the haze from his lame accusations settles. Guess it only takes danger and the fact that he dares threaten me to make my anger soar. "You *are* delusional. Dammit, Austen!"

"I'm warning you, Dom. You better keep your bloody mouth shut like a good girl." There my mind goes, reeling again. What did he just say to me? My anger is reaching dangerous levels now, and I know for a bloody fact that if I don't walk away now, I will say something I'm going to regret.

"You know what, screw this. I am *not* wasting my time with this useless conversation. I will listen to you when you come to your senses," I say dismissively as I turn to walk away.

The chilly night air is no longer calming my dangerously flared temper.

I barely take two steps when an agonizing pain radiates from my side just below my rib cage. I look down, and my eyes widen in horror as I see Austen's blade protruding from my torso.

It feels like the whole universe has come to a stop. I let out a strained gasp, and a painful cry escapes my throat when he pulls the blade from my body.

I clutch at the wound as I slowly turn to face him. The blood runs through my fingers with no sign of stopping.

"Why?" I groan as I struggle to keep standing.

"Now nothing will stand in my way of being the best vampire hunter ever to walk this earth. Your reputation will be ruined after

I tell them how you died," Austen states dryly, inspecting the blood on his blade.

"You really think this pathetic wound is going to kill me? I made it through worse!" Who the hell am I kidding? It's bad, and I know it. I just can't afford to let Austen know it.

He laughs evilly and pulls a gun from the back of his pants. My eyes round in fear, and simultaneously, the anger rises in my chest again. What the hell is it with these people, even the vampires, that they don't adhere to the rules of engagement? I stand frozen for a few seconds, and the moment I hear the gun being cocked, my body comes back to life.

Austen aims it at my head and pulls the trigger. Not faltering once, not even hesitating. I duck as the bullet whizzes past my head, yelping from the pain in my side.

He screams angrily, and I push forward with my remaining strength, rushing him. I have to get the gun away from him. The coward has broken the first cardinal rule of our trade.

Guns are never allowed to be used for the simple fact that the bullet can pass through or past the target and hit a bystander.

I go to tackle him, but my strength fails me; he stops me, grabbing me from above, around my waist, my head pinned underneath his arm. Laughing mockingly, he brings his knee up and crushes it into my ribs, making me scream out in pain. He throws me to the ground and kicks me repeatedly anywhere he finds an opening.

Austen retreats only to catch his breath, looking down at me, broken on the ground.

"You fuck-king traitor," I choke out through short breaths of pain, spitting out the blood that's gathering in my mouth.

"I'm not the traitor, sweetheart. You think no one knows about that bloodsucker you *fight* but never *kill?*" He spits the last few words as he points the gun at me again.

"Austen, please. What the hell are you doing? You truly have lost your damn mind," I grit out as the pain becomes more than I can handle with the added weight of the betrayal from my best friend.

Austen's eyes become beast-like as he sneers at me. He aims the gun again and pulls the trigger. I don't have time to react as the shot makes my ears ring just before the bullet enters my shoulder.

Screaming from the close impact of the bullet, my body pulls into a ball involuntarily from the ever-loving pain.

A bellowing laughter rips through the night air as my once close friend aims the gun at me yet again.

His head whips to the side when sirens blare close to our location. I get to my feet as quickly as my body will allow. I need to get out of here, or I am going to die at my friend's hand, and he will indeed lie about how I died. I have no doubt about it. I stumble into the darkness of the trees surrounding the grounds. There is a hidden entrance to an alleyway behind the tree line. *If I can just slip through there, I will be fine,* I lie to myself.

An angry bellow vibrates over the sirens. Austen must have turned back and noticed my lack of presence.

I force my wrecked body to get to safety. My weakened state does nothing for the anger that's still burning red-hot in my chest. That bastard is going to get what's coming to him. Austen just made an enemy he never knew he could handle; if I survive this, he will be sorry.

"Shit," I mutter to myself as I lean against a dirty wall of one of the buildings in another abandoned alleyway in the city. I spit the blood from my mouth as I try to catch my breath. My stomach churns from the taste. I have somehow made it out of the schoolyard without Austen finding me, and I still don't really know how. *What the hell am I going to do?*

I can't go home; Austen will go looking for me there. At this point, I don't know who I can trust.

I groan as my vision starts to blur. I'm losing way too much blood. With the way my knees try to give out on me, I will not be able to make it much further anyway.

Tears run down my cheeks as I slide down the wall to the filthy alley floor, leaving a smear of blood as I go down. These tears have nothing to do with pain or sadness but everything to do with anger and hatred.

Lifting my top, I assess the damage the asshole has done to my side, and I cringe at the jagged edges of the wound. The bastard literally twisted the blade when he withdrew it from my body. The beating he let loose on me makes my body scream in agony every time I move, and it really shows the hate he's been building up, and that makes the hate in my heart manifest even more.

I feel my shoulder next, where the bullet entered. I breathe out a sigh of relief when I find it's a through and through, which is good. Not great, but now I don't need to worry about digging the bullet out.

My breathing is quick and uneven, and it hurts so damn much. *Shit* ... I close my eyes and lean against the wall, trying to keep my breathing even. It is getting more difficult, but I need to stay focused.

I can feel my strength seeping out with the blood I'm losing, and that makes panic want to rise in me, but I can't let it happen. Panic will only make it worse, so I try to find a focal point: some rats eating near the dumpster in the alley.

I look only at them, think only of them and not my injuries. Not the pain. Not the betrayal. And definitely not the shit show my life has turned into. I clench my jaw as my emotions get the better of me. It's not working. The agony of my side wound makes me whine miserably.

I will die here if I don't get up and out of the filth. I lift my hands from my side, and the blood keeps bubbling out of the wound. *Shit.* I need to find a place that is not on the VHA's radar. But where?

My brain is foggy and doesn't want to work correctly. Coughing, I laugh bitterly at the irony of my situation. Dominica Salvatore, the Reaper of the vampire world, perishes not because of the creatures she hunts but because of jealousy.

How the hell did I not see this coming? How did we get to be here? I've always had Austen's back, and I would have given my life for him at one point. It looks like I am not as great at reading people as I thought I was.

The breeze picks up, and my whole body trembles. The more I shake, the more it hurts, but I realize that I don't feel the cold, and my body shakes for an entirely different reason.

No, of course not. I roll my eyes. *Why will it be that easy?* My inner sarcastic voice doesn't help my situation.

I take another shaking breath, letting it out slowly. My body is shutting down, and I can feel it. I'm going into shock; I know I am losing blood fast, but I didn't think it was this fast. I can't stay here. I can't give up so easily.

Wincing from the pressure in my ribs again, I force myself to get up with the help of the concrete wall.

Come on, you have to move. You aren't some weak damsel in distress. You are strong and resilient. This is just a scratch.

The pep talk to myself is cringeworthy at best, but I really don't care. If it's the only thing making me get to my feet and move my ass to safety, I will do it again.

Pressing against the wound in my side, I force my feet to move. It's a slow and painful process, but I drag one foot before the other. The tears keep streaming down my face as I force my body forward, every muscle and nerve ending screaming in protest, but I force it aside and keep moving.

I must be making some progress, but my heart sinks in my boots when I look up. I haven't even moved a few feet, and as if my body hears precisely what I'm thinking, it gives in, and I slump to the ground.

Black spots appear in my vision once again. This is it.

I never feared anything really, but lying here *alone* dying, I realize that I don't want to die, and the fear envelops my mind as darkness envelops my senses.

CHAPTER SIXTEEN

DOMINICA

I'm jolted. The pain radiating through my body confuses me. My senses are in hyperdrive—or let's just say as much as they can be—when something or someone starts rummaging through my pockets.

I grunt, and the person gasps just as I open my eyes—with difficulty.

"Wha-what the hell are you doing?" I croak, and my throat feels like sandpaper when I swallow. I move to sit up but moan painfully as my body reminds me that it's not such a clever idea.

"I thought you were dead. You weren't breathing," a male voice squeaks. I frown, closing my eyes again. It's taking a lot of energy to keep them open and the black dots that are threatening my vision at bay.

"Did you even feel for a pulse before you thought it best to ransack my dead body?" My voice is weak and trembling, and it's pissing me off. I hate sounding weak.

Silence.

Wait, how am I still alive? I really thought I would not wake up again. I move my hands slowly to my side and touch the wound lightly. I almost hurl at the pain shooting through me. It feels like the bleeding has stopped, but how?

My confusion gets the better of me, and I am overwhelmed by the memories of what happened flooding my mind again.

I focus my thoughts on the present. However, I do not have the strength to fight the emotions associated with my betrayal.

I listen intently for any sound from the man who was here, but everything is still silent. Maybe he ran off.

"No, I suppose I didn't," he says, startling me as he shuffles closer. "I know I should have, but I am a desperate man and need money. This is the worst thing someone can do, but I didn't have any other choice."

He is crouching next to me with an odd look in his eyes. He looks torn, and I know why that is.

Like he said, he's desperate. So, what's he waiting for? I am helpless, lying here dying still.

"You are in awfully bad shape, miss. And I, um ... " He trails off, and I know exactly what he is thinking. I'm not going to make it, so he might as well just take what he needs and leave me to die.

I try to laugh at his pathetic face. This is why I have lost my faith in humanity, although I do everything possible to protect them from the danger lurking at night. Most of my kind have lost the ability to give a damn and go out of their way to help another.

The laugh comes out as a violent cough, and I try to curl into myself to stop the overwhelming amount of agony.

"Then what the hell are you waiting for? I can see it on your face. You already decided to take what you want—" Another coughing fit racks through my body, cutting my words off.

His hand touches my shoulder as the fit leaves my lungs, and I frown up at him, and tears run down my face again. This time, I *am* crying from the pain, and it's becoming unbearable.

"Something tells me you don't believe in kindness anymore, miss." His voice is almost a whisper, and it sounds nearly like he is talking more to himself than me.

"Hmm," I grunt, spitting out the blood pooling in my mouth again. "Something like that."

"Well, I don't have much left to give, but I can help you get to a hospital." I look up at the man and see him for the first time. He is worse for wear, but the fear and uncertainty I saw in his eyes just a few moments ago have changed into something else.

"Come on, miss, let's get you off this floor," he tells me as he works his arm under my neck and the other under my knees.

I cry out the moment he lifts me. "Please, no. Just leave me here. I can't take it anymore." I frown at my words. It doesn't sound like me, but the pain is getting the better of me.

"No, miss, you need a doctor, and I am not leaving you here."

"I can't go to a hospital," I groan as I clutch my side. "The guy who did this is going to look for me there," I plead as he carries me out of the alley. "Just take me to a gas station and get me some bandages so I can patch myself up."

"Miss, I don't—"

"Please, I'll be fine. I just need to get cleaned up, and then I can find my way to my doctor friend," I lie. For someone who hates lying, I'm becoming well-versed in it.

He narrows his eyes at me but doesn't say another word as he nods, carrying me out of the alley.

CHAPTER SEVENTEEN

XAVIER

I've been walking around the city for the better part of the night, and I must admit, it helps a little. The claustrophobia I felt in the compound seems so silly now, and now that I've had some time to think, I know I can't give up on Alex and his misguided ways.

I can't believe that after all this time of trying to avoid *precisely this,* I eventually find myself in the middle of conspiracies and conniving assholes. I don't have time for this, and I am not one for this kind of childish behavior. If I wanted to rule the vampire world, I would have taken the job centuries ago.

I turn left on Spruce Street and stroll up the walkway toward the highway, kicking a rock while I figure out how to work with Alex and the voices of non-reason at his back. A drop of water falls on my cheek; it's drizzling as I walk down the busy highway. The water is cool on my skin. I embrace every drop as it drenches my clothes. It washes away the weird night, and it makes me feel invigorated.

Okay, enough lollygagging. It's time to sort out the shit with Alex so I can move on. Hopefully, I will never have to deal with the VHA or any hunter, for that matter. I sigh as I change course, slowly making my way back to the compound.

Alex slams his fist through the wall while I tell him my ultimatums for staying and helping him after what happened.

I told him that for us to work together in this, I need him to not go behind my back and plan any more suicide missions against the VHA, not until I smoke out the rat among us.

Alex pulls his face in disgust and glares at me. "What makes you think there is a rat in my compound?"

I raise my brow as I cross my arms over my chest. I hate that there is little to no trust between us now, and I can't believe it happened right under my nose. I try to push down the frustration building in my chest once again.

"We are getting off topic here. You need to get a hold of yourself, Alex; we won't be able to take the VHA down if you do not get a grip," I tell him, unimpressed with his tantrum.

"Fine, but don't think this topic is resolved. Back to the bigger problem, then. How much more are we supposed to suffer at the hands of that bitch? I do not care how, but you need to take her out and do it now!" Alex yells, a vein throbbing in his neck.

I can't remember Alex ever acting this way. I don't care for his attitude, but I tolerate it, for now. He's lost, and like I said, the drive to do something, *anything*, just for the sake of doing it, is making him act irrationally.

As much as I want to eliminate Dominica Salvatore, she isn't our only problem. Yes, sure, removing her from the equation will make our lives much easier, but she's one of many flies in the pudding.

Something isn't sitting right with me, but I can't quite put my finger on it. The hatred in this room is centered solely on one hunter and not the entire Association.

I don't know; maybe I *am* imagining things, but it's been bugging me since the night we heard about the bombing, and it only solidifies after last night's events.

"Alex, I'll take her out, but our main problem is her entire Association. You know I'll get vengeance for Sofie and the rest of our kind, but we need to think bigger than just one person."

Alex, who had started pacing his office, whirls around to look at me, pure hatred and murder on his face.

"Are you trying to defend your little *toy*, Xavier? Are you having second thoughts about killing that woman?"

"No, Alex, but you seem to think that by taking her out, you are going to solve all our problems—"

"It sure as hell will solve them!" he yells at me now as he storms closer. I don't budge from my stance. He doesn't scare me, nor has he ever been able to intimidate me. Alex stops right in front of me, the tip of his nose almost touching mine. He breathes heavily through his clenched teeth, his fists are balled next to his sides, and his stare is venomous.

I roll my eyes at my friend. "What will it solve then, hmm? Please enlighten me on how killing Dominica Salvatore will solve our problems with the VHA?" I say, unexpectedly calm. "And for Pete's sake, Alex, back off. You don't scare me, and you never have. Don't you think we have enough drama between us for now?"

Alex glares at me for a few seconds before he ambles back to his desk, sighing heavily and pushing his hands through his hair.

"I don't know why I'm acting like this. I feel so out of control of my own body. It's like my emotions are going haywire, and that freaks me out," Alex mutters, his back still to me.

I let my hands fall to my sides as I stride over to him and place one hand reassuringly on his shoulder. Alex drops his head, and a sob shakes him as he cries.

I feel the sadness from him coursing through me. This is the first time he has really mourned his sister. He tried to keep it at bay until we got vengeance for Sofie's death, but it's been over a month, and he hasn't shown any form of remorse.

Alex's whole body shakes as the sadness crushes him, and he sinks to his knees. I follow him down, crouching at his back. Nothing I say will make this better; I can do nothing to take away his sorrow. I wish I could because then I could rid myself of these emotions that are threatening to destroy an empire that has withstood the changes of time.

I squeeze his shoulder and rise from the floor. I'm about to help him up when someone bangs urgently on the door. Alex whips his head toward the door and scowls at it like it's the door's fault he's sobbing like a baby, but then he looks pleadingly at me.

I huff as I nod, a silent answer that I will handle this. I walk to the door as the person on the other side bangs again. Now I'm bloody annoyed.

I rip open the door, and the guy on the other side glares at me when he sees it's not Alex but the one they are trying to get rid of. "What!" I bark at the council member, the same one who has been a thorn in my side since the first day I got here.

"Where is the king?" he says irritably.

"The king is indisposed at this time. What the hell do you want?"

"I don't answer to you, *traitor.* Now move so I can speak to the king," the council member says, moving to push past me, but I widen my stance and cross my arms over my chest, blocking his way.

"How dare you—"

"Lucien, just spit it out. Dammit!" Alex bellows as he rises from the floor. "Let him in, Xavier, it's fine. Thank you."

I let a malicious grin creep onto my face, and my eyes darken as I watch Lucien. I don't move for a few more seconds. I guess I'm doing a power play, and it's childish at best, but I can't help it. Stepping backward, I slowly turn to where Alex has taken up his seat behind his desk again, and I stop beside him.

Lucien doesn't like the move very much. He scowls at me, his lips paper-thin. *My* lips pull effortlessly into that same threatening grin, and I place my hand on the back of Alex's chair.

Lucien moves closer to the desk and starts to protest, but Alex holds up his hand, and Lucien cuts off from spewing bullshit. It only makes the grin on my lips spread into a beaming smile.

"What is it, Lucien?" Alex asks, sounding annoyed.

"We received word of the Reaper's location," Lucien says slowly, his eyes never leaving mine.

The asshole watches me for a reaction at the mention of Little Deadly, but my face doesn't move except for the very disturbing smile that's still lingering. It's starting to unnerve Lucien as his eyes jump between me and Alex.

"The Reaper was seen moving toward an alleyway and then again at a gas station near the middle of the city," Lucien says, now concentrating on Alex, unable to stare me down.

"Are you sure?" Alex asks, all his attention fixed on what Lucien is telling him. "Yes, sire, we have confirmed the sightings before bringing it to you." Alex leans back in his chair, huffing a relieved sigh. He turns to me and says, "Will you be able to take her out now?"

I lower my gaze to his and watch him before answering, "Yes, just give me a few soldiers, and we will make quick work of it."

Alex nods, turning to Lucien and ordering him to get it done. Lucien opens his mouth to protest again but shuts it just as quickly when Alex gives a rumbling growl. He nods and bows before making his way hastily out of the office.

When I walk to the front of his desk, Alex asks, "Are you sure you will be able to finish the job this time?"

I huff a sigh, pushing my hand through my hair. "Yes. Now, stop wasting my time. I have a hunter to kill," I declare and half smile as I turn to leave.

"Please don't disappoint me, Xavier. I need you to kill her. She can't live one more day." Alex sounds concerned, and I frown when I reach the door, looking at him over my shoulder.

"I will do my best."

CHAPTER EIGHTEEN

DOMINICA

"Miss, please, you need to get to a doctor. These wounds are severe, and I have limited knowledge on how to dress wounds and stop the bleeding," Joss tells me frantically as he holds gauze to my bleeding side while I cling to the basin in the dirty bathroom of the downtown gas station.

I groan as he pushes against my side. My breath comes in short, quick bursts as I fight to keep the nausea and dizziness from consuming me.

"You're doing g-great," I struggle to tell him. "W-we just need to slow the bleeding enough so I can show you how to bandage the wounds. Then I will go to my doctor friend to patch me up, okay?"

Joss looks at me unconvinced but keeps his grip on me as he pushes against the wounds harder.

We got the formalities out of the way when Joss carried me to the gas station. He told me how he got himself into a lot of trouble when he started gambling, and he couldn't pay the loan sharks anymore. He was forced to flee and leave his family behind as the people who were after him threatened them, and he couldn't see another way out.

I guess I should be glad that he thought of robbing me; otherwise, I don't think I would have been able to get myself here. Not that *here* is a whole lot better than where I was.

The bathroom is filthy as hell, and if I do manage to stop the bleeding, I run a very high risk of infection. I can't let myself think like this. I won't be able to get myself to safety if I keep lingering on what else could go wrong tonight.

"Miss, I beg you. Please, just let me take you—"

"For the last time, Joss, call me Dom." I grit my teeth as my hand slips, and Joss tightens his hold on me. "And I told you, I can't go to a hospital. The guy who did this has connections to all the emergency care facilities. I can't risk it. If he finds me, he will definitely finish the job." I grunt as I push against my shoulder.

"Who would do something like this? I mean, should I be worried for my own safety now?" I look up at the scrawny man holding me up, and my heart aches for him. He will definitely run in fear if I tell him what I do for a living, never mind that the person who was supposed to be my backup and friend for life did this out of spite and jealousy.

"If we can get me bandaged up quickly, we can go our separate ways. They will never know you helped me; I promise."

My answer is vague, and it doesn't seem to convince him, but he puts a smile on his face. "Thank you, I can't let my family suffer more than what I already put them through, and I get the sense that your business is more dangerous than what I ever got myself caught up in in the past."

I snort, and as soon as I do, I regret the small action immediately. I hunch over, grabbing my side when it feels like my ribs are caving in on themselves.

"Shit, Dom."

Joss adjusts his hold on me and keeps me up when my hand slips from the basin a second time, almost sinking to the floor.

"Argh, shit," I breathe out. "I'm fine. Just give me a minute." It takes me almost ten minutes to calm my breathing enough so I won't pass out, and with the help of Joss, I stand slowly so we can continue to try and stop the bleeding.

I still can't believe that this is my fate. To be honest, I never thought this would happen, and the fact that I did not see it coming pisses me off more than anything else. I try not to linger on the thoughts. It's useless and repetitive. No matter how unbelievable it is, I can't change what's happened.

I close my eyes and wait for the pain to become bearable, and when it does, I make a mental note to handle the hurt and anger accordingly.

I lift my shirt to see the bleeding has slowed. I smile a little, looking up at Joss only to find a look of absolute horror on his face. It catches me off guard, and I look down to see what he's staring at. My skin is covered in my blood, and the jagged gaping wound above my hip doesn't look good, not to mention the skin that's not bloody and cut up is black from where Austen's blows landed on me.

"It's not that bad, I promise. Will you please go get some more gauze from the shop and some more bandages and something to clean the wounds with?" I ask him, trying to sound calm and to get his attention away from my injuries.

Joss looks up at me, still horror-stricken, and his face pulls in disgust. He looks at me like something is wrong with me and then back at the hole in my side.

"What do you mean it's not that bad? Dammit, Dom. You have a gaping wound in your side, and it looks like you were run over by a car. You must have at least three broken ribs on that side, if not more, and you act like this is normal," he says exasperatedly as he points to my body.

I close my eyes in defeat, trying to hold back the tears that try to force their way out occasionally. "I know, okay, I know. But I can't think that way, or my body will shut down. And to be honest, this is something I'm used to, but I've never been injured this badly."

Joss just looks at me still trying to figure out if my answer is good enough. I sigh and almost curl from the pain again. *Shit, when will I learn that small, frustrating gestures aren't something I should do?*

"Don't ask, okay? Please, Joss, will you just help me get these cleaned up, and then you will never see me again," I plead with the man still holding me up.

After a few seconds, he huffs and nudges his head toward the toilet. I look over my shoulder and instantly want to throw up. This place hasn't been cleaned in a while, and now I have to sit on that filthy thing. I look back at Joss and give him a slight nod.

"Ready?" he asks me, knowing full well this is going to hurt like a bitch. "As I'll ever be, I suppose."

Joss picks me up again, and I grind my teeth, trying to suppress a scream; when he sets me down, I can hardly contain it, and a sob slips past my lips.

"I'm so sorry, Dom—"

I hold my finger up in the air, stopping him from blubbering, and clutch my side. "Not you, okay? Just go get the supplies, and if there is any form of a painkiller, I would not mind," I huff as I look up at him again, forcing a smile.

"I'll be right back, okay?"

"Mm-hm, I'll just be here."

A light tapping on my cheek wakes me, and I struggle to open my eyes. When I do, I look up at Joss's worried face, and I'm confused.

"Oh, thank goodness." Joss huffs a sigh of relief, lowering his head as he clutches my face.

"What happened?"

"I thought I lost you there for a moment. When I got back here, you were slumped against the wall. You passed out, and I couldn't wake you." Joss's worried tone sounds like it's climbing a few octaves the longer he speaks. "Are you okay?"

"Hmm, you don't maybe have water with you?" I say as I sit up painfully, and Joss takes his hands from my face.

"Yeah, I thought you might need some. Here." He grabs the bottle from the bag, opens it, and hands it to me.

My hands shake as I take it from him and slowly bring it to my mouth. I take a few sips and wince as the cold water runs down my split lip. Shit, I haven't even considered that my face might also look like my body. After taking two more sloppy sips from the water, I hand it back to Joss. "Could you get anything else?"

"The only cleaning stuff I could find was vodka, I don't know if it will work. I've seen in movies they use it, so I thought it could work now," Joss says hopefully.

I huff a laugh and wince again, *dammit.* It's not ideal, but it will surely help to numb some of the pain if I drink it.

"Don't always believe what you see in movies, Joss. Unfortunately, it won't really do the job, but for the time being, it can work. Come on, help me up so we can get this over with."

Joss purses his lips, takes the bottle of vodka from the bag, opens it, and sets it down beside me.

"I think you should stay seated. I can't help dress the wounds and keep you up." I huff my agreement and watch as he takes the gauze, bandages, and a hoodie from the bag and sets them on the now empty bag.

"This is going to sound pervy, but I need to remove your shirt to clean the wounds better. Will that be okay? I got you this for afterward," he says, picking up the hoodie from the floor.

Smiling weakly, I only nod, and he starts to help me slowly remove my shirt. I try not to cry out every time I move, but it proves difficult, and I can see that it bothers Joss.

It feels like forever until we get the torn fabric—of what used to be one of my favorite shirts—off my body, and Joss's eyes widen as the full view of my battered body is exposed.

"Fuck me," he breathes as his eyes roam over me, and he pushes his hand through his hair. "How the hell are you still alive?"

I close my eyes, feeling more vulnerable than I've ever felt in my life, and it's not because a stranger is seeing me semi-naked. It's because *I* don't even know how it is that I'm still breathing and the fact that, in my condition, I am not the strong hunter I've always thought I was. It humbles you a little when you aren't able to do the stuff you take for granted every day.

"Been asking myself that same question since I felt you rummaging through my pockets." I smile weakly.

Joss lowers his eyes as the shame washes over his face. I didn't mean to make him feel bad, dammit. "Hey, it's okay. I don't blame you. I'm glad you did that because who knows what would have happened if you didn't find me."

He smiles sadly but doesn't say anything further on the subject as he takes the bottle of vodka from the floor. "Do you want to take a sip of this before we start?"

"Yeah, maybe I should down the whole damn bottle, then I won't feel a thing," I groan as I take the bottle from him.

Joss shakes his head disapprovingly as I take three big gulps of the alcohol and it burns down my throat and stomach. My muscles relax somewhat after the third swig, and I hand the bottle back to him with a nod.

Joss doesn't hesitate as he takes the bottle and pushes me back gently to expose the wound on my side. He tips the bottle, and the liquid pours over my exposed flesh, making me scream. He moves to my shoulder next and dumps a generous amount on it.

I can't stop the tears from running down my cheeks as he goes back to the wound at my hip and repeats his motions.

"I'm so, so sorry, Dom. Shit." Joss keeps on apologizing every time I cry out. I hardly hear him through the throbbing of my blood in my head and the hammering of my heart as my body struggles to deal with the onslaught of pain on top of what it already feels.

I sway, and my vision blurs as everything turns dark.

I crack my eyes open when fabric is pulled down my body. I groan and try to sit up, but two gentle hands push me down.

"Hey, glad you decided to stay a little longer," Joss says, trying to sound lighthearted but failing miserably.

"Shit, I passed out again, didn't I?" I ask, my voice raspy. "Yeah, which was good, I think. I could actually clean out the wound at your side without causing you more pain. The one in your shoulder doesn't look too bad, but I think you have more than three broken ribs, and I suspect that your collarbone, where you got shot, is cracked if I look at the amount of bruising and swelling there. I'm no expert," Joss says as he gets up and throws away the bloody gauze and the empty bottle of vodka.

"Thank you," I whisper. "You will never know what this means to me. I hope I can repay you somehow."

"No need, Dom. You made me realize that I can do something and that I don't need to give up on myself. I mean, look at what you endured, and you are still fighting."

I'm happy he sees it like that because I am fighting with every ounce of my will not to just let go. I don't know where I will go from here or how I will manage. It feels like I want to just give up and let death take me.

I don't, though, and if it's for the simple reason of none other than the determined look on Joss's face, then that will be what I hold on to. If I can give hope to just one person to do better in life, I will take it.

"I'm happy you feel that way. Now, if you could just help me up, we can go our separate ways like I promised."

"Maybe I should make sure you get to your doctor friend. I don't like the thought of you being helpless and alone out there," Joss says as he washes his hands and dries them on his pants.

"Don't worry about me. I'm no damsel in distress. I can take care of myself." At that, Joss snorts, crosses his arms over his chest, and looks me up and down.

"Oh, go away. *This* does not count. If you knew what my job entails, you wouldn't be looking at me like that. Now, will you please help me up?"

Joss snorts again, rolling his eyes at me, but he takes my arm and helps me get up. I sway a little as my head spins, and Joss raises a brow as he watches me.

"I'll be fine, okay? I don't want anything to happen to you, so you need to go before me, so no one sees you leave with me," I tell him as I struggle to pull the hood of the hoodie over my head.

Joss slaps my hand lightly and takes it from me, pulling it over my head so my face is covered in darkness.

"Are you sure?"

"Yes, now go."

Joss hesitates for a few more seconds before he turns and walks to the door. He looks at me over his shoulder one more time before walking out of the washroom.

I gnash on my teeth as the pain makes my head spin and my stomach churn. I breathe through the nausea, steadying myself against the basin. I wait for another few minutes before slowly limping to the door.

It's proving more difficult to walk than I thought as I struggle to lift the leg with the wound on my side. I limp out of the washroom and inhale slowly as the night's cool air hits my nose.

Okay, time to think, Dom. What the hell am I going to do now? Maybe if I can get to a hotel and just rest for a bit, I can devise a plan to stay hidden until I'm healed enough to confront Austen and get my life back. It all feels like too much shit to handle now, and I can't cope; my brain is mush from the blood loss, and I can't think straight.

I groan from the ache in my ribs, but I halt the sound that comes from my chest as I hear a howling scream rip through the night. My hand instinctively goes to my thigh where my daggers are typically strapped, but I grab at thin air, and the realization hits me. I left them at home because I was too eager to get to my friend and fix things. My face pales as I hobble closer to where I heard the sound come from.

I round the corner of the washroom building, and there on the ground lies Joss, his throat ripped out and his body now surrounded by at least nine vampires. I cover my mouth with my hand, moving out of sight as a sob slips out.

No, no, no.

How could I have let this happen? Shit!

"What the hell is going on here? Why did you kill that human? We are here for the Reaper, not to draw attention to ourselves," one of the vampires says.

"We can smell that bitch on him, but he said he didn't know who we were talking about." I peek around the wall again, suppressing a groan. The vampires smell the air, and I know with the amount of blood on my clothes and the open wounds, they will pick up on my scent quickly.

I'm utterly defenseless, and I have nowhere to hide, not that I will be able to move fast enough anyway. I scan the ground for something I can use to defend myself, even if it is just to take out one before they kill me. I spot some broken metal pieces from a busted car or something lying by one of the dumpsters, and I force my body to move.

Just as I bend down to pick up a piece of metal, cackling laughter comes from behind me.

"Well, well, what do we have here?"

"It looks like we might have found ourselves an injured hunter by the smell of things. I have to say, *hunter*, your blood smells different from the normal ones. It makes my mouth water," the vampire taunts me, but I keep my head down, cradling my injured arm. I've hidden the metal piece between my bent arm and body as I straighten slowly.

I hear them sniff the air, and the moment they do, the air thickens as silence falls around me.

"Boys, I think we found ourselves the Reaper," one laughs maliciously as he walks closer to me.

I back away slowly as he advances on me. My back hits the wall behind me, and I cry out.

The vampires surround me and start to laugh menacingly as they walk closer.

"Go get him. We're on strict orders. Only he may kill her." *He? He, who?* I'm in so much trouble.

I watch in horror as one of the nine turns and walks out of sight. Maybe I can coax them into fighting me, and it'll be over before the others return.

"Shame, never knew you were so low on the food chain that you had to ask for permission to feed," I groan again as I taunt them, my voice weak and pathetic.

The one who ordered the other to leave hisses at me and storms forward, grabbing me around my throat.

I gasp and groan as his nails dig into the back of my neck. He lifts me and then slams my back into the wall. I cry out, and the vomit pushes up my throat, black spots appearing in my vision. I choke, and he slams me against the wall again, wringing out my cries of pain. Smiling every time.

I can't take much more of this assault. I pull the piece of metal from its hiding spot and drive it into the vampire's heart with the bit of strength I have left.

He howls out in pain and drops me to the ground. The other vampires rush to his side as two grab me by my arms and pull me up to my knees. I cough violently and taste blood on my tongue before it runs down my chin. My consciousness slips, and I fight to stay awake.

"What's going on here!" a voice booms from far off, but the vampire walks up before me. Why does that voice sound familiar?

My mind can't grasp what the hell is going on since it's trying its best to cope with my body screaming from the onslaught.

My head lolls. I don't have the strength to hold it up as I try to keep from passing out. After a few seconds, long, cold fingers grip my chin tightly, painfully, and wrench my head up as the other rips the hood off my head.

I try to focus on the face now mere inches from mine, growling, but it's pulled away too quickly. The vampire I stabbed roars as he pulls out the metal from his chest. He storms toward me and slaps me across the face with so much force my face rips out of the cold grip and the blood that pools in my mouth splatters on the wall next to us. My ears ring, and all my senses go numb.

"Let her go. Let's give the Reaper here a fighting chance," the familiar voice laughs, and I lift my head weakly when the recognition hits me.

Xavier ...

CHAPTER NINETEEN

XAVIER

Walking out of Alex's office, I feel somewhat defeated. I can't explain it, but something is stirring in the air, making me unnerved.

Three cars and nine other vampires wait outside when I leave the compound building. I inhale deeply and let my breath out in a huff.

It looks like tonight will be the end of another chapter in my life. That vixen was sure fun to play with, but for the sake of my kind and their king, I need to follow through this time.

Walking down the steps, one of the nine opens the back door of the middle car, and I get in. Two vampires follow, and the third gets into the driver's seat.

"Could you pinpoint exactly where she is?" I ask Damion, who is now seated next to me. "I think so, yes. Someone told one of our guys that he saw a man carry a woman into a gas station washroom."

"That doesn't sound like her. She's too independent to let anyone carry her anywhere," I state flatly as I look out the window.

Why does it feel like my chest is closing in on me?

"Yeah, you would know," Damion snorts, giving me a disapproving look.

"What was that?" I snarl, turning my glaring gaze on him. "I've heard the rumors. Sounds like you have a thing for this hunter," Damion snickers. "I will advise you to keep your mouth shut."

Damion eyes me but doesn't say another word. This is just great. Now, I *need* to kill her just to prove a point and to retain my reputation.

I huff out a sigh through my nose as I look out of the window again. It's gloomy tonight, and I wouldn't be outside if I could still feel the cold.

"How long ago did you receive the information?"

"About an hour ago, but our guy hasn't seen anyone leave, so we suspect they are still in there."

"You better not be wasting my time," I tell Damion irritably.

He gives me a sideways glance and purses his lips but says nothing else. Good, I'm in no mood to school this asshole again.

After about thirty minutes or so, the driver tells me that we have reached the gas station where they suspect the guy brought Little Deadly, and my heart beats a million miles per second. I'm not sure if it's excitement or horror, but it doesn't really matter. The faster we get this over with, the faster I can go back to my normal life.

All three cars pull up to the gas station at once, and just as I'm getting out of the vehicle, the washroom door opens, and a scrawny-looking man walks out. His clothes are covered in blood, and he looks like he has seen better days.

"Go and see if there are any hunters or anyone else who can cause trouble tonight. I will contact the spy and confirm if that guy," I point to the man leaving the washroom, "is the one he saw carrying the woman."

Damion glares at me again but orders the rest of the party to do as I commanded. I take out my phone and walk away from them, dialing the number Damion gave me earlier.

"Hello," the voice on the other end of the line greets, but he sounds nervous.

"Yes, this is Xavier. I've seen a man leave the location you gave us. I need you to describe what he looked like and the woman, if possible," I state flatly.

I listen as he describes the man I saw to a tee, but he struggles to describe the woman as he only caught a glimpse of her just before they entered the washroom. He told me the man had left the washroom after a while and returned with a bag of stuff. He's unsure what was in the bag as he didn't want to get too close to them and give himself away.

I sigh tiredly, not having gotten any real information from the guy. "Well, that was helpful," I tell him irritably, disconnecting the call before he can say any more.

I rub my hand over my face as the irritation and frustration make me want to scream when an actual blood-curdling scream comes from where I left the others.

"Shit," I breathe out as I walk back to the cars.

I don't have time to deal with this. Why can't these assholes just be discreet and not draw attention?

I'm about to pass the last car when the driver of my car comes running up to me, a gleeful smile plastered on his face.

"What!" I snap.

"I think we found her. This will be the easiest kill of your life," he laughs evilly. "What the hell are you on about?"

"Just come and see for yourself."

A growl slips past my lips, and I push my phone back into my pocket. I nod, waiting for him to show me where, and he turns and walks back to where he came from. I sigh again and follow him.

He's a few steps ahead when Damion howls out, and I quicken my step. I round the corner, and I'm stopped dead in my tracks.

"What's going on here?" I ask, walking closer and coming to a stop as I look at the person on their knees and Damion with a shard of metal sticking out of his chest.

The smell of blood overwhelms my senses, and I know exactly who the person on their knees is. That scent of her blood will always haunt me.

I inhale deeply, bending down and grabbing her chin with enough force that she would know her time is limited.

I lift her face and pull the hood from her head. I'm frozen to the spot when I look at her bruised and cut-up face. My eyes move slowly down her kneeling body, and fury builds in my chest that I haven't felt before when I see the amount of blood on her clothes.

Damion roars as he pulls the metal from his chest and storms over to where I still have Dominica's chin between my fingers. He slaps her so hard that her blood splatters over my arm and on the wall next to me.

I step back as she heaves and groans. "Let her go. Let's give the Reaper here a fighting chance." I force the laughter from my chest.

The two holding Little Deadly up let her go, and she slumps to the ground, crying out.

"Come on, Reaper. I don't have all day," I say darkly. Dominica clutches her side as she struggles to push herself up from the ground. Her foot slips, and she falls forward again.

"I don't have time for your games, Xavier," Damion spits, kicking Little Deadly as she tries to get up again.

She screams in agony and falls on her back before curling in on herself, whispering, "Just kill me and get it over with, please."

I frown. Are my ears deceiving me? Since when does this force of nature beg for death? It feels wrong somehow, and I find myself staring at her as the tears run down her face, blood covering her mouth, and now starting to seep into the hoodie she's wearing. The scent is so strong, but the smell of her pain overshadows the blood.

Damion lets out thunderous laughter, and the rest of the team joins him. He walks to her, crouching beside her and tilting his head menacingly. "Where is that fighting spirit, Reaper?"

Little Deadly coughs and looks up at Damion. With a bloody smile, she says, "I thought I'd make it easy for you guys since you never could beat me otherwise."

The vampires surrounding her growl viciously, and Damion grabs her around the throat, hoisting her up into the air. Little Deadly chokes as Damion increases the pressure around her throat.

"Come on, Xavier, kill her, or I will do it for you," Damion taunts as he shakes her.

Little Deadly's eyes fall on mine, and the pleading look behind them, coupled with pain and defeat, makes me react in a way I didn't think I would ever do.

Before any vampire can react, I rip their hearts from their chests and go for Damion next. His face pulls in horror, then changes to absolute rage when he sees what I just did, but before he can react, I grip around his trachea and pull it from his body.

He looks at me, horror-stricken, before letting go of Dominica, and she falls to the ground; he grabs his throat before falling to his knees in front of me.

Damion gurgles for a few seconds before toppling sideways as the life leaves his eyes. I look down at my bloody hands and clothing, knowing full well that I have just signed my own death warrant.

I roll my eyes, cursing through my teeth. I've done it now. Dropping the piece of Damion's throat, which I still held in my hand, I slowly make my way to where Dominica is trying to get up again.

I take my handkerchief from my pants pocket and wipe the blood from my hands before crouching beside her. She tries to move away from me but fails miserably.

"Stop moving, dammit," I tell her forcefully as I push on her shoulder so she can lie down, and she cries out again.

What the hell happened to her? I frown, gripping the hoodie and pulling it up to expose the side she's clutching. I spot a bandage around her middle, and it's stained red from the blood. I pull it away from the wound, and my anger doubles, my lip pulling up in a snarl.

"Who did this?" I ask darkly, my hands shaking, and I let go of the fabric.

"What are you w-waiting for," she sneers weakly.

"Oh, shut the hell up, Little Deadly. Tell me who?"

"None o-of y-your business," she says softly before her eyes close and she passes out.

Oh, for Pete's sake. What the hell am I going to do now? I stand and look around at the carnage I left, pushing my hand through my hair as my eyes fall on her face again.

"Look what you made me do," I mutter as if she could hear me.

I sigh heavily, bending down. I push one arm under the bend of her knees and the other behind her back, lifting her up and walking to one of the cars.

"Shit, this is surely going to bite me in the ass," I scold myself aloud as I lay her on the back seat and get into the driver's seat.

CHAPTER TWENTY

DOMINICA

I groan when I crack open my eyes. The darkness that consumes my vision alarms me more than I thought it ever could since there is no difference between my eyes being open or closed. What the hell is going on? I move to sit up but cry out from the pull on the wound on my side. Everything that's happened in the last twenty-four hours comes rushing back, making me much more confused.

I am lying in some sort of bed, and it's warm in the room. I touch my side where the wound is and drag my fingers lightly over the bandage, feeling stitches poking through. My injured arm is in a sling that's fastened around my neck, and I'm dressed in clean clothes, or that's what it feels like.

The sound of a throat being cleared comes from the corner of the room, making me jump, and I groan, clutching my side, breathing in through my nose.

"Glad to see your fighting spirit didn't betray you."

I stiffen as the voice drawls through every word, and my head spins. I remember seeing Xavier at the gas station, but the rest of the memory of him killing his comrades makes me feel like I can't trust it.

Why would he do that? And now I find myself in a room, patched up as it seems, with him not trying to kill me.

"Where the hell am I?" I ask, trying to sound angry, but it takes too much out of me and comes out in a whisper.

I hear the rustle of clothing as Xavier rises from wherever he is and the sound of his footsteps walking closer to me. The movement of curtains and the slight glow of the city lights flood into the room, and I can see some of my surroundings a little clearer now.

It's a spacious area with the bare minimum of furniture. There's a leather couch in the corner with a table next to it positioned so you can enjoy the view. The bed I am in could be big enough to fit a whole family of six. I suppress a snort. Why the hell does any one person need a bed this size?

I look around more and spot a tall mirror standing beside a dresser, and that's about it. I roll my eyes, thinking about the stupid myths of vampires not having a reflection. They do, but only when they want you to see them, so I guess there is some truth behind it. I look beside me, and there is only one nightstand for the bed. It also has basically nothing on it except for a bedside lamp and a glass of water. My mouth goes dry as I see the liquid, and I swallow loudly but don't dare move.

My head snaps to the window when Xavier breathes out a heavy sigh and walks around the bed toward me slowly, meticulously.

I follow his every movement, and when he comes to a stop at my side, I flinch and then scrunch up my face in pain as he reaches for the glass.

"Dammit, stop moving. Then it won't hurt so bad," he says irritably.

I glare at him as he takes the glass and brings it toward me. I turn my head away. A growl ripples in his chest. His lip pulls up, exposing his fangs, only for a brief second before he composes himself, which only makes me angrier.

"Don't you growl at me," I mutter, still glaring in his direction.

"Don't be so damn stubborn, then I won't growl at you. You are looking at this glass of water like it's your only lifeline, and I'm only trying to help you," Xavier growls again, still irritated.

He narrows his eyes at me when I turn my head away from him again as he brings the glass toward me for the second time.

Xavier huffs his breath out through his nose as his nostrils flare and his jaw ticks. "Fine, be stubborn then."

He slams the glass down on the nightstand, and water spills out of it. He turns and storms out of the room, slamming the door behind him.

I stare after the insufferable asshole. Nothing is making sense. Why the hell would he help me?

Pulling my face as I push on the bed so I can sit up, trying not to make a sound, I manage to move my butt backward inch by inch until I'm not lying flat on my back anymore. I shift my leg to the edge of the bed slowly, and I bite my tongue as the blinding pain courses through my body again.

I need to get out of here. I don't trust Xavier not to hand me over to his clan and to let it slip that he found me. My body vibrates from the fear of being unable to protect myself, sending a cold chill down my spine.

I move slowly and after a while of struggling and biting on my clenched fist to stop from crying out, I manage to stand.

I move toward the door agonizingly slowly, stopping every now and then to catch my breath and to listen for movement on the other side of the door.

Who am I kidding? It's a damn vampire, and they already make little to no sound at all. I'll just have to push through and hope he left so I can escape.

I reach for the door to open it, but it's wrenched open from the other side, making me yelp in surprise and jump back, instantly regretting the movement.

On the same note, my body really doesn't like the movement, and my knees give out. Before I have time to even think about falling, strong arms wrap around my body, effortlessly catching and picking me up.

"*Dammit, Little Deadly!* What the hell are you doing?" Xavier scolds me as he carries me back to the bed, lying me down carefully and sitting down next to me.

I'm so caught off guard that I reel, and I'm at a loss for words. He pulls my shirt up and curses under his breath.

"You pulled the stitches with your little endeavor there."

"What?"

"I said you pulled the stitches, and now you've ruined my handiwork of trying to stitch you up so it won't leave an ugly scar. You better hope you didn't do any more damage," he says softly. Anger brews behind his deep, intensified green eyes when he looks at me.

Xavier lets go of my shirt, rises from the bed, and walks to the door. He looks at me over his shoulder, lifts his brow, and says ominously, "Don't let me catch you out of that bed again, Little Deadly. You are in no shape to stand, never mind trying to escape."

Xavier's eyes glint with something I can't describe other than mischievous pleasure when I pull my face in disgust at his threat before he walks out of the door and returns moments later with what I can only assume is a stitch kit in one hand and saline solution in the other.

I snort, showing my disobedience as his eyes fall on me, but I lay my head back on the pillow, not having the strength to try anything.

I'll just have to wait for my body to heal a bit more before I try to escape again.

Xavier sets the stuff in his hands down on the bedside table and sits down next to me, lifting my shirt to expose the wound on my side.

He taps me lightly on my leg, indicating I must turn on my side. Still, I glare at him, not wanting to comply so easily. Xavier watches me for a few seconds, the muscle ticking in his jaw, but he only looks at me. After another few seconds of defiance, I turn.

Without a word, he pushes my top out of the way and gently pulls the plaster with the bandage off from my back where the sword entered. I can't believe the amount of gentleness he is showing while he's working on me.

Who the hell is this man?

I've only known mocking and evil coming from him, and now he rips the rug from under me with how gently he's handling me.

Don't get me wrong, the irritation and hatred still scream behind his eyes, but his actions tell a different story.

"It looks like you didn't pull any stitches here," he says softly, breaking the silence. I hear him pour some of the disinfecting solution into the bowl he brought with the rest of the supplies.

Xavier tears the gauze packet, takes a few pieces, dips them in the solution, and gently cleans the wound.

I hiss when the sting registers, but he cleans the wound like he heard nothing.

After cleaning the back and re-addressing the wound, he again taps my leg lightly and helps me turn onto my back.

I can say or do nothing other than stare at him. He repeats the process on the front of the wound. When he pulls off the bandage, he sighs, rolls his eyes, and shakes his head disapprovingly. "Lucky for you, it's only a couple of stitches."

The silence falls between us again since I don't know how to answer his statement, and he starts to clean the wound.

"Why?" I manage after a while, my voice no louder than a whisper, and at first, I think he didn't hear me. I frown, opening my mouth to repeat it, but he huffs.

"I heard you, Little Deadly. I just don't know how to answer you," he retorts. The frown on my face just deepens, and he looks up at me with a bored expression. "That dent on your forehead will stay there if you don't relax your face once in a while."

I huff irritably and groan instantly from the stupid movement, grabbing onto the covers and biting the inside of my cheek until I taste blood.

Big mistake on my part because Xavier freezes and looks up at me slowly, his eyes darkening. His Adam's apple bobs as he visibly swallows.

How is it that he is cleaning a wound with ripped stiches—that's bleeding, by the way—without even flinching, but I bite the inside of my cheek and he looks like a starved vampire.

"Blood from a fresh wound smells different than the blood from a wound that's been bleeding for a while. I don't know how to explain it, but I suggest you behave yourself. Otherwise, we are going to have a problem here," he tells me through his clenched jaw, turning his attention back to my side.

How the hell did he know what I was thinking? I swallow the blood in my mouth and clear my throat. He still hasn't answered me, and I need to know why.

"This is going to sting a little," Xavier states flatly.

I brace myself when he rests his hand with the needle and thread on my stomach and only nod before he starts to replace the stitches I had torn. It hurts, but not as much as what I've already been through, and besides, I've given myself stitches before.

"You're a tough one, Little Deadly. I'll give you that much," he says, and it sounds almost like there's admiration in his voice.

"Why the hell do you keep calling me that?" I grit my teeth, unable to contain my frustration with that nickname.

Xavier looks up at my frustrated expression and chuckles, not saying anything as he continues on my wound. Ten minutes later, he snips the last of the knotted thread and reaches over to grab some clean bandages and tape.

"Don't you worry your pretty little head about that now. You need rest, and I need to go do damage control since I decided to save your ass and put a target on mine, apparently."

"What the hell are you talking about?" I ask, now more confused than when I woke up. Looks like the memory of him killing his men was true.

"Rest. I won't ask you again."

"Don't tell me what to do, X," I scoff, but he's right. I struggle to keep my eyes open as he finishes with the bandage. Rising from the bed, he pulls my shirt down and covers me with the blanket.

"Such a stubborn hunter," he mocks, shaking his head as he turns to leave.

My eyes are heavy, and before I drift off to sleep, I see him watching me. I must have imagined the lingering look on his face, since that would be impossible, before he quietly leaves and shuts the door.

CHAPTER TWENTY-ONE

XAVIER

I drag my hand down my face, sighing heavily before walking into Alex's compound. They must have surely found the bodies by now, and for the life of me, I don't know what lie I'm going to tell that will sound even remotely believable.

Alex would have my head if he knew the truth: a vampire was harboring a hunter and nursing her to health. I would kill myself too, if I were in his position.

It sounds ridiculous, but the anger I felt when I saw her face—how bruised and battered and weak she looked—I couldn't think straight. Don't even get me started on how her body looked. It took me almost two hours to clean her up and dress her wounds.

I'm vibrating with pure rage, but I have to hide it. It's proving more difficult than I thought, especially when I found her trying to escape. My anger was briefly clouded by surprise. I couldn't believe she was standing on her own after losing that much blood.

That woman surprises me more than I've ever been surprised in my whole existence. It's unnerving, to say the least. I don't like being surprised.

My hatred for her did not outweigh the absolute need I felt to protect her at that moment. I can't even try to explain why. I'm fighting an internal battle. How can you hate someone so much but care for their well-being at the same time?

When the front door comes into view, I purse my lips and force myself forward. The compound is a large Italian-style villa on the outskirts of the city. It's two stories high and extends another three stories into the ground with connecting tunnels for daytime travel. Alex and Sofie were born in Italy, and when he built the villa, he wanted to incorporate everything that was modern when he was a child. I always thought it was a bit much, but I can't deny that it's beautiful.

I trudge up the steps and enter. The moment I do, gasps erupt, and I freeze in the doorway. Alex—who is at the end of the foyer, dressed in his battle gear, if you will, which is basically just black cargo pants, a button-down shirt with extra protection around his chest, and his favorite leather jacket that he only wears when fighting—whirls around. When his eyes fall on me, they widen in surprise, but he immediately narrows them as he walks toward me.

"Dammit, Xavier, where have you been?" Alex exclaims, gripping me in a bear hug. I hug him back, trying to force the enthusiasm that I'm happy to see him too.

"Trying to get back to the compound without being tracked," I lie, sounding drained. To be honest, I am drained, but not in the way he thinks.

"What happened? I nearly lost my mind when I saw the carnage, and there was no sign of you anywhere." Alex pulls away but grips my shoulders as he looks me up and down.

I didn't change my clothes for one reason and one reason only: Dominica's blood. I need him to see me looking disheveled and covered in her blood to make it look like I was in the fight of my life and that I narrowly escaped.

"I had that bitch in my grasp, Alex, and then Damion thought it best that he should get to kill her to get back in your good graces." I drop my gaze, shaking my head once and feigning guilt. "The rest of the men stood with him, and I had to fight them off, but then the VHA showed up. I had to kill Damion. He almost ripped my throat out. I'm sorry, Alex, I didn't have a choice," I lie through my teeth.

I do feel guilty, but not for the reasons I've stated. No, for the fact that I am shaming my own name by lying to Alex and the whole clan. For what? A woman who would kill me in a heartbeat. Who won't think twice about staking me when she has the chance? I could fix this by just telling Alex where to find her and giving him what he so desperately wants—revenge for Sofie.

But I don't. I can't seem to form the words to tell him the truth. I can't get my heart and head on the same page since my head is screaming for me to do the right thing and what a warrior is supposed to do, but my heart sees it as a betrayal.

What has Dominica Salvatore ever done to earn my trust? Then, the image of her pulling her friend off me flashes in my mind.

Ugh, shit!

"Xavier?" Alex asks, sounding concerned. Sounding is the operative word here because he doesn't look it. I shake my head lightly and look up at him, a frown pulling at my face as my heart and mind battle it out.

Alex mistakes my expression for the spoils of what happened last night and ushers me toward his office. I follow him, trying to look defeated and out of it.

"I'm so sorry, Alex. I wanted to get this over with, but all hell broke loose when the VHA showed up, so I had to leave. You must be very disappointed."

Alex closes the door to his office as I tell him my story. He sighs heavily, walks to his chair, and almost falls into it, gesturing for me to take a seat opposite him.

"I was on my way to look for you." Alex pauses. "It seems what you're telling me is true. I smelled the Reaper's blood on the scene when I got there last night, and I feared for your life," Alex says without missing a beat, and I narrow my eyes at him.

I catch myself and soften my face quickly. Alex can't have seen anything other than what was left behind since I know for a fact that the VHA wasn't there and that I was the one doing the killing.

Alex watches me for a few seconds before pulling open the top drawer of his desk, taking out pictures, and throwing them on the desk for me to look at. I keep calm, knowing he will pick up on any fluctuation in my heartbeat.

I take the pictures and look through them. I can't help but frown. Every photo shows evidence of a fight between the VHA and the vampires. The pictures show the carnage, some destroyed parts of the washroom building, and what you would expect to see when our two kinds clash.

Looking up, I find Alex staring at me, his elbows resting on the armrests of his chair and the tips of his fingers pushed together.

Okay, if nothing else, it only confirms my suspicions that there's a rat in the compound, and by the way Alex looks at me, I'm starting to wonder if it isn't him.

Don't be ridiculous. Why would Alex want to ruin his kind and sign up with the enemy? It doesn't make sense.

"I'm happy you are alive and unharmed, my friend." Alex smiles, but it doesn't reach his eyes. Within seconds, it disappears, and a blank, emotionless expression replaces it.

I almost scoff but catch myself. "Me, too."

I pace my bedroom floor, paging through one of my journals. I've been under close watch since I came back. Agitation crawls up my skin, and I can't seem to feel at ease.

It's been two bloody days, and I'm worried about … *No, I refuse to think that.* I stop pacing, look out my window, and down at the increased security patrolling the grounds.

I refuse to worry about that vixen in my apartment. Little Deadly will be able to look after herself. Huffing, I rake my hand through my hair. "Hopefully."

I can't worry about her now; being distracted will get me in more shit than I already am.

Alex absolved me of the killing of Damion, not that there wasn't heavy protesting coming from the council members and especially from that dickhead, Lucien.

He wants me locked up and executed for the death of their brethren, but Alex made it clear that nothing of the sort will take place, and if one of them even tries to make an attempt on my life, there will be hell to pay. So, naturally, they came to a compromise that I would be under house arrest for a few days since the council didn't trust me.

So much for being absolved, right? Feeling like a damn caged animal doesn't help my resolve, either. I've never been treated like this. It sets me off, and I want to rip someone's throat out. Three soft knocks sound on my bedroom door, and I wrench it open with a rather uninviting snarl on my face. "What!"

Tasha's eyes widen and she steps back quickly. I sigh angrily and roll my eyes at her as I step aside for her to enter my "cage." She hesitates for a few seconds, and when I turn my irritated gaze back on her, she hurries into the room.

"What do you want?" My words are harsher than I intended, and Tasha flinches as I slam the bedroom door shut behind her.

"I-I'm so sorry to bother you," she stutters as she fidgets with her fingers, not looking at me. "I am hoping there is something I could do for you?"

An irritated growl leaves my lips, and I push my hands roughly through my hair, not saying anything. It's not that I don't want to;

it's just that all words fail me. How can Tasha possibly do anything valuable for me?

Tasha throws her weight from one foot to the other as she waits a few more minutes and then looks up at me when I still haven't answered her. She's uncomfortable, and I'm trying not to let that action set me off. Since I can't get out and clear my head, I've been struggling to keep my anger at bay, and remaining calm gets more and more difficult with each passing second.

I know it's not just the fact that I'm being locked in here, for goodness knows why, but it's because of that damn woman in my house. The more I worry about her, the angrier I become … at myself.

Tasha catches my attention again when she fidgets with her shirt and looks around nervously. I have this nagging feeling that this could be a trap.

"Did Alex send you here as a spy?" I ask her eventually, advancing on her. Her eyes widen even further, and she steps back. With my senses being shot, I can't stop the malicious grin from creeping onto my face. Trust is fleeting in this damn compound, and I'll be damned if I let this human girl deceive me.

"N-no, no! I swear, I'm here on my own accord," she sputters under my intense glare. "Why would Alex or any council member, for that matter, allow you near me if they don't trust me?"

"The king asked for a volunteer blood source since you haven't fed in a while, and I said I would do it," she explains quickly.

I narrow my eyes, still advancing on her like prey. My muscles tense and release as I roll my shoulders in anticipation. "*Why?*"

Tasha swallows hard as she backs up until her ass hits my desk. She looks down. Big mistake. I pin her to the desk, and she yelps. "I-I just want to help—" Tasha gasps when I wrap my hand around her throat. A scream threatens to leave her, and I cover her mouth with my hand. The muffled cry doesn't travel very far as I sink my fangs into her neck. Losing all semblance of control is a real struggle.

The strong, lingering scent of Dominica's blood on my clothes makes me go crazy as I drink from Tasha. The poor girl doesn't know what hit her as my grip over her mouth gets harder, and I pin her against my body harshly with the other.

Tasha moans painfully and grips my biceps tightly. After a few seconds, her grip weakens. I need to let go of her now, or I will kill her. My hands shake, and I pry myself from her neck.

Stepping away, I let go, and she slumps to the ground. I place as much distance between us as the room will allow, turning my back to her. My fangs ache and my heart pounds, my breathing harsh as I push my hands into my hair, gripping it tightly.

I'm being overrun by bloodlust. It's a foreign sensation. I've never felt the absolute need to slaughter to feed as severely as I do now. Not to mention what Little Deadly's scent is doing to my self-preservation.

"Tasha," I warn with a low growl in my chest. "You need to leave, or you won't survive this time. I can't control my bloodlust."

"But I want to help … " Tasha argues weakly. I look at where I left her. Shit, we are going to have a problem.

Tasha is on her knees on the ground, clutching her neck. At first, I'm rooted to my spot, but I force myself to walk to her. Tasha is pale, and I move her hand from her neck. I roll my eyes and curse inwardly. The bite I left was brutal, and my fangs tore from her neck, and now it won't stop bleeding. There is so much fear on her face it sickens me.

"Dammit!"

I quickly bite into my wrist and push it against her mouth. She gasps, squirming, and tries meekly to move my wrist away, but I clasp the back of her neck with my other hand as I push my wrist harder into her mouth.

"*Drink!*" I bark in a demanding growl, and she swallows the blood pooling in her mouth immediately. *This is my own bloody doing.* Pressing my lips into a thin line, I shake my head once, cursing again.

There is a reason why vampires don't give our blood willingly to just anyone. A blood bond is something we don't take lightly and there are many ways for the bond to form.

Yes, that's how you turn someone, by draining them and then feeding them your blood, but the other reason is that the person gets linked to you for the rest of their existence or until the human dies.

Then there is a part that's lesser known, and it's that our blood can heal wounds completely if we don't want to turn someone. Vampires do it rarely since we don't want the bonded baggage, but I can use Tasha, so saving her seems like the logical option.

The worst part of all—which is even lesser known and borders on being a myth—is when you fall in love. You are bound for life, but then there's the fine print.

Meeting your soul's equal is so much worse. When you share blood with the one you love, something happens to your heart and mind that is inescapable. There's no taking it back, even if your partner dies. What's created between two beings in that moment can never be undone. It's a nexus, an everlasting bond, one that can kill you if and when your partner dies.

If it doesn't kill you, and this is the part every vampire fears, you are reduced to something much less than what a vampire once was. Not quite a vampire, not quite human, not entirely living. It's difficult to explain since I've only heard the legends and rumors of it. It's almost the same as the silent vow you make when giving your word. The consequences aren't as severe, though.

I swear, when you think of it, being the undead needs to come with a bloody manual since it's so much more complicated.

Tasha swallows twice more before I take my wrist from her mouth. Her cheeks glow, and her brown eyes look brighter as if a light was coming from within her—*damn vampire blood.*

She inhales deeply, closes her eyes, and smiles as the wounds on her neck heal.

I sit back on my heels, waiting for it, and after about five seconds, Tasha yelps, grabbing her neck again.

"Ow! What was that?" she asks, bewildered. "Did you just turn me?" The constant panic in her voice gives me a migraine. I really don't have the strength to deal with this.

I close my eyes and shake my head slowly as I huff out in defeat, rubbing at my temples. How do I keep getting myself deeper into these kinds of shit when all I'm trying to do is get out of it?

"No. I only healed you, but it comes with a price. Like everything else in this life," I state flatly but mutter the last bit under my breath.

Tasha gets up from the floor and walks to the mirror in the bathroom, gasping when she sees the red X on her neck just below her jaw, where her carotid artery is.

Tasha turns, shocked and clearly at a loss for words, as she just stares at me.

"You're still human. Unfortunately, when a vampire doesn't turn you, he marks you with his blood. We are linked now, which means … " I trail off as the defeat and tiredness hit me at once. "You belong to me now."

"I don't understand," she mutters, frowning.

"You are linked to me; no vampire may touch you. The downside is you will belong to me until your last breath."

"So, like your partner? Like a mate bond?" she breathes.

An involuntary snort leaves my mouth. *Humans,* I think to myself, rolling my eyes. "No, vampires don't have mate bonds per se; we have something entirely different. When I do get a partner and give her my heart and blood, I'm forever linked to her. She will be able to command me like I am her slave if that's what her heart desires, and when the time comes when she isn't in this world anymore, I will either die with her or be reduced to something much less than what I am now," I explain reluctantly. "So, my dear Tasha, as I just explained, there is a big bloody difference, and that's why I would never allow myself to love *anyone.* I'm not capable of it, anyway."

Tasha's shoulders sag somewhat as the severity of the situation sinks in. I can't help but feel sorry for her. It's almost like a prison sentence.

"Shit," she whispers, trailing her fingertips lightly over the X on her neck.

"Yes, shit is absolutely correct. Believe me, I like this just about as much as you do, but here we are. You wanted to help, and this is what it gets you. Becoming a fucked-up vampire's property."

She huffs a sigh as I speak, but the look on her face doesn't turn to terror like I thought it would. No, it turns to something like … determination.

Letting her hand drop to her side, she walks toward me, kneeling in front of me. She takes my hand and smiles up at me.

Oh crap. I know *that* look.

"I'll be by your side until … um, I'm not. I promise. I'll never betray you; maybe one day you will see that love isn't such a bad thing," she says, smiling shyly.

I pull my hand from hers and rise from the floor. It's times like these when I absolutely despise what my kind is capable of doing. Tasha acts like a drunk lovesick puppy. It fades after a few weeks but unnerves me more than anything else.

Once again, I walk to the opposite side of the room, as far from Tasha as I can get. I huff out a breath through my nose, now turning to her. "Listen, I need you to do something for me," I tell her quickly, ignoring the statement she made moments ago. "I need you to go to this address and see if the woman there needs help. You can't tell anyone where you're going or what you intend to do. Just make sure she is okay and has everything she needs, then come back here as soon as possible."

The frown on Tasha's face is one of confusion, but I catch a whiff of jealousy.

"Who is she?" Tasha rises and crosses her arms in front of her chest. "Dammit, girl. I do not have time to play these childish games—"

"But you said, just a couple of seconds ago, that you don't have anyone and can't love someone, and now you sound concerned for some woman," she interrupts me, pacing the floor. The angry look on her face makes me clamp my jaw shut as I try to suppress the snarl threatening to pull on my lips.

I quickly close the distance between us and grab her shoulders forcefully, shaking her once. "For Pete's sake, Tasha. Don't go looking for shit. Either you do as I ask or get the hell out."

Tasha's breathing picks up as she looks up at my now almost black gaze. I warned her not to be here, and now she's pushing buttons that should be left alone.

"I-I'm sorry, I didn't mean to … "

"Stop apologizing and just do what I asked. That's all I need from you now. When you return to the compound, come find me."

Tasha's eyes never leave mine as I tell her exactly where to go and what she should do when she gets there.

"The woman in the apartment is injured badly, but there is nothing wrong with her senses, so please be careful. Announce yourself when you enter."

I force my warning on her again. She needs to understand and not take what I tell her lightly. Dominica is like a wounded animal now; those are not the good kind to be around. I don't think she will harm a human, but she might act before realizing what's happening, and I can't afford to lose my only ally at this stage.

It's foolish to trust Tasha so unquestioningly, and I know the severity of her betrayal if she decides to go against me, but I can't think like that now.

The absolute need to ensure Little Deadly is okay is like an ache in my chest. This woman is driving me insane. I can't place the feelings unraveling inside me, and it concerns me that I can't just get rid of her.

Tasha still watches me with those fearful eyes, which makes me somewhat concerned for the poor girl. What the hell is going on with me?

I grit my teeth, and when Tasha gasps again, I realize my grip on her has tightened more than I intended. I loosen my grip on her shoulders slightly. She needs to fear me and not want to be near me. That's the only way I'll be able to make it through this stupid-ass mistake I made.

"Do you understand, Tasha?"

"No, not really. Who is in that apartment, and why are you sending me to someone that might kill me?"

"When she sees you are human, she won't harm you, that I can promise you. My kind unnerves her; believe me, she won't think twice about taking us out. That is why I told you to announce your presence, and it won't be a bad idea to let her know you are human."

"Xavier, please. I don't want to do this," Tasha says after a pause, tears threatening to run down her cheeks.

I sigh, closing my eyes momentarily before looking at her again. "You will be fine. I need you to do this for me."

Tasha lets out a shaky breath before she nods quickly and wipes the tears from her eyes. "Okay, I'll leave at dawn when everyone has settled in. I'll return as quickly as I can."

Pursing my lips, I give her a curt nod and let go of her shoulders. Tasha forces a smile, but I can sense her horror. She takes a deep breath before she leaves my room.

Rubbing the back of my neck roughly, I turn and walk to the window. *I need to get out of here.* I'm really starting to feel like a caged animal, and unlike Dominica's wounded animal theory, mine is a lot more dangerous the longer I stay here in these conditions.

My thoughts aren't even cold when my bedroom door bursts open, making me whirl around and snarl at the vampire standing in the doorway.

Great, here we go.

CHAPTER TWENTY-TWO

DOMINICA

Austen is at my throat, ripping and tearing, while Xavier and his cronies surround us, laughing. The laughter is dark and menacing. I've never heard anything like it. I try to push Austen away, but he only lifts his head. His mouth and his clothes are covered in my blood, and he gives me the most evil of feral grins. I try pushing again, but this time, my arms are spread wide, and I have Xavier and the rest of the vampires biting into my flesh …

I startle awake, my hands reaching for my daggers as my breathing comes in short breaths. I grunt, grabbing at my side, regretting the movement at once. The images are so vivid, I struggle to discern what's real and what's not.

My breathing is ragged and labored as I try to calm myself, my screams and the laughter from the vampires still ringing in my ears.

The bloody nightmare has my body covered in a cold sweat, and I'm confused about my surroundings before the memory of Xavier stitching me up comes to mind. It feels foreign, the angst and overwhelming need to get away, but when I remember how gently he worked on me, I struggle to get to the *actual* reality.

I relax into the pillow again, taking deep breaths to calm my heartbeat. I rub my face, pulling my hand down and letting it fall on the bed, staring at the ceiling. *Dammit!*

I look around the room again, the night sky stretching out before me when I look out the window. How long was I out?

Terror creeps up my spine and starts to crush my chest as the thought takes life, and it makes my stomach churn. How could I let myself fall asleep and be so vulnerable with a damn vampire near me? Not to even mention that it's not just any vampire, it's *Xavier.* Yeah, he teases and is playful, but there is nothing playful about his reputation and how he fights. The last time he had his hands on me, he nearly ripped my throat out.

I reach for my neck quickly, feeling for puncture marks but coming up short. I only feel the scar he left, and I trace it absent-mindedly. I know for a fact that Xavier can't resist my blood, so why did he now? He told me countless times that if he ever got his hands on me again, he would drain me dry since my blood was calling to him. What the hell does that even mean?

Come to think of it, I've never seen any vampire react to blood the way they do to mine. It's eerie, and it makes me utterly uncomfortable.

Maybe I'm just imagining it since a bloody vampire said it. I mean, really, blood is blood. A humorless chuckle bubbles from deep inside me, making me wince again.

Okay, weird train of thought. I rub my eyes with my uninjured hand when my stomach growls, and I huff out a moan. *Great, just what I need now.*

I groan as I push on the bed with my uninjured hand, feeling the stitches pull at my wounds. I need to take it slow, and I hate it. I shuffle backward as slowly as possible, trying not to move too much.

After what feels like hours of struggling to sit with my back against the wall, I rest my head back, closing my eyes briefly and catching my breath. Why does it always take so much energy out of you when you're injured?

Granted, I haven't ever been injured this badly before, and I still can't believe I survived.

The burning sensation from my wounds pulls my mind back to the present, and I lift my top. I strain to look down at my very ugly torso and notice the bandages are bloody from when Xavier last stitched me up, but the blood is dark, which means it's dried, and the dressing hasn't been changed recently. Could I really have been out so long?

I take in my bruised body, and the wave of anger coursing through me makes my stomach churn. Or is it the fact that I haven't eaten that makes me want to throw up? I'm not entirely sure.

I force my thoughts away from the images that pop up in my mind again from the nightmare and try to focus on the here and now.

Speaking of which, surely Xavier heard me waking up since it wasn't really graceful, so why hasn't he been in here? The thought that I don't know where the asshole is lingering and that he can pounce at any second adds to the uncomfortable feeling still hugging my chest.

With great difficulty, I manage to get off the bed and stand, gripping the bedpost for stability. I must have been out for a few days since I feel stronger than when I tried to escape. Not to the point where if I need to protect myself, I won't writhe in agony if I do, of course, but I don't feel like I want to pass out every few seconds.

I take a deep breath, which earns me one of those lovely stabbing pains in my ribs, before walking to the door agonizingly slowly. I strain my ears for any sounds coming from the other side, which there aren't, and carefully open the door.

The room beyond the threshold of the bedroom is eerily dark, with absolutely no light streaming in anywhere. I wait by the door, leaning on the doorframe, catching my breath so my eyes can adjust. When they do, I look at what I can now make out as an apartment. The living area and kitchen are in front of me. The style of the apartment is modern, with a black-and-white kitchen, chrome taps, and door handles. But, like the bedroom, it's lacking that homey feeling.

The living area has the same style: bare, with only a couple of couches and a coffee table in the middle. Two throw pillows are on the bigger couch, but that's about it.

I don't really know what I was expecting to see or find. I mean, I am in a vampire's residence and have nothing to compare it to. Vampires typically live together in a coven and not alone, so this is a first for me. Ignoring the obvious other firsts that I've experienced since the fight ...

I swallow hard. Damn this, I don't know what to think or how to feel anymore. My whole world has been ripped apart, and the pieces have scrambled so much that I'm not sure where they fit.

Pushing these unwanted feelings down so far that I don't have to deal with them now, I peer around the doorframe, making sure that there are no surprises lurking, and force my body to move toward the kitchen.

I'm starving, and my throat is so dry I can't think about anything besides water. I move around the couches blocking my way, and when I get to the basin, I don't even think twice as I bend over, open the tap, and drink straight from it.

Only when I have my fill do I let myself feel the pain screaming up my body. Damn this, hunters heal faster than a normal human. Why are my wounds still not even remotely better than what they were?

I hate feeling weak and being reliant on anything or anyone. Now I find myself in my enemy's apartment of all places, after my *friend* and *ally* betrayed me.

I close my eyes and let out a huff of laughter, ignoring my body's protest, as I lean with my ass against the basin. I couldn't even make this shit up if I wanted to. If you had told me a week ago where I would find myself now, I would have thought you crazy and driven mad by some sort of magic since no human could think up this kind of scenario.

Never mind the fact that my enemy killed his own team to save me. What the hell is that about? There must be some hidden agenda. Nothing else makes sense.

I feel flustered as the thoughts loop endlessly in my head, and I can't come up with a reasonable answer to explain whatever *this* is.

"Screw this," I force through my clenched jaw as I rub my temples.

My head is throbbing, and I don't have the energy to work this out in my mind, which means I need to ask Xavier what the hell he was thinking.

When he did this, he made life a hell of a lot harder for both of us, and clearly, he didn't think it through.

Don't get me wrong, I am thankful I am still breathing. What is getting to me is the fact that nothing is making sense, and with that, the image of Joss on the ground with his throat ripped out after I promised him that he would be okay surfaces. *Poor Joss.* Tears burn my eyes at the thought of Joss. What angers me even more is that I won't be able to make the shitheads pay since Xavier killed them already.

The more I think of that moment, the more my chest aches. I can't let this get to me. I've never let myself feel after a human life was snuffed out because it breaks me every time, killing off a part of my soul and making me dead inside.

Pinching the bridge of my nose, I huff out a sigh of frustration when keys rattle on the other side of the door just as someone pushes the key into the lock and turns it.

Shit, I'm unarmed and in plain view of the front door. I push myself away from the basin, looking around frantically for a knife or something to defend myself with when the door swings open. I stiffen as the light from the hallway spills into the still-dark apartment, and I squint. The light makes it difficult to see who is standing at the door, and I can only see the person's silhouette.

I drag my eyes away from the figure in the door, who seems to stop moving. I quickly scan the counter again, spot the block with a couple of butcher knives on the kitchen island, and force my body to move.

I moan in pain as I pull the strap of the sling over my neck to free my injured arm. Grabbing a knife, the burn on my side from the stitches pulling makes me bite the inside of my cheek hard enough to taste blood.

"Who the hell are you, and what do you want?" I ask with sheer rage, but my voice betrays me as it comes out shaking and weak.

Nice one, Dom.

I point the knife at the person still standing frozen in the doorway. The figure stays silent, and after a while, my hand and arm start to tremble from the weight of the knife. It wasn't the best idea to hold the weapon on my injured shoulder's side, but I don't have a choice; it's my dominant hand, and I can't take any chances. Not now.

Clenching my jaw, I force every ounce of my being to keep the knife up and grasp my side in pain, feeling the slight tear of the stitches when I raise the knife higher.

The person gulps audibly as their hands shoot up in surrender. "My name is Tasha. I'm human … " the figure says, her voice high.

The girl trails off, but I only narrow my eyes at her, not saying anything since I know my voice will betray my pain if I do.

"I'm going to step into the apartment and close the door, okay?" The girl waits for my answer for a few more seconds, but when she doesn't get one, she walks forward slowly and pushes the door shut with the heel of her foot.

The moment the door shuts, the room is shrouded in blackness, and my heart slams against my chest. The darkness overwhelms my senses, and I want to kick my own ass for not thinking it through.

The absolute terror running through me unnerves me so much that my body trembles. To my surprise, there is no rustling of clothes, no echoing of footsteps as the girl stands entirely still, and I frown when my eyes adjust to the darkness again.

"You didn't answer my question," I mutter, my hand shaking as the weight of the knife becomes heavier.

"I did, but I think I should be clearer. Xavier sent me to check on you. Unfortunately, he won't be able to come himself since they are keeping him under house arrest," Tasha says with a shaky voice.

The sneer on her face throws me as she speaks, but the moment her eyes fall to mine again, they shift, and I can actually see her pupils dilate. She talks about Xavier as if he is warmth itself, but when she looks at me, it's the total opposite.

Is this girl afraid?

Of me?

I will revisit her statement about Xavier later when I can control my limbs properly and know exactly what her agenda is. I look from her to the knife, now dangerously close to falling. I lower my hand just as my legs start to tremble, and I curse out loud. I sink to the floor with a painful cry.

The girl, Tasha, rushes to my side just as I pull my hand away from my side, covered in blood.

"Fuck," is what I try to say, but what comes out is a painful "F-fllk."

"Shit, are you okay?" she squeaks when she sees the blood.

"Hmm," is all I can manage. My vision blurs, and my consciousness is about to make a hasty exit.

Tasha jumps to her feet, looking around frantically. "Where the hell is the light switch in this damn place?"

"Don't know," I breathe out, returning my hand to my bleeding side.

Tasha runs to the door, feeling along the wall. With a click, I'm momentarily blinded again when she finds the switch and turns the light on.

"I'm so sorry. I should have told you to close your eyes. Come let me help you—" Tasha extends her hand to me, but I pull my arm out of her reach, moaning as the agony screams in my shoulder. "Please, I won't hurt you. Let me help you."

I give her a sideways glance, unsure if I can trust her. To be honest, I don't think I would be able to trust anybody ever again, but I can't get up on my own. "Fine," I force through my clenched jaw.

Tasha huffs a sigh of relief and smiles warily at me. "I am sure this will hurt, but I will try to do it as gently as possible, okay?"

"No, just do it so we can get to the couch." I groan, and my head lolls as my vision blurs again.

"As you wish." Tasha grips my arm and pulls it over her neck; her other hand wraps around my back and grips my broken ribs, and I cry out again. She doesn't falter or hesitate when the cry leaves my mouth and grips my wrist around her neck, lifting me off the floor.

I struggle to get my feet under me, but after a few seconds, I'm up, and we are walking to the couch.

"I think I've pulled the stitches again, and I need to stop the bleeding so I can clean the wounds. I don't know where the supplies are, though," I tell Tasha as we reach the couch, and she helps me to lie down.

"I'll see what I can find."

I try to concentrate on my breathing. So much for feeling stronger, since now the little bit of energy I did have is dissipating. I haven't eaten in, I don't even know how long, and with the constant blood loss, my body struggles to heal. Reality hits me, and I know it's my fault for not healing faster. Looks like *this* is where stubbornness gets me.

Tasha rummages through the apartment, and after a while, I hear her yell out, "Aha," before rushing back into my line of sight. "Okay, I've found some," she says triumphantly.

"I've heard so, yeah," I scoff.

Tasha narrows her eyes at me. "I've also gotten the sling for your arm, so we can rest your arm in it again like it's supposed to be."

I let out a defeated sigh and only nod in agreement. Tasha sets out the gauze and cleaning solution. "Okay, so I assume your arm is injured, hence the sling. Are you injured anywhere else?" Tasha asks hesitantly.

"Right side and shoulder," I say, breathing harshly. Tasha nods and helps me turn on my uninjured side, then pulls up my top to look at the now bloody bandage. The absolutely devastating feeling of depending on a stranger does *not* sit well with me. I want to scream and lash out, but for obvious reasons, I bite my tongue and let her do what she needs to. Tasha examines the wound in front and then at my back, pulling in a quick hiss of air through her teeth as her eyes roam over my bruised body. Moving to my shoulder next, she lightly pulls the top down from my neck, trying to look at the bandage there.

"We need to get your arm out of the top. I was hoping not to move you a lot, but everything is bleeding," she says as she touches the wet part of the fabric over my shoulder.

I sigh again, not really wanting to expose my naked body to just about anyone; yet again, I don't really have a choice, do I? It's becoming a regular occurrence.

Tasha kneels next to me and, with as much gentleness as possible, helps me get out of the bloody top, pulling a face like she's the one in pain. When I eventually manage to pull my arm from the fabric, she gets up and walks to the bedroom, only to return a minute or so later with a blanket, handing it to me.

This is just terrific, I think to myself, rolling my eyes as Tasha removes the bandages and cleans the wounds.

CHAPTER TWENTY-THREE

DOMINICA

Being propped up by pillows and cared for still irritates the living daylights out of me. But to avoid putting my body through another round of stitching and to give it time to heal, I bite my tongue and let Tasha make me something to eat.

She cleaned my wounds thoroughly and with so much gentleness it surprised me. We were silent the whole time. When Tasha covered each wound with a new bandage, she got up and took one of Xavier's shirts from the closet.

I pursed my lips and raised my eyebrows when she handed me the piece of fabric, a distasteful scowl on my face.

"You need a clean shirt, and this is all there is. So, am I helping you get into it, or are you going to do the naked thing?" Tasha said, a hint of amusement in her voice.

What the hell is her problem? Does she think this is funny? There is no joke in refusing to wear my enemy's clothes.

I rolled my eyes and only gave her a curt nod. Tasha tilted her head, frowning, waiting for me to answer her.

"Fine," I snapped irritably.

Tasha huffed a laugh and made her way over to me, helping me get dressed.

The smell of Xavier is overwhelmingly strong, and what pisses me off is that the scent on the shirt unnervingly makes me feel at ease.

"Can I get you anything else?" she asked, but my stomach growled so loudly that it made her stop mid-sentence and raise her brow. "Seems like you haven't eaten."

That was an understatement, but I still didn't answer her, so she helped me turn onto my back, propping pillows behind me, and then went to the kitchen to get me something to eat.

So this is where I find myself: lying on a damn comfortable couch, waiting for something to eat, which is being prepared by somebody I hardly know. I was surprised to hear that the fridge was fully stocked, which means Xavier had to have gotten food when I was out cold since vampires don't eat, which is obvious. The thought of him making sure there is food for me is hard to swallow.

I mean, what the hell?

My senses are so screwed. I would never allow anyone with connections to a vampire to prepare food for me, and this girl has strong connections with a particular one.

"Here you go." Tasha sets the plate with a grilled cheese sandwich down on my stomach.

When the sandwich's aroma hits my nose, I can practically feel my mouth water, but my instincts are screaming at me. I look from the plate to Tasha and narrow my eyes at her, still keeping quiet.

"Is something wrong? Don't you like grilled cheese?"

"I do, but I don't trust that you haven't poisoned the sandwich or something," I tell her bluntly.

Tasha's eyes widen in surprise as she looks at me bewildered. "I would never."

"How would I know that? I don't know you, and what's worse is that you work with Xavier even though you state that you are human."

She narrows her eyes at me now. I've offended her, but I really don't care. "Don't you think if I wanted to harm or kill you, I would have done it when you were on the ground or when you were lying with your back to me when I cleaned your wounds?" Tasha says, her voice getting louder as she speaks.

I frown. That's a valid point, but it could be false pretenses. *Ugh, what the hell is wrong with me?* My gut is telling me that she's telling the truth, but the extreme reality of the fact that the one person I trusted the most turned against me doesn't help much. It's screwing with my senses, and it's a dangerous thing if I'm not able to trust my gut anymore.

I sigh, closing my eyes and resting my head on the pillows. The silence in the room is deafening. I should say something but can't bring myself to do it.

When I eventually open my eyes, Tasha sits opposite me and watches me intently. "Look, I don't know what happened to you, and I can see that you are finding it difficult to trust, but I would never hurt someone. I know what it's like to be scared and unable to protect yourself … " Tasha trails off, her eyes trailing my face and then my body before they fall to her fidgeting hands. "The only conclusion I can come up with is that you were abused by the looks of your bruises, and that sucks."

I huff out a breath in annoyance. This girl is *so* barking up the wrong tree. "How long have you known Xavier?"

"Um, not too long, but I sort of owe him my life. He saved me from … " Tasha trails off again. Her eyes widen momentarily as if she said something she wasn't supposed to.

I raise my brows, waiting for her to finish, but she smiles apologetically and changes the subject immediately.

"If you need someone to talk to, I'm willing to listen. I know we've just met, but like I said, I know a thing about being abused and feeling like you don't have power over what's happened."

I let out a snort, turning my head away from her. Not because I am ashamed that she thinks I was abused but that she isn't wrong about feeling like I don't have control. And that has always been one of my weaknesses. I *never* let anything be *out* of my control.

"Thanks for the concern, but I wasn't abused."

Tasha's frown deepens when she narrows her eyes, and recognition hits. I don't think she recognizes *me,* but she can put two and two together.

"You don't know who I am, do you?" I ask flatly.

Frankly, I'm a little relieved she doesn't recognize me since the humans who do, the ones who know what lurks in the night, usually look at me with so much fear, like *I'm* the creature that will snuff out their lives, scared that I will kill their vampire "friends." Others try to challenge me to show me they can do my job better than I ever could.

It's irritating as hell on both ends. I don't care for that attitude, so for Tasha to think that I was some helpless woman who was abused and was saved by a kind and loving vampire—I just know that's what she's thinking—agitates me.

Not so much the part that I was abused, since there is so much pity in her eyes when she looks at me, but more the part of being saved by the vampire.

See, just as I thought, Xavier is making my life even more difficult than it already is and needs to be.

If it ever comes out that I was saved by the vampire world's renowned hunter-slayer, my reputation, the little I have left, will be completely ruined.

"I'm sorry if I offended you. I just assumed that you are a victim of abuse," she says slowly, trying to keep whatever it is she's feeling out of her voice.

"Listen, like I said, I do appreciate the concern, but I wasn't abused."

"I don't know what to make of what you are telling me, but I don't like where my conclusions are leading me. Are you insinuating that Xavier did this?" Tasha gestures up and down my body with her hand.

"No, I'm not. Is it really upsetting to think Xavier might have done this?" I ask, avoiding her question somewhat. It seems the best idea for now, but when I speak Xavier's name, it almost comes out as a snarl.

"Something tells me you aren't a fan of him, but what you fail to understand is that he is the kindest vampire I've ever met—"

A snort slips out before I can stop it. I clear my throat and just stare at her dumbfounded. Tasha clearly doesn't like my little retort and scowls at me.

"I can't for the life of me understand why you would react like this after he clearly saved you," she exclaims as she gestures to me again. I shake my head and roll my eyes before looking at her again.

Tasha huffs her annoyance, folds her arms across her chest, and falls back into the single-seater couch she's sitting on. She turns her head away from me, looking out of the window, and there at the base of her throat is the source of what I couldn't fathom.

"You drank from him, didn't you?"

"Excuse me? That's private," she says, her voice squeaky now as she covers the X with her hand.

"Look, do you know what happens when you drink from a vampire?" My patience with this girl is wearing thin. Can someone be any more ignorant?

"Yes, Xavier explained it to me. I'm now tethered to him," she says, and the sheer amount of affection there tells me that she must have drunk from him recently.

"Yes, but did he tell you that this *love* you feel for him now is a side effect of the blood?"

"That's not true. How would you even know?" There's uncertainty in her voice.

"I know things that will give you nightmares for the rest of your life," I mutter more to myself, but she catches it and sits forward in her chair.

"Come to think of it, how did you know Xavier is a vampire? I haven't mentioned anything about that, and it's a closely kept secret," Tasha asks, now looking at me like she's suspicious of me.

Well, honestly, she probably should be since I am the one who kills the creatures she and all the groupies love so much.

I pull my tongue over my teeth, annoyed at the conversation now. The grilled cheese is cold on the plate as I look down at it.

"You have, actually. Remember telling me, 'He's the kindest vampire?' " I mimic her tone of voice but with a slight difference: my face has an ugly sneer, whereas hers had an affectionate smile.

Tasha clears her throat when she realizes her mistake and lets the silence fall between us for a while. I revel in it. Talking about Xavier that way makes me want to chew out my tongue.

"Are you going to eat that or not?"

I give Tasha a sideways glance before taking half of the sandwich and cautiously bringing it to my mouth. Well, I'm either going to starve to death, or a grilled cheese will kill me. I take a bite, and my eyes close involuntarily as a hum slips past my lips. When I open my eyes, Tasha is smiling triumphantly.

I narrow my eyes at the sheer delight on her face but continue eating. Grilled cheese has never tasted so good in my life. I blame it on the hunger.

She waits until I clean off the plate before taking it from me and goes to the kitchen to place it in the basin. She sets a glass of orange juice down on the coffee table so I can reach it before returning to her seat again.

The silence drags on for another few minutes. "So, are you going to answer me?" Huffing out a sigh, I say, "I'm very much a part of the world Xavier is, so it's necessary for me to know."

"What do you mean 'a part of his world'? You can't be a vampire; otherwise, you would have healed by now … " Tasha's eyes dart back and forth as she tries to make sense of what I just told her. After a few seconds, she gasps and gets to her feet quickly, placing as much distance between us as she can, now glaring at me. "You're a vampire hunter!"

I laugh dryly, tipping my imaginary hat. "Yup, the vampires know me as the Reaper. Ever heard of me?"

Tasha's eyes widen even more, and the absolute horror on her face makes me want to laugh.

"Why would Xavier save the one hunter he and all the vampires fear the most?" she asks softly, not looking at me.

I let out a snort and wince before I say, "Don't let Xavier hear you say that. He's not as nice as you think he is." Tasha objects, but I shoot her a glare. She huffs and starts to pace the floor. A heavy silence falls again, and this time, I can't keep quiet. "Why the hell are you more afraid of me than you are of him? I mean, really? I bust my ass every night to make sure humankind is safe just to get this reaction every time."

Tasha doesn't answer me right away, and after a while, I just shake my head, feeling the headache return, accompanied by soul-crushing tiredness.

I lie my head on the pillows again and close my eyes. I really don't have the strength to convince this girl that her misguided ways are going to end up with her throat on the ground.

After a few minutes, Tasha's footsteps echo through the nearly empty apartment, and then she throws the blanket from earlier over me.

Cracking my eyes open, I watch as she takes a seat on the same couch as before, lies her head against the back of the sofa, and closes her eyes.

The tension is heavy, but I'm thankful she's leaving me be. I need rest and healing, so I let myself drift off to sleep.

"No … no … "

Light tapping on my cheek makes me jump as my eyes flash open, my body entirely covered in sweat again, and I grip my aching ribs as I try to reel in my ragged breathing. I hunch over sideways, letting out a strained groan and gritting my teeth.

"You were having a nightmare. Are you okay?" Tasha's voice comes through the cloudiness in my mind, and I frown up at her, not quite seeing the full features of her face.

"Here, drink some juice," she says, handing me the glass.

Clearing my throat, I blink up at Tasha again, trying to get my eyes to focus. The nightmares are so vivid, and every time I wake from them, it takes me longer to get back to reality. I take the glass from her. The same images loop in my mind, the ones from my earlier nightmare.

"I'm sorry for waking you," I mutter, sipping the orange juice.

"It's fine, don't even worry about it. That nightmare seems like it's haunting you," Tasha states, waving her hand almost dismissively as she sits beside my legs at the bottom of the couch.

I stiffen and tilt my head. If she notices my reaction, she doesn't show it as she leans her arm over my legs and rests her elbow on the sofa and her head in her hand. Tasha watches me for a few seconds, then lifts her brows at me in a "well" kind of gesture.

I don't even know how to answer her because she wasn't wrong. I feel like I'm reliving it over and over again, like the night I was actually attacked. Every time I wake from them, it's like I can *feel* the sword entering my body and the blows Austen left on me. How is that even possible, and how do I even begin to explain that to someone, let alone someone I barely know?

Taking another sip of orange juice, I stay quiet. I can't explain it; she wouldn't understand. At least the disgusted look on her face has disappeared.

"Are you done?" she asks when I rest my head back on the pillow.

"Hmm." I only hum, looking past her at the door.

Reaching over, she takes the glass from me and places it back on the table. Tasha's eyes dart between mine, and she chews on her bottom lip when she sits back.

I catch the movement out of the corner of my eye and shake my head. "Just spit it out."

"Sheesh, rude much," Tasha scoffs.

"No, I'm just cutting across the bullshit. Say what you wanna say or ask whatever you want to because this nervous behavior isn't working for me."

Tasha snorts, folds her arms across her chest, and glares at me. "Are you sure you aren't a vampire? And that wasn't my actual question, by the way."

What the hell? How can she even insult me by asking me that? As if Tasha can read my expression exactly, she giggles and says, "Okay, clearly I've insulted you. Please forgive me. That wasn't what I meant. You're just … I don't know. Just as blunt as all of them, I guess."

Shaking my head in a get-to-the-point way, I wait for her to spit it out.

"So, my question is, how exactly do *you* know Xavier?"

"That's a stupid-ass question. I've told you what my job is, so it's obvious that we would have crossed paths some time or another since he's a hunter killer, and I make it my life's mission to go after those assholes who hunt my kind," I tell her, shrugging and then wincing.

"Maybe you should keep the sarcastic movements to a minimum for now," she whispers, an amused smile on her face.

"Don't get snarky. I wouldn't have to use sarcastic movements at all if you weren't asking me stupid questions."

"Well, if you just answer my questions, I don't have to dumb them down for you," she snaps back.

"Listen, lady, I don't even know you. Why the hell would you think I would give you my life's story? Haven't you been listening? I'm a *vampire hunter,* I don't trust easily, and after what happened … " I cut myself off quickly and bite my tongue as the anger builds in my chest again.

Closing my eyes, I take deep breaths in through my nose, as deep as I can manage, and blow it out slowly.

"Look, I can see that this is difficult for you, so I—"

The door bursts open before Tasha can finish her sentence, and she and I jump off the couch.

Tasha's face pales as she stares at the door, but all I'm feeling is dizziness as the pain shoots through my body, and I double over, letting out a strained cry.

I look up slowly, and in rushes Xavier, bloodied, sunburned, and clothes torn. Xavier curses as he rushes to me, catching me just as my knees give out.

"I apologize. I didn't think," Xavier states flatly as he picks me up bridal-style and carries me to the door. "We need to move." I can't even protest because the numbing pain makes it difficult to think straight.

Xavier looks over his shoulder to Tasha. "Get some supplies and a first aid kit and meet me at the car."

Tasha still stands white-faced as she stares at Xavier.

"*Move, Tasha,*" he barks before walking out the door with me in his arms.

CHAPTER TWENTY-FOUR

XAVIER

"What do you want, Lucien?" I snap at the council member. The look of pure evil joy and hatred is plastered over his features as a wicked grin meets me when my words leave my mouth. He strolls in, hands behind his back, as he looks around at the contents of my room.

I, on the other hand, am standing next to the window, arms folded over my chest to hide my balled-up fists. My face is an entirely different story altogether since I can't do anything to hide the sneer on my lips and the anger and annoyance behind my eyes.

"Well, well, how the mighty have fallen." Lucien smiles maliciously, the entirety of his fangs showing. "I've come to take you to the lower level for interrogation. I don't believe anything you are saying, naturally. You might be fooling our king, but you're not fooling me."

Lucien has always been a little delusional. He behaves like he is in charge and doesn't like when he is corrected. His features match his attitude to a tee. He has chin-length blond hair, a mouselike appearance, and is short and scrawny. His dark brown eyes look dead and, in contrast to his extremely pale features, the only sharp edge to him is that pointy nose that he loves to poke into people's business.

"I'm not going anywhere, not if my king doesn't command it," I tell him forcefully as the guards loom by the open door.

"Oh, the king doesn't even know. I am going to surprise him with the information we're going to wring out of you the moment you break. And believe me, my methods of pulling information out of traitors are quite unique."

My lip pulls up in a snarl as I stare at him, trying to not lose any semblance of control. I am not going to give him a reason to act on his plans and sick thoughts. Hell, if he thinks he's going to take me without a fight, he's got another think coming. Does this asshole even know who I am?

"Like I said, *Lucien*. I'm not going anywhere with you."

Lucien lets out a burst of laughter as he turns and nods to the guards. A few moments later, four large, pissed-off vampire guards enter the room, making it clear that they mean business.

"You don't have a choice here, Xavier. Either you come willingly, or they will break your body enough that we can transport you without much fuss," Lucien snickers.

Snorting, I roll my eyes, letting my arms fall to my sides. I shake my head slowly as I inhale the now tension-filled air, catching the scents of the guards.

A wide grin spreads over my lips. "There won't be much of a fight now, will there?" Lucien's smile mimics my own, probably thinking I'm the one that's going to lose.

"So, what will it be?" he asks, seeming pleased with himself. "I think I'll take my chances."

"Very well," Lucien scoffs, his smile fading somewhat as he gestures to me with his hand, giving the guards permission to take me.

The first one snarls at me as he stalks forward, looking very much like one of those gym guys who only works on his upper body strength. I roll my eyes. Don't they know that your strength isn't just in your arms?

I stand my ground, widen my stance, and brace for the onslaught, only raising my brow as he stalks closer.

The first guard swings his fist toward my face, and I dodge it easily. He swings again, right and left, but I dodge it again, smirking when his eyes meet mine.

He roars and storms me, grabbing me around my waist as he goes in for a tackle. I bend forward at the impact, grabbing onto the waistband of his pants, pulling it upward, making him lose his footing, and he stumbles, trying to right himself quickly.

I bring my knee up at that exact moment and slam it into his rib cage. I hear bone crack at the force of the blow, and an *oof* sound escapes his mouth just before he heaves and lets go of me. I let the bastard fall to the floor, kicking him in the head. The other three guards lunge at me when I step over their friend, and I make quick work of them.

Within a few minutes, they lay sprawled out on my bedroom floor, bleeding, some broken, and at least one dead.

I haven't gotten off entirely unharmed as one of the assholes got a few blows in with his nails and the other a few shots to my ribs. I can feel it ache but also can feel them heal.

When the last bastard hits the ground, I look up at Lucien. His expression almost makes me laugh. The look on his face can only be described as terror, but he is trying to hide it with fury, which, in his case, he fails miserably at.

It's important to understand that every look you want to sell needs to come from your eyes, no matter what emotion it is. Hatred, evil, dismay, hell, even love and affection come from your eyes. If you want people to believe what you are selling them, you need to look the part, and believe me, Lucien is doing a shitty job at hiding his true emotion and an even shittier one at trying to mask it.

His hands tremble, and his mouth slacks from the likely surprise of the events while his eyes scream fear as they jump from the fallen guards to me, then the door, and back to me again.

Even the stench coming from him is screaming fear. Either he never learned how to mask certain scents or he just doesn't know he can do it, which is weird. When you become a vampire, it's one of the first things you're taught or that you learn yourself.

Tilting my head, I step over yet another one of the guards, making my way to Lucien. "You next?"

Lucien's eyes widen, and he stumbles backward. "You are fucking insane!" he yells, baring his fangs now.

Does this asshole really think that little pathetic gesture is going to scare me?

I take another step toward him, and he stumbles back toward the door more. "You will pay for this, you piece of shit," he spits, but I tilt my head menacingly in the other direction, smiling now. At that, Lucien turns and bolts out of the door.

Huffing a quick sigh of relief, I drag my hand through my hair. I need to get the hell out of this place, and I need to do it *now.* When this asshole gets to Alex, he is going to spit a lot of bullshit, and I can't take any chances. Not now, at least, not with the uncertainty that Alex might believe him and actually lock me up.

I inhale deeply and exhale through my nose. Some parts of my body ache more than others as I move, and when the dull throbbing in my side makes itself known, I wince slightly when I look down. I haven't seen any of the guards pull a weapon, but it's now lodged in my side. And by the way it's starting to burn, and the feeling of my flesh being eaten away, I know it's silver.

Grunting and cursing inwardly, I grip the handle of the dagger that's lodged hilt-deep in my side, and after taking a few breaths, I yank it from my body. A strangled sound escapes my mouth. *Dammit, this is going to slow me down.*

Without giving it another thought, I wipe the dagger on my pants and shove it into my belt. Grabbing my jacket, I rush out of my room toward the compound's front door, and to my luck, no one is there to stop me. I pull the door open, and the heat that streams in knocks my breath from me momentarily. Squinting, I watch as the darkness starts to fade to hues of violet, then yellow, orange, and red as the sun rises.

Oh, shit.

And here I thought I was lucky. Bellowing voices and thundering footsteps echo in the halls of the compound. My time is up. "Shit." I take a few quick breaths and run into the rising daylight.

Getting inside is one of my biggest priorities since I will be useless to anyone if I'm dust. The sun scorches my face and back as I run. The gash on my side struggles to heal as the sun takes all my energy. If I don't get out of it soon, I *will* be dust. Not even to mention that I haven't fed in quite some time, so there's that. And evanescing is out of the question with my weakened state.

Rounding a corner, I huff a sigh of relief when my apartment building comes into view.

The vampires at the compound won't risk their lives to come after me now. I don't know how long they will wait before coming for me, and the sound of Alex's voice bellowing through the halls just before I took off makes me think he isn't going to stay put for long.

Damn, Lucien. I should have ripped his heart out, and now I'm dealing with unnecessary heat.

Pun intended.

I can't believe I let myself be fooled by Alex. *Dammit.* I'm already going to face shit for helping a bloody vampire hunter, and now I have Lucien to thank for the extra grief added to the pile.

Speaking of shit to deal with, I totally forgot that I sent Tasha to check on Little Deadly. I hope for the life of me that their encounter went well and that I won't find two more dead bodies in that apartment.

At that thought and the sun bearing down on me, I push myself to move faster, or at least as fast as my draining body will allow. I need to get to them and get that bloody hunter out of that apartment, or all my efforts will be for nothing.

I still can't understand what went through my mind the night I saved her. I acted out of instinct. It must be.

Storming into the apartment building, I roll my eyes at myself. Instinct, my ass—I know precisely why I saved her. The attraction toward that woman is ridiculous. We are enemies and deadly ones at that. For all I know, the feelings of attraction are only one-sided, and who am I kidding? She would drive those silver daggers through my eye and then a stake through my heart.

I snarl inwardly as I take the stairs two at a time. My speed is nonexistent. *Why do I always have to get the apartment at the top of the building?*

My thoughts are all over the damn place as I get to the last landing of the building. I pull open the door to the stairs and quickly make my way to the apartment.

The closer I get to the door, the more this looming dread closes its claws around my heart. I feel it coming from every corner, and my tired, paranoid ass doesn't think as I burst through the apartment door.

Tasha jumps up and retreats to the back of the living room, her face pale. At the sound, Dominica jumps up from the couch and, quite frankly, moves too quickly for someone with her injuries, which, by the smell lingering in the air, are still fresh. I can scent the newly opened wounds. She curses and doubles over before her knees give out. I'm at her side just before she falls and quickly gather her in my arms. Tasha hasn't moved once in the small window of time this happens.

I make my way out of the apartment and order Tasha to get some supplies since I haven't had time to gather first aid supplies in the other safe house. Why would I if I never need it? I never thought I would have a human, never mind a damn injured hunter, to care for.

Tasha doesn't move, and the irritation creeping in my chest doesn't help when I snap at her, "*Move, Tasha.*"

The poor girl snaps back to reality. She inhales quickly and rushes to the bathroom, and I carry Little Deadly to the parking garage.

"I can walk on my own, you know," Little Deadly's pain-filled voice comes in a whisper. I look down at the woman in my arms, and for the first time since I met Dominica Salvatore, she seems small and fragile. I don't want to lose my head in this instance, so I don't voice my opinion. I know for a fact that she is anything but small and fragile. I'm generally on the receiving end of her wrath.

"Oh hush, Little Deadly. We don't have time for you to leave a blood trail, and we both know this way is faster." Little Deadly stiffens in my arms, and a smirk spreads on my lips. When I dare glance down at her, my heart almost slams to a halt, and my dick strains against the zipper of my pants.

Oh, for heaven's sake, now is not the time for this.

"Don't call me that," she forces through her clenched jaw and grips her side tighter. That killer look flashes in her eyes, and I snicker.

"Fine, for now, I will let you have some reprieve. But know that the name will return when you are on your feet again. Deal?"

Little Deadly doesn't answer me right away, clearly struggling to concede. "Fine," she huffs.

I chuckle at the look on her face. This force of supernatural nature will make my life more hell than anything I've ever encountered. I know that without a doubt.

To my surprise, Little Deadly rests her head against my chest as I make my way to the waiting car. Her labored breathing and trembling body worry me, but she doesn't make a sound or complain once.

I've known vampires with less restraint, and they are immortal. The apartment door slams shut on the three landings above us, and I hear Tasha's footsteps as she runs down the steps to catch up with us.

"You really did a number on that girl, didn't you?" Little Deadly whispers as I descend another flight of stairs, and I find myself somewhat annoyed at the question.

I frown but don't look at her since I can sense nothing but disgust radiating from her. "I have no idea what you're talking about," I state flatly, going down another.

"Don't play dumb, Xavier. Why the hell would you let that girl drink from you? I never pegged you for the groupie type, but here we are."

Snorting, I say, "Have you been losing sleep on my comings and goings, Little—"

"Don't you dare," Little Deadly scolds, interrupting me.

I shrug, and she winces. "Shit, sorry. Serves you right for interrupting me."

"You made a deal not five minutes ago. If you can't stick to something so trivial, how am I supposed to trust you?"

"Let's get one thing straight. You don't trust me and never will, so let's be honest here and get that out of the way so we don't try to fool one another. It's safer if you don't trust me since *I* don't trust *you,*" I force out in a snarl as I look down at her.

Little Deadly's hands ball up in fists, and her back goes rigid as I continue, "It's harsh, I know, but it is what it is."

"Thank you for reminding me," she bites out.

The silence that falls between us then is heavy with everything we want to say but don't since I'm too tired to bicker and she's in too much pain.

As I push open the door to the last stairwell, Tasha joins us, slightly out of breath. When I look back at her, she smiles, but the smile fades as her face pales again.

Turning in the direction Tasha is staring, the same dread from earlier crashes over me.

The door to the parking garage is at the bottom of the staircase, but what lies beyond that makes me halt my steps. My suspicion is confirmed when the dark outline of a vampire shoots by the door's window.

How the hell did I not sense them, and how did they find me so fast?

"Dammit."

Dominica tenses and looks up at me before her gaze follows mine to the door. "Who the hell are you running from, Xavier?"

"It doesn't matter. Can you stand?"

"Of course, I can stand. I've been trying to tell you that since you picked me up in the apartment."

"Hunter, this isn't the time for playful banter. I need to know you will be able to carry your own weight if trouble comes our way, and I need you to be able to get to the black Mustang at the back of the lot if I can't take you there." I rush through my words, scowling at Little Deadly as I set her on her feet, then turning my attention to Tasha before taking out my phone and sending her a location. "Don't wait for me. Get yourself and Miss Huntress here," I try to mock, but Little Deadly only glares at me, "to the car and drive to this location."

"What the hell is going on? What's behind that door?" Tasha's panicked voice sets my nerves on end.

"I don't have time to explain."

Dominica winces and leans against the wall. I raise my brows at her, and she scowls at me before flipping me off. "I am fine. I don't need you to fuss over me," she grits.

"Could've fooled me." I roll my eyes, folding my arms over my chest.

"Fuck you, Xavier. You have no idea what the hell I went through. So don't judge me." The anger builds in her eyes and voice, so I place my hands up in front of me in surrender. I would love to know more about that subject, but now is not the time.

"The vampires behind that door are ruthless and have no mercy. They would stop at nothing to kill you both, not to mention what they will do to you, Miss Salvatore, if they manage to capture you—"

"I can look after myself, you arrogant bastard. Don't try to patronize me."

"Uninjured, yes, but in the condition you find yourself in now, you will only be a liability. So do us both a favor and get your stubborn ass in that car," I growl at Little Deadly, baring my fangs.

Little Deadly makes a distasteful noise in her throat, rolls her eyes at me, but nods in agreement after I raise my brow at her.

"Don't hesitate. Keep your head low and move quickly," I tell Tasha as I move for the door. "I can't be distracted by you two, so do as you're told."

Tears rim Tasha's eyes, and she nods as she tries to suppress a sob. Little Deadly was right: I did do a number on Tasha, and now it's going to bite me in the ass.

Groaning, I give Little Deadly a quick once-over before bolting through the door.

CHAPTER TWENTY-FIVE

DOMINICA

I find myself more irritated than I have been in quite some time, even more so by this bloody vampire. Xavier's cold touch still lingers on my skin like a cool summer night whisper, and I can't shake the heat that builds in me. The cold and heat are so opposite from one another, but I can feel them lingering together, mixing like long-lost lovers.

It doesn't make sense.

"Are you okay to move?" Tasha says softly, wiping the tears from her eyes. I look at her with a frown, and she tilts her head before nudging it toward the parking garage.

"Um, yeah, I think so."

Pushing myself away from the wall with the opposite hand, I manage to stand upright and take a few steps before my breath rushes out of me and my knees buckle.

White-hot fury burns in my veins from frustration that I can't even walk properly and get *myself* to safety. Tasha ducks under my arm to help keep me upright, adding insult to injury.

"Come on, I'll help you," she sobs again.

"Why the hell are you crying?" My anger at my own lack of assistance is boiling over, and now, unfortunately, Tasha is feeling the blunt force of it.

"I'm scared, and I don't know if Xavier is going to be okay—"

"Oh, for Pete's sake, Xavier can handle his own, believe me, and second, crying will only draw unwanted attention to us, so please just suck it up." The harsh tone in my voice makes me cringe, but this girl needs to grow the hell up and get a hold of herself if I have to count on her for our survival.

"You are a real *bitch,* do you know that? People wouldn't dislike you so much if you could show just a semblance of compassion." Tasha sniffs but wipes her tears on the back of her hand.

"Story of my life," I mutter more to myself. I bite my tongue to keep from crying out when she tightens her grip on my ribs and moves us toward the door.

"Ready?"

I only manage to nod before Tasha opens the door as quietly as possible. We move through the door and weave through the cars as the sounds of fighting and flesh-tearing echo through the space. We duck between two cars just as two forces clash three cars down, and a horrific hiss rings out before an unearthly scream fills the space but gets cut off just as quickly.

Dammit, we are in the heart of the attack, and if we don't move now, we won't be able to make it to the car undetected.

When we entered the garage, I only got a few seconds to scan our surroundings, and our path to the Mustang wasn't covered. The deeper we get, the fewer cars there are, and our available hiding spots progressively dwindle.

I hate hiding, I *loathe* it, but Xavier is right. In my current state, I will only be a liability to everyone here. "Tasha, we need to move before the fight gets closer to us—"

Tasha screams, and icy bony fingers wrap around my throat, hauling me into the air and slamming me against the car behind me. The sheer force of it knocks the breath from my lungs. The fingers around my throat tighten as the face connected to the hand comes into view.

Instinctively, I reach for my daggers, but my hand closes over empty air, and panic envelops my mind.

The vampire forcefully twists my head to the side and drags his nose up my neck, inhaling deeply, pulling back, and coming into view again with an unmistakable smile on his face.

"Well, well, didn't I stumble onto a treasure." He turns his head to his friend at his back, and it's only then that I spot the other vampire and his grip on Tasha.

"Can you guess who this lovely mess is that I have here, Samual?" The vampire chuckles as he slightly steps out of the way, just enough for Samual to lay his disgusting eyes on me. "In my hands, I have what our king is looking for. By the looks of things, his trusted friend had her tucked away all this time." Dragging his eyes over my injured body, he tsk's and says, "You won't put up much of a fight … Pity."

The other vampire, Samual, cackles and pulls Tasha closer to him. "This little slut I've seen at the compound a few times. Isn't her sister the king's new plaything?"

"You are quite right, Samual; our dear king will indeed be pleased with our catch tonight."

Think, Dom, think.

I frantically look around for some kind of weapon before spotting the first aid bag in Tasha's hands. She clutches it to her chest like some sort of lifeline. There must be scissors or a knife in there—anything sharp will be preferred—to get us out of this situation. I've never been so desperate for my weapons in my life.

Tasha screams and fights the vampire, clawing at his wrist when he moves her to me. He slams her into the car next to me before sniffing the air; his head snaps to me, his pupils dilate, and I swear his mouth waters.

"Did you open a wound there, sweetheart?" Samual purrs, licking his lips.

"Now, now, fellas." I force myself to sound cool and calm even though my body protests the onslaught, and the pain threatens to make me lose consciousness. "Don't get carried away. Like shit face over here said. Your king is looking for me, and I know that he wants me alive."

The vampire who has his hands around my throat hisses at me, slamming my back into the car again, and this time, I can't keep from crying out.

"Don't be so sure there, *Reaper,*" he spits the word and snarls, "our king is only interested in having you brought to him alive if possible but will settle for your body. And who's to say you didn't fight, and we had to kill you?" The sneer on his face is laced with disgust and a deadly promise.

"Maybe we should taste her just to ensure the rumors about her blood are true. It sure as hell smells delicious," Samual says, flashing those sharp teeth with a massive grin. His eyes dance with excitement and hunger at the thought of feeding from me.

"Don't you dare put your mouth on me," I warn, but unfortunately for me, the normal conviction behind my voice is missing. The asshole's grip tightens like a snake, and my fight to keep my vision from blurring takes precedence.

Samual throws his head back, laughing, but vampire number one tilts his head, still watching me with those unnerving eyes, and braces his free hand on the roof of the car behind me before lowering his face to mine, snarling so much that his saliva hits my face.

"You have no say here, blood bag. When will your race understand that you will never be more than food, and the fact that you try to hunt us like animals makes killing you so much more fun?" A slow smile creeps onto his lips before he snaps his teeth in my face.

I force all my willpower not to show any emotion while this bloodsucker has his face so close to mine. "Seems only fair, as you started hunting my kind first. Besides, the feeling of your cold corpses turning to dust around my stake gives me more satisfaction than anything else in this world." I shrug, keeping that white-hot fury from earlier beneath the surface, and my vision clears.

With the vampire so close to my face, I summon all my remaining strength and slam my head into his.

His grip loosens around my neck as he stumbles backward, cursing violently, and I drive the heel of my palm up into his nose, hearing bone crack before bringing my knee up and kicking him in his crown jewels.

My cry of pain tangles with his scream, and his friend lunges for me as I push myself away from the car, tackling me to the ground. My head slams into the concrete, and I'm disoriented. I can't concentrate on the vampire on top of me, pushing my head to the side as he pins me to the floor. Tasha's distant screams make my head hurt even more, and somewhere, I register the panic building in my chest when Samual's fangs scrape against my neck.

His tongue licks at my skin, and he laughs like a starve-crazed animal. I can't gather my thoughts, I can't see, and for the life of me, I just want the blinding pain to end.

A deep, vibrating, vicious growl rumbles from behind Samual, and Tasha's screams cut off abruptly.

Within seconds of the growl reaching my ears, the weight of Samual is ripped off me before blood hits my face.

I vaguely make out images of Tasha scrambling to her feet before Xavier's bloody face clouds my vision. Groaning, I try to lift my head, but firm hands push me down. "Don't move." Xavier's voice sounds strained and filled with worry.

"Tasha, bring the car here. Hurry, we don't have time to waste. They were only the first wave. We need to get the hell out of here," Xavier snarls.

"But you're hurt—"

"I'm fine, do as you're told." The sneer on his face is clearly frightening when Tasha gasps, scrambles to her feet, and runs to the car.

Blinking, I try to get Xavier into focus, but the splitting headache won't allow me to. I attempt to sit up again, but Xavier scolds me. "Will you, *for once,* not be so bloody stubborn and let me help you."

"I've already let you help me plenty," is what I meant to say, but Xavier's chuckle lets me know that my words came out scrambled and did not make a lick of sense.

"Come on, Little Deadly, let's get you out of here." Xavier picks me up slowly and chuckles again when I mumble my protest at him for calling me that. "Hush now." I have no choice but to obey. My feeble attempts at scowling at him only make my head hurt worse. I concede and let him win this round. He carries me, cradled to his chest, toward the oncoming Mustang, and my consciousness begins to slip, but just before everything goes dark, he says softly, "Looks like I wasn't wrong with the name after all."

I'm walking in the maze, and a piercing scream howls through the night. It sounds like Austen. Panic crushes my chest as I take off running in the direction of the scream. Skidding to a halt, I listen hard while looking around for any form of a clue to get to my friend.

The scream howls out again, now closer. I sprint after it, rounding a corner left and then right. I round one more corner, and a blinding pain explodes in my side, and I grind to a stop. Looking down, Austen's sword protrudes from my side. I look up slowly, following the blade to the hilt. A hand clutches the pommel, and I look up at my friend's distorted face, smiling back at me.

"Where have you been, Dom?" He twists his head in a way no human is supposed to. The panic now crushes my lungs as he steps closer. His hand still clutching the pommel of the sword and twisting it slowly.

I scream and try to retreat, but I'm frozen to the spot. "Why didn't you just let me finish the job? You could be free now."

His inhumane eyes meet mine just before ripping the sword from my side. Laughing menacingly, he picks the sword up and drives it into my chest—

The grip on my shoulders, shaking me, wakes me. I'm breathing so hard that drawing in enough air to properly fill my lungs is challenging.

"It's a nightmare. Calm down, breathe."

Xavier?

I can't concentrate enough to discern where I am, and for a moment, I forget what happened. The panic raging in me from hearing my enemy's voice throws my head into a flat spin.

My eyes snap to him, but his face is shrouded in the darkness that fills the room. The memories of the last few days flash through my mind, and I take a deep breath. My heart still hammers against my chest. Absentmindedly, I reach for my chest, feeling for the wound that felt so real, but there is no hole, no jagged flesh, and no blood.

A sigh of relief slips out with the building sob, and I want to kick myself. Shuddering when I pull in a shaking breath, I reach for my face, and when I touch my cheek, my fingers are wet from the tears that still stream down my face.

The sorrow from my broken life and friendship, and I don't even know what else, crushes my chest so much I'm heaving from the weight of it, and yet my heart feels so empty.

The sobs spill from me as the tears still pour from my eyes. Every sob causes the pain in my body to flare, but I don't have the fight in me to care.

Cold, firm fingers brush against my face before I feel them push behind my back and under my knees, and I'm lifted from where I lie. Xavier brings me to rest in his lap so gently, it's unnerving. He folds his arms around my trembling body and gently hugs me to him as I bawl my eyes out.

When was the last time I let myself cry, not to mention like this? Absolutely losing all semblance of self-control. And what's worse is that my enemy, the one vampire I despise more than all of them combined, is comforting me, *and I'm letting him.*

What the hell is happening to me?

Xavier doesn't move, doesn't touch me other than his arms caging me to him. He doesn't say anything. I wonder if he's even breathing. I cry and cry and cry, and when I have no more tears left, my ragged breathing starts to fade.

My headache has escalated to a full-on migraine by this point, and my body is screaming, and though I feel like I could exchange my current body for a new one, my heart feels lighter somehow, and then the exhaustion hits me like a landslide.

When I wake again, I'm in bed, and the light of the new day streams into the room. I groan when I move my stiff body, but I feel a lot better than before. My shoulder feels better, and the sting in my ribs and side isn't as bad as it was.

I clear my throat and hear movement outside the bedroom door before it clicks open softly. Tasha appears in the gap between the door and the frame. She scans the room, and when her eyes fall on me, she smiles brightly.

"Oh, thank goodness. You're awake." Huffing a sigh of relief, Tasha pushes the door open more and strides in, sitting on the bed beside me. "How do you feel?"

I rub my hand on my face and say, "Better than I should, I guess." My voice is hoarse, and my throat scratches when I swallow.

Tasha reaches toward the nightstand and hands me the glass of water, seeing me struggle to swallow. I push myself up on my pillows a little and am confused when the level of pain I'm expecting doesn't register. The sting from the wounds is still there but feels more like a shadow lingering.

"How?" I ask, reaching for the glass and all but gulping down the water. "You had us worried there for a while. When we arrived at the new safe house, Xavier brought you in and cleaned your wounds after you passed out, but you didn't wake."

I frown at Tasha while she tells me what happened. My confusion isn't so much that I was out cold for goodness knows how long but that Xavier hadn't told Tasha about my meltdown.

My cheeks heat at the thought of the moment between us, followed by earth-crushing embarrassment. Tasha keeps talking like she didn't just see my cheeks flush bright red.

"Xavier got grumpier with every passing day that you haven't woken up yet. I really thought you weren't going to make it."

Tasha's face gets gloomier as she tells me about Xavier's mood. All these feelings and worrying about me are overwhelming. I have this sinking feeling that Xavier's crappy mood has nothing to do with me.

"How?" I ask again, this time pulling Tasha's attention to me.

"How what?"

"*How* did my wounds heal so much? *How* long was I out? Just … *How?*" My voice cracks on the last "how," and I clear my throat again, leaning my head on the pillows.

"Oh, well, you were asleep for four days. I thought Xavier was going to rip this place apart." Tasha cringes but continues, "Since you weren't moving and straining yourself so much, I think that helped your healing. It's quite impressive. I didn't know hunters also possessed accelerated healing powers."

Without thinking, I roll my eyes at her statement and move to sit up more before answering her. "We need fast healing for what we do. If we didn't heal fast, we couldn't protect the humans from the beasts at night."

Becoming a hunter has always been a dream for me, ever since I learned why my parents were never home at night. I'll never forget the night I found out what they did for a living. I snuck out of the house and followed them to a cemetery of all places. The moment the vampire attacked, I watched in awe as my mom took it down. When my parents discovered me there, I was in a world of trouble, but I couldn't stop asking a million questions. I was sold the moment my father told me about the accelerated healing and longer lifespan. Little did I know how fleeting that could be.

I stretch my sore limbs a little and hiss as my ribs protest with the movement.

"They aren't all beasts," Tasha says softly.

"I'm starting to see that," I agree, thinking of what Xavier did. "Where is Mr. Grumpy Pants, anyway?"

Tasha's eyes meet mine, and worry flashes behind them but disappears quickly. "He, um, he locked himself in the other room last night."

"What? Why? I thought he would revel in the chance to come and gloat." A scowl settles on my face.

"Yeah, well, I haven't heard anything from that room in a while," she says, her mind going somewhere else before looking at me again. "You must be starving. What can I get you?"

I shake my head in confusion. What isn't she telling me? But at the mention of food, my stomach growls so loudly that Tasha giggles, gets up from the bed, and walks to the kitchen. "I'll fix you something."

Ten minutes pass, and I am getting restless in this bed, so I throw the covers off with a wince and get up. My head spins, and it feels like I'm going to hurl.

That's what happens when you don't eat for a few days.

I sit back down and wait for the lightheadedness and nausea to fade. When it does, I look around the room. This one has a little bit more warmth to it. The couch in the far corner looks like you can melt away and never get up again. The bed is large, and the covering is soft as silk and welcoming.

The scenery outside is absolutely gorgeous. We aren't in the city anymore—that much is clear. The white-tipped mountain in the distance catches my eye, and then the birds chirping draw my attention to the adjoining forest just outside the window. The grass is a beautiful green and stretches as far as my eyes can see. It gives me a sense of serenity. I close my eyes and inhale deeply, feeling that calm spread in my veins.

The feeling is so foreign. Is this what peace feels like? I shake my head to rid myself of something I know is not meant for me and rise slowly. This time, nothing spins, thank goodness. I make my way to the door and stop dead. This isn't an apartment. It's a cottage. Like my room, the furniture here is soft, plushy, warm, and welcoming. There are a lot of similarities between the previous place and this one, but unlike the cold, calculating feeling I got there, the feeling of home echoes in my chest here.

"Where are we?"

Tasha yelps, spinning to face me, her hand on her heart and the other holding a ladle in defense. "You scared me, shit." I smile apologetically.

After a few deep breaths, she lowers the hand with the ladle and says, "You're up! That's great, but please take it slow."

Pulling a face, I decide it's not worth the argument since I'm no child. "Where are we?" I ask again, wandering around the small living space.

"We are in a cottage that belonged to my mother's great-aunt. When she passed, my mother left it to me and my sister. We never really came here, so I told Xavier we could use it since not many people know about it, and clearly, his safe houses aren't so *safe*."

I chuckle, "Clearly."

Walking around the poofy couch, I spot a short hallway, dark and gloomy, and at the end, a heavy oak door.

"Where is it you said Xavier locked himself up?"

When Tasha doesn't answer, I look in her direction, and she watches me warily. I realize that I've balled my fist and that my shoulders are tense. Forcing myself to relax visibly, I raise my brows at her.

"In that room you are staring at. I don't know what's wrong with him. He doesn't answer me, and like I said earlier, I haven't heard one sound come from that room in the last twelve hours." Tasha moves to the small dining area and places a bowl of stew on the table. My mouth waters when the aroma of the food reaches my nose. I huff an irritated sigh, looking at the door one more time before making my way to the table. My hunger outweighs everything else at this moment. I'll deal with Xavier later.

The image of him holding me the other night flashes in my mind, and I cringe. *Xavier.* The damn bastard is making me worry about him. It feels like I don't know who I am anymore. The uneasiness of the situation is getting to me, and I'm starting to question my entire existence. *I don't have the strength to think about that right now.*

I take a seat and inhale the delicious smell of the food in front of me. Tasha returns with her own bowl and a plate of freshly baked bread. I frown up at her and she laughs nervously. "With Mr. Grumpy not being the best company and you out cold, I had a lot of free time. And besides, I bake when I'm nervous."

I take a bite from the stew and feel my insides melt. It's that good. The bread isn't half bad, either.

I eat my fill and sit back in my chair, clutching my injured arm as I watch Tasha. She inclines her head as she chews, and I huff air out through my nose.

"Thank you. It was delicious."

Tasha swallows and picks up another spoonful of stew but pauses before taking a bite. "You're welcome," she says, narrowing her eyes. "What?"

I analyze her and then look around the small cottage before my eyes linger a little too long in the small hallway. I look back at her just as Tasha pulls the spoon from her mouth.

"Why are you here?"

Tasha frowns as she chews but doesn't make a move to answer me as she eats another spoonful of her stew, so I continue talking. "Your life is threatened by him and now the target is a lot bigger with me in the picture."

Tasha shrugs as she swallows. "My sister was taken by the king, and I thought if I could bargain with him, he would set her free, but he saw me as a backup for when he was done with my sister and took me, too."

I try to keep my face neutral with that statement.

"And Xavier?"

She sighs, setting the spoon down in her bowl and resting her arms on the table. "Xavier was the first vampire in that hellhole who showed me an ounce of kindness. It won't seem like kindness to you, but what he did saved me from the more brutal ones there."

I contemplate Tasha's words as I listen to her talk. Xavier has never been kind a day in his life, not while he ripped my team members to shreds, not when he tried to rip my throat out on our first encounter, nor on any other encounter for that matter. Then, the other night flashes in my mind again, and the conflicting feelings in me make themselves known yet again. I pinch the bridge of my nose in frustration.

"It seems like you don't believe me."

"I don't know what to believe anymore," I mutter, staring at my empty bowl.

"Are you going to tell me what happened to you?"

My eyes snap to hers, and my mouth goes dry from the thought of telling her what happened. "I don't want to talk about it."

"Well, I'm here if you wish to talk—"

Tasha stops mid-sentence when we hear the heavy oak door from the room down the hall open. The atmosphere in the room chills, and on instinct, my back goes rigid. I get up quickly—too quickly, causing my head to spin again, and I stumble backward, grabbing hold of the chair for stability. My vision goes white for a split second, and when it clears, Xavier's strained face is inches from mine, his hands clutching my waist.

I inhale quickly and step back from him instantly. His lip pulls in a snarl, and his face is drawn, but he releases me and shoves his hands in his pockets, retreating from me.

"Glad to see you're up." Xavier nods in my direction, and I only nod in return. Something is wrong here since the chilly atmosphere has become heavy with his presence. I take in the entirety of him. He looks disheveled and … starved. His lip twitches as his nostrils flare every few seconds, his jaw ticking as he clenches it. Xavier's whole body is tense. Every muscle seems to clench and relax with difficulty.

I drag my eyes up to his face, to his eyes, and I have to force myself not to react on instinct when his gaze connects with mine. Xavier's eyes are wholly black as the darkest night, and his skin is paler than usual.

Narrowing my eyes, I slowly step backward, making my way around the table. I place as much distance between us as I can as I slowly move to the kitchen. His head jerks to me, and he tilts it slowly, following my every movement.

"When was the last time you fed?" I ask slowly, carefully, as I spot the blood stain on his shirt at his side and the unhealed cut on his neck.

Xavier's eyes narrow on me, and the deadly calm in his voice makes my hair stand on end. "What are you doing? Don't provoke me, Reaper," he says, now unable to keep the snarl from his lips.

"When?" I push, still moving to the kitchen. I saw a knife there earlier and need to get to it.

Xavier's eyes flick to Tasha, and he visibly swallows before snapping his eyes to me just as my fingers close on the knife's hilt on the kitchen counter.

Xavier's voice goes deadly low, and his eyes darken. "I'm warning you. Provoking me now will not go well for you or for Tasha."

Tasha, who hasn't moved or said a single word since Xavier appeared, gets up from her seat slowly and looks from me, with the knife in my hand, to Xavier, whose lip is pulled up so far I can see both his fangs gleaming.

"Tasha, move to me. Now," I say carefully.

"No, he won't hurt us. I know him—"

Xavier tilts his head menacingly at Tasha, and his lips pull up in a disturbing grin, fangs still wholly visible.

"Have you ever been near a starving vampire before?" My voice is soft and calm, with a hint of anger, and I never take my eyes off Xavier. "Not to mention one who is injured."

"No," she says, scared now.

"I have, and I have proof of how savage said vampires can be." Tasha snaps her head to me, and I tilt my head to the side, exposing the jagged scar at my jugular.

Tasha's eyes round in fear, and she moves toward me. However, her movements are sloppy, and she bumps into the table, causing the spoon to clatter from the bowl.

"Shit," I exclaim as Xavier launches himself toward Tasha, snarling like a wild animal. His eyes are crazed as the frenzy takes over his mind. Tasha screams and runs to me but trips over her own feet.

Xavier is on her a split second later, snapping his jaw as she screams.

I move, driving the blade of the knife into his back. Xavier howls in pain, and that crazed gaze pins me. He gets up from Tasha and slowly stalks toward me. I back away, and the first night we met flashes in my mind from how similar the situation is. "Tasha, get me another knife."

"No, please don't kill him." Tasha's frantic plea is like sandpaper to my skin. Xavier had nearly ripped her throat out and is now coming for me, but she begs for *his* life.

"Tasha, get me the damn knife, or we both are going to end up drained," I snarl and look at her.

I realize my mistake too late when my back slams into the wall behind me, and Xavier snaps his teeth at me.

My scent isn't helping since I completely smell like a hunter. Not any hunter, but the Reaper. Xavier only sees me as a threat now, and I let Tasha distract me. I brace myself for impact when he tightly grips my hair, wrenches my head to the side, and smells the air as a growl rumbles from his chest.

Xavier is inches from my throat, and his body jolts against mine before he slumps to the ground. My breathing is ragged as I look around the room. My eyes land on Tasha, who clutches a heavy cast-iron pan, the one she just knocked out Xavier with.

Relief washes over me, and nervous laughter bubbles out of me. Tasha frowns as she lowers her weapon. I can't stop the laughter, and Tasha joins me after a while.

I laugh and laugh and laugh until my jaw and muscles hurt, and the ache in my ribs makes me groan.

"Next time, don't hesitate. If I tell you to move, do it. I know you think you know Xavier, and I have to give him credit that he can subdue his hunger for as long as he did and suppress basic vampire nature, but by doing so, he just placed us in more danger."

Tasha sighs and walks to the kitchen counter, plopping down on one of the bar stools. The pan still clutched in her hands.

"I need you to get silver chains. It's going to hurt him like a bitch, but we have no choice. Not until we figure out a way to get him blood." My eyes fall on Xavier's unconscious form, and for the first time in my life, I feel a tinge of regret for what I'm going to do.

"Are you sure we should do that? He's already injured, and the silver will only weaken him more."

Stepping over Xavier, I make my way to Tasha. I take the pan from her and place it on the counter. "Yes, I'm sure. I know what I'm doing, Tasha. If I wanted to kill Xavier, I would have done it already. I just want some time to think of a plan without worrying that he is going to rip our throats out."

Tasha's eyes find mine, and she nods slowly. "Okay. I trust you." I want to laugh at those three little words. Three words so small and meaning nothing on their own, but put them in that order, and it's the most dangerous thing you can do, especially in my world. Trust is feeble and overrated. Trust is what got me here. It's something I will likely never do again, but here is Tasha, naive as hell. But I only smile at her and nod.

I won't crush her heart and ruin her trust. It doesn't mean I can't be there for someone and let them trust me when mine was shattered too many times.

"Thank you. Now, please, hurry. If he wakes and we haven't tied him down, we will be in a lot of trouble."

CHAPTER TWENTY-SIX

XAVIER

"Do you think the chains will hold him?" Tasha's voice breaks through my haze-filled mind.

I struggle to open my eyes. Where the hell am I? It feels like my energy is being drained from me in a way that will kill me if I don't move. But when I do, a searing pain rips through my body. It comes from my wrists and ankles.

"I'm not taking chances. Silver has never failed me before," Little Deadly says. My surroundings get clearer, and I look down at myself. Silver … I am bound in bloody *silver.*

I can't contain the snarl rippling from my throat when I snap my head up and look into Little Deadly's eyes. Those damn beautiful, *deceitful* eyes.

I snarl again, pulling against my restraints, and regret it immediately. The more I move, the harder it becomes for me to breathe. The silver cuts into me like a red-hot knife through butter.

Wait … Silver isn't supposed to make me feel like I can't breathe. The bloodlust hits me so hard I have to keep myself from biting through my own tongue.

"Xavier, are you lucid?" Little Deadly's stern, cold voice filters into my ears. I look up at the hunter again, this time seeing a very frightened Tasha behind her.

I swallow past the frenzy in my veins and lock my eyes with Little Deadly's. "*Yes.*" The former word comes out in a snarl, my lip twitching, and my fangs ache.

I fucked up royally.

So much for trying to help the damn woman standing in front of me when I am just as dangerous as the vampires I ripped off her the other night—if not more.

Little Deadly walks toward me slowly and crouches before me, resting her arms on her legs. I take in the woman, but all I can focus on is the vein in her neck, pumping blood through her body.

My mouth waters, but the frenzy rises when I spot the scar at her jugular. The one *I* made when my fangs ripped from her throat, how many years ago? My restraint on the bloodlust wanes, and I swallow hard.

"When was the last time you've fed?"

I force my eyes away from Little Deadly's and look at Tasha, who gulps.

Little Deadly looks behind her at Tasha and then back at me, and I snort at the frown on her face.

"What's wrong, Little Deadly? A little confused there?" All pleasantries are out the door when the bloodlust beast in a vampire is stirred awake. Mine has been awake for the last four days.

She ignores me and rises, walking to Tasha. "When, Tasha?" Tasha looks from me to Little Deadly and says, "If I'm correct, he last fed from me. The night we um—"

Little Deadly tilts her head slightly and looks at me when I chuckle darkly. "When I was buried balls-deep in her, is what she is trying to say."

The emotion on Little Deadly's face is one I never thought I would see. It's there and then gone so quickly that I barely noticed it, and the surprise sobers my mind somewhat.

Hurt ... There was hurt in her eyes.

What the hell would she even feel hurt over? We hate each other's guts. Killing me has always been her number one priority.

Little Deadly clears her throat and turns to me. The look on her face is like a punch in the gut. Her lip curls in disgust as she says, "When was that, exactly?"

"I, um—" Tasha fumbles.

"For Pete's sake, Tasha. Tell me when. I don't need details. I just need to know *when*."

"I'm not sure when that was. A few weeks ago, I think."

"Sounds about right," I groan when another wave of hunger hits me.

"This is just awesome," Little Deadly laughs sarcastically, throwing her hands up and wincing.

For the first time, I notice that she is dressed in dark blue jeans and a white shirt—*my shirt*—and her arm is no longer in the sling.

"Why do you say that?" Tasha asks, wringing her fingers nervously. Little Deadly clutches her shoulder and starts to pace, keeping her face in the shadows of my room.

That's right. We're in the room I locked myself in. No sunlight reaches this room, and the dark oak door is perfect for keeping someone like me locked up if they are weakened enough.

I pull at my restraints again, cursing violently.

Tasha squeaks and steps back until her back is against the wall. Little Deadly—true to the name—gives me a death stare, and her hand reaches behind her back, staying there.

"I suggest you refrain from moving so much. You will only harm yourself more."

"What's your plan now, *Reaper?* You have me where you've always wanted me. Why wait? Why not take the killing blow now and be done with it?" I smirk at her when she clenches her jaw.

Little Deadly ignores me and turns to Tasha. "You know that when a vampire feeds while screwing, it's not really feeding, right? They need the blood to be the only source of attraction when they do feed. That's why they feed directly after having had their fill from sex."

How the hell does she know this? As far as I know, that is a closely kept secret unless one of them infiltrated far enough that someone blabbed. I snarl in Little Deadly's direction.

"So, when did he last *feed?*" She carries on with her questioning without even flinching. Tasha frowns, and her face pales slightly. At least she knows the trouble we're in if I don't get blood soon.

"Um, the night I met him. Maybe a few weeks before the other time." Tasha averts her eyes, unable to look into mine or Little Deadly's livid ones.

Actually, Tasha is wrong. I drank from her the night I sent her to the apartment. So why the hell is the bloodlust so overwhelming? Then it hits me. I've been trying for a week now to keep Little Deadly alive. The smell of her blood, added to the injuries I've sustained, is screwing with my senses.

After a few minutes, Little Deadly pulls her hand through her hair and curses. She turns toward me and watches me with those damn eyes that drive me insane.

"So, what now?" Tasha whispers.

"I don't suppose you know where to get donated blood, do you?" Little Deadly looks over her shoulder at Tasha who shakes her head, eyes wide.

"I can give him some of mine again—"

"*No.*"

"But—" Tasha argues, pushing off the wall and walking around Little Deadly to stand between us. Tasha's back to me.

A low, dangerous growl vibrates through my chest as I pull harder at the silver chains holding me down. The bloodlust is starting to take its toll, and I don't know how long I have until it consumes me. The thought of losing myself frightens me. I've only once been close to losing myself, and that was the night I first saw Little Deadly. I've never let myself reach that point after that night. Not because of what I did to her but only for the fact that she almost killed me because of it.

"Dom? Please, we can't kill him. I beg you, please don't—" Tasha's voice cracks, and she sobs, grabbing Little Deadly's shirt.

Little Deadly doesn't take her eyes off me as Tasha pleads for me. I don't know what's more pathetic: the human girl bonded to me, begging for my life, or me letting her.

The air in the room seems to chill, and I know my fate is sealed. Little Deadly will get her all-time kill tonight despite everything I've done to protect her.

Who am I kidding? I told her not to trust me, and now, moments away from being taken by the bloodlust, she demonstrates why every vampire is afraid to cross paths with her.

Little Deadly grips Tasha's wrists tightly and pulls them from her shirt. "I need you to leave and lock that door. Do not, under any circumstances, open it unless I tell you to. Do you understand me?"

"What! No, please—"

"Tasha, you said you trust me. I need you to do that now," Little Deadly says, still watching me with those anger-filled eyes.

"What are you going to do to him?" Tasha whispers, turning to look at me. The tension-filled silence following her question only confirms my suspicion, but when Little Deadly opens her mouth, her words aren't what I expected.

"Your blood won't be strong enough to sate him. Therefore, the only blood at our disposal that is strong enough is ... *mine.*"

Tilting my head, I smirk at the beautiful, deadly Reaper who's about to offer up her blood to me. The thought of her blood coating my tongue sends a thrill through me, and my fangs ache. The bloodlust hits me full in my chest, and I snarl viciously, my mind filling with a blood-red haze.

CHAPTER TWENTY-SEVEN

DOMINICA

Every cell in my body screams in protest when I tell Tasha I'm giving my blood to Xavier. All my training bucks in my mind, and my body even recoils at the thought. But deep inside my heart, I feel this pull. Something I haven't felt before. Like it's the right thing to do, without a doubt. But then there's the feeling of betrayal when these two told me about their night-time *fun.*

I couldn't understand why my heart felt like it was being ripped from my chest, but I shoved that feeling down so deep, hoping to never see it again.

The smirk on Xavier's face when the words left my mouth made me think twice, four times even, about whether I should do this.

Tasha gaped at me, her chin almost hitting the floor, and was about to say something when Xavier started to thrash in his restraints.

I've only taken my eyes off him for a split second, but when I look at him again, that smirk has vanished, replaced by a snarling mouth with razor-sharp fangs.

His onyx eyes now have a red hue to them as he pins me with his gaze.

"Tasha, you need to leave. *Now.*" I don't give her time to argue more as I push her toward the open doorway and shove her out of the room. "Remember what I told you. You do *not* open this door unless *I* tell you to."

I barely see her nod when I slam the heavy door shut and after a few seconds, I hear the dead bolts snap shut from the outside.

Great stuff, Dom. What a situation to find yourself in. Some hunter you are. The words ring through my mind, and somehow, they sound exactly like Austen … and Brian. I shove the voices out of my head and approach Xavier cautiously, forcing my body to move in the direction of the hungry, blood-lusted vampire. No, not to kill him but to *feed* him. *Go figure,* I think to myself, rolling my eyes.

Reaching behind my back, I pull the knife from where I shoved it into the loop of my belt.

The action catches Xavier's attention, and he snaps his jaw at me, pulling at the chains.

Xavier bucks, but the chains hold firm when I stop before him. He narrows his eyes at me as he tilts his head from one side to the other, his chest heaving. Those teeth still bared. The action is nerve-racking, to say the least. I take a deep breath, trying to calm my racing heart and convince myself I can do this.

It's now or never.

I take the knife and place the blade against my neck, nicking the skin. Warm blood trickles down my throat, and Xavier stops thrashing. His eyes pinned to the wound on my neck. His heaving chest rises and falls every few seconds, his eyes crazed, but he goes completely still when I straddle him.

"I know a part of you can still hear me, so listen carefully. You'd better take control of your own bloody body, or this is going to be your last day on this earth," I say as I poise the tip of the knife at his heart.

He doesn't move, doesn't breathe as he watches me with those unnerving eyes and tilted head. The knife won't be enough to kill him, but he is sitting on a wooden chair, and a knife to the heart would still incapacitate him long enough for me to end him.

Xavier snaps his jaw at me again, and I grab him by the throat. "*Get control of your body, Xavier, or so help me.*"

He bares his teeth but doesn't move, and I let go of his throat. I drag my finger through the blood, now pooling and staining my white shirt, and pull it across his lip.

He inhales sharply and closes his eyes as his tongue drags over the blood. I feel his body tremble, and when he opens his eyes again, the red hue has subsided a little.

"Get the hell off me, Reaper." The snarl on his face is vicious and like nothing I have seen him do toward me before. Xavier has never called me Reaper, only that damn annoying nickname.

I snort, and a ghost of a smile appears on my lips before I move forward on his lap until my chest is flush with his. Something warm stirs in my lower stomach and sends pulses of pleasure through me.

What the actual hell?

Swallowing visibly, I try to force the feeling away, but it seems to linger with my heavy breathing, which causes my breasts to move against Xavier's hard, muscular chest. My nipples peak, and heat stirs lower down.

This is absolutely ridiculous.

I lower my neck to Xavier's mouth, and a string of vulgar curses leaves his mouth before he fights to turn his head.

I never in my life thought I would fight to force a vampire to drink from me, but here we are.

"Dammit, Xavier. *Drink.*" My voice is hoarse but firm. Xavier turns his head to me, and the pain I find in his eyes makes no sense at all.

Deciding to address that issue later—the list just keeps piling up—I concentrate on the task at hand.

I push my free hand into his hair and grip it tightly—the other still gripping the knife, which is pointed at his heart—and pull his mouth to my neck.

"*Now,*" I order, but the conviction leaves my voice.

The tension-filled silence and heavy atmosphere make the anticipation for his bite so much worse, and then he strikes, sinking his fangs into the already jagged scar at my throat.

Gasping at the sting, I grip the hilt of the knife harder and grit my teeth. My hand trembles, fighting with all I have not to give in to my training and drive the knife into Xavier's heart.

Xavier groans and sucks harder. Every muscle in his body relaxes with each swallow of my blood.

The sensation from his teeth and mouth on my skin awakens parts of my body I never knew possible, placing me in a trance. My tightened jaw slackens, and so does my grip on the knife. Xavier laps at the bite on my neck before biting down again, pushing his hips upward.

A moan slips from my mouth when his rock-hard erection pushes against the now aching, wanting spot between my legs. I roll my hips and drag another groan from his chest.

What the hell are you doing, Dom? that small voice in my head shouts, but it doesn't sound right.

I roll my hips again, and Xavier growls, trying his best to push closer to me. My body molds to his, wanting his full attention. I find myself imagining his mouth on my aching nipples, the swollen bud between my legs, that tongue and teeth on my inner thigh—

A loud clang rips me from the drunken, lust-filled haze, and I snap my eyes open. *When did I close them?*

To my horror, I find my hand empty and the knife on the floor. Xavier hasn't stopped drinking, and my head begins to feel foggy.

How could I have been so stupid? I'm in so much trouble. Dammit. Oblivious to any sound or distraction, Xavier bites down on my neck again. I wince. I need to get him off me. I gather all my strength and push my now-free hand into his hair, trying to pry him from my neck.

He snarls, and the panic I've been taught to control threatens to cripple me. "Xavier, let go. You've taken enough." A low rumble in his chest is my only answer.

I try my best not to let the panic show in my voice since it's now creeping through my entire body. "That's enough, Xavier." I pull at his hair again.

My training is flawless, and I can quickly escape this situation, but all my tactics usually leave the vampire in a pile of dust. The thought doesn't sit well with me, so now I'm left with the alternative.

The alternative is ... *I don't know.*

Begging is out of the question since it will only make matters worse, and second, I *never* beg, especially not a vampire.

My heart hammers against my chest, and my mind draws a blank. Xavier bites deeper, and the fogginess threatens to overwhelm my senses.

Just before the panic in my veins totally overshadows every rational thought, I remember the chain in my back pocket.

I let go of Xavier and reach behind me as he still pulls mouthfuls of blood from me. I yank the chain free from my pocket and wrap it around his throat. The chain is just long enough to choke him with it.

Xavier rips his mouth away from me at the burn from the silver. The moment his mouth is lifted from my neck, I get up and push away from him.

Obviously, I didn't think it through, and before I can register, I fall backward on my ass when my knees give out.

Xavier hisses at the now-added silver, but I pay him no mind as I push against the wound at my neck. With so much of my blood drained, my adrenaline rush has now entirely run out, and exhaustion creeps closer.

I blink a few times, hoping to push it away long enough to get out of this room, but with my still-healing wounds and the sudden blood loss, it proves impossible.

My head spins, and my consciousness ebbs away. When I sag to the cold floor, Xavier curses and strains against the silver again.

Muffled banging irritates my ears, and I try to open my eyes. My eyelids feel heavy, and my body is drained of all energy.

Bang, bang, bang.

Bang. Bang. Bang.

The incessant banging makes me groan, and I open my eyes.

"*Dom!*" I can barely make out the muffled voice screaming my name over the banging.

What the hell happened?

Another voice catches my attention, the one in the room with me, low and threatening.

"Open the door, Tasha. *Now.*"

My head feels thick and cloudy. I swallow slowly. My throat feels like sandpaper. "Dom said not to open the door unless she says so." The panic is still thick in Tasha's muffled voice.

Chains whine under pressure, and then another string of vulgar curses on a growl clears my mind a little.

I turn on my side and push to sit up, but my limbs tremble—no, wobble is more accurate. Clenching my jaw, I push on the floor again, wincing from the pain in my aching, cold body.

"Don't move," the voice I now recognize as Xavier says softly, still laced with danger. "You've lost a lot of blood. Just stay still." Xavier looks at the door. "Tasha, I will not tell you again. Open the damn door and take these damn things off me. *Now.*"

Seconds tick into minutes before Tasha's muffled voice comes through the door. "I can't. I-I promised Dom I wouldn't open this door unless she says it's okay."

Xavier's answering roar sends a chill down my spine, and the hairs on the back of my neck stand on end. Tasha yelps on the other side, but still, no locks click open.

The deathly silence that falls after Xavier's temper tantrum clears my head more.

"Open—" I don't know if she can even hear me. I can't get my voice to go louder, but I clear my throat and try again. "Open the door, Tasha."

My eyes fall on Xavier, and I'm met with a burning *green* gaze. A burning determination to get out of his restraints and do what exactly? Finish me off?

The bolts and lock on the door click, and then Tasha's running steps echo in the room. To my astonishment, she runs to me first.

"Lie down, Dom. Shit." She pushes me down and turns on Xavier. "How the hell can you do this to her?! You know she's not fully recovered!"

Tasha gets to her feet and storms toward Xavier—who, if I might add, is glaring at Tasha like she is enemy number one, her face red from anger and her hands on her hips.

Xavier works his jaw so hard I'm surprised I don't hear teeth cracking. When Tasha eventually stops wailing on him, he snarls at her, voice low and full of violence. "Are. You. Done?"

Tasha's eyes round in fear, but she doesn't back down as she keeps glaring at him. Maybe now is a good time to step in between them. I turn to my side again, slowly, and push myself up into a semi-sitting position.

Xavier turns his head in my direction and tilts it to the side as he narrows his gaze on me. "You have some nerve."

"Don't you dare talk to her like that. She saved *you* and both our asses," Tasha says to Xavier, motioning to me and her.

He turns that predator's gaze on Tasha again, and she steps back once before planting her feet.

They glare at each other while Xavier still pulls on his chains. My head sags, and I reach a heavy limb up to touch my neck. It seems the bleeding has stopped, but the bite mark hurts like a bitch.

"Let me heal you."

Soft steps move to me, and I lift my eyes to see Xavier staring at me as Tasha kneels beside me and inspects the wound on my neck.

My ears must be ringing because why the hell would he say that? My voice is still weak when I say, "You are out of your mind if you think I am ever going to drink from you. I have probably already lost my status as a hunter. What do you think they will do to me when I have a mark like that on my throat?" I nudge my head in Tasha's direction.

"Fine. Then you can suffer." He growls, flashing his fangs as he talks through his teeth. I narrow my eyes at him but turn my attention to Tasha. "Will you please help me up?"

"Are you sure you should stand?"

"Tasha, I am a hunter, for Pete's sake. If a bite from him the last time didn't keep me down, why should this one?"

I reach for her hand, and she helps me up. I stumble a bit but stay on my feet. Xavier's eyes flash when I do, but it's gone in a split second. I frown at him. I swear I saw worry there, but I chalk it up to my fog-filled mind and ask Tasha if she can draw me a bath.

I need to wash the feel of Xavier off my skin, and hopefully, the images from earlier will wash away with it.

Tasha looks hesitant but nods and walks out of the room. Xavier doesn't acknowledge her and doesn't even watch as she leaves. His eyes stay pinned to mine, then drift to my neck, and he swallows.

"This will never happen again." I lace my voice with as much disgust as possible. "If you can't control your bloodlust, there will be none of this bullshit next time. In that state, you pose more of a threat to me and Tasha than the vampires out there. I will not be a blood bag to your kind. This is my only warning."

Xavier doesn't move or even flinch at my words. I wait for a reply, and when he doesn't answer me, I shake my head in disappointment but slowly walk toward him. He doesn't take his eyes off me as I bend down, pick up the knife, and push it into the loop at the back of my jeans.

I reach for the chain on his neck and take it off slowly. Xavier only clenches his jaw and closes his eyes. The only way he will show his pain.

Next, I remove the ones around his ankles and then the ones wrapped around his torso. The little energy left in me depletes quickly, and I need to leave this room. I've shown enough weakness in front of Xavier. He is still my enemy—a necessary evil at this point, but still an enemy.

I reach the back of the chair and crouch down to undo the silver chain around his wrists. After a few seconds, they, too, drop to the floor. When they do, Xavier's head lowers, and he whispers so low I barely catch it: "I'm sorry."

I'm not entirely sure that I *did* hear it. He moves his hands in front of him and rises from the chair. The wounds from the silver already healed.

I get up from the floor and have to catch myself on the wall behind me. He doesn't move, doesn't reach out to catch me. Xavier just watches me until I'm steady on my feet again and then walks to the door. Xavier pauses for a brief second before walking out into the hall and out the front door.

I sigh, and my knees threaten to give out, but I refuse to let them.

A few moments later, Tasha walks into the room and looks at the empty chair, spinning to look behind her quickly and then back to me.

"Where is he?"

"I let him go. I told him I won't hesitate to take him out next time something like this happens."

"Will that really be necessary?"

I push myself away from the wall and walk to Tasha. "This thing that happened today can never happen again. I am one of the most notorious hunters in this world. I can't afford to let the vampire world think I am weak and that I am a blood whore for any vampire that needs it."

I huff air out through my nose as I reach for the bite on my neck and lightly touch it.

"I don't know why, but the vampires I've encountered all said my blood smells different. Even Xavier. Hunters who become easy prey don't bode well in my world. Only one vampire could sink his teeth into my neck, and that was Xavier. The VHA barely let me back in that night. They had so much testing done on me I felt like a damn pincushion when they were through. Deciding that I wasn't turned, even though I told them that I didn't drink from the vampire."

Dragging a hand over my face. "The VHA will absolutely skin me alive if they find out I gave my blood willingly. Even more so if they knew it was Xavier. I just can't risk that."

The sigh that leaves my lips speaks more of the weight these events place on me than I have ever said aloud.

I push past Tasha and walk to the bathroom. My whole body aches. To Tasha's credit, she knows how to draw a bath. I don't close the door behind me as I strip my clothes and get into the bathtub—filled to the brim with hot water and bubbles.

My muscles instantly relax as the aroma of the bath salts fills my nose.

Hmm, vanilla and jasmine. Tasha clears her throat and enters the bathroom. "I hope the water is fine. I didn't know if you would prefer the water without the salts, but I figured you need them."

"It's perfect, thank you. I don't think my body has taken so much onslaught since I trained to become a hunter." I sink deeper into the water, groaning as the pain subsides and my body warms up.

After a long pause, I say, "I'm glad you're here. I think Xavier and I would have killed each other by now if you weren't."

Maybe we would have, maybe not. I don't know, but I do know that this unlikely friendship saved my life more than once. Everything I used to see as black and white has now become utterly gray, especially when it comes to Xavier.

I still hate his guts, but I'm less likely to spill them now than I would have a month ago.

I look at the door where Tasha is still standing, and a soft smile tugs at her lips.

"I'll go make us some hot chocolate. Take your time, and please call me if you need my help." She walks to where I discarded my bloody clothes, picks them up from the floor, and closes the door behind her as she leaves.

I rub my wet hands over my face. How am I going to get out of this mess? I will not ruin this bath by debating my next moves. I close my eyes and slide my head under the water.

CHAPTER TWENTY-EIGHT

XAVIER

"That damn woman will be the death of me," I shout from the middle of the woods. My tension-filled muscles are coiling like a snake, and I need to rip something's throat out.

I can't believe I got myself into this situation. *Again.*

Little Deadly's taste still lingers in my mouth, veins, and even my lungs with every breath I take. Her blood is crippling.

Not in the sense that it weakens me but that I can't get enough of it. It awakens something in the deepest part of me, and like last time, I will be in deep shit if I don't keep an eye on my feeding schedule now.

The more I think about it, the more it frightens me. Her blood calls to me like barren earth calls to rain.

I knew it the first moment I tasted her blood so many years ago. It's one of the reasons I can't stay away from her. Now, because of my negligence and injured ass, she was forced to give me her blood to save herself and Tasha from *me.*

The taste lingers to the point where I can still feel it run down my throat. I can still feel her heart hammer against her chest. The arousal my bite made her feel made her blood taste even sweeter.

I can't afford to let her—or anyone else, for that matter—find out what her blood does to me.

Dammit! I slam my fist into an old oak tree next to me, and it cracks under the force of the blow. Leaves and dry branches fall from above.

The woods are dark and beautiful. Nighttime creatures crawl around and go about their business.

The blow still echoes through the woods, and every living thing seems to stop breathing. The woods become eerily quiet.

I huff an irritated sigh and turn back to the house when a snapping twig disturbs the silence, and I whirl around to peer into the darkness.

I stand absolutely still, which isn't hard, listening intently and then catching movement to the east of where I stand.

Evanescing into the night toward the movement, I appear mere inches from the creature now grazing the leaves of the nearby tree. Overwhelming relief washes over me. It's inexplicable. The elk only lifts its head when I turn to move away from it. It watches me for a few minutes before returning to its grazing.

I am so tired of looking over my shoulder. It's bad enough that with the VHA out in the world, my kind has to constantly be on the lookout, but now I have the vampire world on my ass as well … It's exhausting.

The cottage comes into view as the trees thin out, and I climb over a fallen tree just to stop short.

The bathroom window is visible from where I find myself in the woods. I step closer to the cottage, but I'm careful not to enter the light from the moon and window, keeping myself shrouded in darkness when I see movement from within.

Little Deadly gets out of the bathtub and makes her way to the towel rack. My body reacts instantly, and I clench my fists. She is absolutely beautiful.

My eyes fall on her slender, muscled back, riddled with scars, and my eyes slope down to her ass. Every inch of her body is exquisitely sculpted and toned from training—in a way that no one will suspect how strong she is. My eyes trail further down to her legs, and then she turns, towel in hand, and walks to the window.

My breath, if it could, would be knocked out of me by the sight of her naked body. I swallow hard as my eyes roam up her thighs and linger on the spot between her legs. *Fuck me.* Clenching my jaw so tight at the images running amok in my mind. My fangs ache, and I find myself wondering what she will taste like when she releases on my tongue.

I shake my head and force my eyes upward but get caught on her full breasts, nipples peaked from the chilly wind blowing into the open window.

Dammit, Xavier, get a hold of yourself.

Little Deadly dries her wet hair before she wraps the towel around her body. Only then is the spell her body cast on me broken.

My eyes move up to her neck, where an angry bruise has formed around the bite. My gut clenches, and I shove one hand in my pocket, the other flexing as the taste of her blood becomes strong in my mouth again.

Little Deadly watches the mountain at the end of the open field when I step out of the shadows, and our eyes meet. She jolts and glares but composes herself before turning and walking out of the bathroom.

Well, since she is looking much better, I think it's time for her and me to have a little talk.

The thought of going head-to-head with Little Deadly isn't something I'm looking forward to. I am in no mood for this talk, but it's necessary. Any day now, Alex could locate us or the VHA if my suspicions are correct. We need to see where we are going from here.

She can handle herself now that she is mostly healed. I shake my head at myself at the thought of her on the floor after she fed me her blood.

I still can't fathom why she would do that. I'm torn. I'm so pissed that she did it, but at the same time, the gratitude I feel can't be explained.

Damn woman. Since crossing paths with her, she has consumed my entire world. I've done everything in my power to pretend that it doesn't, but I'm losing that battle. Now more than ever.

I stroll into the cottage and am met with the two women sitting in front of the fireplace, each with a mug of steaming hot chocolate.

Tasha turns and gives me a quick smile before focusing on the fire. Little Deadly, with her knees pulled up to her chest and the mug between her hands, doesn't even look my way—not when I walk around the couch or drag a chair to sit directly in front of her. She sips her hot beverage and then turns to Tasha to thank her.

In my peripheral, I find Tasha watching my every move. Eyebrows raised. I pay her no mind as I rest my elbows on my knees.

"Thank you."

That catches Little Deadly's attention as she turns to me and only stares. This is going to be more difficult than I thought. She purses her lips and takes another sip from the mug. I have to admit, her silence unnerves me.

"We need to talk," I tell her.

Little Deadly only raises her brows, turning the mug in her hands. If she is trying to irritate me, it's working.

Deciding it's not worth the trouble, I lean back in the chair. I fold my arms across my chest and trail my eyes over her robe-covered body. Slowly—oh so slowly—I trail them down and then back up to linger on her mouth for a minute and then back to her eyes.

I have to keep from laughing when I'm met with blushed cheeks and a genuinely frightening glare.

"If you drag your eyes over me one more time, I *will* remove them. Didn't you get your fill when you watched me get out of the bath like a perv?"

Tasha gasps. "Xavier."

I turn to Tasha and roll my eyes, bored. "Why don't you give us a moment, Tasha?" I order. I don't know if I like that Tasha has grown fond of Little Deadly. I guess I should have expected as much.

"But—"

I throw a warning glare at her, and Tasha shuts her mouth quickly. Nodding, she gets up and walks out of the cottage.

"You are such an asshole," Little Deadly says as she glares at me.

Ignoring her statement, I rest my arms on my knees again and intertwine my fingers. "Are you going to tell me what happened to you?"

Shock flashes in Little Deadly's eyes before hatred overshadows her face. Her eyes become dark at the mere mention of it.

"I don't know what you're talking about." Her answer is short and clipped as she sets the mug down next to her.

I try to keep the violence out of my voice when I ask, "Who hurt you, Dominica?" Little Deadly clenches her jaw so tight that I can hear her teeth straining under the pressure. She balls her fists and looks away from me without answering.

"Okay, let me ask you this then. Why didn't the VHA come to help you when you got hurt?"

More silence.

Little Deadly doesn't move. She only stares ahead of her. Her nostrils flare at my incessant questioning. Come to think of it, the

VHA hasn't sent even one of their dogs to search for their most deadly hunter.

"I need to know what the hell I got myself into here—"

Her head snaps to me, and she scowls. "*You* didn't get yourself into anything. I can handle it."

"Okay," I say, nodding my head. "Then why aren't you fighting to get home? Why stay? Why the hell feed me your blood?"

Little Deadly glares at me but then closes her eyes and sighs tiredly. "I can't go home. Not yet."

"Why?"

"It's none of your damn business, Xavier," she snaps again.

The lack of information and her unwillingness to provide it are wearing my patience thin. Dragging my tongue over my teeth, I push again. "It is my damn business when I am the one who saved you from those idiots who almost made you dinner. *Twice.*" My temper rises with each word.

"I didn't ask you to save me. You are my *enemy.* I didn't have a choice in the matter. I didn't tell you to go against your own kind and help me. That's on you," she says with utter disdain.

I shoot to my feet and throw my hands up in the air. "You are a piece of work. You ungrateful little bitch."

The words leave my mouth before I have time to register them. Little Deadly goes entirely still and drags her eyes to me before baring her teeth and rising slowly from her seat.

"What did you just call me?"

Well, the damage is done. If the only way to get her to talk is to provoke her, then so be it. I'll ride this train.

I turn my attention to her fully and smirk as I say, "You heard me. You. Ungrateful. Little. *Bitch.*"

Dark laughter bubbles out of Little Deadly's chest, and the next moment, she hurls her almost full cup of hot chocolate at my head.

I dodge the cup, but the hot liquid splashes on my shirt and half my face. I hiss at the burn, and when Little Deadly lunges for me,

I barely have enough time to wipe it out of my eye before her fist connects with the left side of my face.

She swings her left fist to my face again, but this time, I catch it and hold her firm. Little Deadly struggles to pull her hand from mine, and I frown at that.

She isn't nearly as strong as usual, which worries me. Have I taken that much blood from her?

"Let go of me!" she seethes.

This time, my breath *is* knocked out of me when she brings her knee up and connects it with my balls. I roar in pain and grab her by the throat, snarling at her as I yank her toward me.

Little Deadly doesn't blanch. Doesn't show an inch of fear. She never has. What happens next is still so wildly unfathomable that I still don't know how it happened.

One moment, we are glaring at each other, ready to rip each other's throats out, and the next, I grip her hair tightly as I crush my mouth to hers.

She freezes for a few seconds, but then her hands are all over me. I kiss her feverishly, teeth clashing as our tongues battle it out.

I draw a sharp breath, and a growl rumbles through my chest as she drags her hand down my chest and grips my length through my pants.

Letting go of her hair, I rip the robe open and let it fall to the ground, and to my utmost pleasure, I find her completely naked.

A wicked smile creeps onto my lips as I take in the beauty of the woman before me. Little Deadly doesn't wait as she grips the top of my button shirt and rips it open. Buttons flying in every direction. She yanks my shirt down and then goes for my pants next.

"A little enthusiastic, aren't we?"

"Shut the hell up, Xavier, or this is going to stop," she snarls as she yanks my pants down with my boxers.

I put my hands up in defeat and step out of my pants. Little Deadly drags her gaze down my body and back up again, smiling in approval.

"Shall we get on with it?" I mock, and she slaps me across the face. Snarling, I move fast. I wrap my hands under her ass and haul her up. She yelps and wraps her arms around my neck as I fold her legs around my waist.

I push my hand into the back of her hair, grab hold of it at the nape of her neck, and pull her head back to expose her throat.

Little Deadly goes completely still when I drag my nose down her jaw to where my teeth were just a few hours ago.

I struggle to swallow, and my mouth waters at the thought of sinking my fangs into her throat again.

"Don't you dare bite me again," she warns, and I laugh darkly against her throat.

I leave light kisses at the bite and make my way down to her breast. I latch on, and she arches her back when I suck the peaked nipple into my mouth.

I suck and flick it with my tongue until she writhes against me. Only then do I move my attention to the other until she gasps.

Feeling the need to be inside her so strong I might lose my mind, I move to the wall and slam her back against it. Little Deadly gasps and wraps her hand around my throat, pushing me away far enough so I can look at her.

"If this is a struggle for dominance, Xavier, I can promise you, you will lose."

"Is that a challenge I hear in your voice … *Little Deadly?*" I snarl and rip her hand away from my throat. I grab the other and pin them above her head against the wall with one of mine. I wrap my free hand around her waist and align myself.

She scowls and opens her mouth to protest, but I smirk before driving into her. Little Deadly screams and arches her back off the wall.

"More," she breathes, and when she levels those lust-filled eyes with mine, I damn near lose my mind.

Drawing out of her slowly and thrusting in again, I feel that foreign thing in me pull—pull so tight it threatens to snap. With every thrust into her, the thing in my heart grows tauter until it snaps into place, and I nearly lose all sense of myself.

I drive into her, again and again and again, until she screams my name when she's thrown over the edge of her pleasure. Moments later, I follow her over that edge, and I sink to the floor.

When I release her hands, she slumps against me, and I lie us down on the soft carpet next to the fire.

"What the hell are you doing to me?" Little Deadly says as I brush her hair out of her face.

"I can ask you that same question."

She covers her face with her hands as nervous laughter bubbles from her. When she eventually lowers her hands, she only stares at me, and there is a spark in her eyes that I haven't seen before.

I am so royally screwed, it's not even funny.

CHAPTER TWENTY-NINE

DOMINICA

What the hell have I done? The thought loops in my mind whenever I look at Xavier, who is now dressed and sitting in front of me.

I've always known how dangerous Xavier is, but the danger he poses *now* is, in a way, worse than before.

I can't understand how I got myself into this mess. Sleeping with the enemy is an understatement. Once can be seen as a lapse of judgment, but *five times* in a matter of an hour is *insane.*

I should feel ashamed, but I just can't seem to conjure up the feeling.

Poor Tasha.

My cheeks flush bright red at the thought of the poor girl who clearly heard what happened in her cottage. Even if she didn't, she could not miss the carnage we left. She didn't look pleased when we called her back into the house. I smiled apologetically, and we all took a seat at the dining room table.

Every time the cunning vampire looks at me, it sends my blood rushing to my cheeks and down to that traitorous spot between my legs.

Xavier still irritates the living daylights out of me—but something in me has changed. I'm grappling to hold onto my hatred for him, but it seems to fade with every heartbeat. *Could it be possible for me* not *to hate him?*

"So, are we only going to stare at each other or what?" Tasha scoffs and folds her arms across her chest. She is clearly annoyed by us, and I can understand why. The fact that she's still newly bonded to Xavier's blood and, in part, to him probably feels like a betrayal. The atmosphere is heavy with disdain. After our lapse in judgment, Xavier's temper flared. His mood is brooding and dark. When Tasha dared to ask what happened, he nearly lost it.

"No." The only answer Xavier utters.

His irritated tone toward Tasha is pissing me off. He glares at her, and somehow, his mood gets worse.

"You don't have to be a dick, Xavier," I snap.

Xavier turns his burning gaze on me, and his eyes flash before he grits his teeth and snarls, "If she can stop being so incessant and just mind her damn business, I wouldn't have to be."

My eyebrows pull together. "What the hell is wrong with you?"

"Nothing." Xavier slams his fists on the table and rises suddenly. "I'm going for some fresh air. When I return, you'd better be ready to give me the information I need."

"Screw you."

"You already did," he snorts and evanesces.

My eyes widen in shock, shooting to Tasha, whose face goes sour. She turns on me and gives me a glare that could melt the entire world's icebergs. "I thought you were sworn enemies. But you just couldn't resist, could you?"

Now, *I'm* getting frustrated. "We are, and it's none of your business. All I am going to say on this topic is that whatever happened today, the feeding and then … " I roll my eyes. "The fucking will never happen again. *Never.*"

Tasha snorts as she gets up from the table and walks to the kitchen. “Whatever you say.”

This is ridiculous. I don’t have to explain myself, not to her and especially not to Xavier. He has become more and more grumpy with every passing breath.

My thoughts threaten to doubt my performance, but I squash the idea quickly. Xavier probably regrets it just as much as I do. I’m just handling it better.

Yeah, that’s it. I roll my eyes at myself for thinking like a damn lovesick puppy. “Do you want some coffee?” Tasha says from the stove, her back to me.

“If it won’t be too much effort. Thank you.”

After a few minutes, she turns and looks at me. She huffs and fidgets with her fingers before she says, “It doesn’t make sense … the way he looks at you.”

“Don’t go looking for something that isn’t there, Tash, please. It’s probably because of my blood. And it *was* just sex. There is nothing there.”

“Hmm.”

“Can we please not talk about this anymore? It’s bad enough that I have to look at sourpuss when he’s here. Can we just put this behind us?”

Tasha chews her bottom lip and gives me a slight nod. “Okay.”

“Thank you.” I inhale deeply and huff it out, feeling somewhat relieved. *Can this day get any worse?*

Xavier *appears,* and I nearly have a heart attack. He scowls at me and then at Tasha. His mood darkening still. “Ready?”

“No.”

“Dominica Van Helsing Salvatore, do not push me,” Xavier says darkly, gripping the back of his chair.

My back goes rigid at the mention of my full name. A name *no one* is supposed to know. The one I’ve been working my ass off to distance myself from. The one that lost its popularity over the years since my ancestors mostly died out. But only a few still knew the true meaning of it, deep within some circles of the VHA and Old Vampire communities.

I open and close my mouth a few times as the words fail me and only manage, "How?"

Xavier chuckles menacingly. "Know thine enemy."

I slowly rise from my seat and rest my hands flat on the table, leaning forward. I look Xavier dead in the eyes, searching for goodness knows what.

"Well, *thine enemy* says *bite me,*" I say, flipping him off. Not my best comeback. I cringe inwardly at the holes I dig for myself.

"You make it *so* damn easy." He smirks while also leaning closer to me. Tasha clears her throat and sets my mug of coffee in front of me before taking her seat and sipping from her own.

Deciding that this will not end well if I let him bait me further, I pull back and take my seat again, thanking Tasha for the coffee.

Xavier watches me for a few seconds before turning his attention to Tasha. "I'm sorry if I offended you or if I'm being rude. I'm struggling to deal with this troublesome m—" Xavier cuts himself off and stares at me.

"Troublesome what?" I ask, intrigued.

"Nothing," he says, baring his fangs and shoving his hands in his pockets before turning toward the fireplace.

"What time is it?" I ask Tasha.

"Why?"

"Because maybe he needs his beauty sleep?" I shrug as I take another sip from my coffee.

Xavier only shoots me an irritated look over his shoulder before returning to the table and sitting down again.

"No one is sleeping until we know why the VHA isn't looking for you and how you ended up mortally wounded before I found you."

"You aren't going to let this go, are you?"

Xavier only lifts his eyebrows at me in a "not a chance" manner and makes himself comfortable.

"Maybe Xavier has a point," Tasha says softly from behind her cup, and I shoot her a look. "Hear me out. I know it must be difficult for you to talk about, but if we are going to survive the vampires after us, we need all the information."

"I don't see how my misfortune with people has anything to do with our current situation. That falls on him." I nudge my chin in Xavier's direction. "I didn't ask him to save me, although I am grateful he did. I did not ask him to take me with him when he ran from whatever the hell he's running from."

Xavier's nostrils flare, and vicious anger builds in his eyes. "I'm in this mess because of *you.*"

I roll my eyes and shake my head. "And how do you reckon it's my fault?"

"Because of you and that damn Association. Alex is hell-bent to have your head on a platter after you had to go and bomb the compound his sister was in. He sent me to bring you to him, but—"

I am flabbergasted. What the hell is he talking about? Then I remember the briefing, where Brian said they had intel that a high-priority target was eliminated.

"But what, Xavier? You've had multiple chances to take me to Alex. Why haven't you?"

"Something didn't feel right, and I wanted to get to the bottom of it. I can always take you to Alex if it is revealed that all the evidence is true." Xavier shrugs and crosses his arms over his chest.

"Damn you. I had nothing to do with that bombing."

"And I'm just supposed to believe you?" Xavier snorts.

When I heard about the compound being blown up, I knew something didn't feel right, and now some of the puzzle pieces are being shifted into place. I am being set up, but by whom exactly is still a mystery.

"Believe what you want. It doesn't matter either way. I am on my own whichever way this plays out," I mutter as I stare at my cup.

"Ugh! You infuriating woman!" Xavier snarls, slamming his fist on the table.

"Don't be a dick, Xavier," Tasha mutters and gives him a sidelong glance before turning to me. "Take your time."

I laugh dryly and lean back in my chair. "Fine, you want to know what happened? I was ridiculed by my boss and practically fired for your stunt at the docks that night Silvia was killed. Because *I saved you.*" I pause, catching my breath, my heart pounding. "And then I got run through with a bloody sword, wielded by my *best friend.* The only ally I had left. He wanted something I couldn't give him, and everything just got worse when he thought I had helped you—" I shove my hand in Xavier's direction. The tears brim in my eyes as I feel the betrayal and the pain from every wound Austen inflicted on me, surface. "Helped you kill his partner.

"Austen lured me out to the schoolyard and tried to kill me. He drove his sword through my torso and *twisted* it for good measure. And then, to top it off, he kicked the living shit out of me before he shot me." My voice becomes softer, but the fury in it lingers. "I barely got away and thought that dying would be better than living with all of it, but then, by some cruel twist of fate, someone found me and helped me, and *your cronies* ripped his throat out. And who would be the one to save me then? Of all people, it had to be *you.*"

I'm not even trying to hide my disgust at the whole situation. I'm heaving from the pressure in my chest, the anger threatening to consume me, along with the sorrow.

When I finish, neither of them makes a sound. The only sounds are the crackling fire and the soft patter of rain on the roof. I didn't even notice. I close my eyes and cover my face with my hands as the sobs tear through me.

It's exhausting, all this crying, all this betrayal. If I could go back to when I first started training to become a hunter, I would tell myself never to trust and never let anyone in.

Xavier hasn't moved since I told them about Austen. He still isn't moving. His face is hooded and dark, and his knuckles are white as he clutches the arms of his chair.

The wood snaps under the pressure, and Tasha jumps up from her chair, moving quickly to me.

I shove my chair backward but don't get up, placing the ball of my foot against the table. If he loses his shit and lunges, I can buy us some time if I shove the table at him.

Xavier's lip twitches, and he tilts his head eerily, narrowing his eyes as they fall on me.

"*What. Did. You. Say?*"

"You heard me. I am not going to repeat it again."

A deep, dangerous growl rumbles low in Xavier's chest before he evanesces.

CHAPTER THIRTY

DOMINICA

Two days have passed, and Xavier still hasn't returned to the cottage. I am getting worried, but at the same time, my anger at his dismissive nature outweighs the worry.

The little information I got from Tasha has been mulling in my head. The hit on my head came after the death of the vampire king's sister. Every piece of evidence points to me. The only problem is that I didn't do it.

So, who did, and why place the blame on me?

I slipped out of the cottage last night after discovering that the nearest town is about thirty minutes away. I took Xavier's Mustang—seeing as he clearly didn't need it—and went to an internet café.

I logged into the VHA server using Austen's login, but not before I scrambled the IP address. I have no doubt they will trace it back to the café, but it will give us some time to get our shit together. Three days max.

The files were all sealed, but the information I did manage to obtain didn't say much about who blew up the specific compound. What stood out to me was the source of all the anonymous tips.

It seems they were given by a vampire. Why the hell would the VHA take tips from the enemy? Something is very wrong, and the dread I felt the night Silvia died settles in my stomach. I logged out as soon as possible and returned to the cottage.

Hence, my irritated state. There is no Xavier, and our time is running out. Tasha, who looks like a coiled spring, keeps herself busy baking in the kitchen. We haven't spoken much since Xavier vanished.

I turn to her after pacing the floor for the thousandth time—not believing that I haven't made a trench in the floor. "We need to get ready to leave."

Tasha doesn't answer as she takes the seventh batch of cookies out of the oven. Only then does she say, "We can't. Xavier hasn't come to get us."

"Let's face it. Xavier has abandoned us. Likely feeling that I'm too much of a liability to have around and is probably planning to bring Alex to me so I can pay for my sins or whatnot." I shrug and plop down on the couch.

"Don't say that. Xavier won't do that."

I snort but stay quiet. I don't have the strength to argue with Tasha. Every nerve ending in my body is on edge, and the impending danger lingers in the air like a disgusting odor.

"We need Xavier to protect us," Tasha softly says.

"Pfft, we don't. I am back to my full strength. *I* can protect us."

"How?"

I purse my lips and narrow my eyes. That question doesn't even warrant an answer. I clearly haven't made a good impression in my injured state. Speaking of which, my wounds are all almost completely healed. All but the one in my neck. My strength is back up, and so is the need to get to the bottom of everything.

I need to get to my apartment and stock up on weapons if I am going to keep the heat off our backs. I don't feel comfortable not having my daggers on me.

"Dominica?" Tasha says, sounding annoyed. "What's going on? You haven't listened to a word I've said."

"Sorry, what?"

"I asked, how you plan on keeping us safe without Xavier?"

"Listen, I know I wasn't able to hold my own for the last few days, but I will be able to now—like I always have," I tell her, staring at the fire.

"If you say so."

"Thanks for the confidence," I scoff, rising from my chair and walking to the kitchen. I grab a cookie from the baking tray, still warm and absolutely delicious, and shove it into my mouth. I have to give it to Tasha. She really knows how to make comfort food.

"What's the plan, then?" Tasha turns to the boiling kettle and makes us each a cup of coffee. She then puts more cookies on a plate and sets them on the coffee table.

Taking her cup, Tasha sits on one of the comfy couches. I take my cup and join her, taking a seat on the armrest of the opposite couch.

I tell her about the information I gathered when I left the previous night.

"I wondered where you went. I thought you left me, too," she whispers just before sipping her coffee.

"We are in this together. I won't leave you until I know you are safe." Tasha gives me a small smile and takes a bite of the cookie she just took. Worry still ebbs in her eyes, her shoulders still tense. She chews her bottom lip, looks at me, and says warily, "What about Xavier?"

I roll my eyes and get to my feet, strolling to the window overlooking the woods and the mountain. It's dark out, but the moon is full and eerily lights up certain parts of the grounds and woods. The perfect setting for a horror movie.

I laugh silently at my impeccable thought process. *Always seeing the bright side of things, aren't we?* I think to myself.

"What about him?" Remembering the question when Tasha clears her throat.

"Don't you feel guilty about leaving without him?"

I turn and frown at her. "I think I repaid him well enough." Without thinking, my hand drifts to the bite in my neck, and I trace the two holes lightly with the pads of my fingers.

It still stings when I touch it, but not as bad as the night it happened. I still can't believe I let him drink from me.

That thought leads me to the next, and oh boy, does my body react to it. My core heats up like molten lava. Flashes of Xavier's mouth and hands on my body make my lower abdomen coil in pleasure. My cheeks heat, and I find myself rubbing my thighs together at the thought of his hands there, on that spot, the one that he so expertly knows how to work. The same one he used to make my body feel like jelly at the number of times he made me climax.

"Dammit," I mutter and have to turn my back to Tasha.

"Sorry, what was that?"

"Nothing, just thought of something." Understatement of the century. I didn't just think about it, no. I lusted after it, reliving every second of it.

The conflict in my mind, heart, and even my body is driving me insane. I don't know how to feel about Xavier anymore.

He showed kindness and compassion—*so much compassion.* And there I lose my train of thought as the images flash again.

Get a hold of yourself, Dom.

But then the memories of him brooding after everything happened also surface, as did the way he reacted after I told him what Austen did to me. It's almost like he got the intel he needed, finding out I am alone with no backup. No one would come for me if I was in trouble. Like he knew this was the time to get back into Alex's good graces.

My heart aches at the thought of him betraying me like that. Actual hurt. The kind that cripples. The kind I felt when Austen did it, but in a way so much worse.

I turn my attention back to Tasha, if only to distract myself from Xavier. She watches me with raised brows and says, "Looks like he got under your skin."

"Xavier has always had the privilege of doing that. No other vampire has ever made me so mind-numbingly livid at their presence."

"That's not what I mean, and you know it," Tasha scoffs.

I narrow my eyes at her. "I *don't* know what you mean. The only thing I feel for Xavier is annoyance, and when he pushes me, I feel absolute hatred, but nothing more."

"Hmm, keep telling yourself that. If you keep lying to yourself, you will regret it." I huff an irritated sigh and swallow my annoyance, now directed at Tasha. I don't like this conversation. I do not need to explain myself.

"Okay, so we both slept with Xavier. Big deal." It's a colossal deal in my case. "We can't dwell on it. I'm sorry if I hurt you by doing so, but you need to remember that the feelings you have for Xavier aren't real. You only feel them because of the blood bond," I tell her and tap on my neck, the exact spot where the X is marked on hers.

"How would you know?" she mutters and looks to the fireplace. I sigh and walk to sit next to her. Only when she turns to look at me do I say, "I know because I've seen it happen a million times. Girls lose their minds over it sometimes. The vampires who do link humans to them are cruel and sadistic."

"Not Xavier."

"No, not Xavier. I will give it to the bastard; you were extremely lucky. What I know of Xavier is this," I say, thinking it best to choose my words carefully. "He's a loner. A vampire like that doesn't like loose ends, which never ends well for the human hanging around. Xavier has more of a heart than I've ever seen in a vampire, especially one who has lived as long as he has."

"How long?" Tasha asks, her eyes wide at the mention of his age.

"I'm not entirely sure, but from what I gathered from our records," I say, trying to recall the exact document, "he has been around a long time, since before the American Revolutionary War—"

"Are you both really this bored that my age needs to be what you talk about?" I startle at the voice and jump to my feet. Xavier steps out of the shadows in the kitchen, his hands in his pockets and his face drawn.

"Where the hell have you been?" I snap, trying to calm my racing heart.

"I didn't know the VHA's records even went that far back," he says, ignoring my question.

I narrow my eyes and glare at him. Tasha jumps to her feet and runs to Xavier. She slams into him and throws her arms around his neck while shoving her nose into the crook of his neck just below the jaw, sobbing.

I'm frozen to the spot, my heart still hammering in my chest. Annoyance takes root once my heart eventually calms down, and I pull my mouth into a thin line as the weirdest feeling crawls out of the depths of somewhere dark—*jealousy.*

Are you kidding me? Jealousy isn't something I am used to feeling, and the little green monster sets its hooks deep into my soul.

Xavier doesn't move either. When Tasha embraces him, he doesn't remove his hands from his pockets. He doesn't even look at her. What he looks at … is me.

No, *look* is not the correct word for it.

At first, I thought there was hatred behind those dark eyes, but then again, I have seen hatred in them before, which isn't quite the same as this.

Tilting my head, I try to decipher the look he gives me. To be honest, it's unsettling. My brain struggles to comprehend the conclusion I come up with.

It's hunger—not the feeding kind, no, but absolute *want.* The kind that you can't live without.

I shake my head in disbelief and close my eyes to gather my thoughts. But when I open them again, there's nothing of the previously tortured look, nothing but loathing.

He smiles, and I can tell I wasn't supposed to see that emotion. The smile is twisted and a warning, one without words, one that will send some lesser human running in the opposite direction.

"Where have you been, Xavier? We almost left without you," Tasha says, pulling back and looking up at him.

"Were you now?" he says, unimpressed, lifting his brows as he looks down at Tasha before lifting his gaze back to me.

"Yes," I snap. Gone is the bemused feeling from just a few minutes ago, replaced by the familiar pissed-off one.

"And why is that?" Xavier steps away from Tasha and toward me. His gaze roams the entirety of the cottage before dragging it up my body.

He saunters toward me, but I step back, and with every step, he comes closer. Every movement, every look, screams predator.

Xavier gives me an amused smile, still walking toward me slowly until my back hits the wall behind me, and I'm cornered. A smile tugs at the corner of his mouth as he stops mere inches from me.

How the hell did I let this happen? All my focus is on his stance and the look on his face. I didn't notice him herding me into the corner.

This is dangerous. Xavier only confirms my thoughts when he chuckles darkly and says, "Seems like you are losing your touch, Little Deadly."

Heat pools below, and my body comes alive with him so close. I clench my jaw at the mention of the nickname and shove him away from me. Xavier steps back twice and smirks. I blush instantly before moving away to the other side of the room—as far as possible in this tiny living space.

"What is your problem?" I fume.

Tasha, now glaring at me, storms in between me and Xavier. She turns on Xavier, and that glare falls on him.

"I don't know what's going on between the two of you, but you need to get over it. We have bigger shit to worry about."

CHAPTER THIRTY-ONE

XAVIER

"Where were you?" Tasha asks me again, still glaring at both of us. I narrow my eyes at her, and my lip twitches as I suppress the snarl. "Out." My mind flashes with the memory of two nights ago.

I just couldn't look at the hurt and betrayal on Dominica's face any longer. The more I watched her crack and reveal what that bastard of a friend did to her, the more I had to keep from going into the lion's den and killing him. Even that egotistical boss of hers.

So I left. Evanesced. For two days.

*I had to get my shit under control. That bond that snapped into place when we made love—*can I even call it that?

Love.

If that's what it was—and for the life of me, I wish it wasn't—I am going to suffer.

I dragged a hand over my face, swigged the whiskey in the tumbler I clutched in my fist, and looked out at the city.

Who am I kidding? I knew what it was, but the thought scared me. The mate bond—*the very* rare *mate bond.*

I don't recall ever hearing of one in my lifetime. It's not just any mate bond. It's two destinies entwined from the very beginning of their existence.

I sighed, clenched my jaw, and threw the glass into the fireplace. The fire roared to life from the few drops left in the tumbler.

Why I didn't realize that it could be a possibility was beyond me. Everything made sense now. The pull toward Little Deadly that first night we crossed paths, and in every other interaction we've had, it wasn't only hunger that I felt—it was her.

I rose from my seat and walked over to the fireplace. I leaned against the mantel with both hands as the fire settled into that low ember burn.

What am I going to do? This can only end in disaster—Me and her can never be. *I gripped the mantel with so much force that it crumbled in my hands. Luckily, this was one of my many apartments I have across the city—the one I wanted us to come to next. It's already in shambles since Alex had already thought to look here. They destroyed everything.*

Time got away from me, and I didn't realize that two days had gone by. Panic enveloped my mind when I did.

I evanesced back to the cottage to find Dominica and Tasha talking. I didn't show myself immediately, still trying to school my features so as not to show what my body was screaming.

It didn't work.

The moment I stepped out of that shadow, my heart and that taut tether pulled me to go to her. But I didn't—I couldn't.

Dominica saw it in my eyes; she must have because her face pulled in confusion. So, I focused my attention on Tasha, and the immediate irritation of her touching me in front of Little Deadly helped me hide that feeling—the need, the want.

I stroll leisurely to the kitchen counter and pick up a tray of cookies before looking at Tasha over my shoulder, and I raise my brow.

Maybe it's best to ignore Little Deadly for the time being until I can figure out how to deal with this mess.

But try as I might, my gaze keeps going to where she stands at the other end of the room. Her weary eyes follow my every movement as she stands, feet shoulder-width apart and arms loose at her sides, ready to strike at a moment's notice.

"I bake when I'm nervous," Tasha says, her tone clipped.

"Clearly." I set the tray down and move to the dining room table, sitting down and motioning with my hand for them to also sit down.

Tasha looks at me and then at Little Deadly before slowly walking to the table and sitting opposite me.

Little Deadly shakes her head and just crosses her arms over her chest.

"As you wish." I lean forward in my chair, place my elbows on the table, and intertwine my fingers.

"I apologize for evanescing while you were telling your tale. I had somewhere to be and a few things to sort out."

Little Deadly narrows her gaze on me again and says venomously, "Like leaking my whereabouts to your master."

Anger flashes through me, and I snarl at her. "Don't you *ever* insinuate that I am a traitor. I have *no* master. Nothing will ever have me in its snare, and *nothing* will ever control me."

Lies. All lies.

I am a slave. A slave to a bond I didn't ask for but one I realize I would protect, even from her. The only master I will serve is … *her.*

I don't break our stare for a few more seconds before deciding it's not worth explaining.

Shrugging, I relax back in my chair. "We need to plan our next move."

"Our?" Little Deadly scoffs.

"Ours. Yours. It doesn't matter, but we need to establish what will happen next. Preferably before Alex and his cronies find us—you," I drag on.

The silence ticks by, and when Little Deadly doesn't answer me, I push some more.

"They know that I helped you. If they didn't, they do now, especially after the other night. So, like it or not, we are in this together. I am enemy number one for the VHA and now my own kind. If you prefer to do this on your own, then so be it." I shrug. "I can get Tasha to a place where she can be safe, and I can disappear. But let's be honest, it's not in your nature to shrink away—"

"You know *nothing* about my nature. So don't you dare sit there and try to talk to me about who I am. You don't even know me." The disgust and anger overshadow the trauma behind her eyes. She tries her best not to show it, but it's there.

"I know what I need to know. Especially about an enemy." *And more about you than anyone else,* I think before I continue. "Like you know every possible piece of information you could find about me. That's what makes you an excellent hunter: not just your skill wielding a blade but the fact that you can obtain information others can't," I say, with no trace of a smile. I am not trying to compliment her. I am only stating the obvious to establish the point I'm trying to make. "Like myself. I have not lived as long as I have because of luck."

Little Deadly snorts but doesn't utter a single word. Tasha only watches us. Disgust and fear behind those eyes.

Good.

Tasha needs to see the real me, who doesn't do well with groupies, like I told her the first time we met.

"Like you said the other night. You don't have anyone since your friend turned against you, and so did the Association—"

"I never said that," Little Deadly snaps.

"Don't be so sensitive. I only imply that you have me on your side, so use it." I shrug. Little Deadly opens her mouth but shuts it again. She closes her eyes, and after a minute or so, she straightens and lifts her chin.

"Fine. Just until we get to the bottom of this shit show." I smile, bowing my head slightly. She doesn't return the smile, doesn't even acknowledge the gesture. Of course, she doesn't.

Little Deadly huffs air out through her nose and sits as far away from me as possible, and I only lift a mocking brow.

Ignoring me, she settles in her seat and says, "I have a theory. I've had a bad feeling ever since the docks, the first bombing, and it only intensified the night you killed Silvia."

I don't react to the jab she so clearly wants to land, so I tilt my head in anticipation.

Little Deadly tells me about the source giving information to Brian and Austen and how the intel always lacked vital parts. She tells me about her little outing last night, and I have to keep myself from reacting. From snarling at the thought of her getting hurt again, alone without backup.

She tells me that the VHA may or may not be on their way already. She covered her tracks as far as she could, but they were good at deciphering encryptions.

My brows pull together, and the hairs rise at the back of my neck. The VHA is indeed notorious for uncovering traps. I let my thoughts wander. Didn't Alex tell me that they leaked information? It's unusable information, but information nonetheless.

Why do I get the feeling that the VHA and the Vampire Society aren't so enemy-like as they make it seem?

I tell her my thoughts and what I've seen in the compound with Alex. Little Deadly only frowns but doesn't interrupt. She works her jaw as the pieces of this demented puzzle start to align.

"We need to get more information before we can do anything. It is all speculation at this point, and if we want to do anything about the corruption in our world, we need to be sure," Little Deadly says, rubbing her temples.

We make ourselves comfortable and discuss our next moves. Seeing as the VHA will be on our tails in just a day or so, we decide that we need to move to another place and get to planning how we are going to expose the corrupt parties.

Five hours later, we have a semblance of a plan. Tasha isn't thrilled about what we decided but agrees that it's best for her and her sister's safety.

Tasha will send word to her sister that she managed to get away from me and that she knows our location.

Knowing Alex, he will send Tasha's sister first to see if it's a trap, which will work in our favor to get her out and get Tasha and her sister to a safe house far away from here.

Three hours in, Tasha couldn't stay awake anymore and excused herself. I only nodded and watched as Little Deadly's body stiffened.

The thought of being alone with her is driving me up the wall. I can't concentrate, but I managed the last two hours by letting her do all the talking.

I, on the other hand, wage a war within myself. I nearly bit through my own tongue to keep from telling her. I dig my nails into my thighs to keep from going to her and laying her on this very table. Spreading her legs and—

I swallow hard. That sound of her moaning my name seared into my mind. "Xavier?"

I realize I'm panting, and I let go of my thighs. Blood drips to the floor, and Little Deadly's eyes widen, and she rushes to me.

"What the hell?" She kneels before me and lays her hand softly on the already-closing gashes.

I sharply inhale through my nose and shoot to my feet at her touch. That damn touch *will* and *can* bring me to my knees. That damn touch is so dangerous it can conquer an entire kingdom. Because I will lay waste to it if she wishes. I would lay every vampire at her feet, every VHA member.

The thought makes me pale—paler than I am naturally—and I storm to the fireplace. "Don't touch me."

Little Deadly gapes at me, still kneeling before the chair I was in moments ago.

"What's going on with you? I don't understand," she says softly.

"What don't you understand? I don't want your hands on me. What we did the other night was … " I trail off, not entirely sure what to say. Seeing the hurt on her face breaks me, but I can't afford her knowing how much I want her. How much I want to go back to that night and never burst that bubble, even if it was *just* sex for her.

"Was what, Xavier?"

"Was getting you out of my system and to say that I bedded the Reaper. When I return to my people, it will do *wonders* for my reputation."

Little Deadly watches me studiously before she slowly rises, and a dark smile creeps onto her lips as she nods her head slowly.

It's all an act. I know it, but I can't shake the anger when she says, "Glad to be of service. Just think how popular I will be among your friends. I welcome the target on my back. It will help me kill even more of your kind."

Little Deadly turns on her heel and walks to her room, closing the door behind her, but not before I catch how she folds her arms around herself and how her face falls.

Closing my eyes, a breath shudders out of me at the closing click of her door. I am such an asshole.

CHAPTER THIRTY-TWO

DOMINICA

I can't deal with this anymore. I miss the time when my only worry was how many vampires I had to kill. The whiplash Xavier gives me every time we interact makes my head spin.

One moment, he's caring and protective—which in itself is difficult to deal with—and the next, he acts like the rest of the vermin.

Why do I even care?

The hurt and disappointment clutching my heart make no sense—no sense at all. Tears escape my eyes. Crying seems to be becoming normal for me with Xavier near.

I wipe it away on the back of my hand when I sit on the edge of the bed. How am I supposed to work with him? We can barely have a decent conversation without going for the throat. Literally and figuratively.

I rub my chest, hoping the action will soothe the pain behind it.

Working together can only work if I keep my focus on what I need to do to get away from him. So, I try thinking of every possible way to complete this "mission."

The sooner we can sort out our sides and set things back to how they are supposed to be, the sooner I will be rid of Xavier.

The twinge in my chest makes me double over. *What?* The thought of never seeing him makes me feel sick. I visibly swallow as the exhaustion I managed to push away for the last two days crashes over me. I crawl into bed. Sleep consumes me when my head touches the pillow.

When I wake, it's still dark out. Sleeping has only made me feel worse. How that's even possible is beyond me.

I rise like a zombie from a grave and feel the exhaustion still coursing through my whole body. I scrub my hands over my face and get out of bed. Walking to the closet, I wrench open the doors and am met with two options. The jeans I wore earlier with the white button-down, which is still Xavier's—or the dress that belongs to Tasha's sister.

There wasn't much left of her and her sister in the cottage since they never really returned after their mother died. Tasha told me as much, and I didn't want to pry. The clothes they did leave aren't something you would catch me dead in. So, I opt for the same outfit as the previous day. I'm grateful that Tasha washed it while I was in the bath. Seeing that, I would rather walk naked than wear a dress.

I get dressed and walk out of my room. The living room is dark, with a bit of light coming from the moon that spills onto the dining room table. Tasha is still asleep on the couch, and there is no sign of Xavier.

I wait for relief to appear, but I'm only met with disappointment, and it angers me to the point where I have to suppress a frustrated growl.

The pain in my chest isn't something I've felt before, and it throws me. I don't know how I'm going to get through this. Working with Xavier and having him as an ally when we can barely look at each other is like a horrible one-night stand that won't end.

I sigh. I need to get my head straight. I'm not the kind of person who normally lets my emotions dictate my actions. I never have been. But these last few days have been nothing other than exhausting.

No matter how hard I try to convince myself otherwise, the pain in my chest doesn't subside.

I peer down the hall to the closed oak door and listen for movement. When I hear nothing other than Tasha's light snoring, I take the keys to the Mustang and open the front door to the cottage as silently as possible.

I step out into the chilly night and make my way to Xavier's car. The bastard is fast enough on his own, so he won't need his car.

I get in and start the engine. I tap on the car's navigation system and enter my address. I might as well get a head start on this plan. And I won't be doing that without my weapons.

I turn on the headlights, and when I look up, my heart almost stops beating entirely. In the driveway in front of the car stands Xavier, legs shoulder-width apart, hands shoved in his pockets, and a dark, dangerous look on his face.

The frustration in my chest only intensifies, and I roll my eyes, sighing heavily. I fall back in my seat and cross my arms over my chest, glaring at him.

Xavier's emotionless expression unnerves me. He tilts his head menacingly, pulls his hand out from his pocket, and beckons to me with his fingers. His motions slow and meticulous.

This asshole is starting to get on my last nerve. Who the hell does he think he is, beckoning me like I belong to him?

Xavier's lip twitches, anger flashes behind his eyes, and he runs his tongue over his teeth, lingering for a moment on the sharp fang. He then points his finger down in a "here, now" motion.

White-hot fury explodes in my chest. I place my hands on the steering wheel and grip it tight enough that my hands ache. I put the car in drive and slam my foot on the gas.

The engine roars loudly as the tires spin, and the car flies toward Xavier. The fury in my veins makes me really not care if I run him over.

Xavier waits until the last second to step out of the way. I smile triumphantly as I look back in my rearview mirror. But no one's there. "Where the hell did you go?" I mutter to myself.

The next moment, there's a thud on the roof, and I startle. I clench my jaw irritably. Why can't he just get the message?

Without giving it another thought, I slam both my feet on the brake pedal, and the car screeches to a halt. Xavier flies from the roof but lands gracefully in a crouching position. He rises slowly and swats the dirt from his pants, looking extremely bored. It only sends my irritation limit through the roof.

I push open the door, get out angrily, and slam it shut so hard I'm astounded that the window on the door didn't shatter. I don't know what I'm going to do, but I do know this bubbling anger is driving me, which, in hindsight, isn't such a good thing.

Xavier is in front of me in the next second. His hand wraps around my throat, and he slams my back into the car.

"What are you trying to do, Little Deadly?" he sneers, his face so close to mine that our noses almost touch. The moonlight falls on half of his face, and I catch the glint on his fang when his lip curls.

It should send fear and terror through my veins, but all I feel is cold, brutal hatred—a feeling so familiar that it grounds me somewhat.

"Isn't it obvious?" I sneer right back, pushing into his hand and choking on it. His grip on my throat doesn't let up. He narrows his eyes as he drags them to my mouth. His nostrils flare, and his Adam's apple bobs as he swallows—*hard.*

Xavier doesn't answer me, and his gaze burns as he takes me in. His lip still twitches as if he's trying to control himself.

We don't move, and after what feels like an eternity, I grit out, "Get your hand off me." Xavier's lip pulls up in the corner of his mouth, almost smirking, but he doesn't move. How I wish I had my bloody daggers with me. He won't be this close with one in his throat.

My eyes round at the thought, and I close them quickly. Hoping that he doesn't see the fear that shoots through me. *What the hell is going on with me?* Ever since we slept together, something has changed between us, but more so—in me.

It frightens me more than anything else, and I don't want to give the thought any more attention. I'm too scared it will reveal something I'm not ready to admit. It's easier to hate. Yes, hate is something to hang onto, especially when it comes to Xavier.

"I'm not going to tell you again," I warn. My voice deadly as I stare into those deep green eyes.

Xavier's gaze slowly drags from mine to my mouth again and then back up. Amusement plays over his face as he pulls his tongue over his bottom lip, and my breath hitches in my throat.

What the actual hell?

Like the fear, my bewilderment is clear as day. In all honesty—if I must be, and I really don't want to be—Xavier always had *some* effect on me, but not like this. *This* is just absurd. I don't even know how to explain it properly. But if I must, it would be something like my body reacting to him like a flower to the scorching sun. Okay, now I'm just being bitter, but I wish my body wouldn't react at all.

He smirks at me as if he has come to the same conclusion—a dangerous one—before letting his hand fall away from my neck and steps back twice.

The wind picks up, intensifying the cold, empty feeling in my chest from his absence. My hair blows in my face, but I don't move, trying to calm my racing heart.

Xavier might have moved away from me, but his burning gaze doesn't. I swallow hard and grit my teeth.

"Where are you going?" he asks, his voice calm and collected. I can't say the same about the storm in his eyes.

"Home."

Xavier's eyes flash with anger, and he snarls low in his throat. "Are you trying to get yourself killed?"

"Why the sudden worry about my safety?" I cross my arms over my chest. "Just because you saved my life when I couldn't doesn't mean I'm helpless. *You,* of all people, should know that," I snap irritably.

His jaw ticks, and his nostrils flare before he closes his eyes and says slowly, "Don't patronize me. We had a plan, and you are shitting all over it."

"I am trying to get weapons, if you must know. *My* weapons, to be exact. I don't need your permission." I sigh angrily. "I let you take care of me, and I think I repaid you in full for your … *kindness.*" The word comes out like venom. "Like you said last night, you got what you wanted to sate yourself and solidify your reputation." Xavier winces, but I act like I didn't just see it. "You bedded the Reaper, wasn't that what you said?"

"That's not what—" he starts to say, but I close my eyes and place my hand in the air. "Don't," I force out through my clenched jaw. "Let's not pretend, shall we?"

"Little Dead—"

My eyes flash open at the nickname, and lucky for Xavier, he shuts his mouth. "I will say this only once. What happened the other night was a mistake and will *never* happen again."

Xavier's eyes flash again, and his lip pulls up in a warning. But he stops himself. The wind picks up more and flicks my hair around like a whirlwind. I push it behind my ears as the chill of the night raises my skin in goose bumps. I don't know how long we stare at each other, but the silence gets on my nerves. I need to not let this bloodsucker get to me, not if we want to carry out this plan and work together.

"I need my weapons, Xavier. I can't do this without my daggers," I say, my voice almost pleading when I break the heavy silence. "I need this"—I motion between us—"to be over so I can move on with my life. This delusional 'partnership,' if that's even what it can be called." Shaking my head, I huff air out through my nose. "And I need *you* to not look at me the way you are now."

My voice trembles on the last part, and I curse myself for it. Xavier cocks his head and folds his arms across his chest. A smug look on his face.

"How do I look at you?"

I sigh, closing my eyes. "Like you don't know if you want to kill me or screw me. And frankly, I would prefer the former."

"Does that frighten you?" His voice rumbles through his chest, and when I open my eyes, I'm not looking into the deep green anymore but those of a predator.

My back goes rigid, and I roll my eyes. "Nothing about you frightens me. Though it does irritate the living shit out of me."

He *absolutely* frightens me, but not in the way he is supposed to. No. That stupid thought crawls out of the box I shoved it into earlier, and I force it back down. Snuffing it out before it has time to settle and unnerve me even more.

Xavier chuckles darkly, but his eyes, those damn pools that have me in their current and won't let me go, don't share the dark humor. They, in fact, betray more of his mood than I think he realizes.

As if he hears my thoughts, Xavier snarls and closes his eyes. When he opens them again, there is no emotion behind them. Just black pits of … nothing.

I look away from him and push myself away from the car. Turning, I open the door, but he slams the door shut and cages me with his body against the car.

An involuntary shriek escapes my mouth and my mind reels. My back is pressed to Xavier's front, and he crushes me to the car harshly.

The cold of the Mustang seeps through my clothes, chilling me to the bone, and the metal handle of the door bites into my hip.

"You are not leaving this cottage. Do you understand, *Little Deadly?* Don't make me lock you up," he growls his warning, low in his throat. His chest vibrates from it.

"I am not your pet. Get the hell off me!" I push back, but he only increases the pressure, and I bite the inside of my cheek not to yelp from the pain of the handle digging into my hip now.

Xavier towers over me. His chest is broad against my back, yet his lean body makes him look smaller. He lowers his head to my ear, and I startle when I feel his breath.

My traitorous body comes to life, and the heat pools between my thighs. Xavier snakes his hand up my back and into my hair, gripping harshly at the roots, and yanks my head back. Tears pool in the corners of my eyes, but I bite my tongue to keep from crying out.

Xavier lowers his mouth to my throat and drags his fangs over my jugular. I stiffen. The fight between lust and disgust in my body is ongoing when he pulls his tongue up my throat and groans.

"No, you certainly aren't my *pet.* You are so much worse. You are my *hell.* Torment placed on this earth to damn me even more than I already am."

My brain lags at his words. What the hell does that even mean? My breathing comes in short huffs. I'm not entirely sure if it's pleasure or pain, but when Xavier snickers in my ear, it all gets replaced with that same white-hot fury from earlier.

I close my eyes and take in a shaking breath. Xavier still has my hair gripped tightly. I take another breath, steadier this time, and then I strike.

I shove my elbow back into his lower ribs as hard as possible with my limited range of movement. Air escapes through Xavier's mouth, and his hand slacks on my hair.

This is going to hurt like a bitch, but I don't hesitate. I push on the car and drive us back before ducking under his arm and turning to face him.

The hairs pull from my scalp, but I push the pain away as I grab onto his arm. Then his grip tightens again, and he growls.

I bring my knee up and connect with the most vulnerable part of him. He bellows a roar of pain and releases me enough for me to pull out of his hold completely.

"You fucking bitch," he seethes.

"I warned you not to touch me." My chest heaves as I talk between breaths, trying to calm my hammering heart.

I plant my foot square on his chest and kick. Xavier grunts as he falls backward. I don't waste another second and turn to the car again.

I yelp as his arms wrap around my waist, and he spins me to face him so fast that I become disoriented.

Xavier growls viciously and grips my throat, hauling me into the air. I choke and try to kick him in the chest again, but he crushes me to his body.

"You are making it extremely difficult *not* to kill you," he grits out, his face too close to mine.

Before I can anticipate his next move, he throws me over his shoulder and evanesces me to the cottage.

My stomach turns, and I have to swallow the bile in my throat when he sets me down in the living room, my world spinning.

I stagger to the back of the couch, trying to ground myself. I've heard about the effects on humans and hunters alike when vampires move with someone at that speed. It's horrendous. Now that I've experienced it for myself—no, thanks.

Xavier is there quickly, steadying me, holding onto my waist. It's like his hands on my body burn through my disoriented state, and I round on him. Swinging my fist, I hit him square in the jaw, sending his head to the side. He whips his head to me, a growl rippling from his chest so loudly that it vibrates through the house, and the danger behind his eyes sends an unwanted chill up my spine.

Tasha jumps up from the couch and glances around the room, bewildered, before she spots us, her eyes round in fear. "What the hell is going on here?" she squeaks, her hand on her heart.

We don't move from our stance, glaring murderously at each other.

"Will someone please tell me what the hell is happening?" Tasha asks, annoyance creeping into her uncertain tone.

Xavier drops his hands from my waist, stepping back, and then the sting registers. He gripped my waist so hard it's starting to bruise. *Bastard.*

But I dare not show him the pain in my body. I move for the door, and he steps in front of me again.

"Do you want me to make good on my threat?"

"Fuck you."

"WHAT THE HELL IS GOING ON?" Tasha yells now.

"Little Deadly tried to sneak away, and I stopped her." Xavier doesn't take his eyes off me and shoves his hands in his pockets.

"What?"

"I wasn't sneaking away," I grit through my teeth at Xavier before turning to Tasha. "I wanted to go to my apartment and retrieve my weapons. But this asshole thinks I owe him my existence for saving my life."

"I never said that," Xavier snaps, his face dark.

"Not nice when someone makes up shit, is it?" I snap at him, and his lip curls in a vicious snarl.

Tasha sighs tiredly and rubs her eyes. "What did I miss?"

"Nothing—" I start to say, and Xavier snorts, rolling his eyes. "Don't," I tell him venomously before turning to Tasha again. "I wanted to get my weapons, that's all. I am not the kind of person who abandons missions and my team. But I'm also not the kind of person who goes into a fight without my weapons. They're a part of me."

"Didn't you think it wise to maybe just tell me you wanted to do that?" Tasha says, looking hurt.

I sigh frustratingly and walk to the window. The sky turns hues of oranges and pinks as the sun rises. "I wasn't thinking clearly," I mutter. I rub my hands over my face and turn to Tasha again. "I'm sorry."

CHAPTER THIRTY-THREE

XAVIER

I pace the floor of the dark room behind the heavy oak door. Whoever built this damn cottage made sure a vampire couldn't move about it during the day with the amount of sunlight streaming into every room except this one. Makes me think that maybe Tasha's parents knew about our existence. I ball my hands into fists and dig my nails into the palms of my hands, drawing blood.

I can't say my irritation stems from how this cottage is built or that Tasha's parents may or may not have known about my kind. I close my eyes, and all I can see is Little Deadly.

A growl ripples through me, and I slam my fist into the wall. *That damn woman.* Why would this be my fate? Why on earth would I ever be granted a mate bond with a bloody *hunter?* A Van Helsing hunter, to be exact.

Dominica makes my blood boil. It turns to black sludge at the thought of her. Images of her flash in my mind, and the way her breath hitches at the slightest movement of my tongue being dragged over my lips. The noises she made when I was buried deep inside her for hours. And just like that, my dick hardens, contradicting everything I am trying to *make* myself feel toward that infuriating woman.

Then comes the images of her face when I told her I only slept with her to rid myself of the tension and for my own reputation.

It was the first time I saw the broken and fragile side of Dominica Salvatore. I can't say that I enjoyed it. Not like I always thought I would when I *tried* to break her in the past. I like it even less that the cause was because of me.

This screws up everything I've thought I could return to and so much more. I know exactly what will happen to me if we don't complete the bond and, even worse—what it will do to me when she accepts and then eventually perish.

I punch the wall again, this time without conviction, and drag my hands through my hair.

I couldn't control myself when I saw Little Deadly sneaking away. I should've just let her leave. In one instance, I try to push her as far away from me as possible, and in the next, I act like a possessive beast.

Well, it's basic vampire nature: being possessive, not to mention when a female belongs to you.

Shit!

I inhale deeply and have to stop mid-breath when the scent of Little Deadly's blood hits my nose again. The smell still lingers, but I don't have a choice. There is no other room dense enough where sunlight won't end me.

Older vampires, like myself, can be in sunlight for a few minutes, but it drains us. Younger ones can't be in the sunlight at all. They turn to dust within seconds.

I swallow and force the bloodlust away. I need to feed. It's been three days since I had blood, and I usually can last longer, but like the last time I had some of Little Deadly's blood, I'd gone nearly crazy when I didn't feed within a couple of days. This time, I had a lot more than just *some* of her blood and the hunger claws at me.

It feels like the sun will never set. I need to get the hell out of here and find a blood source. Our time is running out, and the VHA will be here any day now. I can't be bloodthirsty and out of control when they do.

I start pacing again when there's a knock on the door.

"What?!" I bark, and Tasha's trembling voice comes through the door. "We, um—" Tasha clears her throat and speaks louder. "We might have a problem."

I storm to the door but don't open it. "What do you mean we might have a problem?"

"Well, Dominica just left."

A string of curses leaves my throat, and I rip open the door. Tasha yelps and jumps back, her hand on her heart.

"I wish you would stop doing that."

I move to step out, but Tasha holds her hands out in front of her to stop me, and I glare down at her.

"It's still light out, and I told Dom she can go. She needs space from you and your overbearing ass," she tells me, trying to sound stern, but her voice fails her when her eyes fall on my gaze.

"Please tell me how it's possible that you are bonded to *my* blood, but your allegiance is with the Reaper." The venom in my tone makes Tasha tremble again, but she doesn't back off.

"I don't know what you want me to say," she says, folding her arms in front of her chest.

The panic in my veins feels like my heart will cease pumping. I have no way to contact her since she doesn't have a phone, and what if she gets in trouble and can't call for help? I clench my jaw hard enough that I feel my teeth crack.

Little Deadly decided to leave on her own, and she has always been able to hold her own. The rumbling in my chest makes the pictures on the walls vibrate. I feel the possessiveness pull and morph into something ugly, and I simply can't let that happen.

"Tasha, how is your strength?" My voice is cold and harsh.

"Fine. Why?"

"Brace yourself," is all I rumble before I move and sink my teeth into her throat.

Tasha screams, but it dies off quickly. I have her jaw clenched in my hand, having pushed her head aside and her hands pinned behind her back in that same instant.

I drink my fill, making sure not to take too much. I can't risk Tasha's inability to get herself to safety when the VHA decides to show up.

I pace the living room floor, my hands flexing at my side. I'm just about to rip this house apart. My temper and mood are nothing other than a black hole, and I warn Tasha to stay as far away from me as she possibly can.

The sun has almost disappeared behind the snow-tipped mountain, and I'm seconds away from losing my mind.

When the sunlight disappears, I turn to Tasha, who hasn't taken her frightful eyes off me.

I open my mouth to tell her to get ready to leave when the cottage door bursts open, and Little Deadly rushes into the room. Her eyes are wide but not from fear.

"They found us and are on their way here," she says hastily. "Five black SUVs picked up on my whereabouts, and I couldn't shake them."

My gaze narrows on her, and I suppress the urge to rush over to her and look at every inch of her body to make sure she isn't harmed.

I force myself to stay still, and it proves more difficult when my eyes roam over Little Deadly's full, delicious lips, down to her throat, where I can see her heart beating quickly and then her breasts. Those absolutely succulent breasts fit just perfectly in my hands, like they were made just for me.

I shake my head once. *Pull yourself together.* But I can't seem to tear my gaze from her chest, which rises and falls quickly as she tries to calm her breath.

"Did you hear me?" Little Deadly's gaze pins me, and I swallow a groan.

"Did you lead them here?" I ask darkly, trying to hide my lust-filled voice and morphing it into something similar, like loathing.

Little Deadly clenches her fists, and I can see them tremble, but when she speaks, it's calm and calculated.

"If you want to insult me like that, I don't see any future where we can work together. So, you need to tell me now, Xavier. We don't have time to waste."

"What are you asking exactly?"

She huffs out a breath through her nose. This time, speaking through her clenched jaw. "If you don't trust me enough to believe that I will never betray anyone, then this," she gestures her hand between us, "is a waste of time. We can't be looking over our shoulders with the enemy surrounding us and worrying about an ally turning on us. Decide, but make it quick."

I can't seem to find it in me to tell her that I trust her entirely, but in the same breath, not at all, but not because we are enemies—or supposed enemies—no. I can't trust her because I don't trust myself when it comes to her. She can break me with one command; I simply can't let that happen. How can I trust that she won't turn on me? And just like that, I know it's utter bullshit. Little Deadly would rather die than betray *anyone*—even me.

Hurt flashes behind Little Deadly's beautiful eyes so quickly that I'm not entirely sure I saw the emotion there. She rolls her eyes and shakes her head, turning her attention to Tasha.

"Tash, please—" Little Deadly walks to Tasha slowly. She places her hand over Tasha's—covering the bite—and removes Tasha's hand. The atmosphere thickens when her breath catches in her throat.

I brace myself when Little Deadly's shoulders rise slowly as she inhales a breath, and when she turns to face me, her eyes scream bloody murder.

She hasn't looked at me like that in a while, and it still sends a chill down my spine. I smirk, shrugging one shoulder, and move around the couch to the front door.

The next moment happens in slow motion. My instincts warn me milliseconds before Little Deadly's dagger whooshes past my face, almost taking my nose with it. Tasha lets out a strangled scream. Then, the thud of the dagger digging deep into the thick wooden panel of the home's structure.

I look at the blade and then at the red-faced, fury-filled woman. I rub my hand over the tip of my nose, feeling the red liquid seeping through the small cut. My eyes flash in anger. "Cutting it a bit close there, aren't we?"

"Just close enough," she says softly. I know better than to assume the softness in her voice is weakness. Oh no, when Little Deadly's voice goes to a whisper in situations like these, it's cataclysmic.

You do not screw with her. But like every other time, it draws me in. The thrill of the danger in her eyes only vibrates stronger in my blood. This is why I never could go through with killing her. This exact moment, this exact expression, this exact electrified feeling.

How can anyone just snuff it out?

I turn my full attention to her now, sauntering closer. Little Deadly's shoulders stiffen, and her grip on her dagger tightens. When I advance on her, she doesn't move back, never has, and probably never will. She only tips her chin up to look at me.

"I've never thought of you as a blood-lusted beast, but looking at Tasha and what you did ... " she trails off, shaking her head disappointedly.

Dammit, how am I supposed to tell her what's happening to me without revealing anything? How her blood and her essence draw me to her and make me the beast she wants to deny I am when I can't have her.

A snarl slips past my curled lip, and I only narrow my eyes at her before looking over her shoulder at Tasha.

Tasha's face is so pale. I'm not sure how she's still conscious. I took too much. I can't trust myself and my control. The one I've worked centuries to get—is shot.

I open my mouth, but a loud explosion comes from right outside the cottage. The strength of the blast shatters the windows and throws us backward.

CHAPTER THIRTY-FOUR

DOMINICA

I throw my hands up to shield my head just in time. Debris and glass fly directly at me and lodge into my arm when I go down.

My ears ring so loudly that I can't focus when long fingers wrap around my wrists and pull my arms from my face.

Xavier's panicked face fills my gaze, and I can see his mouth move, but the ringing is still so loud that nothing he says filters through.

I cough and stumble to my feet, looking around frantically for Tasha. She was just beside me. Where the hell is she now?

Utter chaos filters through the ringing in my ears, sending my instincts into hyperdrive.

"Are you hurt?" Xavier's hissing voice comes to me next, and I whip my head in his direction.

Gunfire and another explosion sound from outside, and I'm thrown to the ground again. Xavier covers my body with his as bullets whiz past us.

A dull, sickening thudding sound comes next, and Xavier groans painfully. Something warm soaks through my top, and I look in horror as Xavier stumbles off me, holding his side.

Blood! Shit!

My head reels as I reach out to Xavier and pull him back down to his knees. The stupid idiot is going to get himself shot again. I wrench his hands away from his side and tear his shirt to assess the damage. I hope I will find the wound already healed—but it's not.

It only means one thing. And if I'm right, we are in so much trouble. I look up into Xavier's pain-filled gaze, and he nods, his jaw already clenched, and he braces for what I'm about to do next.

I swallow hard and then dig my fingers into the hole the bullet made. Xavier's groans of pain fill my ears, and he slams his fist on the ground just as I pull the *silver* bullet from him. *Not good. Not good at all.*

Seconds later, the hole in his side heals, but it's red and inflamed, meaning the silver has already been absorbed into his system.

"We need to get the hell out of here. Where is Tasha?" Panic fills my voice as Xavier hunches over.

The gunfire ceases for a few seconds, and I whisper-yell for Tasha. I strain my ears, and in the next moment, she squeaks from behind the kitchen counter.

My eyes lock with Tasha's, and I motion for her to crawl to us, but she shakes her head, trembling.

We definitely don't have time for terror. I look behind me at Xavier, who sways. "Go," he mouths.

I lower myself to my stomach and am leopard crawling toward Tasha when the hairs on the back of my neck rise.

"Reaper," a cold, ominous voice calls from just outside the cottage.

I freeze and slowly turn my head toward the sound. My gaze falls on Xavier, and his eyes are dead, emotionless, as his lip curls into a snarl.

"Come on out, Reaper. We can smell you in there."

"Who the hell is that?" I mouth to Xavier, but Tasha's sob makes my blood run cold. It takes three heartbeats before Xavier looks at me and mouths, "Alex." How the hell did the vampires find us?

I was expecting the VHA. Something doesn't make sense, but I don't have time to linger on the thought when the window shatters, and a hand grenade rolls into the room. Shit!

I have seconds to react. I lunge for the bomb and grab it, throwing it in the direction of the broken window, but the grenade detonates, and the blast burns my skin as it forces me backward again. My body slams into the kitchen counter, and my head hits the side of the counter. Xavier's scream barely registers as my world goes dark.

A murmur fills my ears, and then a loud clanging as something hits metal and sends me shooting upright from my unconscious state. I groan when, seconds later, my head throbs in protest along with my aching body.

Firm, strong hands clutch my arms, and my heart is sent into an overload of panic when the last images I can remember run through my mind.

I react without giving my brain and eyes time to adjust and slam the palm of my hand into the chest of the person clutching me.

The man—or, at least by the sound of the deep grunt, confirms that—stumbles back and lets go of me. I throw my legs over the bed. Again, I'm speculating here since my vision isn't clear enough to discern precisely where I am and get off stumbling.

"Dom!"

That voice. It sends chills down my spine as every muscle in my body seizes before regaining memory of survival.

"Calm down, please. We're only trying to help you. You've been out for a while." That voice grates at my insides. The concern there surprises me, but we both know he has no right to be.

I shake my head and blink and blink and blink until I can make out my surroundings.

I've backed up as far as possible when my back hits a solid wall behind me. I keep my hand out in front of me, warning anyone who comes near me that it would be a final, fatal mistake, while I rub my temple with the other.

My head throbs so badly I want to hurl. I shake my head again, trying to take in what's before me. The VHA infirmary. My brows pull down, and my head protests from the action. How the hell did I get here?

That bloody voice makes me forcefully swallow the bile rising in my throat when he says, "Dom. Shit. I've been so worried. Are you okay?"

Am I okay? Did that bastard really just ask me that? I drag my gaze through the room until it falls on the one person I thought I would never see again. His look of worry and concern is so sincere that I wonder if the last few weeks really did happen.

I let my hand fall to my side and trace the scar there, the reminder that it wasn't a bad dream etched into my skin.

"Austen," I growl, but it becomes a confused question.

Austen's eyes follow my hand, and his hands ball at his sides as anger flashes behind his eyes—briefly—so briefly that my confused brain thinks it must not have been there.

Austen approaches me slowly, and my back stiffens. I reach for my daggers only to find that I'm stripped of my weapons—*again.* Why is it so hard to just leave my shit alone? *Dammit.*

Austen takes another step in my direction, and I glare at him. "Don't," I force through my bone-dry throat.

I move to sidestep him, but my head spins, and I lose my balance. I fall and brace myself for impact since I can't tell up from down, but it doesn't come. Strong arms catch me, and the nausea building in my chest only pushes its way out when Austen touches me.

He sets me down, and I turn on my knees. My stomach turns, and I dry heave. Austen rubs my back gently, and that only makes the heaving worse.

"Don't," I heave. "Touch," heave. "Me," heave.

Austen ignores me and barks, "Bring her a glass of water and stop staring." Within minutes, Austen presses a glass to my dry lips, and I all but gulp down the water. As soon as the welcoming liquid hits my throat, my mind clears, and I stumble to my feet again, stepping away from the traitor on the floor—as far as I can.

I narrow my gaze on him as he rises slowly. His hands are out in front of him in defense. "Where the hell am I?" I croak. My instincts tell me exactly where I am, but my mind doubts everything. I can't connect the dots yet, and I hate that feeling. Everything is so far out of my control.

"Let's get you back in bed, and then we can talk. Okay?" Austen says, stepping toward me again. His hand still outstretched.

"If you want to keep your fingers, wrists, and arms uninjured, I'd suggest you stop advancing on me. I'm confused as hell, and that makes me dangerous. You, of all people, should know that." I glare at him, then at his hands, and back at Austen again.

"Dom, please. I'm only trying to help you. You were fighting that bloodsucker that killed Silvia, and he almost killed you. You were out for more than two weeks—"

"What?" I shake my head in disbelief. "That's bullshit," I seethe. "You and I both know that's the biggest load of bullshit you're trying to sell."

"Please, Dom. Listen to me. I don't know what happened in your mind when you were out, but I'm telling you the truth." Austen looks at me with pleading eyes. I can't believe this asshole.

"Stop spewing bullshit, Austen. Xavier didn't harm me. *You* did." I force the last part through my clenched teeth. My chest feels like it's going to cave in on itself, and my heart is trying to keep it from doing that at the rate it's hammering.

Austen closes his eyes in defeat, lowering his hands to his sides. He turns to the other people in the room. "Give us the room, guys."

Panic hits my chest again. "No!" I all but yell, and everyone stops dead and stares at me. "Don't leave me alone with him."

My head is still throbbing, and I can't think clearly enough to anticipate his movements. "He will kill me if he is alone with me."

"Dom, please. I will not hurt you. I swear on my life," Austen says, the hurt and pleading in his voice catching me off guard again. "Please, just let me talk to you alone. I think it will be better."

I'm silent for a long time, and no one moves until I nod my head once, still glaring at Austen. I replay the events of the night Austen almost killed me in my mind. Yup, it's real. So why is he acting like it all played off in my mind? My thoughts go to the cottage and the grenade that exploded. Shit.

Xavier. Tasha.

I glance around the room quickly when Austen's back is turned to me. There's only one hospital bed. No sign of either of them. Though I doubt Xavier would've received medical attention. But the VHA wasn't there. Alex was.

My head throbs again. It feels like someone is trying to hammer their way out from inside my skull, and I have to swallow bile again.

As soon as the door clicks shut and Austen and I are alone in the room, I snap, "Where are they?"

Austen tilts his head in confusion. "Where's who?"

"Don't you dare patronize me. You know exactly who I'm talking about."

"The vampire and his assistant?"

I only glare at him.

"Dom, I hope you aren't suffering from Stockholm syndrome. Please tell me you're still you?"

My exasperation boils over, and I can't help but roll my eyes. "What are you talking about?"

"What's the last thing you remember after Silvia's death?" Austen asks cautiously. I look at him bewildered, but my curiosity gets the better of me. Fine, let's indulge his delusion.

"Being called into Brian's office. Being suspended because I pulled you off Xavier. Then you asked me to meet you at the school grounds … " I trail off, swallowing. My hand drifts to my side again. "You attacking me—" I clench my jaw and scowl at Austen.

"Shit," he mutters.

"Shit is a bit of an understatement, but okay," I huff bitterly. My voice cold.

"It's even worse than I thought. They altered your memory—"

"That's bullshit!" My statement lacks conviction. My energy drains from my body as it does from my voice. I shake my head as fog fills my mind.

"It's not, Dom. Please, just listen," Austen says. Caution still lingers in his eyes as he tells me of the events after Silvia's death.

I stare at Austen, my mind reeling. Uncertainty now replacing confusion. My mouth feels clammy and dry. I can't place the sudden onslaught of confusion and my mind's fogginess.

Wait a minute. The water. My skin breaks out in a cold sweat, but Austen keeps talking like nothing is wrong. My heart slams against my chest, and I force myself to calm my breathing.

"You went out to look for the bloodsucker who was responsible for Silvia's death. You found him and his cronies at the school grounds. They attacked you, and you were injured real bad, but you managed to get away. Some guy found you and took you to a gas station. He helped you get cleaned up. We saw it all on the surrounding surveillance," Austen adds quickly when he sees my confusion deepen as I tilt my head and frown at him. I rub my eyes and try to fight the fog building in my mind. I can't lose consciousness now. This is really, *really* bad. Everything he's saying is correct except for minor changes here and there.

He sounds so convincing, and as he continues, I find myself starting to doubt my own account of the events.

"I was worried out of my mind when I saw you on your knees outside that gas station, but Brian sent a team as soon as we saw you being carried into that place. The team arrived when the vampires surrounded you, but they were too late to get to you. That *fiend* took you, and I almost lost my shit." Austen touches my shoulder when I drop my head. I'm grasping at the images. "A few days ago, I got an alert that my password was used in an alternate location, and I knew it had to be you, sending for help."

No, that's not right. I went to that café to get intel on the rat in the VHA—or did I? Yes, I did, or maybe not.

Dammit, why can't I remember? My eyelids feel heavy, but Austen shakes me, and I open my eyes again.

"We tracked the movements at the café and then got a glimpse of you getting into a black Mustang. Brian sent out a small team to do recon, and they tracked you to that cottage. I almost rushed in there to get you, but Brian restrained me. That bastard who took you was outside talking to his king. Sound surveillance picked up on what they said just before we surrounded them."

I can't. This isn't right. That's not how it happened. I know it's not, so why am I doubting my own memories?

"Dom, are you okay? You look pale," Austen says, resting his hand on my cheek. Why am I letting him touch me? I can't think straight.

"No, you're wrong. That's … " I shake my head again, my fingers digging into my temples. "That's not how it happened."

Austen scoffs and continues, "The bloodsucker was telling his king that he faked saving you to get you to trust him and that you were ripe for the taking. He said he even went as far as to bed you for his reputation."

I gasp, my hand covering my mouth. "What did you say?"

"He said he fucked you beyond tomorrow to rid himself of the tension."

"No," I whisper. Tears sting my eyes. It can't be. I look up at Austen and find pity behind his dark eyes. "How do you know this?"

"We have recordings of them talking. I can play it for you if you don't believe me." I swallow again, then shake my head no. I don't want to hear it. I can't. I can't relive the hurt Xavier put me through when he said that to me.

My heart aches, and it feels like a hole the size of the Grand Canyon opens in my chest. My breathing picks up as I start to hyperventilate. I clutch my chest as the tears run down my cheeks. I rack my brain, trying to sort through everything that's happened until now. I am trying my best to leave out the parts Austen told me and not let it taint *my* version of events. But for some reason, the fog in my mind makes it difficult to do just that.

Focus, Dom. You need to focus. I press my fingers harder into my temples to the point where I want to scream from the pressure. It helps a little as some parts of my memories start to align.

Wait. Xavier said that to *me* and no one else. So, how did Austen know about it? Somewhere in the back of my mind, my inner voice screams for me not to believe what anyone says. Not to drink any more "water" or any liquid offered to me by these people. And the more I try to grasp at that distant voice, the louder it becomes until the illusion Austen tries to sell me shatters, and I'm left bare to reality.

My memories are the real ones.

My gut tells me this is part of why the VHA and the Vampire Society have the same spy. They are a lot closer than two enemies are supposed to be. I school my face and let the tears fall. If I'm going to get to the bottom of this bullshit, I need my traitorous friend to think that I believe him.

"What happened? How did you get me out?" I sob.

Austen watches me for a few seconds before answering me. He's hesitant, but then he sighs. "We bombed the place and captured that fiend and his human assistant."

I let a shuddering breath slip past my lips, playing my part until I can get to Tasha and, hopefully, Xavier.

Xavier … Shit. My heart sinks. If I know Brian and Austen—and I do—they wouldn't just kill Xavier for the death of Silvia. No. They will torture him until he's seconds from death. And I hope with everything in me that he's still breathing. A fist tightens its grip around my already panicked heart at the thought of losing Xavier.

I increase the pressure on my throbbing head. All of this is too overwhelming. I need to know if Xavier is still alive.

When I open my eyes and look at Austen, he watches me warily. I need to play this right. If I sound too eager, Austen will know I'm not buying his story.

"That's good. Did you kill them?" I inhale deeply, blowing out my breath slowly. Bracing myself for the answer.

Please. Please say no.

"No."

I almost sob from relief but manage to stay somewhat emotionless. Austen rises from the floor and holds out his hand to me. I reach out to take it, my hand trembling as I grasp it. I don't even have to fake it—they *are* trembling.

"Come, I need to show you something." We start for the door, and Austen places his hand on the small of my back. I force my body not to react to his touch.

"The girl is in custody, and we are busy debriefing her before we establish if we can send her back to her life before the vampires—"

I zone out when Austen starts talking about the protocols. I almost roll my eyes. Like I don't know them. I hope Tasha has her wits about her and plays her part, too. We didn't fully cover what to do if we got captured by the VHA. We were supposed to do that before heading out to another safe house. But things didn't quite work out the way we planned.

"—kill him." I'm ripped from my mind and stop dead when the two words register. "Sorry, what did you say?" I turn to look up at Austen.

"Weren't you listening?" Austen asks, annoyance lacing his tone.

"My head is pounding, Austen, and I'm struggling to focus. Forgive me if I don't absorb everything you say—" I cut myself off when his eyes narrow. I swallow and apologize quickly. "The pain is making it difficult," I tell him, tapping my temple and forcing a wince. "Please repeat what you just said."

Austen huffs his frustration but drags a hand through his hair as he pushes into my back with the other to start walking again. He waits until we round a corner to the interrogation rooms for the vampires when he says the words that make my blood thicken in my veins.

"Brian and I thought we would give you the honor to kill the bloodsucker."

CHAPTER THIRTY-FIVE

DOMINICA

My ears ring, and my heart pounds. I force down the sob that threatens to spill past my lips as I look through the two-way mirror into the interrogation room. On the floor, on his knees, is a bloodied Xavier. Covered in silver chains. His wrists are chained and fastened to the floor, pulling his arms out to the sides. His ankles and just behind his knees are shackled to the cold concrete floor. His face is so pale, contorting in pain, and there is no doubt in my mind that they forced liquid silver down his throat.

I know the protocols for interrogating a vampire. I know from experience that one this powerful and guilty of killing one of our own will receive the worst of what the VHA can offer.

Tears sting my eyes, and I have to force them away too. I can't show compassion for Xavier. Not as I turn to look at those who are in this very room with me. My back stiffens at the sight of all the big shots of the VHA seated in the room. Their gazes skim over me but never fully linger. It makes me feel like they are avoiding looking at me for a particular reason. Almost like they are in on something I'm not.

Brian rises and walks toward me, opening his arms to welcome me. He embraces me in a crushing hug, and I bite my tongue to stop myself from lashing out. I don't return the gesture, and when he releases me, I step back out of his reach, only to bump into Austen.

I freeze, and my throat bobs as I swallow. I force a scared look on my face. Milking the victim card seems like the best idea for now. As long as they think I'm doubting myself, I can maybe, *maybe* get us out of this mess.

How? I do not know yet.

"How are you feeling, Dom?" Brian asks me but doesn't wait for my answer as he looks at Austen. "Is she back with us? How is she?"

"It took a while for her memory to return, but she's fine. It looks like a concussion from the blow and a few minor cuts and bruises, but otherwise unharmed. Her blood tests also came back negative," Austen says. He steps closer to me and wraps his arm around my waist. Almost protectively. I clench my jaw but fold my arms around myself as I close my eyes, releasing a shuddered breath, just for good measure.

Right, the blood test to determine whether I'm turned. Stupid assholes. If Xavier had fed me his blood and drained me, I would have turned already. They wouldn't need a test to tell them that. But the bite marks on my neck are still fresh, requiring tests.

"It's so weird to see her so timid and afraid. Are you sure he didn't break her?" Brian asks Austen again before raking his eyes over me.

Timid? Yeah right. Glad that my acting isn't as bad as I thought it was. I bite the inside of my cheek hard enough to draw blood to keep from speaking, and seconds later, there is commotion in the entire viewing area. Head members jump to their feet. Everyone stares at the two-way mirror.

I dare a glance in that direction, and my heart sinks. Xavier has lifted his head and bared his teeth as he stares directly at the mirror. Or is it at me? I swallow the blood, and his eyes—those wholly black eyes—follow the movement of my throat. Well, that answers that question.

I fake a gasp and step away from the glass and closer to Austen—with difficulty, I might add. Austen's gaze falls on me, and I force my body to tremble. Austen tightens his grip on my waist, and the next moment, the glass of the two-way mirror vibrates when Xavier growls low and dangerous.

I frown. Wait, Xavier's reaction doesn't make sense. Why the hell would he act so possessively over someone who's his enemy? It can't be over me. It must be because two hunters have entered the interrogation room.

Every fiber screams that I need to test the theory, and I fake another sob. Austen wraps his arms around me, pressing my back to his chest, and kisses my cheek. The glass rumbles again; this time, more guards and hunters rush out of the viewing area when Xavier strains against his chains. He snaps his jaw at the glass, and his lip twitches in that very pissed-off way I've come to know is Xavier's signature, for he's about to rip out throats.

My head spins, and the all-too-familiar overwhelming feeling hits my chest again. I've grown fond of the stupid vampire, but I wouldn't kill someone if they were touching him. And then I remember the night when Tasha told me they slept together and how I wanted to kick her ass for even feeding him, never mind sleeping with him.

Am I falling for my enemy?

It can't be. No, please, no. But then another unwanted memory makes itself known: the way Xavier held me when I broke down, how he softly and tenderly cleaned my wounds and nursed me back to health. He protected me valiantly and painted a massive target on his back because of it.

But then again, he said I was just something to get out of his system. The way he acted after he drank from me and after we fucked. Crass, I know, but I don't know how else to put it. It certainly wasn't lovemaking, that's for sure.

Shit, I don't know what to think or feel.

My head aches so much I'm struggling to see clearly. Xavier strains again, and then I hear a sickening thud, and my head whips to the men surrounding him. Every single man has a bat and is beating the shit out of Xavier.

The renewed trembling in my body isn't from fear or uncertainty. It's pure rage, and I have to stop myself from reacting. But every blow they land on him makes my blood boil. My breath comes in quick bursts as I try to rein in my temper.

I need to get the hell out of here, or we will both be dead because I'm seconds away from running out of this room and into his to kill the bastards hurting him.

My thoughts startle me. I don't know what is happening to me, but the need to get Xavier out of here overwhelms any other rational thought. But before I can act on them, my attention is pulled back to the present when Austen hugs me again and then steps away. "I need to go deal with that shithead so you can kill him and get this over with."

"What?" My panicked-filled voice echoes in the room, and Brian narrows his eyes at me, and so does Austen. I clear my throat, rub my temples, willing my heart to calm. "Please just get me out of here. I'm going to throw up. I don't feel well, please, Austen." I step to Austen and feign my knees giving out. Just as I expected, Austen rushes and catches me before I hit the ground.

He scoops me up and carries me out of the room to the infirmary. When he sets me down on the bed and wipes the tears from my face, I don't know what to do with the anger in my chest. The tears are genuine. I thought about faking them, but they just started flowing down my cheeks. The devastated look on Xavier's face breaks me. The one I saw just before Austen carried me away.

"Shh, Dom. You're safe. Okay? He can't hurt you; I promise." Austen wipes my hair out of my face, and I let him.

"Please just leave me alone. I—" I shudder and take a shaking breath. "I need some time for myself."

Austen inhales deeply, huffing his breath out on a sigh, and nods somberly at me. "I'll give you a few minutes," he says as he turns and walks to the door. Austen pushes down on the handle but doesn't open it right away. I wait, but he doesn't move or say anything for a while.

The seconds tick by, and then I see the muscles on his back ripple as he visibly tries to relax. A few moments later, he slightly turns his head to look at me over his shoulder, and I have to suppress a curse when I catch a glimpse of that same look he had the night he almost killed me.

I knew the bastard was acting, just like me. But what I'm struggling with is why. Why go through the trouble to act like Xavier had hurt me? Why not just kill me and take my place in the VHA like he said he was going to?

What is his endgame?

And then it hits me, just like his words do when he says with little control, "But, Dom. You *are* killing that vampire. And it will happen today." Austen wrenches open the door and walks out, closing it behind him again.

I huff out the breath that's lodged in my throat. Horror and disgust ripple through me. "Shit," I say softly. "What the hell am I going to do?"

I can't kill Xavier. I won't. That much has been clear since the day he saved me. What I can't wrap my head around is the way he reacted. I didn't think he could smell my blood in his weakened state, let alone react to it. But the possessive way he reacted still sends my mind into a flat spin. I mean, really.

When I can get my mind to conjure up a semblance of an escape plan, he and I are going to have some words. If he doesn't end up with one of my daggers in his chest first.

CHAPTER THIRTY-SIX

DOMINICA

The danger looms and breathes down my neck. My time is running out, and so is Xavier's. I don't doubt that Tasha's death is looming also. She has Xavier's mark on her neck, so they definitely will not let her go. They will keep her locked up for the rest of her life or use her as bait to draw out other vampires. I wouldn't put it past them. They did it in the early years of the VHA, but who says they haven't been doing it still?

Everything I ever thought was true and pure about the VHA has turned out to be a lie. So, no, I don't think Tasha is as safe as Austen wants me to believe she is.

I've come up with a shitty patched-together plan to get us out of here—one I believe will absolutely fail, but I don't have another choice. It all rides on the schedules of the guards. If I remember correctly, there should be a shift change in about five minutes if the clock in the infirmary is on time. I will slip out and see if I can't get into the control room with the surveillance cameras. Once there, I need to find the cell where they keep Tasha. From there, I'm not entirely sure how I'm going to proceed.

I guess I'm going to have to wing it. It's not one of my favorite things to do, but I don't have a choice.

The clock strikes seven, and I quietly open the infirmary door. I peer out into the hall, and it's completely empty. Thank goodness. I step out and tiptoe my way to the control room.

Voices echo down the hall, and my heart nearly climbs out of my chest. I slip into the dark room and close the door behind me as silently as possible. The voices grow louder as they near the door, and I brace myself to take them out if they enter. But they fade again as they move down the hall and away from my position.

A strained breath of relief escapes my lips, and I turn to the monitors. I don't have long. It takes the guards about fifteen minutes to get to their stations, and I only have five minutes to spare.

I run my eyes along every monitor until my gaze gets snagged on one specific one. It's not the one I was looking for, but one so intriguing that if I choose to listen in on the people talking in that room, I won't have time to search the others for Tasha.

But I can't let this go. I tap a few keys on the keyboard in front of the monitors, and the sound comes on for that specific monitor.

My jaw clenches as the two men talk in hurried, hushed voices, and my heart beats a million miles per second.

"Does she suspect anything?" Brian asks Austen.

"No, I think the mind games worked. I've told you this many times, but Dominica Salvatore is a sad excuse for a hunter. She has always been easy to manipulate, and this time was no different." Austen shrugs, his expression bored.

"And you think she will be compliant long enough so my brother won't suspect anything?" My breath hitches in my throat when a third voice—a female voice—speaks from the shadows in the room.

I can't make out a face, only her body and the clan ring on her finger. She's a vampire. An old one at that. Only the old ones are allowed to wear them. I tap a few more keys and zoom in on the ring. Where have I seen that image before?

Austen laughs. "There is no doubt in my mind. We just need to move fast enough that if she does suspect anything, we can handle it accordingly."

"I agree. The sooner we get rid of her, the better. Dominica may be many things, but she's still resilient," Brian huffs.

My insides feel like they are turning to liquid. Have all of them been against me this whole time? I don't have time to wallow in that truth when Austen speaks up again. "Good thing that vampire was so willing to tell us about their fuck session. I've never seen something show so much disgust for having sex with a person. He couldn't wait to tell us how badly he wanted to scrub that memory from his mind. How she threw herself at him. He was so willing to use her to get into Alex's good graces that he lied to her about their plan to get that Tasha girl's sister out."

My lungs stop working entirely. The metaphorical knife twists in my heart at Austen's words. It can't be true. Xavier wouldn't, but he said so himself. *He would use the knowledge that he slept with the Reaper to boost his reputation.*

My world crashes in around me as yet another betrayal cripples me to the point that I can't breathe.

How was I so stupid? I trusted without even realizing it. I trusted Xavier, and he betrayed me even after he heard what Austen had done to me.

And then a distant memory comes to my mind. The one where Xavier carried me out of his apartment and told me *not* to trust him. But I did. I even started to like him.

Tears form in my eyes, blurring my vision, and I don't even move when the door to the control room gets kicked in and I'm wrenched out of the chair.

I can't stop the tears that run slowly down my cheeks as the guards bind my hands behind my back and pull me up to my knees.

Austen enters the room, but I can't seem to care. I was sorely mistaken if I thought I felt empty when Austen betrayed me.

The chasm in my chest is so enormous I don't know if I'll ever feel again.

"Well, well. Still so bloody predictable, aren't we, Dom?" Austen laughs. I don't react as I stare at the floor.

He bends down and grips my face forcefully, squeezing. I don't even flinch when he rips my head up.

"I told Brian you would betray us. And here you are, looking for what exactly? Certainly not a way to help your people end the one vampire causing trouble. No. You're probably looking for a way to get them out, right?"

I don't look at him as the tears still run down my face, and I struggle to keep breathing. Austen lets my face fall and then back-hands me so hard my ears ring. "Answer me!" he yells.

Blood runs down my split cheek, and I lift my head slowly. "Do whatever you want. Just get it over with," I say, my voice defeated just like the rest of me.

"Oh, no. You seem to misunderstand. You are in for a nasty surprise. Everything you do from now on will determine if what lies ahead for you will be difficult or not." Austen wraps his hand around my throat and hauls me to my feet. "Bring her."

The two guards grab hold of my bound arms so hard I feel my skin bruise under their grip. They don't need to force me to walk because I'm not resisting. My brain seems to have stopped working. It only makes sure my lungs and heart still do their job.

My vision blurs as the tears keep spilling. When I blink, I find myself in the interrogation room with Xavier, but all I feel is emptiness. The betrayal from him was too much.

Austen appears in front of me again and wrenches my head up. "Focus, Dom. You need to listen, or this will end badly for you."

"I don't care," I whisper. Even my voice has lost the will to fight.

"Oh, you better start caring, or I'm feeding that slut who's bonded to this asshole to one of the other vampires we have captive."

My eyes shoot to Austen with a deadly glare, and he smirks at me. "There you are."

"What the hell do you want from me? You got what you wanted. Kill me and get it over with." The tremble in my voice is unmistakable, but it's still dangerous, and I couldn't be more thankful.

At the sound of my voice, Xavier groans and tries to lift his head, but Austen punches him hard enough that his head lolls again.

A spark of rage shoots through me, and Austen's face lights up. "Ah, there it is. I thought I had seen compassion for this beast earlier, but I wasn't sure. This will be so much sweeter now."

"Fuck you," I grit out.

"No, darling, not after that filth's dick was in you. I'd rather a vampire drink from me than fuck you," Austen laughs evilly.

"As if you would be so lucky," I snarl and groan when Austen's backhand connects with the same cheek as earlier. The pain shoots through my eye and my still throbbing head. My vision swims, and darkness threatens to consume me, but I manage to pull myself out of it.

A weak snarl ripples from Xavier's chest, and when I regain my vision, I see him watching me with a painful glint in his tired eyes.

"Little D—" Xavier tries to say, but Austen punches him again. This time, I lunge, without thinking, at Austen, but the guards rip me back and push me down on my knees. My actions surprise me just as much as him.

What the hell was that?

"Enough," Austen snarls, then pulls a stake from his back pocket. "Stake the vampire, and we can talk about your punishment."

I glare at Austen and shake my head once. Austen slaps me again, and I cry out. Blood runs freely from the wound in my cheek, and Xavier draws in a weak breath.

"Very well." Austen nods his head, and a guard appears with a glass. I spot the silver liquid and struggle against the guard's hold on me when Austen steps not to Xavier but to me. He holds the glass against my cheek and lets my blood collect and mix with the silver.

"No," I breathe when Austen swirls the glass, thoroughly mixing the two liquids, and walks to Xavier.

"Hold his head back," he commands the guard who brought the silver. He does it without hesitation. The guard fists a handful of Xavier's hair and wrenches his head back. Xavier winces but has little strength left to fight. The guard grips Xavier's jaw and forces it open.

With one quick glance my way, Austen smiles maliciously and pours the silver liquid mixed with my blood down Xavier's throat.

Within seconds, Xavier screams and his body starts to convulse. I cry out for Austen to stop, but one of the guards holding me down slaps his hand over my mouth, and I have to watch as Xavier convulses till his body gives out and he slumps forward.

I swallow the bile rising in my throat. No, no, *no.*

Austen turns his attention back to me, the evil, malicious smile still plastered on his face. "Van Helsing blood," he laughs, "mixed with silver, the ultimate poison for vampires."

My jaw drops at the mention of my name. How the hell did he know? "Oh, don't look so surprised. I've known since we were little. I broke into that room your parents always told us we could not enter under any circumstances, and I found so many treasures, including the documents from your ancestors."

I swallow hard. A cold sweat covers my skin.

"I've read the entries on those documents and heard myths about what your blood does when mixed with silver, but I couldn't test it without raising suspicion, but now," Austen shrugs. "I don't have to ask for your permission." He looks at Xavier, and my eyes follow. "Dead the moment the poison mixes with their blood."

"What?" I don't have time to wrap my head around Austen's last statement. The door to the interrogation room opens, and I squint at the light. In the open doorway are two figures. I can tell that one is the woman from the monitor, and the other is Brian as he strolls into the room.

"Finally," Brian breathes. "A deal is a deal. Austen, you are now the head of the VHA mission's department." Brian walks to me and wraps his hand around my throat, squeezing.

I choke as black spots hit my vision. The woman steps forward and says lazily, "I hope you do not forget your deal with our vampire clan?"

Brian scowls at me, and then his hand is gone. "Of course not, Sofie. She's all yours."

To Be Continued.